"Cohen is gnds, atmospheres. Her lang... is a

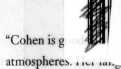

She is a frequent contributor to *The New York Times Book Review*.

ALSO BY LEAH HAGER COHEN

FICTION

NONFICTION

NO BOOK
BUT THE
WORLD

LEAH HAGER COHEN

THE CLERKENWELL PRESS

This paperback edition published in 2015

First published in Great Britain in 2014 by
PROFILE BOOKS LTD
3 Holford Yard
Bevin Way
London WC1X 9HD
www.profilebooks.com

First published in the United States of America in 2014 by
Riverhead Books, Penguin Group, USA

1 3 5 7 9 10 8 6 4 2

Printed and bound in Great Britain by
CPI Group (UK) Ltd, Croydon CR0 4YY

The moral right of the author has been asserted.

A CIP catalogue record for this book is available from the British Library.

ISBN 978 1 84668 971 0
eISBN 978 1 78283 026 9

MIX
Paper from
responsible sources
FSC® C020471

TO OCKY'S 10

AND THEIR

G

Let there be no book but the world.

JEAN-JACQUES ROUSSEAU,
Émile: Or, Treatise on Education

Contents

I know everything.
Half of it I really know,
The rest I make up.
The rest I make up.

MARÍA IRENE FORNÉS, *Promenade*

I

PERDU

One

I HAVE BEEN TOO FOND OF STORIES. Fred and me both. If I were called before a judge, that's the first thing I'd confess: how quick I have been to embrace them, stories, with their deplorable tidiness. Like a bakery box done up too tightly, bound with red-and-white string.

The second thing I'd confess: how I am responsible for Fred's fondness, how consequently he would have to be called blameless.

Oh Fred. Oh Freddy.

I could, would, gladly elaborate. In however much detail would help. I'd describe where it began, on the gray flowered couch where we often sat, half sunk in its cushions, a couch I haven't seen in over a decade, yet whose texture I recall with precision: the way it was coolish on our bare skin, glossy where the fabric was going threadbare and furred on the armrests where it had already frayed. I would testify to this, the fertile bed in which our fondness took root.

But look. Already—I throw up my hands. This is no more than a story itself, the one that goes Ava is guilty, Fred innocent. How eagerly the words spring into shape, winding themselves around a rigid latticework of meaning like the curling tendrils of some plant—like, in fact, the skeletal branches of ivy that crisscross the window here in this room that is not my room, but which belongs to a Mrs. Tremblay, who is not happy about renting it to me.

The fine-boned ivy, whose intricate fretwork clings to the screen, is at this moment holding tight against a lashing wind and pelting rain as if in helpful illustration of my very point, which is to say my problem: the easy danger of stories, their adhesive allure. The way, once a story takes hold, it begins to choke off the view.

I can hear Mrs. Tremblay downstairs now, moving about in her kitchen. Each sound she makes, innocuous though it really may be—the faucet turned on, then off, the creak of a cupboard, the clank of a metal pot—seems to reprove. When she rented me the room yesterday she was pleasant enough, but earlier this morning when I went down for the breakfast that is included in the price of the room her manner was cooler. I can only imagine she must have become more informed in the interim about who I am.

Fred and I have different surnames. He is still a Robbins but I am a Manseau, having taken Dennis's name when we married. Why ever, and with what little consideration, did I shed my own? At the time I felt only impatience to don the costume of a married woman. Ava Manseau. Like playing dress-ups, I thought, although at twenty-five I was no child and should have been more deliberating, less hasty about the decision. But with its echo of *trousseau*, the very name seemed to waft and billow like the creamy organza of the imaginary gown I conjured and altered a dozen times during the weeks leading up to the wedding, at which I actually wore a sleeveless white shift from a consignment store. Too, there was the notion I'd be doing something that would please my husband-to-be. I was so eager, so impatient, to prove my willingness to conform. Later I allowed myself to realize—admit—that

I had ascribed this desire falsely. Dennis never minded whether I took his name or not.

The different surnames explain why Mrs. Tremblay did not make the connection—neither on Monday, when I called about the room, nor yesterday, when, after driving eight hours from Freyburg I arrived on her doorstep here in Perdu, "so far upstate you can practically see Canada out the window," as she announced with a kind of practiced delivery and accompanying hand gesture toward this ivy-choked pane—even though Fred has been so much in the news. She has a squished sort of accent. "Canada" gets flattened into "Kyaneda," and "far" sounds almost like "fire." After a brief tour, during which she pointed out the bathroom with its pink toilet seat cover and matching floor mat, and the old black push-button phone perched on a stand at the top of the stairs ("Your cell won't work. From town it might do, but we don't get any reception at all out this way."), she accepted my check for one week's stay, $196, made out to Mrs. Oliver Tremblay, taking time to read it over before putting it in the pocket of her boiled wool cardigan. I think she must be a widow.

The November rain is blowing sideways, crazing the glass. What is it about extreme weather that gives one the feeling of having traveled back in time? As if the past somehow had more weather; as if weather is one of those things that has dwindled or languished with modernity. It was raining, too, when I arrived yesterday, though more lightly then, the drops as tiny as if pressed through cheesecloth. Still, it was enough to slicken the flagstone path, and when, after Mrs. Tremblay took my check, I went back to the car to retrieve my suitcase, I slipped. One moment I was striding confidently on two legs. The next, my right foot slid forward and my left was no longer aligned in any way useful to holding me up. For one protracted moment the dun-and-gray world seemed shot through with color, and I caught a whiff of something sharp and bright: lemons, onions. Flailing, I managed to right myself, but that oddly invigorating moment of imbalance has stayed with me. Last night when I was trying to fall asleep it replayed several times in my mind and each successive time, rather than intensifying in fright, it seemed softer and more expansive, and finally almost pleasurable, like a dream of flying.

Now the rain is really slashing down. I long for another cup of tea—breakfast was hours ago—but although yesterday Mrs. Tremblay showed me the tray she keeps available in the kitchen for guests, stocked with Tetley, Swiss Miss and packets of artificial sweetener and nondairy creamer, I am reluctant to go downstairs. On Monday, at home in Freyburg, while researching places to stay, a guesthouse had sounded cozier than a motel, not to mention less expensive and more convenient, the nearest motel I could find being twenty-three miles from where Fred is—but I'd pictured something different from this saltbox house with stained siding, hunkered stoically right on the edge of the county road. I'd pictured a place with more than one guest room, and a bar of soap by the guest sink that was not already pared down and riven with cracks, and a proprietress who didn't seem so inconvenienced by, well, an actual guest.

It's not as if I'm stuck. I have the car, could drive to town.

The prospect is not enticing. Four miles in the rain on a snaking one-lane road and then the lone diner where I ate last night. That's the town, as far as I can tell: one diner, two bars, three churches, a handful of storefronts, a dozen shingles hung from front porches—family dentistry, chiropractic, dog grooming, tax prep—and running behind the row of old brick buildings that line the main street, a narrow, foul-smelling mill river the color of a paper clip.

Anyway, once there, what would I do? Sit at the counter on a vinyl-covered stool and stare at the cakes under glass, all the while being stared at by the other customers, who would know at the very least that I am "from away," if not the details of what has brought me. Of who has brought me. I suppose I could ask for a cup to go. And then what? Drink it in the car. Behind the opaque waterfall of the windshield, beneath the rain beating its tiny fists on the roof. Or I could drive back here, bring the tea up to the aseptic stillness of this angular room under the eaves. How strange that would seem to Mrs. Tremblay.

She is shaped, I have noticed, like an eggplant, and her mouth looks permanently pursed, her lips jutting out as if fastened around a sour ball. She'd glance up from—what? her ironing, her coupons, her cross-stitch?—eye me coming in with my paper cup, the shoulders of my coat dark with rain, and be sorry all over again that she'd taken my check.

I reach into my bag and pluck the torn envelope on which I have written the assigned counsel's contact information and the time he has agreed to meet: four p.m. He has one of those inverted names—Bayard Charles—which seems very lawyerly and formal of him. His office isn't in Perdu but over in Criterion, the county seat. I have decided to allow myself a full hour to get there, and still that means I have three hours to slog through before I leave, and the weather has conspired to pen me here.

So I remain, tealess, in this chilly bedroom I think must once have belonged to a daughter or a son, but which has been stripped of any indication; it is a neutered space, pared down to bare essentials and a few desultory efforts at decoration: a faded print of geraniums over the bed; a faded print of a barn and silo on the opposite wall; a dusty succulent in a plastic pot on the rattan table by the window, where I sit with the composition book Kitty gave me unopened in my lap. I have noticed a burn mark on the carpet near the dresser, remnants of tape on the ceiling, and a large rectangle of blue wallpaper deeper-hued than the rest. Even the aberrations are minor, nondescript.

I could not number the scars left on our own house. I'm thinking not only of those we (by which I mean mostly Fred) inflicted, but also of the ones we inherited, marks made by people we never met, but which we came to know as intimately as the freckles, moles, protrusions and concavities of our own bodies. When I was little and the distinctions between familiar and unfamiliar were not yet fixed, explorations of my body yielded at times that which seemed foreign, even that which seemed against me, unfriendly. I remember encountering one afternoon, while studying myself in the bathroom mirror, the irregular topography of the underside of my tongue. Dark-veined and grotesquely anchored to the bottom of my mouth by a wobbly pink tether, it repulsed—this rudely intractable item that was part of me.

Similarly, I remember explorations of our home yielding spots that felt as remote and mysterious and vaguely threatening as anything in my most forbidding dreams: the weirdly gouged section of the upstairs banister that looked like it had had a bite taken out of it; the dinner-plate-sized bulge in the living room wall that seemed evidence our house had at one time been under siege by cannon; the leg of our coffee table that was covered with rows of evenly spaced scratches, as though someone—or something—had scored it with a fork or a set of sharpened claws.

But there I go again. Further evidence of my inability to consider a thing without imagining the story behind it as a needful force, a great petitioning weight.

Mrs. Tremblay might have the right idea with this guest room, after all. Void the space of history's crumbs; annul all suggestive detritus.

Do not feed but let fast the traveler's weary mind. Tabula rasa: the kindest form of hospitality.

It doesn't work on me. In the absence of external grist, my mind turns to the silt it is already carrying around. This room, rinsed of nuance, only sends me deeper into my own thoughts, so heavily dusted—everywhere coated—with Fred.

Yesterday before making my way to Mrs. Tremblay's I went to see the building, long and yellow and close to the ground, set back from the road many hundreds of yards. I didn't realize I'd assumed it would be fenced until I saw it was not. In the slanting light of late afternoon, with the sky raw and low and bristling with moisture, the undulating sweep of grass between road and building had been the flat color of the ocean on a hazy day. Hillocks stood in for waves and rendered the building ship-like. I drove by, made a U-turn and drove back again, slowing, vaguely aware of the possibility of seeming suspicious to anyone watching, only no one was. I saw no movement, no figures, no cars, not even lights in the narrow windows. Just the edifice itself, and a flagpole flying its requisite banner, dark and drooping in the rain, and a sinuous road that must have been the way in but whose course was erased by the tall grass that swallowed it beyond the first rise.

I might really have been gazing at the ocean, for the seasick feeling that rose in my gorge—to know Fred was inside, to be so close and yet unable to see him or even let him know I was there.

I am not allowed in.

New inmates are entitled to one fifteen-minute non-contact visit with anyone they wish during the first twenty-four hours after commitment, but that time window expired yesterday morning before I was able to get here. I learned these rules Monday by going on the website, after discovering he'd been moved from the hospital to the county correctional facility. Henceforth, from what I have been able to gather—or really from what Dennis, who is not only more Internet-savvy but also less incapacitated by this particular news, was able to gather and then pass along—Fred will be allowed two one-hour visits per week, any days except Tuesday and Wednesday. On weekends only, visits are structured according to the first letter of the inmate's last name, the second half of the alphabet falling on Sunday. Also on weekends only, a two-hour visit is allowed if the visitor has had to travel at least a hundred miles, one way, from home to the jail (proof of residency required), but then this takes up the inmate's entire week of visitation in one day. Visits must be scheduled in advance, by telephone or in person with the Lobby Officer, Monday through Friday between four p.m. and nine p.m., or Saturday and Sunday between eight a.m. and two p.m. I haven't yet been able to ascertain how much in advance "in advance" means. And all of this, I ultimately learned, is in any case moot, because visitors' names must previously be placed on a visitation list in order to have their requests processed.

"How do I get on the list?" I asked when I finally got through to a human.

"The inmate has to put your name down." A middle-aged smoker, her voice at once clipped and bored.

"How do I get a message to him to put me on it? He won't know . . . We haven't been—"

"You can tell him by phone."

"I can call him?" A rush of relief. "Is it a different number, or can you connect me?"

A sigh. Then: "Inmates-don't-receive-calls. They-have-phone-time-every-day-he-can-call-you-then. It's-a-collect-call-you'll-have-to-be-home-to-accept-the-charges."

"And if he doesn't call?"

A silence.

Then: "Ma'am. You can write him a letter." Before I could ask she began reciting the address, and it might have been the pledge, she said it so fast and cute. I had to quick find a pencil and beg her to repeat it.

I put a letter in the mail to you, Fred, before going to bed Monday night. I walked down the dirt road to the paved road, a walk you and I took so many times together, you with a long stick in your hand, running it along the trunks of trees we passed. I put it in the mailbox and raised the red flag. The mailbox that sits alone now but once perched in a row of mailboxes, like plump metal hens, which you would strike with your stick, making them cluck and squawk, tapping out your non-rhythms on their silver backs. I don't suppose my letter can have reached you yet.

And where exactly are you, Fred, on this drenched November morning, eight days after they initiated the search, five days after they found you, four days after they found the boy they say you took into the woods? You're some four miles from me, closer than we've been in almost two years. But where are you precisely, in that long, yellow brick building? At one of the windows, perhaps, its own pane crazed by the sideblown rain, looking out at the midmorning darkness? What might you be seeing beyond the storm? The boy? The boy whose only image I've seen is the sixth-grade school photo that has been reproduced in all the papers and on all the television news updates, a very nearly generic image of a boy in a red and blue rugby shirt, yet with something disconcertingly familiar about his look: the unkempt dark hair and full cheeks, the smile just wide enough to reveal the frank thrust of his top front teeth. Not so much rabbity as game-looking, that bite of his. Is that how he looked to you? Game.

As you were always game. Do you remember that, how game you were, back in those days when we played our own game in the woods?

11

But maybe you're seeing something else at this moment beyond the streaming pane, its vista erased by a network of rivulets, replaced by images of whatever it is you did with a different child in a different woods. Is that what you see, not the boy himself but the stages of the event as it unfolded? Do you replay those steps in your mind? What are they, Fred? I need to know. When you see me, will you explain?

Or perhaps you are focused instead not on the event as it occurred but as you'd intended it to occur—whatever your intention was I do not know, only that it differed, must differ, from what actually came to pass. That much is certain. That much about you I assuredly still do know. You are no plotter, no predator. Of all people—you, who were allowed to grow into a natural man, who were not put into a press, are you not, as our parents might say, incapable of evildoing?

I can't help imagining that as you look out your own window at the tossing darkness of this morning, you might be seeing me. Is it ego that binds me to you, makes me see you seeing me? Seeing me beside you, before you, up on the flowered couch, kneeling by your bed, standing over you as you lay on the stone slab in the woods, taking you by the hand, leading you places.

Is it guilt?

Freddy, come. How many times did I urge you on, tug your wrist, yank your elbow, even at the risk of upsetting you? Because as everyone knew you did not like to be touched. I touched you anyway, and you let me. Sometimes. You let me more than anyone else. I was the big sister. I could take your hand, pull your thumb from your mouth, pry the stick from your fist. *Freddy, come on. Let's go.* I could guide you into the woods, out to our special spot. Dress you in silks. Cover your eyes. Prick your finger.

But I never did that: prick your finger. Nor did Kitty. That is one thing we never did.

Or is it our parents you visualize as you look out the window? I see them often, and always in tandem. Even when I picture them physically apart, they remain paired, joined by a kind of invisible thread. You could feel it running between them, this thread, pliable and strong, holding them together, eternally allied through every superficial disagreement.

Mostly I picture them together. In the front seat of the car, the backs of their heads silhouetted against the windshield, hers a good three inches higher than his. On the flowered couch, her feet in his lap, their voices rumbling above us as we maneuvered our toy cars around our father's shoes. I see them diverting themselves from whatever conversation they were having to regard us from a bemused distance, from high in the ether, twirling in the thin atmosphere of their thoughts, their philosophy. Floating above our heads like paper dolls cut from a single sheet of construction paper, their hands joined at the fold. Their free hands extended as if to summon us forward, although couldn't the gesture as easily be interpreted as a staving off, their hands flexed at the wrist, bidding us go be independent?

We succeeded in that, Fred, you and me. We were independent, inhabiting our home like two small grown-ups, or no, like gnomes, solid little earthbound creatures, hiding and tunneling and exploring on our own. We mined every corner of our house for mystery, for treasure. Is that what you see in the opaque surface of your watery windowpane? Our house, with its soft pine floors so quick to take an impression (the many impressions, for example, of your own pounding fists and heels during your frequent tantrums, or the dents you made tapping out erratic rhythms with building blocks or the blunt ends of butter knives); its potted plants, so fiercely healthy, their vines running rampant along shelves and sills and spilling over to snake across the floor; its listing door and window frames, every one just a little bit warped, a little bit crooked, so that nothing ever hung plumb?

When we tired of our house, we'd move outdoors—by then we often had Kitty with us, too—and go scavenging in the tangled meadow and the scratchy woods. We did not limit ourselves to the woods as we found them, but invented within them a realm of our own, a place no one else knew about, no one else could enter or even perceive. It lay, this place, no more than a quarter mile behind our house, but it was unreachable by others. We, too, were beyond reach there. We did as we'd been bid: we acted independently in that realm.

Perhaps this is what you see, staring out your barred window—for I think it must have bars; I see it with bars; I have invented that detail—staring through silvered slashes of rain that light up your memories with the faltering flicker of an old film projector. Perhaps you see what I am seeing now, as I write: Batter Hollow, with its cluster of five mismatched cottages, and the jagged pines spreading densely back for acres, and what we fashioned out there, Fred—you and Kitty and me.

Two

I PLANNED MY ROUTE on Monday afternoon, on an old gas station map spread across the kitchen table, using a highlighter pen to mark my destinations in order: first the building where Fred is being held, eleven miles off the highway and two miles southwest of the black dot that is the town of Perdu; then Mrs. Tremblay's, two and a half miles east of the same. I used the first joint of my index finger to calculate distances as per the legend, and these numbers I penciled above the roads. I tallied the mileage this way.

"Why don't you just map it online?" asked Dennis, behind me. He plunked the kettle back on the stove and leaned over my shoulder.

"That's all right."

"Want me to? I'll print it out."

"No." I closed my eyes and breathed. "Thanks."

I could feel him trying to think what else he might offer, felt the burden of his hopeful hesitancy. Or not his hesitancy, but my own inability to respond. Once it had been a novelty: the idea that I could take care of him by letting him feel he was taking care of me. Once I would have said *yes, please.* Once I thought I could become the sort of person who would find comfort in the usual gestures. Now what I feel most often toward Dennis is sympathy and regret that he has ended up with an irregular wife.

I turned my upper body halfway from my map. "I just like doing it this way, Den." And stayed with my face inclined toward him until he bent and put his mouth to my cheek and rested it there, not kissing, just holding still with his parted lips against me, making a warm chamber against my skin. His blond stubble fine as grains of sand. He smelled of wool sweater and soap and tea. He is lovely with me, patient and undeterred.

Yesterday, rolling by the long yellow building, coasting with my foot off the gas, I tried to feel that Fred was there behind the walls and could not. And because I could not, it gave me the absurd notion that perhaps he *was* not—that perhaps they have the wrong person, someone using Fred's name, someone who might have stolen his identity, while the real Fred is far away and safe somewhere, still in the woods, tramping unhurriedly over sodden leaves, alone and safe from those who cannot understand him.

Also yesterday, for the first time the TV news aired a mug shot of the man they say is Fred, and although there was undeniably a resemblance, the man in the picture looked different from my brother as I last saw him. The hair on his head was cut severely close to the skull, and his face looked whittled, gaunt. More jarring was the darkness of his eyes, shaded beneath a promontory of brow. They had a smudged, exhausted look, a crepuscular quality that went beyond hue or shadow.

Until I saw that photo yesterday, flashed so briefly across the television screen, I had struggled to picture Fred as a grown man. When I last saw him, close to two years ago, he was twenty-eight, but try as I might to recall what he looked like then, I kept seeing him instead as he was when I first began to read to him, when he was little, Freddy, and most mine.

I'd see the two of us up on the sagging gray couch, whose flowers, once blue and red, had faded to variations on gray. I'd see us at ages five and three, me an imperious, middle-aged sort of child, Freddy in diapers still. He was large for his age and slow at everything the world held in regard: toileting, ambulating, speaking, minding. He minded me, though. Or sometimes did. Or nearly did. He minded when I told him to do something he was already about to do. I made a sport of it. It was a game of unwitting cahoots and it was all in the timing: "Take another bite of carrots, Freddy." "Chew, Freddy." "Throw your spoon on the floor, Freddy." "Throw your dish down, too." "Scream." "Turn red."

The fury my game provoked in him seemed evidence he wasn't as slow as people believed. It wasn't exactly fury in any case; it was something else, more nuanced than frustration or anger, for all I had to do was fall silent and he'd leave off having his fit and turn to me with a curious, ripe kind of look—a look whose meaning was not, as I thought the first few times, simply to egg me on. It was keener, more particular. As if he were marking a thing beyond ordinary apprehension, the way a dog can hear a whistle pitched beyond the range of human hearing. And I'd feel between us then—not love, exactly, but a kind of tight excitement, the heady trill of possession. As if he were saying we belonged to each other, were parts of the same one thing.

When we sat up on the high flowered couch, the game worked differently, for there he was liable to mind me whether I'd anticipated his intentions or not. "Get us some books, Freddy boy," I'd say, and likely as not he'd comply, turning onto his stomach to slide backward off the cushions and toddle across the room, his round pink heels going *chud*

chud chud across the floor, his plastic diaper crinkling. He'd squat before the row of milk crates lined up under the windows, from which he'd extract, with grave determination, an armload of books, always more than he could manage, and transport them back to the couch. One or two volumes would drop along the way and he'd go back for them only to lose others, so that by the time he'd conveyed them all back up beside me he'd be panting. "Breathe with your mouth shut," I'd tell him, and automatically he'd bring his lips together and try.

I had to be mean to him when I could.

Our collection consisted largely of Ladybird Books, a few dozen of them, their dry, cracked bindings the colors of oil pastels. Our mother had bought them all at one go at the town library's book fair the year she was pregnant with me. She'd taken care to write the place and date on the flyleaf of every one: Freyburg, New York, June 1974. Published in England, they brimmed with exotic words—lorry and sweetie instead of truck and candy—and for many years, until I was finally allowed to go to public school, I thought aeroplane and colour were the preferred spellings. The stories reeked thrillingly of disobedience and peril. An old woman exhorted an indifferent pig to jump over a stile. A mother goat slit a wolf down the middle and sewed his belly full of stones. Wayward kittens and bunnies were forever smashing tea sets, spilling bags of flour, running away and falling into rivers and streams.

Certain of the illustrations had the power to produce in me a silvery jelly feeling that was disturbing without being disagreeable. A boy peeping over his blankets in horror as rats dashed freely across his bed; a man in jerkin and tights hacking at thorns, his thighs a mess of bloody gashes; a hooded crone hauling herself up a stone tower on a shining rope of hair; a maiden splayed unconscious, cheeks flushed, her ice-blue gown tightly fitted through the bodice. It all lay in store for us, Freddy and me—I remember believing this quite matter-of-factly. Even as I made the distinction between pretend and real (I would not really grow up to become a princess, a witch, a wolf), still I believed the essence of these stories must in some way seep into or prophesy what our lives would become.

Sometimes I wonder how things might have been different if a grown-up had read us those books. Might it have had a mediating effect? What if my own overly credulous renditions bore a kind of unnatural potency? I think of our mother's voice, which possessed, even when speaking about ordinary things, a latent musicality, so that her words might rise and fall, glide and rest, carving out pleasant corners in which my attention liked to nestle. This vocal quality suggested a kind of mastery over the events she narrated, a completeness of perception that let me relax into my own spottier grasp of the world. Had the stories in our picture books come filtered through the voice of our mother, would they have reached our ears tamed, contained, stripped in some crucial way of implication? Would we have liked them as much?

But reading to us was not one of the things in which our parents believed. *Reading*, our father used to pronounce with a kind of hammy horror, *is the scourge of infancy.* Also: *Books! What cheerless furniture!* This he liked to roar in mock dismay upon coming into the room and finding us sprawled on the couch among dozens of said objects. Sometimes, in an especially playful mood, he'd contort his face in a mask of revulsion, as if we were surrounded by actual vermin.

We knew these utterances were not original. I understood them to be the words of "Jay-Jay," whom I imagined to be an old and much esteemed friend of my father's. I was eight or nine before I learned that Jay-Jay was actually the philosopher Jean-Jacques Rousseau, no pal of my father's but his ideological hero, who'd died some two hundred years earlier. His book on education, *Émile*, had been the primary inspiration of my father's own philosophy and, indeed, career. A reproduction of the Maurice Quentin de La Tour portrait of Rousseau hung behind the desk in my father's office, and during my childhood I made a long and thorough study of it, determining always to my satisfaction that Jay-Jay had kindly eyes, a trustworthy forehead, a sympathetic, good-humored mouth.

Much later, in college, when my disillusionment with my father was at its most excruciating, I set out to learn more about the philosopher and his life. It was only then that I discovered that the great philosopher, my father's idol and model, had deposited his own five children in a foundling hospital.

At any rate, our father didn't forbid us to read. For all his blustery protestations, he didn't even discourage it. Simply, books were one of the many things he thought we should be left to discover (or not) on our own.

So it was Freddy and me and no one else up on the couch for long stretches of time, Freddy breathing with adenoidal impediment, the air ruffling thickly around his thumb, which he kept parked in the corner of his mouth, taking the occasional series of rapid sucks before letting it idle again; me enunciating schoolmarmishly (even though at five I had never set foot in a regular school, I somehow had a sense of the role and played it to the hilt). I had been prescribed glasses for amblyopia, and although I reviled them I never thought to rebel, but donned them each morning with a sense of duty that bordered on priggishness. What a homely sight we must have made, the stuffy-nosed and the lazy-eyed, our knees and elbows bumping and overlapping (he did not mind being touched so much when he was very little) as we nested among the cool, gray, disintegrating flowers.

While I read, Freddy sucked his thumb hard and ran the fingers of his other hand over the illustrations, always tracing the pictures with gentleness at first, but often getting overexcited and rubbing faster and harder, scratching at the pictures with his sharp little nails so that I'd have to push his hand away. "Cut it out, Freddy. No. *Stop*." When that didn't work I'd shut the book with a smack.

Then he'd let out a rattling scream of protest—I could see the disgusting dangling thing at the back of his throat—and begin to plead and whine for what had been taken away.

Primly I'd tell him: "Calm down. I can't open the book unless you promise to be gentle."

But this I well knew he could not deliver. He was incapable of reeling himself in once he'd achieved such a state, and things would inevitably devolve into a kicking fight, both of us with our bare legs and heels delivering a frenzy of blows, and the book would sink between two cushions and the poor faded flowers of our battlefield would fray a little more. If our mother was in the vicinity, she'd swoop down and extract Freddy—always Freddy, not me, even as he grew to be the larger, heavier one—from the tumult, but if our father was there he would only stand by.

"Make him cut it out!" I'd demand.

But he'd lean, untroubled, against the door frame of his study, where he would have been working before the commotion roused him. "Better to work it out yourselves." And he'd linger there, considering us from across the room with maddeningly genuine curiosity.

Most of the time, though, we were amicable up there on the flowered couch. Burrowed among those sagging pillows and cushions, we'd lose ourselves for hours, willingly, willfully, not so much poring over as pouring ourselves into the words and pictures, illustrated guides of all that life had to offer: treachery, adventure, peril and bliss. Bright little maps, the books seemed to me, second or third cousins of the road maps we'd pick up at corner gas stations on our impromptu wanderings.

That was something our parents did believe in: vagrant rambles, sprung loose from plan or aim. A few times a year we'd set off on excursions in the car—a rattling orange Dasher with a hole in the floor a little bigger than a Susan B. Anthony dollar (I knew because I'd once stuck one through, to see if it would fit)—with little more than our sleeping bags and tent and a vague itinerary. We'd head for Cape Cod and make it all the way up to Acadia National Park, or set out for Delaware and wind up visiting the wild ponies on Assateague. Wherever we went, when we stopped for gas our mother would disappear inside the shop to pay for the fuel, and she'd frequently come out bearing the same three items: a sack of sunflower seeds, a copy of the local paper, and a road map of the sort that used to be free at filling stations. Sometimes she'd emerge carrying drinks, too, but more often we'd make do with paper cups of warm water dispensed from the big red Thermos jug, with its little hinged spout, that rode on the floor between her feet. She'd pass out cups of water and handfuls of sunflower seeds, and Fred and I would make a game of trying to spit out the hulls, once we'd sucked off all the salt and cracked them open between our teeth, through the hole in the bottom of the car.

The age difference between our parents was nineteen or twenty years, depending on what time of year you made your calculation. Our father was fifty-nine when I was born. I only ever knew him with white hair, but it was a youthful head of white, thick and curly and roughly cherubic. In public school, in tenth-grade English, when I encountered the description of Odysseus's "hyacinthine locks," it was my father's hair I envisioned. He was a few inches shorter and more than a few inches rounder than our mother, built, as one of his admirers had once written in a book about progressive education, like a Dutch oven. Our mother was a painter and dancer and musician. We never called them anything but Neel and June.

They are dead now, both of them, Neel for more than seven years, June for less than two. Even so, it's Neel I find myself addressing in my head this afternoon, Neel I wish I could call from Mrs. Tremblay's heavy black phone out on the landing. Not because I care more about what he would think and say than June, but because I long for his certainties, his conviction.

I set the book Kitty gave me on the rattan table and feel in my bag for a pen. The book is exactly the kind you picture when you think of a composition book: the classic black-and-white-marbled cover, the black tape binding, the blue-lined pages. I've encountered this exact species of notebook a hundred times over the past twenty years, yet it gave me a turn when Kitty put it in my hands Monday night.

I used to love a new notebook. Kitty and me both. At the beginning of each school year, once I had joined her in attending Freyburg Primary, we'd sit on the braided rug in her bedroom and organize our newly purchased supplies with solemn relish. Virginal pencils and unsullied erasers; blocks of crisp index cards; stiff, unnicked rulers; colored pens whose felt tips were perfectly tight and saturated; mini-staplers, which we loaded with their heavy cartridges of metal teeth. The tools of ordering. The promise of that which could be ordered.

Here in Mrs. Tremblay's guest bedroom I open the book's cover, breaking its binding. Kitty and I used to love that sound. Almost despite myself, I bring my nose to the crease, inhale the clean-laundry smell. Then I smooth the book flat on the table.

"I thought it might help." Kitty'd sounded diffident, dropping it off on Monday night, the eve of my departure.

"Help what?"

"Oh, Bird." Her longtime nickname for me, ever since we'd looked ourselves up in the tattered book of baby names we found on a low shelf at the foot of her parents' bed. The fact of its being stored there, bedside, lent it an illicit aura: Were her parents planning more children? Did they alternate between laboring at this effort and consulting the pages of the book? We learned that her given name—Katherine— meant pure, a discovery that sent us into raucous, uncertain laughter (we'd been bumping up against puberty at the time), and mine meant just that: bird. We found the discovery providential: we fit together. Kitty and Ava. Cat and bird.

I stood on Monday night in the front hall of the house that still does not feel quite like home, blinking at Kitty. I had, until her arrival, been sitting in the kitchen, letting it grow dark without getting up from the table to turn on the light, letting the cup of tea Dennis had made me grow cold. The past three days had been long with phone calls, calls at first simply to try to get other phone numbers: numbers that would ring in the right buildings and the right offices, then numbers where a human would actually pick up at the opposite end, then numbers that would lead to someone authorized to talk, someone willing to dispense pieces of practical information such as where Fred was, whether he was all right, what was going to happen next, how I could get in to see him.

So by Monday night, when Kitty drove up from Brooklyn unannounced to see me before I left, I'd been feeling little besides exhaustion. Dennis and I had eaten an early supper, a kind of post-apocalyptic menu—soup from a can, peas from a bag, toast spread with apple butter—after which he'd cleared the table while I sat in a weary stupor, and then he'd gone out while I continued to sit and the sky turned incrementally from purple to black.

When the doorbell rang I went into the front hall to find Kitty already inside, looking faintly dazzling as ever, standing by the door in her dark red wool coat, pink-cheeked, rain glistening on her hair. Her hair is curly as clock springs and made up of every shade of yellow you can think of, from corn silk to yolk, and she has always worn it cropped, which only underscores its allure, as if any more of its glory would be an unbearable excess. She has a wide, graceful prow of a forehead, and high, round cheekbones and a chin with just a whisper of a cleft. When we were girls, Neel, who claimed not to believe in nicknames (he said the term of greatest endearment was a person's own name, unadorned), and who never had one for me or Freddy, used always to call her "Bonny Kitty." Or really: "Bonnykitty," in a single breath, as if it were her given name.

She stood there in the hall, shaking out her salmon-colored scarf, drops arcing in the overhead light, and when she saw me come in her eyes collapsed tenderly at the corners, and I could see her restrain herself from hugging me. "Hi, Ayv." She sounded almost bashful.

I said hi back, squinting in the sudden brightness of the hall and hugging myself around the middle; I'd only just noticed how cold the house was. Dennis and I moved here a little less than two years ago, on the heels of June's death, and we've done nothing yet about the draftiness, despite the fact that this is Dennis's line of work: installing eco-friendly insulation.

"Are you okay?" said Kitty. Always, even on a solemn occasion like this, an undercurrent of laughter in her voice. I've known her far too long to take offense. The semiquaver riding beneath her words, like the edge of a slip peeking from beneath a skirt, is symptomatic of her particular slant of mind, her ceaselessly amused disposition: a thing I have long both envied and held in faint contempt. Even as a child Kitty seemed to possess a keen sense of the fundamental absurdity of life.

Me, I am the opposite. I have a hard time laughing at anything, even that which is by all accounts patently absurd. If her mind has a glittery radiance, mine is dark and loamy, preternaturally attuned to sorrow.

"I mean—not okay, but okay?" she added.

I nodded.

"Well, I brought you something." She shrugged, as if a little display of self-deprecation would make me more likely to accept the gift. "I thought it might help."

And she held it out, the hard-backed composition book with its marble cover, indistinguishable from the ones we used as children in school, the ones all children use in school, ubiquitous, innocuous— and yet I stared to see her extending it so blithely, as though she did not notice it was a replica of the other book, the one in which long ago we had recorded the story of our childhood game, the game we kept coming back to, over and over, the three of us, the game we called Fredericka. I looked at the book she had chosen to bring me on this night and did not take it from her hands.

"Help what?"

"Oh, Bird." She looked at me for a long moment before dropping her gaze to the book itself. To her credit, her ears grew pink.

Kitty is a clinical psychologist. She sees mostly people with anxiety disorders and specializes in cognitive behavioral therapy. I can easily imagine her giving patients homework assignments like writing down their feelings in a notebook.

Now in the hall she recovered herself, raising her eyes again and giving a snort. "Help *that*!" she said, gesturing with a little vaudevillian stamp, as if my reticence was something visible, concrete. "Really, what does Dennis *do* with you?"

Kitty is not only my oldest friend, she's also my sister-in-law, a title I can't quite get used to even though Dennis and I have been married for over seven years. The power of that childhood relationship remains huge, and it occupied my life long before I had any inkling that her much older brother might one day figure in my life, let alone be my husband. For years it was just Kitty and me. Well. Kitty and me and Fred.

I was seven and Fred five when the Manseaus moved to Batter Hollow. The cottages—as everyone called the handful of buildings arrayed in the grassy clearing at the end of a long dirt road—were all that remained of Batter Hollow, the famous experimental school our father started in 1949 and ran, together with his second wife, Margo, until 1973. People referred to our mother as his third wife, but they were never legally married. They met when June joined the faculty during the last year of the school's existence, and although she wore a gold band on her ring finger, they were in fact only common-law spouses. "What did you wear at your wedding?" I remember asking when I reached an age where I found ceaseless fascination in the whole concept of brides and gowns.

"Oh." June gave a small laugh. "We didn't bother with all that."

Batter Hollow is where we grew up, Fred and me (and later the Manseaus, along with the Gann kids and Noah Salinas-Buchbinder), and perhaps as a result of our having been born so soon after the school's closing, the grounds held for us the aspect of an echo, as if only recently abandoned by its most significant players, a place whose key chapters had already occurred before we came along.

The Manseaus moved into one of the end cottages. It had been the Art Barn, back in the days of the school, and one side of the building bore the faded results of the community-wide painting project our mother, as art teacher (she'd also taught music, puppetry and movement), had organized. This mural offered a riotous disquisition on scale, with its stumpy trees, colossal flowers, butterflies the size of dogs, and a diminutive hot air balloon that seemed to hang like a fruit from one elongated branch.

Ours was the middle cottage, a gray clapboard two-story with a mansard roof. It had been the Office; in it Neel and Margo had conducted school business and also lived. The other cottages had been the Classrooms (this largest of the buildings, made of whitewashed brick that had gone rosy-bald in places, housed all the redheaded Gann kids along with their parents and a rotating menagerie of dogs, cats and assorted amphibians); the Annex (this smaller version of the Classrooms, hiding as if shyly behind a heavy veil of ivy, was occupied by the quiet, decorous Salinas-Buchbinder family) and the Shed (a simple wooden A-frame, inhabited by Jim and Katinka, a young couple who made their own yogurt and sweaters and beer). All five buildings bore, over their front doors, pine slabs onto which Neel had wood-burned their names decades earlier. Two more of these handmade plaques hung inside our own house, lettered in the same dusky block writing. They featured Neel's favorite lines from Rousseau's *Émile*. In the front hall: LET THERE BE NO BOOK BUT THE WORLD, and above the towel rack in the downstairs bathroom: THE BLESSINGS OF LIBERTY ARE WORTH MANY WOUNDS.

When Dennis and I first moved back to Freyburg, prompted by my wish to be close to my mother toward the end of her illness, we were tenants at will in a rickety railroad apartment in the center of town. After June died, we surprised ourselves by deciding to stay; that's when we moved back to Batter Hollow itself. We inquired after the only one of the old cottages still standing, the former Annex. It had stood vacant for years, and the land company sold it to us on the cheap. Once the ivy was cut back and a new roof installed, it proved to be in remarkably sound condition.

"I just thought," Kitty continued, then stopped short and exhaled impatiently. "Well, if you don't want to talk to anyone. It might help. Writing stuff down."

That's all she'd intended. Something therapeutic, something kind. No double meaning, not a wink at the past. She probably hadn't thought twice in the drugstore or stationery store, wherever she'd stopped on her way up from the city to purchase the notebook, simply grabbing the first one she saw in all innocence, and why not? Why shouldn't the object, ubiquitous as it is, have lost its special charge?

She looked down again, her brow pleating almost quizzically, as if trying to work out what the book was still doing in her hands, and at that point I said thanks and tugged it gently from her.

"Dennis home?"

"He took my car in. Said it could use oil."

At this we exchanged small smiles. We both knew he would return having gotten not only the oil changed but the tank filled, the fluids topped off, the air pressure checked, who knew what else—the tires rotated, the wiper blades replaced? At any rate a bottle of spring water would have materialized in the cup holder, and maybe a chocolate bar on the dash. That was pure Dennis: thoughtful, practical, modest.

"What are you doing about work?" Kitty asked.

Work: I am the Singalong Lady at a dozen area libraries and pre-schools. I drive around with my guitar and a big red duffel bag bulging with rhythm instruments, some of them relics of the old Batter Hollow School stash, and lead the little children in story-songs, nursery rhymes, handclap games. There are things I love about the job and things I don't. One of the things I have come to like less and less is the way I am greeted at each venue: with a sense of fraudulent excitement. "Look, it's the Singalong Lady!" cry the grown-ups. "The Singalong Lady is here!" And the children say, "Hooray!" on cue, and they clap the way babies clap: all their fingers aligned. Sometimes the littlest ones sit on their caregivers' laps and have their tiny hands clapped for them.

Although I did not choose the name (I inherited it from my first employer, a daycare in a church basement), I don't mind being called the Singalong Lady. Its flamboyant silliness is so unlike my usual comportment that I think it must be good for me, an antidote to some aspect of myself I think of as flawed.

"Canceled," I told Kitty. "Called everyone and said I can't come this week. A family crisis." A dry little laugh at the grotesquerie of using this stock phrase. At having occasion to use it.

"So you'll be back next week?"

I shrugged.

"Are you worried, Ayv?"

Too inane to dignify even with a shrug.

"I could still come with you."

Also inane. Besides her patients she has Dillon at home—thirteen months old, with five white teeth and a bulldog grin, blue-black hair going every which way—yet I knew the offer was real, not simply a gesture, and if I'd said yes she'd have found a way to come with me to Perdu. She still would, even now. If I were to go out into the hall this minute and lift the heavy black receiver of Mrs. Tremblay's phone and dial Kitty and tell her I need her, she'd figure out how to be here by tomorrow. She'd reschedule her appointments and call in the grandmothers to babysit, or get Tariq to take time off work, or else she'd bring Dilly along, port-a-crib, umbrella stroller and all.

The thought of her actually pulling into the driveway, of her red Mini jouncing over Mrs. Tremblay's cold, wet gravel, and then of her, Bonny Kitty, here in this room, flopped sideways across the blue-and-mauve bedspread, filling the air with her fleet chatter, as soft and reassuring as the sound of knitting needles, or else, and equally willingly, with her supple, attentive silence as she listened to me finally unburden myself—what a thought!—listening with that look I know so well, the one I imagine she wears as she absorbs her patients' stories of woe, attending deeply and without judgment to these strangers, her clients, of whom I am sometimes (if I admit it now) jealous. I can picture all too clearly her look of earnest, almost simian compassion, and the image, the very idea of Kitty monkey-faced with empathy, is enough to make me laugh aloud here in this hard cold room, but the noise that barks out of my chest is too loud and unnatural, and the sound dies and the room feels emptier.

What to do now but uncap the pen and take up the book she has given me?

But with care, with caution.

I must be vigilant against making this a story.

Three

THE MANSEAUS MOVED to Batter Hollow while we were away on one of our jaunts, thereby giving themselves the aspect of interlopers. At least I remember thinking of them this way when we got home that day in late August, after a week or two on the road (I think we'd gone to the Green Mountains), to find an unfamiliar Volkswagen bus parked in the gravel crescent that served as a parking area for all Batter Hollow residents, and oddments of furnishings and boxes strewn in front of the Art Barn. Batter Hollowans hardly conformed to the standards of lawn care observed in the conventional neighborhoods of Freyburg, so the sight of a single rocking chair or easel or upturned stained-glass lampshade or even naked iron bed frame set down on the unmown grass would not, each item taken in itself, have seemed particularly strange. But amassed together, alongside so much else that smacked of the personal and the private—a pile of shirts laid on hangers across a bureau; a crate packed with household goods: syrup, cornstarch, shampoo; a terrycloth dog resting its ear on the cardboard flap of an open box—these artifacts seemed evidence of things gone awry.

I think there must be something inherently disquieting about seeing objects that are by nature domestic and interior plunked down on naked earth under open sky. I was seven; I knew nothing of disaster apart from the idly glimpsed newspaper photo, the random snippet of televised footage. I had no frame of reference for such a sight that should have made me find it disturbing, and yet I did find it disturbing; I had a sense of troubling disarray and a longing for quick order and explanation. While I stood there, puzzling, beside the car—I had just emerged after long, cramped hours and the lavender-colored air of early evening floated welcomely between my sweaty clothes and my skin—three men appeared from around the side of the Art Barn and traipsed right through the chaos. When I saw they were laughing, I was taken by surprise.

They had a circusy air. One was tall, one regular and one short, and they were all built like wrestlers or acrobats: lean and smoothly muscular. They wore loose dark pants and sleeveless undershirts, except the short one, who was shirtless. One was bald and one had a brush cut and one a ponytail no longer than a thumb. They waded through the high grass and clumps of browning clover and began gathering armloads from among the items left out front, and here it was as if my fancy, my idle association with the circus, held prophetic power, for the tall one hefted the gleaming white base of a table lamp and flung it casually toward the medium-sized one, who snatched it out of the air in the manner of a juggler, one-handed and graceful, and tossed it up like a baton so that it twirled, a long white bone against the fading sky, before he caught it again.

"You see that?" I said to Freddy. We had fought during the car ride so relentlessly that June had at last repositioned a suitcase on the back-seat to act as a barrier wall. Our fights tended to follow a certain pattern: Freddy would do something to get on my nerves, generally something in the realm of noise production: tapping things over and over with his fist or foot, or clicking his tongue or vocalizing in some tuneless, tedious way, and I would tell him to stop. He would ignore me. I would instruct him more sharply, to no greater effect. Eventually I'd pinch him, hard, on the back of his neck, upon which he would shriek and windmill his arms at me, or else bang his head against the window.

On our ride home this day, once the suitcase barricade had been implemented, Freddy had fallen asleep against it. Now one cheek bore the angry-looking mark of its metal latch.

"Ah?" he said, which was Freddy for *what?* as well as *yeah*, as well as a slew of other words.

"Those men doing tricks."

"Ah," he agreed, speaking thickly around his thumb, and then, "Ah 'ook!" When I looked I saw two of them had hoisted the ornate iron bed frame into the air and were walking it around the side of the Art Barn, and this, too, looked like a circus act, the way the metal slats, aloft and moving, sliced up the blue-gold light of the lowering sun and bobbed along the dusty green of the trees edging the path. We watched the bed disappear and then the third man, the short one with the stub of ponytail, rested the lamp base on top of two large cardboard boxes and finessed them into the air as if they were packed with cotton candy. I didn't think they'd even taken note of our arrival, but this last man turned his head and gave us a nod as he rounded the side of the building, and even though the movement was limited to his neck, it had the dapper flourish of a bow.

I looked at Freddy and he blinked a kind of acknowledgment without looking directly at me. He rarely looked directly at anyone. Even when he turned his face to you, his eyes would slide off over your shoulder or, more disconcertingly, focus on something nonexistent around your jaw. Tiny bubbles of spit had gathered between the corners of his lips and thumb. I used his elbow as a lever to yank the thumb out, a motion I had performed hundreds of times. Depending on his mood, it could result in a full-blown fit, but now he simply replaced the thumb, hardly bothering to scowl. We turned toward our parents, who were preoccupied with unloading luggage from the back of the Dasher.

"What are those people?" I asked.

Neel finished working the bag of tent poles from its designated space and set it down with a little grunt before turning to Freddy and me, giving us, as usual, his full attention when he did: hands on hips, head tilted contemplatively—not in contemplation of the answer, but in contemplation of the question. He had a way of delaying speech by bringing his lips in tight against his teeth, as if our most basic questions were transmitted materially into his mouth and required parsing with the most intricate and involving work of his tongue before he could answer. This initial hesitation was his response to almost any comment or question put before him, and throughout my childhood I took it for his native temperament; only later did I see it as a habit he had formed consciously, through discipline.

"What do you think?" Typical Neel answer.

"Ah-ma, ah-magic thow," Freddy slurped.

Neel seemed to consider this possibility with a judicious cocking of his head.

"Do you know them?" I persisted, and then, too impatient to bother with Neel, appealed directly to June: "Did we know about them?"

From behind Neel's shoulder my mother gave a nod. New neighbors, then. No one had lived in the Art Barn for a long time.

"Who are they? Are they all moving in? Is it just those men? Are there any kids?" What I didn't let myself say: Is there a girl?

I had been yearning for a girl for as long as I could remember, had been actively, strenuously awaiting the arrival of a friend. No less romantically than Rapunzel in her tower pined for rescue did I pine for this idealized being, a kind of alternate me, a me outside of me. Sometimes I would pretend my reflection in the bathroom mirror was she, or contained her, or was a conduit to her, that shining one who would somehow at once be my familiar, my deepest intimate, and at the same time exist thrillingly apart, beyond my will and my ken. She'd have a store of knowledge I did not have, and a willingness to convey it, and an appetite to hear my secrets in kind. She haunted me, this figure whose absence I felt physically as a small precise knot in my chest.

We had a book within whose pages I spent countless childhood hours. It was titled *What's Your Name?* and contained twenty-one paintings by Edna Eicke. All of them had originally appeared on the cover of *The New Yorker*. It was easy to get lost in the images, each of which managed to suggest an entire world and cast of characters with the most particularly observed details: the bent stick with which a rain-slickered boy poked the gutter; the placid stance of a lone pumpkin seller watching the empty road at sunset; the tiptoeing excitement of a girl in a party dress as she peered impatiently through the curtained pane of her front door. I spent hours "reading" this book: gazing at each painting until I seemed, in some serious, definite way, to enter it. The experience was mysterious and ecstatic, involving the sensation that, having surrendered myself to the imaginary world, I attained a state of merging with it.

Looking back now, I am a little mortified by my own sentimentality, for there was something insipid about the art: all those nicely groomed white people full of quaint gentility. All those painted shutters and double chimneys, those wide lawns and spired churches. But the sanitized ideal was part and parcel of what I loved. It fed that part of me that held out an indistinct hope for a more neatly ordered world than that which I knew. Come to think of it, what drew me was not so much the images' sentimentality as their promise of convention, something I craved throughout childhood, a memory that evokes anger as well as shame.

The title painting was my favorite. Centered in the foreground stands a girl in a red-striped dress, facing away from us, her hands clasped behind her back. She has for the moment forgotten about the teddy bear in the doll perambulator by her side, and is looking instead through a rather weathered picket fence into the expansive yard next door, where another girl stands, this one in a straw hat and little blue jacket, cradling a doll in the crook of her arm and regarding the first girl with equally open interest. Behind her, two movers are just hefting a bureau up the front steps of a house on whose porch a woman oversees their labors. A third mover heads down the stone walkway toward the street, where (presumably) a moving truck stands ready to disgorge more possessions.

The title of this painting, as I have mentioned, is *What's Your Name?* and the artlessness of this appealed to me, too. It seemed to confirm that despite the rather formal, restrained postures of the key characters, the crux of the matter was friendship. Too, that the slightly grave atmosphere was not a sign of wariness, but rather of the girls' recognition of the occasion's enormity: the birth of friendship being no less momentous than the instant of falling in love.

Something of this enormity rose up in me while I stood outside our tired orange Dasher at the end of the day at the end of our trip at the end of the summer. The cooling engine pinged. I was gathering myself to receive further information about our new neighbors, information I knew would not be forthcoming from Neel or June, but which I would have to seek out for myself.

"Come on, Freddy," I said, again grasping his elbow, but more gently this time, using it not to yank out the thumb but to lead him along as I crossed the gravel crescent and then the thistly grass. When we got within range of what would have been, if this wasn't Batter Hollow but a regular neighborhood with distinct property lines, the front lawn of the Art Barn, we stopped. Freddy separated from me and went straight for a box of kitchen things set under the sassafras tree. Squatting before it, he extracted a wooden spoon as assuredly as if he'd put it there himself and began banging away on the cookware.

"Fred-*dee*," I admonished in a low growl, but didn't bother to go on. Any attempt on my part to intervene would be useless. Only June might pull him away from a find like this, and even then the prospect of diverting him peacefully was less likely a scenario than something punctuated by screams and snot and dripping tears and saliva dripping, too. I had watched him once as he succumbed to the vortex of one of his frequent tantrums, regarded him from the doorway with a mixture of disdain and disquiet—for even then I had an inkling that his strange behavior implicated me, too—and witnessed a long, glassine string of saliva stretch across his howling mouth and dangle, languorous, from a shining white eyetooth, until it broke off and landed on the carpet: a dark dot of drool.

The last thing I wanted on this sultry August afternoon was for a big Freddy flare-up to interfere with my reconnaissance, so I simply stood back and willed him to bang less loudly on the pots. Sunlight shone through the mitten-shaped leaves of the sassafras tree and dappled him where he squatted, wholly absorbed by the sounds he produced. This was what other people failed to see: for all that his noise-making might seem haphazard, imbecilic, there was sense to it, real deliberation in the phrases he sounded out. I knew it from the way he sped up and slowed down, and chose to repeat some patterns and vary others, and also from the lost, listening look on his face. He wore green plaid shorts and a holey T-shirt and curls clung to his nape, sticky with sweat.

A great splintering crash came from inside the Art Barn. I whipped around to see, but there was only the serene-looking building, with June's old mural splashed familiarly across the side, and an indecipherable silence. Then: raucous waves of male laughter, impaled by a lance of womanly imprecation. Another, shakier silence descended, this one quickly broken by more laughter. Then footsteps descended the creaky stairs. A woman's exasperated summons: "Kitty! Kitty!" The voice was somehow low and high at once: deep in pitch but overlaid with a sonorous lilt. It made me think of milk caramel. "Kitty!" the voice cast about. "Where have you gone to now?"

I thought: *At least they have a cat.*

Then the speaker stepped out onto the porch. She was big-bosomed, big-waisted, big-armed, with small feet and a blue and white flowered dress, and her hair lay in pale swirls around her head like buttercream icing on a cake. Almost automatically, I stepped forward so as to put my body between Freddy and the woman's line of vision, not really to hide him from her notice (the continuing clatter of spoon-on-steel would have made that futile in any case) but perhaps to delay whatever repercussions might ensue. The woman seemed harried, but in the mildest way, as though to be harried was part of her everyday bearing, like a familiar garment she wore comfortably loose. Sighing audibly, she squinted out across the grass, shielding her eyes against the setting sun with one hand. She came to a stop facing in our general direction. "Kitty!" she called more pointedly, peering over our heads. "Are you up a tree?"

Despite my worry over this woman's possible remonstrance when she realized Freddy was beating on her cookware (though my worry, like her harriedness, perhaps, was so well worn it made little impression on me), I was interested in what she'd said. A cat up a tree: that was like something out of a book. A fire engine comes and a ladder gets hoisted and a jolly, dependable man in red hat and shiny boots ascends.

"Kitty," the woman called again, her voice now sharp and practical. "I *see* you. I see your shoes plain as day."

Overhead the branches gave a rustle. I turned my back to the woman in the flowered dress in order to follow her gaze, searching among the boughs above me, which began dipping this way and that as if the tree itself was responding.

Then something dropped from the leafy canopy, landed on the ground with a thwack. A shoe. Brown, buckle undone. It raised a little cloud of yellow dust where it fell, and was followed by the other, and then a heavier scrabbling than a cat could cause, and this is how Kitty Manseau entered my life: barefoot, feet first, born of the lower branches of a sassafras tree, metamorphosed before my blinking eyes from feline to human form: a girl my size in pin-striped conductor's overalls, her flaxen hair cut shorter than Freddy's yet declaring itself very brightly in little sprigs that stuck out all around her head.

She landed gracefully, in fact cat-like, on the dirt. She ministered to the sole of one foot by bringing it to waist level, spitting on it, and rubbing at it with her thumb. Only after releasing it back to the ground did she meet my eyes and give a nod. "Hi."

"Hi," I echoed. "What's your name?" If I blushed a little, saying it, hearing it for the parrot job it was, the line in the book, the title of the very painting into which I half did believe I magically had entered, she didn't seem to notice.

"Kitty. I live over in that flowered house there." And then, with studied nonchalance: "My bedroom's got a sink."

I observed her and she stared back, all confidence, her lean arms and her pert, puckish face. Her yellow hair was lighter than her tanned skin. So were her eyebrows, pale as pollen, and her eyes. She was like the inverse of me. Everybody in our family had dark eyes. Hers were chicory blue, and narrowed at this moment; she had her chin angled up so that even though we were the same height she seemed to peer down at me.

That flowered house.

"It's called the Art Barn," I informed her. "And it isn't really yours." I meant to be firm but nice, to assert my own claim without contaminating the chance of friendship, but even as I spoke I felt a queer misgiving. For the first time I wondered who did own the Art Barn, and all the Batter Hollow School buildings, and for that matter the land itself, the great, slovenly meadow that stretched out between the cottages and the dark woods that ringed it. I'd always assumed all this was ours. But were we really the property owners, or had it been just the school itself that belonged to Neel, not the physical buildings but only the idea, only the part that had dwindled to stories and photographs, names and dates, memory's dry artifacts?

"Is too," she said, without any special force.

For a second I could think only of shoving her. Then I got an inspiration. "My mother," I told her, "is the one who painted those flowers."

Sometime earlier, around when the first shoe had fallen from the tree, Freddy had stopped picking out rhythms on the pots and pans and drifted over to stand nearish me, dragging the long-handled wooden spoon behind him. Now I could hear him breathing in his cloggy way just beside my shoulder. "We've been inside it," I added, "about a hundred times. Me and Freddy here." I jerked my thumb at him.

So it was only natural that we transferred our gazes—Kitty and me both, the first thing we ever did together—to him.

PART OF THE PROBLEM with Fred's being big for his age was that it made people think he was older than he was, which in turn made him seem even slower than he was. Just that day, on our way home from Vermont, we'd stopped for lunch at a roadside diner. While we waited to order, Freddy played with the individual plastic tubs of syrup and jelly that sat in a little basket, emptying a few syrups onto the table before June, taking note just as he was going for another, whisked the basket away.

You could see the rage boil up inside Freddy. His color rose and a vein stood out blue in his neck. I braced myself for a tantrum, but then Neel mused, in the idlest of tones, "I wonder if a person could paint with that?" and Freddy dropped his gaze to where Neel was looking, and sat back on the seat of the banquette and began to draw his finger through the syrup puddle before him. The tabletop was gold-flecked Formica, and Freddy was quickly engrossed in the whorls of golden syrup he made over the gold flecks. He skated a finger through the viscous stuff, becoming wholly absorbed, his mouth open, his tongue stuffed between his teeth.

When the waitress came to take our order she took one look, said, "Oh—lovely," and yanked a damp cloth from her apron. "Don't you know better than to play with your food?" Her voice was penny-bright with false cheer. Her elbow jerked near my face as she wiped at the sticky mess. "A big boy like you."

"He's only five," I explained.

Freddy, against all odds, had not begun to bellow in response to the devastation of his artwork. Apparently shocked into inaction, he only stared up at her, agape.

"I would've thought he was two," she pronounced, stuffing the rag back in her apron pocket. "Five." She snorted. "Five's plenty old not to make a mess."

His head bent and his thumb slid into his mouth.

Now I think she must have just been that way, that brassy with everyone, a no-nonsense sort whose regulars looked forward to being charmed by her rough banter. But at the time I was aghast. Such intolerance, such lack of tact—I wasn't used to anyone addressing Freddy this way. When he acted out in public, most people carefully ignored it. Sometimes they'd act flustered, embarrassed, as if the transgression were theirs. Later I came to understand this had something to do with Neel's reputation, the respect people had for him, even if they disagreed with his methods. On the rare occasions when people did express disapproval of his behavior, it was always surreptitious, a comment uttered just beneath their breath or behind the shield of their hand. Never before had I encountered someone brazen enough to pass judgment out loud and in no uncertain terms with Neel and June sitting right there, and the fierce indignation I felt toward the waitress in that moment mingled, confusingly, with admiration.

In general Neel did not intervene. In general he was against intervention. But now, in the most dulcet, encouraging tones, he leaned across the table and said, "What had you been making there, Freddy?"

June flashed him a look, which he declined to notice. Then I saw her turn and gaze apologetically, or in a kind of appeal, toward the waitress, but the waitress, too, would not catch her eye; she only dragged out her order pad and jabbed at the end of her retractable pen.

"What was your drawing of, hm?" coaxed Neel.

For a long moment we waited then, all of us growing increasingly uncomfortable except for Neel, who seemed wholly untroubled.

"What's that?" he urged, as if to say, "Beg pardon?" although Freddy had not made a sound.

"Ah . . ." Freddy let his thumb slide wetly from his mouth. Still with his face looking down at the spot where the syrup had been, he said, "Ah, ah-cow."

That this was false must have been transparent even to the waitress, although she could not have known what to the rest of us was obvious: the fib's inspiration. Just before turning off the highway for lunch, Neel had pulled the Dasher over onto the shoulder so that we could all get out and have a good look at a herd of grazing cows.

"What do cows say, Freddy?" June had prompted. She'd picked him up, heavy as he was, the better for him to see, and they stood close to the fence, with its five rows of wire strung between wooden posts like a musical staff. June had been teaching me to read music so we could play recorder duets.

"Moo."

"That's right."

I stood a little away, pleased with my discovery of how the fence resembled the empty staves in my music notebook. "Look at the fence," I began, tugging June's skirt, but saw I did not have her attention. Never mind. I would practice alone, practice the mnemonic she had taught me for the lines of the treble staff, trying to hear the notes in my head as I touched my finger to each row of wire in turn: "Every . . . Good . . . Boy . . ."—going from a crouch onto my tiptoes as I reached for the highest two rows—". . . Does . . . Fine." *Fine* delivered a nasty jolt, weirdly fizzy and spiked. I thought at first I'd been stung by a bee. I studied my finger; it bore no mark. The tears that sprang to my eyes were due more to surprise than pain. I squeezed the finger in my other hand and looked around; no one had seen.

Neel, squinting across the pasture, his hands deep in the pockets of his rumpled canvas pants, said in his mild way, pleasant yet corrective: "Cows do not say moo."

And they had not. We stood there smelling the sweetish, prickling mixture of grass and manure, and took them in: they were massive and brown, magisterially placid except for their switching tails. Their eyes big as plums, the bones of their haunches sharp as coat hangers from which their pendulous bodies hung.

We'd stood in a row before the fence, our various heights, it occurred to me, like notation, like the notes missing from the bare staff. No one but I knew the top wire was electrified. I began to hope someone else would touch it. I began to hope Neel would. He was always saying we should learn through experience. A secret, greedy pressure built up in me as I concentrated on the back of his curly head, stared hard at his tanned, creased neck, willing him to rest a hand on the fence's uppermost wire.

He removed his hands from his pockets. I held my breath. "Well," he exclaimed, giving a clap as he turned around. He rubbed his hands vigorously together and seemed to look shrewdly in my direction. "Who's hungry?"

I blushed, and bit my sleeve.

UNDER THE SASSAFRAS Kitty and I stood, a minute or two into our relationship, tenuously united for the first time in the joint act of regarding my little brother, whose own eyes flitted back and forth between us and then away—Freddy whose gaze was forever unmoored, forever listing. Watching him was like watching a ship take on water: under our collective appraisal something seemed to mount within him. Kitty couldn't have known it then, but I recognized the signs of his growing tension, and could guess where it might lead.

Neel and June were nowhere in sight. The bulkhead doors leading to the cellar had been flung open and they had both gone belowground to store the tents and poles in that dank space I loathed, with its low ceiling jiggly with cobwebs and its curious, sour clay smell. We were not entirely beyond the purview of grown-ups; from the corner of my eye I saw the wide woman in blue ambling across the grass toward us.

But I never took my gaze off Freddy while Kitty and I stood and stared at him, because to do so would have been to sever something, this little game we'd begun when we turned, in concert, to look at him, or which perhaps we'd begun earlier when she first tumbled out of the tree, or earlier still when the first shoe fell, when she was still half-cat and I was enchanted by the idea, and now that I had entered this game with her I had to stay. We looked at Freddy. His sloe-eyes went glassy. They fixed on something invisible between us. We had him trapped. We were all very quiet and still under the canopy of mitten-shaped leaves, but the power we held over him was vibratingly real. Visibly he took on more and more of whatever it was we were transferring to him: nothing else but our attention, yet such a deliberate, substantial sort of attention that it seemed to swell him with actual mass. And I had the impression that Kitty, innocent as she then was of Freddy, nevertheless had an inkling of what was happening, what kind of effect we were having on him, so that when the inevitable happened, it seemed to me I wasn't the only one who bore responsibility. Kitty, no matter how genuinely surprised she sounded when she cried out, no matter how true the pain—and it must have been painful, from the pale blue egg that rose up almost instantly on the crescent ledge of bone beneath her eye—was implicated, too.

Moments before Mrs. Manseau reached our little enclave under the sassafras tree, Freddy raised the long wooden spoon he'd been trailing in the dust all this time, arced it up over his head and brought it down in front of him, displacing the air with all his might but not a trace of anger—acting on pure impulse and nothing else—until it met with an audible crack Kitty's heart-shaped available face.

Four

COLD AND HUNGER finally impel me from Mrs. Tremblay's mauve-and-blue guest room around noon.

In an effort to remedy the first, earlier this morning I'd pulled the coverlet off the bed and wrapped it around me as I sat at the rattan desk, writing in the marble-covered book. Kitty had been prescient. Or not prescient, smart. At any rate, writing does seem to help. And once I began, the words came fast. Really I should say they came fast and slow, because the act of writing plunged me so wantonly down slippery avenues of thought that frequently I found myself not writing at all, but having come to an unbidden halt and gazing into the middle distance between the page and the rainy windowpane, my mouth open on a half-formed word with which my hand had been unable to keep pace and from which my mind had careened many seconds or even whole minutes earlier like a horse having thrown its rider. Until, coming to, I would begin to write again, transcribing the raw, unruly stuff of memory and imagination as best I could into letters, sentences, paragraphs. I kept up this spasmodic progress long enough to fill a dozen pages before dropping the pen, queasy with the realization that I was doing again what I'd sworn against: molding the fluid stuff of life into form.

I sat rigid then in judgment upon myself, with the stiff bedspread wrapped around me and my arms folded across my chest, until I realized I resembled one of the pair of Indian dolls that had been passed down through generations in June's family. June said her paternal grandmother had always claimed Oneida lineage, but we had no documentation and June herself seemed somewhat skeptical. Still, I took pleasure in believing it, fervently, all throughout my childhood. (Why? Out of simple-minded romanticism? Or because the story seemed to explain my own persistent and inarticulable feeling of otherness?)

The dolls—a man and a woman, each about a foot tall—were not for playing with. They stood on a shelf in the living room in their doe suede moccasins and heavy woven blankets and long, coarse hair that June said probably came from a real horse's tail. Their faces were molded of glue and sawdust and what I loved most was the unalloyed sobriety of their expressions. They looked as though nothing you told them could possibly make them blink or turn away.

On occasion June would let me take them down, though never when Fred was around. I could be trusted to handle the dolls gently, to inspect how their cotton print shirts had real tiny buttons and tiny pointed collars; to confirm that the beaded necklace the man wore went all the way around his neck; to stick my finger up under the woman's skirt and feel that her legs ended in a block of wood; to press— lightly—their middles and hear and feel the straw stuffing give. She knew I would never force off the stitched-on blankets to see whether they really had arms. I would never break their legs, trying to make them walk or sit. I would never take them into the woods and leave them there to have their faces washed off in the rain, their bodies twisted, their hair plucked out by birds.

But oh, help: I am telling a story. I am telling a story and I must not. What do I know of what happened? What do I know of Fred, my brother, my little brother, now at six-feet-two and nearly two hundred pounds my big-little brother, from whom I have not heard in almost two years? What do I know of his relationship to James Ferebee, twelve years old, enrolled in the sixth grade at Arthur L. Humphrey Middle School right here in Perdu, who, according to the papers, had played youth basketball and numbered among his hobbies fishing and rock collecting; who, last Saturday, at Criterion Regional Medical Center, was pronounced dead?

Nothing. Next to nothing. Little more, perhaps, than Mrs. Tremblay down in the kitchen, monitoring her old cathode-ray TV, which sits fatly on the counter beside the breadbox, emitting its endless newsfeed. She had the local news on at breakfast (fried egg, slice of toast, grapefruit half), and though nothing came on about Fred, I was on edge the whole time, listening for the coanchors' jovial banter to break up and resolve itself into a suddenly grim "And now, following up on last week's story about young James Ferebee . . ."

What did I fear they might divulge? I know what conclusion the public has already drawn. What the television reporters are insinuating every time they direct their somber looks at the camera, looks I imagine they rehearsed in broadcasting school, so uniform are they, so perfectly pitched at virtuous condemnation. I know what it means when they say, "In the absence of any request for ransom, authorities can only speculate on possible motives for abducting the child," and, "A spokesperson for the boy's family describes the suspect as a loner who kept odd hours and preferred the company of children to adults."

A man drives a boy into the woods, disappears with him there for days, until one is found alive and one is found dead, and where no story is proffered people rush in to make one. It's unavoidable, inexorable, water swirling into a ditch. We are at the mercy of our own narrative impulses. We must have story at all costs.

My story is this: Fred is no predator.

Which does not mean he is incapable of doing harm.

I look at my watch: not even one. More than three hours before I'm due at the law offices of Bayard Charles.

I cannot stay in this room until then. If nothing else, I will need lunch. I stand and the bedspread slips from my shoulders.

The stairs, with their flimsy iron banister that moves beneath my hand like a loose tooth, lead directly into the living room, where Mrs. Tremblay looks up from the plaid recliner on which she sits with an object in her lap. Not a cross-stitch, not coupons, not even *Reader's Digest*, but a heavy, serious-looking book, a library book, from the crackle and glint of its acetate jacket. The story I have been telling myself about her needs adjusting. She says nothing, merely looks at me, neither friendly nor unfriendly. I want to ask what she's reading but instead wipe my palms on my pants and say, "I . . . I'll be heading out now," then remain stupidly on the bottom step like a child waiting to be dismissed.

She gives a nod, her lower lip tightly molded around that phantom lemon drop, her finger marking her place in the book. It is so quiet in here, so small. The house with its neat and orderly furnishings shrinks tighter around me. Mrs. Tremblay does not return to her reading but continues to regard me. From somewhere in the very still room comes the sound of a clock I do not see. Each tick a tiny *tsk*.

Until, shaking free of my paralysis, I stumble down the last step into the little foyer where my coat hangs. While I am shoving my arms into the sleeves, Mrs. Tremblay calls out, "Know where you're going?"

Close to a panic—if I answer I will expose the reason I am here, expose once and for all my dreadful link—I thrust my feet hurriedly into my boots, yank open the door and call back, "All set, thanks!" before stepping gratefully into the cold rain.

THE ROAD FROM MRS. TREMBLAY'S into Perdu undulates darkly in a crevice between forested hills. The wind has dropped but rain still falls steadily and in the lowest places my tires send up pearly plumage. I keep my speed low, wipers high. Yellow road signs show silhouettes of swerving cars and zigzag arrows, of trucks pointing down steep grades and of leaping deer. Once when we were small, June paid a tall man at the Freyburg street fair to cut our silhouettes, Freddy's and mine, from black paper. The man wore suspenders and worked with tiny, long-handled scissors, and snipped out our likenesses unbelievably fast. I remember he had a waxed mustache, too, so wide it stuck out past his face like the whiskers on a mouse. My silhouette came out just like me, all the little protrusions and recessions of my profile faithfully noted, including the eyeglasses I still wore then and the slimmest outcropping of paper for my eyelashes. The artist complimented me on sitting so well.

Freddy's was a vaguer likeness. He would not stay put on the little canvas camp stool, but wiggled back and forth until it collapsed; when it was set up again, first he straddled it, then hunched, then, briefly submitting to the artist's entreaties, did sit up straight—only to keep pulling at his lower lip and rubbing his eyes. Then he had a sneezing fit which made him "fall" off the stool. When he got to his feet, he had ropes of snot hanging from both nostrils. June rummaged for tissues in her bag; by the time she found one, he'd wandered off to another booth, whose wares—delicate stained-glass objects displayed on a table—he immediately began to handle, and June had to pay the silhouette cutter in a hurry so we could run after Freddy before he broke any.

For many years they hung, our silhouettes in oval frames, side by side in the upstairs hall: my features neat and tidy, Freddy's softer, slightly lumpy; his hair a strange, clownish nimbus, mine molded neatly to the contours of my head before diverging in a braid down my back. Facing each other, our silhouettes did what Freddy and I could never have done in real life: held each other's unbroken gaze, the very emblem of interconnectedness. But when turned back to back they gave off an embittered aura, an air of excommunication. I am the one who used to switch them around on their picture hooks, depending on whether I loved my brother or hated him on any given day. June must have noticed but never commented on the inconstancy of their orientation.

I wish it were Fred I was driving toward now, instead of this Bayard Charles, his "assigned counsel," whose law offices are in another town. He hadn't even met Fred yet when he finally returned my calls late Monday afternoon. He spoke slowly; I had the sense he was groping between words for the thread of his own thoughts. "Frederick Robbins…" he repeated when I reminded him why I had called, "… Robbins…Oh, yes. Ugly business. So you're the sister?" I could hear papers being shuffled. His breathing made me picture a heavy man, and his voice had the same squashed quality as Mrs. Tremblay's, his vowels flat as the pennies Kitty and I once laid on the Freyburg railroad tracks in anticipation of the commuter train.

We'd been ten that afternoon, at the beginning, and in some important way the height, of our power. Holding hands, we'd backed slowly from the tracks, never letting our vision stray from the five copper coins glinting in the autumn sun, even as the engine approached, mounting in volume and also in something else, a kind of invisible charge, bearing down on us, louder and louder with an accompanying thrust of wind, making us shriek wild crackling ribbons of laughter, and then it was *there*, directly in front of us, a rushing, and we yelled as it stormed by.

In the wake of the train—a kind of elastic lucidity that marbled the air as the whipped-up red and brown leaves settled slowly back upon their beds—we went looking for our pennies. We scoured the rails and ties and the leafy gravel and everything seemed to glint like copper, fooling us, until at last, running our fingers through the clumps of weeds, we did find one, elongated and effaced of any markings.

Freddy had wanted to come and we wouldn't let him. "You're not old enough." In the end we staved off a tantrum only by promising to bring him back one of the flattened pennies, but we never did turn up any of the others. Years later I read that pennies can shoot out like bullets when struck by the wheels of a train, and imagined a disc of copper lodging in a shinbone or eye. I realized what a lucky thing it was neither of us got hit, and how stupid we'd been to stand so close. Back at Batter Hollow, when Freddy demanded his due, we told him we couldn't give him the penny. "We don't even have one apiece," I reasoned.

"And we did all the work," said Kitty.

Whenever he was upset Freddy reddened almost hydraulically, the color rising to mottle his neck, cheeks and ears in succession until it bloomed around his eyes. On that day, as he struggled visibly to fight back tears, I thought about what we'd promised and how much self-control it must have taken for him not to tag along after us, and I began to feel the labor of his restraint as if it were my own, and I felt something else, too: his good faith in us, his innocence, how deep it ran and how unchecked it was, and I understood there was something wrong about this and frightening, how even at his age I'd had more circumspection, and the squashed penny burned in my fist.

But, "You won't get your way by being a baby about it," said Kitty as his eyes filled, adding in her matter-of-fact way, "This is why we didn't let you come."

For several seconds battle was waged on the vacillating planes of Freddy's face. Then he mastered himself; the tears never came, and as if he'd somehow transferred his turmoil to me, I was the one fraught with competing emotions: fury at Kitty, shame at my own inability to challenge her, relief that Freddy was back from the brink and we wouldn't have to give him our penny.

Five

HERE IS A STORY—the story—we grew up with, the one we were nursed on and cut our teeth on, the one that housed us and rocked us to sleep and gave shape to our days, our doings, our forays into the woods behind our home and into the wider world. The story that shaped our sense of who we were:

Man is by nature good.

Though nowhere woodburned into rough pine and nailed up on the wall, these words might well have been. They might well have decorated every cottage, every stone, every tree trunk around Batter Hollow, for they were writ large in every part of the landscape that was our home: in the absence of rules and routine; in the trust Neel and June afforded us and the self-reliance they instilled in us; in the way our own appetites were encouraged to develop freely, without either approval or disapproval.

We were free children. Or Free Children, for this was official parlance, just as Batter Hollow had famously, for nearly a quarter of a century, been a Free School—no mandatory instruction, no required classes—and when the school closed down and we came along, we were freer even than the old students had been, for there was even less structure, and no division at all between school and life.

Neel, after two childless marriages and half a lifetime superintending hundreds of children not his own, found in us, Fred and me, an opportunity at last to put his beliefs fully into practice, around the clock, from birth. I don't mean to say he saw us as experiments, or even that he was more theoretician than father.

And yet. He did seem to regard everything as if through a haze of philosophical curiosity, as if everything under the sun was an experiment, all life experiential, all knowledge empirical, and—this was the crux of it—all experience productive of information and therefore good.

Once I came to him pincushioned with nettles. I must have been five, maybe six. I'd fallen down in the grass only to find both palms and one side of my face on fire with pain. I remember running into the house, its dimness after the bright outdoors rendering me half blind, and barreling clumsily toward the cool, camphor-smelling air of his study, where I knew I'd find him. I was screaming all the while in a way that frightened me, reminded me of my brother. I was hysterical not only because of the pain but with a sense of outrage that something in our own backyard could injure me so. By the time I reached his study Neel was already on his feet and charging around his big, heavy desk, on whose corner he smacked his hip, which made him let out such a roar that for a second I was surprised into silence. Then I resumed crying and he carried me into the kitchen, sat me on a stool and assessed my trouble.

Once he'd determined the cause of my anguish, he calmly fixed a paste of baking soda and water, which he applied with the basting brush to all my red welts. As my sobs subsided, he asked me questions about what had happened, displaying deep, Neelesque interest in the most minor details of my account. I could feel him drawing me out, could feel his subdued pleasure as I shared my impressions, transforming happenstance into understood experience.

When I finished unburdening myself, he squinted up at the ceiling as if marvelously deep in thought, then asked if he might accompany me outside so I could show him where I'd fallen. When I pointed out the spot, he bent and—first taking care to wrap his fingers in the handkerchief he always kept neatly folded in a pants pocket—plucked the leaves of the nettle, one by one. "I wonder," he said, "if we can make soup out of these." Still hiccoughing a bit, not at all sure I liked the idea and liking even less the fact that the nettles rather than my injury now seemed to occupy his attention, I followed him nonetheless back into the kitchen.

We did make nettle soup, with leeks and butter, and the story became oft-told. He used it in lectures, and it got recycled in a feature article profiling notable figures in progressive education, and later requoted in a book. It wasn't only Neel who got mileage out of it; I'd tell it, too, at gatherings of old friends, when getting to know new ones, once at a Batter Hollow reunion. I told it at his memorial service, in fact, framing it, then as always, just as Neel had, making it a story about the things he believed most deeply: that learning is born of experience, that suffering is a valuable teacher, and that all nature's offerings, even those with the capacity to hurt, may be viewed without horror if only we adjust the angle of our perception.

There is one detail I never included, though it was the part I liked best, as well as the reason, I believe, the incident lodged itself so squarely in my memory. In fact, the reason I know my memory is real, not simply a construction based on hearing it so often recounted, is that this aspect of the story was never included in any of the tellings. It is simply this: the look on Neel's face when I first came into his study, just before he banged his hip on the desk. The look he wore while striding around it, not yet knowing what was the matter, just moving as fast as he could toward the banshee sound I was making: a look of utter, ashen terror.

We grew up godless. I learned this only later, once I'd started going to public school and having regular interactions with the more mainstream citizens of Freyburg, kids whose families had Christmas trees or menorahs, whose weekly attendance was required at Sabbath dinner or Sunday services, girls my age who wore on slender chains around their necks tiny gold crosses or Stars of David, and who, no matter how raucous or mocking or harsh they might be on the soccer field or in the cafeteria (the caf, as the older girls thrillingly called it), were invariably glad to explain, when asked, the meanings of these symbols in clear, apprising tones that made me hopelessly jealous—of their jewelry, yes, but even more than that, of their . . . I don't know, *membership*. The way they spoke—the lavish surety with which they related captivating accounts of murdered babies and gentle beasts, of anointing with oil and wandering in the wilderness, of angels who rolled back stones and angels who guided a child's hand to a white-hot coal—created in me my first sharp awareness of impoverishment, of being both an outsider and beyond the pale.

"Don't you *know*?" they would marvel, eyes widening, when I inquired about some aspect of their story that should apparently have been obvious (*Who are the chosen? It really turns to blood? Why couldn't they eat the apples? What's crucify?*), but here again, even the brashest and most supercilious of my peers would respond with a munificent patience they did not otherwise possess, as though it were on loan from another source. Whether such largesse was a mark of their concern for the egregiousness of my ignorance, or whether it signaled a special goodness engendered by religion, either way I was left yearning for what I did not have, and blaming Neel and June for the deprivation.

"Why don't we go to church?" I demanded at home, causing Neel to widen his eyes theatrically and work his lips ruminatively, a performance of contemplation. Then he went into full Socratic mode:

"Why do you ask?"

"Everyone else does."

"Everyone?" He raised his bushy white eyebrows. "Really?"

"Basically. Most people. Church or temple."

"And you'd like it if we went, too?"

"Yes."

"In order to be like everyone else?"

But I was too clever to let him lead me down that path. "No, Neel. Not to be like them—because *I* think it's important."

"What's important about it?"

I hesitated, then came up with what seemed to me a trump card: "God."

It must have been a good answer, because he tacked a little to the left. "And what is it you'd do at church?"

"Pray."

"What does that mean, 'pray'?"

"Talk to God."

"Can't you do that anywhere?"

"It's not the same as if you do it in church."

"What's different about it?"

And so on, until I was ready to heave my knapsack at him.

In the end, though, they decided I should be allowed to experience it for myself, and a few weeks later June took Kitty and me to Quaker services on the other side of the county. I asked June to braid my hair, and Kitty and I both wore skirts and buckled shoes instead of our habitual jeans and sneakers. We rode silently along bumpy back roads, the snowy fields bathed in a thin broth of winter sun. I pressed my mittened hands together in my lap. My scalp felt tight with the braids.

The Friends' Meeting House turned out to be a plain white clapboard structure with a wide front porch and inside, an austere room with wooden benches arranged in concentric circles. There were only twenty or thirty people there, all of them grown-ups, many of them elderly, sitting mostly in silence for what felt like hours. Every now and then someone would stand and say something uninteresting and sit back down again. I was as bored as I'd ever been in my life. I played with my tongue for a while, tried to see if I could count my teeth with it. I kept thinking how lucky it was Freddy hadn't come, how if he were there he'd be making noise, using his fingers as drumsticks, kicking rhythms against the bench in front of him, wailing if June tried to make him stop, and how the people, the Friends gathered in this room, would turn their elderly grim faces toward him, toward June, too, and Kitty and me, and silently determine that Freddy was wicked and June negligent, and Kitty and I distasteful by association, and how they wouldn't understand about who he was, how unmanageable his ways, and how beyond his control because so thoroughly a part of him.

These thoughts made me feel still and mysterious and ancient and sad, almost worthy of my tight braids and skirt and buckled shoes, and when at last people started shaking hands with those sitting near them, and we stood and stretched our stiff cold limbs, I felt as if I'd aged years since I'd woken up that morning.

Then we all filed into the back of the building, where there turned out to be a warm kitchen with applesauce bubbling on an industrial-sized stove and homemade bread and honey—and children! There had been other children there the whole time, off in some other room where they'd been given yarn and sticks for making God's eyes, which they now displayed happily to their parents. Kitty and I exchanged a look of wordless indignation: apparently we'd missed out on the fun part of church. We bit into our bread and honey with sullen relief.

That was not quite my only foray into formal religion. But for all intents and purposes, I grew up with neither a belief in nor even a rough impression of God. Except that no child grows up entirely godless, not unless deprived of the presence of those first, most tangible of gods: our parents. And they were real eminences, Neel and June. You might think parents who followed the creed of allowing their offspring total freedom in exercising their own judgments, their own curiosities and desires, would seem less god-like than other parents—those who more closely direct, intercede and proscribe. But which is more almighty—an ultimate controller, the author of every stroke and flourish, or a prime mover, one who sets life in motion and then bears witness as we exercise free will?

I only know that to me they seemed the more powerful, the more all-knowing, for their remove, for the myriad ways they refrained from ordering or mediating or salving. Although in this they were not equals. Even at a young age, I was attuned to June's ambivalence, the way her actions sometimes seemed to call Neel's own into question.

Once, at a birthday party for one of the Ganns, all the Batter Hollow kids were outside setting off Alka-Seltzer rockets: plastic film canisters in which water and bicarbonate of soda were mingled to combustive effect. It was an unseasonably cold spring day, the air packed with a raw, meaty dampness. Our hands and lips were purple by the time we finished passing around the hose, and as we began to insert the little antacid tablets (the older Gann kids referred to these, knowledgeably, as ammo), a sleety rain began to fall. Our fingers were so numb that the canisters were difficult to seal, but at last we got the rockets capped and lined up along the gravel crescent. Then one by one, with thrilling pops, they sprang into the air high above our heads, trailing white spume.

My jaws ached from chattering and my hands were icy talons, but I remember the giddiness of our laughter as we emulated the whoops of the big kids; remember the sheer glee of being able to shoot things into the air and the pleasure of conspiracy, for we were doing this all on our own, no grown-ups. Our only supervisor was the eldest Gann, a bony-chested teen who'd recently started sporting a beret and a pretty decent Che Guevara mustache, and who exuded such a thrilling air of guerrilla competency that the string of successful explosions felt at once anarchic and ordained.

Into this resplendently adult-free zone stepped June, intruding through the dripping grass in a pair of green rubber boots and a slicker, her arms laden with hats, gloves and scarves scooped from the old steamer trunk that had for decades functioned as the Batter Hollow School lost-and-found. On this cold, wet day, June wove nimbly among us and the detritus of our rockets, laughing a little at her own hennish impulses but earnest in her mission. To the older kids she simply handed protective gear, but with us younger ones she actually stretched the woolen caps over our heads and fitted the mittens onto our uplifted hands. No one protested. If none of us had thought of abandoning our rockets to go inside, we were no less grateful for the warmth she offered us now.

Then across the meadow came Neel, the rain plastering his curls against his head so that he looked like an aged Kewpie. Arms pumping, he strode toward the gravel crescent calling, "June, June!" in an imprecatory tone. "June, please. Let them ... Don't inter—" but here he halted both speech and stride, and it was comical, really, the way he stood there sodden and slowly folded his arms, as if in a futile bid for dignity, over his round chest.

What had stopped him was the fact that June had finished. She'd distributed her whole armload of warm things, with nary a complaint from any of us kids—even the oldest, mustache-sporting Gann had accepted a long mustard-colored scarf. Neel stood there in his defeat, some yards off, trying to make a joke of it by fully embracing the ludicrous figure he must have realized he cut: stout and soaked, with rivulets streaming past his bushy white eyebrows and making him squint. He gestured ironically toward June. "My sweet helpmeet," he said, biting off the end consonant theatrically.

Laughter exploded among us kids. Freddy, at my elbow, positively brayed. I did not understand the joke any more than he must have, any more than the others must have—even the older ones, I think, couldn't have known precisely what was funny—but it seemed necessary to laugh, and a giddy carillon of sound rippled up and down the line. We recognized the feel of comedy, the rhythm of a punch line, the well-oiled choreography of a pratfall, which is what Neel effectively turned it into, never mind that he remained planted where he stood, upright, heedless of the freezing rain.

June laughed, too, softly, or maybe she only smiled, an inward, chastened smile. I was standing near enough to hear the drops pattering off the waterproof poncho; alone among us she was dressed to repel the weather.

An ache welled in my throat. I understood its origins no better than I'd understood why I'd been laughing moments before, but I reached suddenly for one of June's bare hands, and squeezed it in my own now gloved one.

ON THE ROAD TO CRITERION, I descend around a curve and a white wing of water rushes at me, beats violently against the windshield and driver's-side window. I must have gathered more speed than I meant to, coming downhill, hurtling toward my appointment with Bayard Charles, toward the promise of getting one step closer to Fred, and sliced too fast straight through this deep puddle that has responded by rising up as a mad swan. I lose control; the back wheels pull to the right and the rest of the car follows, skidding sideways onto the shoulder and then off the shoulder, scraping up for screeching yards against a wall of banked earth. All the rhythm instruments, still in their duffel bag in the backseat, join in the fracas with great clattering and rattling before I manage to bring the car to a stop.

In the seconds that took, my shirt has become soaked. My top lip is damp with sweat, my hair sticking to my neck. The air bag didn't inflate, so the impact couldn't have been that severe, but my heart feels woozy as a candy heart dissolving in liquid. The wipers are still going, all out of tempo with time, which is suspended in a bubble of stillness. I assess. I feel unnaturally high in my seat, thrust toward a brightening overhead; the rain is lessening. Is that true? Yes, the downpour is thinner now, and pale breaks striate the clouds. My sense of elevation is real, too, I realize, a function of the rear right side of the car's canting low, either because the wheel has sunk into the wet ground there or because the tire has gone flat. As my heart reincorporates into something more solid, I mentally scan my body. I locate only two, anomalous complaints: my throat hurts, for no reason I can fathom except my esophageal muscles must have clenched in fear, and my left knee throbs for reasons I can't make sense of at all; it's as if it got banged against the door, but the impact was all on the right side of the car.

Dennis, I think, wanting him here. And then: *Fred*. With a crumpling realization. *What am I even doing here, Freddy? How can I possibly help?*

Now, just now, like an echo of the water that smashed against the windshield, the hopelessness of my expedition breaks over me—a wave of futility, humility. In the turmoil of the past several days, my only thought has been to rush to Fred's side. But what is it I think I'll accomplish by being there? I see Dennis's kind, watchful face, his blue eyes carefully devoid of skepticism, the way he looked at me Monday afternoon as I sat at the table, mapping my route by hand while he stood with his mug of tea, ready to offer his opinion if asked, ready otherwise to keep it to himself, with that innate sense of chivalry that is so large a part of why I fell in love with him.

I see Kitty, too, being careful. Not quite as careful as Dennis; she was bolder, with her gift of the composition book and her chiding impatience—"Oh, *Bird*"—but nevertheless refrained from saying what she, what both of them, must have been thinking: this is a fool's errand, and I, the fool.

We learned of it Friday. Dennis heard first, while out on a job. Back in Queens he'd worked for a green energy consulting company. Since moving to Freyburg, he's started his own business, Lo-Impact Solutions, installing environmentally friendly home insulation. About half the time he's out on the road, doing consults or installing hemp flax or recycled blue jeans in people's walls and ceilings and floors. On Friday he was doing a renovation project, and at midday the owner happened to be eating his lunch and watching TV in the next room. There Dennis was, unrolling batts of post-consumer denim and cutting it to fit between the wall studs in what would be a new playroom, not really paying attention to the noon news being broadcast only a few yards away, when his ears pricked up at the sound of Fred's name.

The story concerned a search that had been under way since late Tuesday, upstate in the Meurtriere Mountain area of Criterion County, along the Canadian border. Emergency personnel along with civilian volunteers were looking for a twelve-year-old boy who'd been reported missing Monday evening after failing to return home from school. Several witnesses reported seeing the boy in a white Toyota pickup just blocks from his middle school, and by Tuesday afternoon police had located what they believed to be the vehicle in question, which by then had been reported stolen by the boy's grandfather, near one of the trailheads at Meurtriere State Forest. After nearly three days of searching, authorities announced they'd located the driver of the stolen truck, believed to have abducted the boy on his way home from school. A white male in his early thirties, he had, they said, been transported under police guard to an area hospital where he was receiving treatment for unspecified injuries. Meanwhile, the newsreader concluded, the search for the missing boy went on.

All of this Dennis held inside his mind as he finished the job without haste. I marvel to think of it, how he worked another four hours at the client's house, always, being Dennis, measuring twice to cut once, stopping maybe, once the batts were all in, to sit in the van and eat the cheese sandwich he'd brought from home, then heading back into the house to staple-gun the vapor barrier into place, carefully overlapping the plastic sheets at the seams and as carefully cutting them around the switch boxes and outlets. He'd have loaded up the van when he was done, then returned to the worksite with his broom to sweep any errant staples and scraps of plastic, then his vacuum to suck up all the stray fibers and cotton dust, before coming home to me with his burden of news.

He found me, Friday night, standing at the stove sautéing eggplant and celery and onion, and he turned the burner down before placing his hands on my shoulders, his thumbs on my collarbones. The deliberateness of his touch, the purposeful, steadying weight of his hands describing a kind of circle there, as if to brace or contain me, was so unlike him that I knew before he spoke it was something very bad.

"I heard a story," he began, "about your brother."

"A story?" I repeated, confused.

"On the news."

"About my brother?"

"I think so." And he relayed in his quiet, unflinching voice what he'd heard about a man named Frederick Robbins: about the mountain and the boy and the white Toyota pickup, about the search party and the hospital and the middle school and the witnesses and the police guard and the wooded trails and the below-freezing temperatures and the continuing hunt for the missing child, and all the while I had the strange sensation that I was Fred, that I was standing in Fred's body, had taken his place that I might hear these words as the guilty party in his stead, and so I willed myself to let them in, I steeled myself to hear the worst, and when Dennis did not end by saying what I was sure must be coming—that Fred or the boy was dead—I felt a kind of reprieve that was like exhaustion, and the wooden spoon I'd forgotten I was holding clattered to the floor.

It seemed to me then that I had been bracing for news like this all my life.

What I said: "That's not Fred. How could it be? He's on the Cape with Dave."

I hardly know Dave Alsop, the grown son of former Batter Hollow students and a former student himself—although he came right at the end, for just the last few years of the school's existence, before I was born. I met him at Neel's memorial service and remember him only as lean and taciturn, reeking of tobacco but pleasant enough, with a lazy ginger stubble and a housepainting business on Cape Cod. For a month or so after Neel died, Dave hung around Batter Hollow and made himself useful, repairing things, splitting firewood, cleaning out gutters. June, who'd known him as a little boy with bright red hair who'd shown up often at her folk dance and pottery classes, spoke gratefully of his presence during that time. And four years later, when she knew she was dying, she had reached out to Dave, made arrangements for Fred to go live and work with him. I didn't know all the particulars, only that Dave had agreed to provide room and board in exchange for work; that June had left instructions for a sum of money to be transferred into Dave's bank account each month, and that I had been relieved Dennis and I weren't being asked to take care of Fred.

Dennis knelt and picked up the spoon. "I called Dave." Sometimes Dennis uses a voice that makes me think he's working not to spook me. "He says he hasn't seen Fred in months."

The first present Dennis ever gave me—I was seventeen and beside myself with the heady implausibility of Kitty's twenty-four-year-old brother noticing, let alone wanting to impress me—was a necklace he'd made out of a tiny spirit level and a thin leather cord. Besides my wedding ring and a pair of earrings, it's the only piece of jewelry I have from him. I reach for it now, not around my neck but around the rearview mirror where it always hangs, and where, in the aftermath of the skidding stop, it continues to swing back and forth with frantic energy, like a pendulum divining something of great magnitude. I still it between my fingers, then lift it over the mirror and hold it parallel to the earth so that the bubble centers between the rings. A car pulls up behind me. Puts its hazards on.

Someone comes toward me through the rain, man or woman I cannot tell until he's at my side. Slightly built guy in an army-green raincoat, hood up, blinking through a pair of metal-rimmed glasses. Two knuckles tap the window. I lower it and the rain leaps in like sparks.

"You all right?" He's standing with both hands at his sides. His face, back in the recess of his hood, looks clean-boned, disciplined. He might be forty-five, a young-looking fifty.

"Yes . . . yes." The rain feels fine on my face.

"Nobody hurt?" He glances into the backseat, where I have only my Singalong Lady equipment: my guitar and the duffel bag full of percussion toys. "Car all right?"

"I think so."

"See if you can get it up out of the ditch there." He gestures with his clean-shaven, square chin and I turn to see what he means, but all I can see is the reddish earth wall, veined by roots and shrubby growth. I realize the reason I'm angled up so high must be the right rear tire's having sunk into the mud between the paved shoulder and the embankment, rather than the result of a flat, a piece of news for which I have wits enough about me to be glad. "See if you can get out," the man says again, backing up a step. I put the car in gear, foot still on the brake. "Try it," he prompts.

I hesitate. "I'm scared I might hit you."

He takes another step back. It's very Dennisy, the way he does this: pure gallantry. I can see he finds the precaution unnecessary, yet he takes the step courteously and without comment, as if out of deference to what must be my own glaring cluelessness.

I take my foot off the brake, gingerly apply the gas pedal, do not budge. "Try giving it more gas," he says. I do. No good. I can feel the wheel spinning. He moves around to the back of the car, then returns

to me. "You've got about sixteen inches," he says, holding up his hands
to show me. "Try reverse, then real quick gun it forward."

I try it. This time the car rocks back and lurches briefly forward
before becoming stuck again in the exact same place.

"Again."

I repeat the sequence, still to no avail.

"Let's see if I give it a push." Before I can protest he's gone around
behind. I turn to see him sidling into the narrow space between the
rear bumper and the banked, rocky soil. Laying his hands against the
slippery trunk. "Okay!" he shouts. I step on the gas and feel the wheel
spinning, feel the car rocking from his pushing; he's pushing not evenly
but rhythmically, in waves. I depress the pedal lower and the wheel
spins faster, shriller. I let up. He yells something. I look around.
Through the streaming rear window he's all wavy green. "Try again,
don't stop," he shouts.

I comply, depressing the pedal longer and harder, and the rocking
keeps up, the heaving to and fro, until, absurdly, appallingly, I find I
cannot suppress an embarrassed grin. The motion transports me back
to the coin-op kiddie rides they used to have outside our local Grand
Union. There were two: a pink hippo and a blue race car. We'd come
out of the store and pester June to let us ride them, only to wind up, on
those rare occasions when she did produce quarters, having to endure
the experience, as uncomfortable as it inevitably turned out to be. The
painted seats were burny hot in summertime, and the grinding motion
of the machines tossed us herky-jerk, but more than that, it was weirdly
degrading—for there was something about it we both craved. This realization was my private shame. I'd look over at Freddy being buffeted
roughly on his hippo, and he'd look over at me—his gaze vacant and
wild, and it was clear that we were alike in this abnormal way, in our
desire for vigorous motion that was purely impersonal, that came from

motor and metal rather than muscle and skin. For although I, unlike Freddy, did not overtly shun the touch of others and never went into paroxysms of agony when subjected to it, the truth is I did not like it. The truth is, I understood Freddy's aversion more than I'd ever admit.

Now, caught on the side of this rainy county road, I am flooded with the fact of my own ridiculousness. I feel redly silly, clown-nosed, bucking back and forth in the driver's seat while my Good Samaritan heaves away at the rear bumper. It's as though, having realized at last the full measure of my foolishness—the heedless way I've flocked to Perdu, flung myself headlong toward rescuing the brother I barely know anymore and who I am very afraid might have done something irremediable—I'm now stuck here in exaggerated, slapstick fashion: a risible one-woman cavalry with her tire wedged fast in a ditch. Everything seems suddenly mawkish, over-the-top, even the rain, even the lessening of the rain and the brightening of the greenish sunlight trying to force itself through the clouds.

Then I am free. The car leaps forward; all four wheels land on asphalt. I touch the brake, put it in park, get out to thank the man. From the thighs down he's Jackson Pollocked with reddish-orange mud.

"Oh, sorry!" I say. "Thanks for everything, for stopping—*really* thanks, I don't know what I would've done. Can I give you something for your trouble, at least to get your pants cleaned—?"

He waves me off. His eyeglasses are speckled with rain. He returns my handshake with a hard, brief, sopping grip that nevertheless communicates bashfulness, refusing my characterization of his help as anything noteworthy. "Take care, now," he says as I get back in my car. His speech has the same flattened-vowel syndrome that marks Bayard Charles's and Mrs. Tremblay's, only now it seems less an affliction than a winsome fillip. "Have a safe rest of your trip."

Six

CRITERION HAS nickel-an-hour parking meters and an oblong town green with a painted cannon in the center, beside a peeling flagpole. The law office, according to the notes I penciled on the back of an envelope, is above the Ready Barber Shop, which I spot across the green by its spiral pole. The rain has stopped and the air has gone crackly, as if any residual moisture in it has contracted into unseen veins of ice. I put two nickels in the meter, then inspect the side of my car. It looks clawed, but I don't see any major dents and it drove fine, the twenty-odd miles from Perdu. I'd like to talk with Dennis, and I see my phone's getting four bars, but its clock tells me I'd better postpone calling till after I meet with the lawyer.

Next to the barbershop there's a pizza place and I remember how hunger is part of what propelled me from the guest room at Mrs. Tremblay's, but even if my mishap with the car hadn't left me with no time to eat, I realize I no longer want to. A grinding anxiety has supplanted the empty rumblings. I cross the street, double-check the number on the door, go inside. The narrow stairwell leading to the second floor is darkly paneled and smells of bananas.

Three doors lead off the landing. One is featureless. Another has an oval plaque bearing the numeral 2. The third holds a pane of frosted glass on which is stenciled *Bayard Charles, Esq.* I knock once, try the handle. Inside, a young woman sits behind a cluttered desk reading a paperback. She looks up with minor curiosity.

"I have an appointment with Mr. Charles?"

"Oh. I'll tell him." She stands and, bringing the book along, her finger holding the place, goes to a door behind her desk. There she turns, remembering. "Your name?" I can see the book's cover has a picture of a pouty brunette in a nurse's uniform from yesteryear, with one of those starched little caps and an apron.

"Ava Manseau."

She disappears through the door but leaves it partly open, and I can hear when she says, "Something like a Miss Minso is here?"

Almost everything in the office is, like the stairwell, darkly wooden: the uncarpeted floor, the paneling, the desk and various area tables and chairs, none of which, other than the secretary's recent perch, is available for its usual purpose, each being already over-whelmed by Pisa-esque towers of books, folders, binders, notepads and general flotsam. The chair nearest me holds a partly used ream of copy paper, a car charger, and a white paper bag emblazoned JABLONSKI & BROS. PHARMACY. Beneath all the clutter, the shapes of more substantial items declare themselves mutedly: a row of wooden filing cabinets, a huge old photocopy machine, a treadmill evidently not in regular use—stacks of fat file folders are piled on the belt.

This, then, is the rest of the cavalry. My nose has started to run. I grope in my coat pocket for a tissue, to no avail.

"You can go on in." The young woman has returned. She smiles a little this time, her doughy cheeks showing pretty, thumbprint dimples, and resumes reading her book even before she has finished lowering herself back into the chair. I make my way toward the communicating door, high-stepping over various books and boxes.

The inner office smells more intensely of bananas, and something syrupy, too, like cough medicine. The man behind the desk is impressively tall. He's older than I expected; his domed head and large face are mottled with age. Standing, he reaches across the desk. His handshake is strong. "Mrs. Minso," he says. His voice has the resonance of an old-time radio announcer's. I imagine him promoting Brylcreem, Jell-O pudding, Chesterfield cigarettes. "Bayard Charles."

"Hi. I'm Ava—*Man*seau, actually."

He squints at me with a faintly quizzical smile, as if he's either dubious about what I said or else deprecating himself for being slow to place me. His eyes are small and bright beneath the heavy folds of his lids; when he squints the little chinks of blue all but disappear.

"Fred's sister," I add.

"Yes . . ."—he stretches the words out as if evaluating their veracity even as he utters them—"you're Frederick Robbins's sister." And he emits a sigh so gusting, so devoid of restraint that I want Kitty to be here so she can poke me, and I can poke her, and we can hold back giggles together. Instead I sniff and rummage again for a tissue, with no greater success than before. "Have a seat," he offers. I sit. "And you came up here from—?"

"Freyburg." I wipe my nose with my fingers. "Down in Putnam County? About eight hours."

"Nice," he says, courteously if without giving the impression of having heard of either.

"I spoke with you Monday?"

"Monday, yes . . ." He sorts among some papers on his desk, shuffles through an alternate pile, then swivels to a side table and moves about more loose sheets. "Monday, Monday . . ."

"Mr. Charles, have you seen Fred yet?"

He swivels his chair back to face me and gives a delicate grimace. "No, not yet. Haven't had a chance. I expected to get over there today, but something came up. An emergency, really, bank foreclosing on a dairy farm. Over in Rudolf. Tough. Been in the family four generations. Very tough. He's in Afghanistan, she's here taking care of three children and a mom who had a stroke."

His words pave the way for an expression of sympathy, but I find myself unable to come up with one. Of course the contours of the story he described sound terrible, yet I feel nothing in relation to it, feel incapable of sympathy or even clear thought, conscious of nothing save the visceral sensation of slipping, falling, my feet fumbling over disintegrating ground. Some reasonable part of me advises that an expression of sympathy for the family in question might show him we are not monsters, Fred and me, that we, too, are worthy of his consideration, and yet: "A foreclosure," is all I am able to say, dumbly, working to sort out the meaning of this. "But you're a defense lawyer."

"Oh, well, I do some criminal defense, sure, along with some civil suits, some real estate, some estate planning. Trusts, wills. Divorce settlements. The gamut. Practice like this, we get to do it all." He smiles and the bags pouch up under his eyes in a way that seems designed to appeal, a bid for my sympathy. "We get a cross section," he adds, spreading his mottled hands in the air before him, as if the spirit of helpfulness dictates he ought to demonstrate the size of the cross section. Apparently it is the size of a bread box.

"But you are a public defender?"

"Well," he says, in his impressive rumble, "I'm in the assigned counsel program—that's how it works up this way—and I do what I can for 'em, take what cases I can. Get an awful lot of them, to tell the truth. We're overrun." He places a palm on one of the high stacks of paper before him.

"Oh." The air hangs dense with odors of banana and cough medicine and I'm still in my coat, my coat still damp, my nose still runny. I must look badly dismayed because the lawyer reddens slightly.

"We do what we can," he reiterates encouragingly, leaning forward. "Those of us in the program. It's voluntary, so. I wouldn't do this work if I didn't believe in it. Fourteenth Amendment. Equal justice under the law. Regardless of means. That's not the founding fathers, you know, that's Pericles. Cradle of civilization. Problem is, the caseload doesn't allow for me to meet with every indigent client in advance of court dates. The resources simply aren't there."

On a mechanical level my hearing is operating fine; the phonemes and everything are coming through, but I seem to be processing their meaning at an awfully slow rate. Now I repeat the word, "indigent," for example, sampling it with my own mouth. It fairly cuts my palate. I cast my eye at the great litter of paper, all the ruffle-edged legal pads, gaping manila folders, dusty black binders and sheaves of photocopies, newspapers, warped magazines and yellowing journals; also at the framed photographs on his desk, their blank backs turned to me so that I can only imagine the clean, congenial faces of his relatives posed in obliging semicircles at family gatherings; also at a little row of prescription bottles up high on a shelf, and a bottle that looks like aftershave, and another of Pepto-Bismol, unmistakably pink. The single, narrow window reveals a lowering, smoky darkness, through which the lights of shops across the green shine as faint and small as the ends of cigarettes.

A telephone warbles in the outer office, not an electronic sound but a real old clapper-and-bell: *brrrrring brrrring*. Mr. Charles glances toward the door. I touch the inside of my wrist to my forehead and rest my eyelids. When next I open them, Mr. Charles has produced a box of tissues and positioned it at the edge of the desk close to me. I take one, only to clutch it in my hand and say—surprised at how rapidly and with what honest strength the words emerge—"I came to see my brother, Mr. Charles, and I haven't been able to do that yet, and also I came to see if I could help, I thought you were helping him, and that maybe it would be good if I could explain certain things to you, things that would help you help him, you know, and I'm not at all good at this but now I don't even know if you are helping him, but maybe, if not, you could help me at least, because I don't even know how to get in to see him, and I've been here since yesterday. And I haven't seen him in so long."

"Oh." He gives a single, condoling cluck of his tongue. "Mrs. Manseau."

"It's Ava."

He acknowledges this with the slightest of nods. "The particulars of the case, your brother's case, let me be honest, are pretty tough. On paper, of course," he qualifies, as if anticipating my interjection. "But, ah, *on* paper, I'll be straight with you, they're tough. We may do worse than consider a plea."

"A plea?" Such a shy little pansy of a word. A plea, please. Please is the magic word, even Dilly knows that. It sounds like it should signal hopefulness, but I can tell from the excessively gentle way he says it that it is, in fact, a blow.

"Yes, well, I haven't yet had a chance to assess the particulars . . ." He gets to rummaging again, this time standing up to check through yet another stack of folders on a different table, eventually striding over to stick his head through the doorway. "Lisa, honey, do you by any chance have the Frederick Robbins folder out here?"

At last—an anticipatory current of relief. Now he is getting the folder. Now he is going to do something, tell me something, make things clear. I notice the tissue still crumpled in my fist and use it on my nose.

In the doorway, Mr. Charles says, "Thanks, sweetheart," returns to his desk with a not very fat manila folder, and sits down again, spreading it flat before him. I don't like his calling his secretary honey and sweetheart, don't like having to make my appeal to a man who thinks that's the way to address women, but I tell myself it's just cultural, that if I'd grown up in his time and place, I wouldn't think anything of it. The truth is, I am a foreigner here. When in Perdu, etc. So long as I don't judge his ways, perhaps he won't judge mine. I concentrate on engendering goodwill toward him, even as I hope for his in return.

But he opens the folder and when I crane to see its contents I spot, amid the photocopies and forms, newspaper clippings, and then my earlobes burn because I know what all the articles say, what kind of story they tell about Fred and how far short they fall of engendering anything like goodwill. They use the words "drifter" and "vagrant." And "drawn." As in "drawn to young children."

"Let's see now," Mr. Charles says in his deep, silty voice as he leafs through the papers and then finds the one he wants: the charges, he explains, and begins to read aloud slowly as if he himself is discovering for the first time what they are.

"Weren't you—I'm sorry to interrupt, but I'm confused. Doesn't a lawyer have to be present when someone's being charged?"

"Hm?" He squints up at me, deepening the creases around his eyes until they recede so far into the folds of skin they are like caraway seeds tucked into a bun. "Well, it looks like they brought in someone from the Public Defender's Office. Ideally, I'd have been there, but I didn't hear from O.A.R. until after arraignment."

"O.A.R.?"

"Offender Aid and Restoration. They provide the affidavit of indigency. Then they fax it down to the guy who runs the whole assigned counsel program, and he gets in touch with me." His tone conveys both his own easy familiarity with the system and his expectation that whether or not I follow every bit of it precisely does not really matter. It makes me think of Dennis explaining something about soffits or joists—the way we both know, as he speaks, that I am going to absorb it only superficially, and also that it's not necessary for me to understand it any more than that.

I wrap my arms around myself and nod: go on.

He resumes reading aloud, presenting the charges and explaining after each count what it means: unlawful imprisonment in the first degree, kidnapping in the second, unauthorized use of a vehicle in the third.

"Unauthorized use—?"

"The Toyota pickup," translates Mr. Charles. "Registered to a Mr. Ronald Ferebee. Maternal grandfather of the deceased. Reported stolen the morning of November ninth."

He speaks of class E and B felonies, and a class A misdemeanor, of minimums and maximums and priors and mandatories and my bones have become glass tubes, my veins brittle pipettes, they are all shivering cold as if a fierce wind is whistling through them and I imagine I am emitting a kind of thinly audible vibrato. I am wretched. Wretched against the backdrop of Bayard Charles's mellifluous recitation, which continues, his tone unmistakably businesslike; he is using what are for him workaday terms, and I grasp finally what I have been stupid not to understand: that his only idea of me—his only possible idea—is as the sister of a person who has been linked to contemptible acts. I am, to him, surely nothing more or less than a member and product of the household that formed Fred.

Those picture frames on his desk, the contents of whose photos I cannot see, only their impersonal, impenetrable backs tilted toward me on their little hinged stands—they contain the people Mr. Charles recognizes and cares for, the individuals whose histories, entwined with his, render them comprehensible, worthy not simply of sympathy but the status of full-fledged humanity. Those clients he started to tell me about, the ones whose farm is being foreclosed on, those people, whether or not he's even met them in person—the father in Afghanistan, the mother taking care of all the little children and the ailing grandmother—they, too, are worthy of his sympathy. Their story comes handsomely wrapped in the American flag, and in the flaggy tropes of farm and family. And the secretary, the one he calls sweetheart, sitting out there engrossed once more in her paperback novel—she, too, has his . . . what, affection? It isn't affection; it's something more substantial, more practical. She has legitimacy to him. She works for him and he pays her and they are part of the same system, the same portrait; they uphold each other's roles and standing in the community. They help ensure each other's worth and so she, too, is safe with him, enjoys a kind of safety within his penumbra. If her brother were in trouble, Mr. Charles would know exactly where that file was kept, would drop everything to help in any way he could, would afford the brother every benefit of the doubt. I am jealous of her, the dimpled young woman with her nurse romance—what did he call her? Lisa. I wish I could make myself Lisa. I wish I were a plump, good-natured girl who'd grown up passing out paper cups of water at the Memorial Day parade and living in a house that hung bunting every July Fourth and walking with my family to church every Sunday and doing all the correct things, all the sanctioned things. I wish it for Fred. Oh, Freddy.

But I am not Lisa. I am Ava. I am from away, as is glaringly obvious to everyone here. We have always been foreigners, Fred and I, always and everywhere and by design; our parents taught us to conceive of ourselves that way, and it has forever been true, and we loved it some of the time, it served us well, and also it has been our enduring loneliness.

Well. My enduring loneliness.

What do I know anymore of Fred.

Seven

THE FIRST SERIOUS DISAGREEMENT I ever knew Neel and June to have occurred about a month before the Manseaus moved into the Art Barn. It was over June's teaching me how to read music. Not teaching me how to play the recorder—Neel thought that was well and good—but specifically teaching me how to read notes on a musical staff. He believed children should learn to play by ear, and mostly under their own tutelage: in the case of a recorder, by fiddling around with the thing, blowing into it and figuring out what happened when you covered up certain holes, in various combinations. In fact, students at Batter Hollow had always been given recorders when they turned seven, and it was a custom to let them do what they would with their instruments, whether that meant taking them apart, using them as swords, blaring into them as hard as they could (although this inclination was generally short-lived—not, Neel would hasten to explain, because there were rules against it, but because everyone else in the community expressed such annoyance that the kid doing it would decide, on his own, to stop), or discovering how to generate actual notes. Sometimes the little ones would appeal to older kids for help, and that was a fine thing, too, Neel said, to come upon a bunch of students of various sizes gathered cross-legged on the ground or sitting up in a tree somewhere, legs dangling from a low branch, melodies and harmonies and squawky odd notes all issuing forth.

But they didn't receive formal instruction in any instrument until third grade; Neel believed that this early period of free experimentation, when the child is unfettered by a system of notation and accompanying specialized vocabulary, was vital. That was how he talked whenever he was speaking at a conference on child development or on a radio chat show, both of which were regular occurrences when I was little, so that already by age seven I was familiar with the sound of such words and even had a notion of what they meant: they meant running barefoot over grass and dirt and sometimes over nettles, running loose-limbed and headlong until your lungs felt spicy and your throat pleasurably sore, and a high singing sound spun around your head like tiny silver bells.

"Well, but Neel, vital to what?" June asked finally on this particular summer day, not raising her voice but not bothering to disguise her exasperation either. She was a serious amateur flutist and Neel played nothing, except, as he joked, the radio.

We were all outside, Neel and June at the weathered wooden table behind our house, sitting over the remains of a bread-and-cold-soup lunch; Freddy and I sprawled several yards away on the worn brick patio. We were playing with a giant saucepan full of water and a collection of rocks. We were mesmerized by the way they turned different colors when submerged. After a time we'd extract them one by one, and lay them on a tea towel in rows or clusters: pearly ones in this corner, jagged ones in that. Sometimes I'd sort them by sex, girl rocks here and boy rocks there, and sometimes by kind and wicked, and sometimes by happy and sad.

Freddy was good at sorting things, too, although at this moment he was more involved in producing rhythm; he held a rock in each hand and tapped them together, slowly at first and then woodpecker-fast.

"Vital to their being free," declared Neel.

I was only half listening, enjoying the rough warmth of the bricks under my bare legs and the cadences of their grown-up speech, which, because I bore no responsibility for understanding it, had the effect of heightening the pleasurable apartness of the little world in which Freddy and I were ensconced: the water bent and bowed in the pot; sunlight curtseyed lopsidedly across it and flecks of mica seemed to waver and rise up, float loose to the surface and break open to become part of the sun.

Freddy plunged one of his rocks into the pot and raised it, dripping, to his mouth. I could hear it scrape against his teeth as he put it in.

"They *are* free," said June. "They have so much freedom."

Neel gave a laugh. "I'm of the opinion freedom isn't something we measure, or mete out in coffee spoons, like Prufrock."

Prufrock was a lovely name. I gave it immediately to the rock in my hand, a slippery bruise-colored thing. "Prufrock," I whispered in its mineral ear. Freddy made a gagging sound.

"You know that's not what I mean." June's voice sounded as if she were trying to thread it through a needle. I glanced up to see her shredding a crust of bread in her lap. Usually I thought of Neel and June as belonging to the same age group: both of them simply parent-age, but every now and then I would be struck by how much younger June actually was. This afternoon she seemed restless. She was barelegged, sitting with her knees apart under her wide gypsy skirt. Her arms were long and cool-looking and her heavy hair hung haphazardly over the back of her chair.

"If you happen upon a child playing in the mud," began Neel, slipping happily into his public voice—it had a bounce to it, a kind of robust, holding-forth cheer—"would you try to improve upon the shining moment? Would you launch into a lesson on pedogenesis? Would you discourse on soil composition or erosion? What would that contribute to the well-being of the child? What end would you have in view? Simply"—he could not resist answering his own question—"to impart."

He pronounced the last unfamiliar word with such derision it made me think of something rude and foolish, like fart, and I laughed and glanced up to see if they were laughing, too. Neel was beaming, but June sat scowling at the litter of crumbs in her lap. Then she swept them brusquely from her skirt. "Why do you do that?" she said. "Pretend like I'm one of your . . . your nuns or your rubes?"

"My nuns?" said Neel, mock-astonished.

I was astonished, too; that was before I knew that Neel had, as a boy, attended parochial school.

June stood. "You know I don't believe in teaching for teaching's sake. And you purposely use words you know I don't know. Pedowhatever. Why do you do that?"

Freddy made another gagging sound.

With sudden suspicion, I stuck my hand under his chin. "Spit."

"I know why," continued June. "It's a way of making it seem like you know more about everything. But you don't. Not about everything. I know more about music, and I think she'd enjoy it, be good at it, hungry for it. How is it freedom to deprive them of instruction?"

Who was this "she" of whom June spoke? Was it—I had a swift conviction—me? Was I hungry for something? Ought I to be? What a peculiar, marvelous idea. I tried to picture the thing I must be hungry for, the thing June had in mind for me.

Freddy's eyes grew awfully round. His mouth gaped roundly, too, a wet black pit.

"Spit," I said again, suddenly frightened.

He made a thrusting, doggy motion with his neck. It was his queer soundlessness that scared me now, that and the strange purpling of his face.

"Spit it!" I ordered, and thumped him hard on the back.

The stone flew into my palm along with a great mess of saliva. I dumped it in the pot, wiped my hand against the weedy bricks. There was a moment of shocked stillness and then Freddy began to wail, his face bunched as a prune and still nearly as dark.

"He's fine," I called quickly. I wanted Neel and June to keep discussing me. I wanted their subject to remain my hunger.

Kneeling close to Freddy, I brought my face into the tangled nest of hair that smelled of his own briny sweat and spoke straight into his ear: "Shut. Up." But the aperture of his mouth only widened, and he yowled so luxuriantly that both parents flocked over to see what was the matter.

Then I hated him. Maybe a minute earlier he had nearly died, but now he was once more the volatile creature who consumed so much of Neel's and June's attention. I stared at him as they flanked him. Those plump little legs I wanted to gouge with my fingernails. That floppy hair, against whose blue-black softness I loved to brush my chin while we read books together, I wanted to yank with all my might.

June picked him up and walked with him into the meadow, rubbing his back.

Neel remained, squatting lightly beside me. Only later would I realize how spry he'd been for sixty-six; then I took it for granted. He cocked his head at me, waiting. He was patient that way, generous; he always wanted to hear your version.

"He put a rock in his mouth." I shrugged. "I made him take it out."

Why should I tell Neel he'd nearly strangled?

The blessings of liberty are worth many wounds.

SURPRISINGLY, the second major disagreement I witnessed between Neel and June also had to do with me and not Freddy. I say surprisingly because compared with Freddy, I was the easy one, the child who caused our parents hardly any trouble. At least that's how the story went for a long time.

The second disagreement arose over Neel's staunch resistance to my wish to follow Kitty to public school, and June's quietly firm opinion that I should be allowed to try it—but it would not occur for over a year.

The first year of the Manseaus' living at Batter Hollow was in many ways the happiest of my life. I finally had a friend, *the* friend for whom I'd been pining: a girl my age who lived next door, who at once fulfilled proverbial expectation and satisfied flesh-and-blood reality. The central fact of this year was that Kitty's parents, like mine, chose not to send her to school. Don Manseau was a former pupil of Neel's, and after he and his wife had made the radical decision to leave New York City and take up residence in the Art Barn, it was not such a great leap for them to allow their youngest child a year of "experiential learning," alongside Fred and me, as well as the Gann kids. (Noah Salinas-Buchbinder, the other school-age child at Batter Hollow, attended Freyburg Primary; as a result we saw less of him and tended to be more shy of one another.) Don, who turned out to be the tallest of the three circusy men Freddy and I had seen moving furniture that first day, and Meg, the woman in the flowered dress with the milk-caramel voice, had both left jobs at a graphic design agency to move eighty miles north and devote themselves to earlier, less practical loves: metal sculpting and stained glass, respectively.

They had two older children, neither of whom lived at home: a twenty-two-year-old daughter in the Peace Corps in Malawi, and a fifteen-year-old son at Clembrook Academy in Connecticut.

"It's a prep school," Kitty informed me, making a face.

"What's a prep school?"

"Strict."

"Why's he go there?"

"It's the right place for him." She said it in a rehearsed way that suggested she was parroting what she'd heard Don and Meg say. For what sort of child was a strict school the right place? I thought her brother must be wild and difficult, impossible to control, worse than Fred. Then I wondered whether prep school might be the right place for Fred, too, and if I should tell Neel and June about it.

But when Kitty showed me a framed photograph of her brother, looking grimly aloof in his navy school blazer and tie—this of course was Dennis—I decided he couldn't be Fredlike at all. It turned out he was the medium-sized of the three circusy men we had seen the day the Manseaus moved in, but I had a hard time putting together the image of this serious boy with that of the loose-limbed, golden-skinned fellow who'd twirled the lamp base like a white baton up into the twilit sky.

Later I would learn that all the men in Meg's family had for generations attended Clembrook Academy, and that while she had not planned to send her own son there, Dennis wound up suffering a painful transition to middle school—where, as a soft-spoken boy of slender build with a fondness for gymnastics and Tintin, he became the target of such vicious bullying (all verbal, predominantly female) that he lost ten pounds and had trouble sleeping—upon which Meg and Don decided Clembrook Academy was worth a try after all. When eventually I received pieces of this story, first from Kitty and then Meg and finally from Dennis himself, I felt protective of the boy in the navy blazer and grateful for the existence of a place like Clembrook. Back then, however, I was happy to follow Kitty's lead and call it Clenchbutt Academy, and to write off her brother as a stuffy prig.

If we had gone to regular school that year, we'd have been in the second grade, Kitty and I. This I had on the authority of Kitty herself, who'd attended kindergarten and first grade in public school in Manhattan, and was thus something of an expert on the subject. Second grade, she informed me with insiderly aplomb, was when you learned cursive and fractions and got to hatch butterflies.

"Neel!" I stormed into our house. June had gone out somewhere with Freddy, but I knew Neel would be in his study, a low-ceilinged room off the kitchen, whose mint-green walls sported not only the portrait of Rousseau but also many framed photographs of Batter Hollow back in the old days. Most of Neel's writings were about the school in its heyday, how it had changed the lives of hundreds of children, how he personally had encouraged the development of modes of inquiry by stepping out of his pupils' way. He never used their real names. Instead, following the lead of his hero Rousseau, who'd written a whole book about his hypothetical pupil Émile, Neel wrote of Jill and of John, and despite the fact that they didn't exist, I came to resent and even despise these two. "Why don't you call them Ava and Fred?" I asked him once.

He laid a hand on my head and looked kindly down at me. "Because you are you and only you."

Now I think this answer is not half bad, but at the time I considered it a dodge.

Most of his small study was occupied by an enormous camphor-wood desk on which sat an almost equally massive IBM Selectric. I could hear its heavy, arrhythmic clunking now as I flung open the door.

Neel looked up with a scowl of which I took no notice (his standard greeting when interrupted in his study, it was mostly an act, a self-parodying performance of a curmudgeon). When he saw me genuinely bristling with indignation, his mouth curved into a grin. Neel loved uninhibited expression in children, regardless of what was being expressed. In fact he always seemed most delighted by uninhibited *negative* expression.

I stuck my hands on my hips: "I want to learn cursive and fractions and I want to hatch a butterfly."

Untroubled, Neel stroked an earlobe: another of his stock gestures. He looked around at the walls of his study, feigning interest in the many black-and-white images. I myself never tired of examining these photos of students and staff doing all sorts of interesting-looking things: trying on masks, putting up a tire swing, making gigantic soap bubbles, painting the Art Barn mural, toasting sausages over a bonfire, building something with straws, running, hugging, sleeping, wrestling. One picture showed Margo, Neel's second wife, kneeling in the community garden, a heap of just-dug radishes on her lap. A short, stoutish woman with white hair and thick glasses, Margo had died before I was born—but not before June joined the school's faculty as its youngest member.

Sometimes I tried to imagine June as she would have been on her first ever visit to Batter Hollow. She went as part of an avant-garde puppet troupe invited to perform for the students. I imagine her willowy and confident, striding around campus with frank curiosity, her hands thrust deep in the pockets of her long peasant skirt. She had no training as a teacher, having spent her early twenties touring Europe with the puppeteers, but Neel liked inexperience in his staff and preferred hiring them as novices, unmolded by what he referred to as a *mania for instruction.* After the performance, June was persuaded to stay on for a few weeks to organize the painting of the Art Barn mural. By the time the mural was done, she'd been offered a place on the faculty.

Neel and June always maintained they had not become a couple until after Neel's marriage to Margo ended, but even before I was old enough to note the careful semantic contortion (they did not say "until after Margo died"), I held the belief that Neel must have been smitten from the start. That June had been drawn to Neel—a man twenty years her senior—strained my credulity not in the least. After all, Neel was *Neel,* bathed in the glow of his admirers' gaze. To me, their offspring, the notion that romance had kindled between them from the moment they had first laid eyes, et cetera, et cetera, could not seem anything but right and true.

I'd never seen a photo of Neel's first wife, Roberta (Robbie Robbins, this had briefly, cinematically made her). June explained that Robbie and Neel had been "ridiculously young" when they married, both just twenty, and that within a year she'd "run away" with a trombonist. I pictured Robbie as an indistinct blur, her hair streaming out horizontally behind her as she ran. Despite or because of how little was ever said about Robbie Robbins, a kind of glamour accrued to her. She seemed a more threatening rival to June than Margo had ever been, and the thought of her made me want to throw my arms around Neel, less to comfort him for having been abandoned, perhaps, than to remind him bodily of where his heart's home lay.

Now, though, standing in the study, I had no desire to comfort or cling to him; he was being, in his deceptively benign way, infuriating.

"What's cursive?" he queried, scraping the back of his fingers against his neck.

"Don't play dumb, Neel. It's that fancy writing grown-ups do."

"Hm." He put on a contemplative face, then rummaged around his desk. "You mean like this?" He handed me a scrap of paper, the beginnings of a grocery list, written in what June liked to call his "abominable chicken scratch." I could barely make out: COFFEE AVOCADO FETA BUNS APRICOTS.

"Not that, but you know what I mean. And I want to learn fractions and hatch a butterfly," I reminded him.

Here he smiled with such delight I knew before he spoke that I must have made a blunder. "Ava, my daughter," he said, "there I cannot help you. A butterfly must hatch itself."

In the end, Neel did teach me fractions over the next several weeks, mostly using ordinary objects that fell naturally into the course of our daily activities: cutting up an apple or dividing a handful of raisins, folding the laundry, pointing out the Dasher's fuel gauge. One night after June washed her hair, she allowed herself to be used as a fractions lesson for Kitty and me both. She sat obligingly on the flowered couch with a towel around her shoulders, and Kitty and I, each armed with a comb, climbed up on the radiator behind her, whereupon Neel talked us through a succession of steps: parting her wet hair down the middle, separating each side into first two, then three, then four equal hanks. Then back into thirds again. "Now," directed Neel, "each of you take the one-sixth from near her face and place it between the other two-sixths on your side." In this way he taught us not only fractions but how to make braids.

Neel correctly interpreted the rest of my educational demands as being less tied to the particulars than to a general desire not to be excluded from the experience of "real school." For that desire he held little regard, but he suggested I appeal to Kitty, who, when approached, was only too happy to re-create the school setting as she remembered it. Up in her bedroom, which had been crafted out of a corner of the barn's former hayloft, she laid out the family's supply of washcloths. These were "mats," she said, for the "students"—some dozen stuffed animals, Freddy and me. We took our seats and then she stood before us with a yardstick and led us in "lessons," singing and spelling, mostly, before sending us to the little sink she did indeed have in the corner of her bedroom, where she watched over us sternly as we washed our hands, then had us sit back on our "mats" where she handed out "snack"—marshmallows snuck from the pantry and spoonfuls of grape jelly she insisted on feeding us out of a jar. "We're not playing babies," I objected. "We're playing school. Anyway I'm not using the same spoon as him."

Freddy, meanwhile, having appropriated the spoon and scraped out all the remaining jelly, decided he was finished with school and wandered out. We watched him go: half the class, if you didn't count the stuffed animals.

"All right, students!" Kitty clapped her hands smartly. "Naptime!"

"How about I be teacher now?"

"You don't know how."

"Neither do you—second-graders don't nap."

"Do too. I've *been* to school."

"My father *ran* a school."

"Not a *real* school."

"Was too."

"Was not."

I shoved her then, partly in defense of Neel but more because it dawned on me that she had knowledge of both worlds—the world of regular neighborhoods and schools, and the world we inhabited here in these five cottages tucked into a woods. I was then just coming to understand how much these worlds differed, how limited and odd my own known world apparently was. The shove was harder than I'd intended and the back of her head knocked against the wall with a crack. We looked at each other in surprise. Kitty raised a hand slowly to her little cap of fair hair, and her mouth began to wobble and her eyes to fill. I fled the house aghast, pounding down the stairs, tearing through the front door and flying over the front steps without touching a single tread. I did not see her again for the rest of the day.

Our first fight.

"What did you think of school?" Neel asked later that evening.

"Ah-like, ah-like jelly," said Freddy, speaking around his thumb. I could understand him easily, but Neel only smiled in a vague sort of way. This was around the time that I was beginning to realize how often other people, even Neel and June, had difficulty parsing Freddy's speech.

"You liked it, eh?" Neel guessed, and turned to me. "And you?"

"It was all right," I said airily, wanting neither to give Neel satisfaction nor to confess how the game had ended.

THAT FALL MIDGETROPOLIS BEGAN. I don't remember who thought up the name; it felt as if we'd discovered the place rather than invented it. That was its glory: how real it was. What greater artistry, what finer power did we yearn for at that age than the ability to make our make-believe real? Coax fantasy to life. Once named, that part of the woods was forever transformed, and I could no longer regard that patch of ground without spying the order, the architecture, hidden within the growth.

Midgetropolis: a glade off one of the paths that crisscrossed the woods maybe half a mile behind the five cottages. It lay in a shallow dip marked off by a dense swath of ferns on one side, a stand of silver birches along the back, and at the low end, a rocky swale that became a running creek after every rain. In places the ground was laid with a bright emerald patchwork of moss; elsewhere it was roots and rotting leaves. To anyone just happening by, it offered nothing visually note-worthy. To us it was a dominion unto itself, bearing no relationship to the world of the cottages, or to Freyburg or New York or for that matter America. It existed apart, immune from the rules and customs of those realms.

It was Freddy, really, who started it all. He's the one who found not only the kettle but the slab. It was October, not bitter yet, but brisk, the air laced with the fragrance of wood smoke. We'd gone looking for salamanders, Kitty and Freddy and me, without success, pushing far-ther and farther into the woods, seeking out the dampest places, and when Kitty went capering off the path into a lush, low-lying area, Freddy and I followed.

We squatted among mossy rocks and rotting logs, turning them over, checking the undersides of leaves, searching for a flicker of or-ange but finding only brown beetles and spiders, until after a while Kitty said offhandedly, "Salamanders can start fires, you know."

I eyed her consideringly. Already I'd noticed her penchant for vol-unteering sketchy-sounding facts on an exuberant array of subjects. The vexing thing was that I could not say with certainty she was mak-ing things up; she had, after all, lived in the city and attended real school, and her fonts of knowledge included not only two older siblings but also a wealth, it seemed, of worldly uncles and aunts and cousins, themselves apparently expert in a great variety of fields.

"With their tongues," she clarified.

"That's not possible."

"Yes it is. My sister's a biologist."

I did not know what a biologist did, but I'd heard my parents speak admiringly of the Manseaus' older daughter in Malawi, and decided against mounting a challenge on this front. Freddy had moved away from us, wading through ferns that grew high as his waist. I could see him running both hands through their feathery fringe. His head, tilted skyward, oscillated slowly back and forth, and he was half humming, half crooning tunelessly, his lips open to the trees above.

"Freddy and I have caught loads of salamanders," I informed her, "and no fire's ever come out of them." All they would do is promenade over our fingers with their astonishing, delicate toes.

"But have they ever stuck out their tongues?"

I could not recall.

"That's why, then."

How certain she was, how assured. She blinked her chicory eyes.

"S'ah!" cried Freddy. "Hey-ah!" Or maybe it was, "Ava!"

"What'd he say?" asked Kitty.

"C'mon."

We scrambled up from the damp swale and pushed through the ferns toward where he stood, in a hidden little clearing checkerboarded with late-afternoon sun. As we approached, a clang sounded, then another, and I could see Freddy striking something with a stick.

Kitty and I reached him and saw what he'd found: a rust-mottled, broken-handled teakettle with a long curvy spout. "Let me see," I said, stilling his arm and picking up the kettle. It was heavy, like our cast-iron pot at home. The bottom was plastered with wet leaves and its lid was stuck fast. "Who left it here?" I wondered, looking around. Freddy let out a chortle and went to thwack the kettle with his stick again, but

I held back his arm, afraid he'd hit me by accident, so he discharged his excitement by beating the ground instead.

It made an odd sound.

Kitty and I exchanged a glance. Freddy beat the ground some more, and it did not sound like earth. We began to kick back the leaves and clear away the vines that had grown over what turned out to be a stone slab the size of a room. "What is it?" wondered Kitty. "A grave?" But it was much too big for an ordinary grave, and as soon as she said it I saw in my mind the giant that must be buried underneath, his massive skeleton moldering in the brown earth, and then for an instant I felt more of them, everywhere: dozens of giants laid out beneath us in warrens beneath the ground, an entire subterranean population of them, and we no bigger than salamanders in their eyes. But when we had finished clearing away the debris, we found no grave markings on the stone. "Maybe it's an entrance," I suggested, "some kind of trapdoor," imagining with pleasurable dread the chamber that might lie under so great a door and what it would hold. But we found no handle or hinges either.

"What *is* it, then?" Kitty wondered.

"S'ah f'oor," said Freddy. He removed his thumb. "Ah-floor!"

Kitty lifted her pale eyebrows at me. Of course he was right. This was a dwelling, or had been. The teakettle still dangling from my hand must have belonged to this place, this ancient, tiny, lonely house, tucked deep in a corner of the forest, abandoned who knew how many years ago, how many centuries back?

We turned slowly around, filling in the details. Stone walls and thatched roof. A big fireplace at one end. A chimney emitting popcorn puffs of smoke. A front door split horizontally, and a bonneted woman resting her arms on the closed bottom half, looking out the open top. With almost no conversation then the three of us set to work, piling leaves into a bed in one corner of the slab, dragging over logs for benches and stools, carrying in stones to mark off the hearth. Freddy found a clump of mushrooms with deep red gills, which we picked and laid for embers. As we worked, the little house itself seemed to spring forward and assist in its reincarnation, so that each task we completed achieved more than the anticipated effect, and when we located, just beyond a thicket of dense bushes, what must have been an old trash heap, we were not surprised; it was as if the house, pleased by our attentions, were yielding its treasures to us. Among the artifacts we found were the working end of a hammer, a button, a spoon, and a glass bottle caked with dirt, which, when rubbed clean on our sweaters turned out to bear letters reading: HOAGMAN APOC SAFE SPIRITS.

We stayed in the woods until the new early darkness caught us by surprise. We'd grown chilly by then, even with our sweaters buttoned and our hoods up. Our hands were red-knuckled and bunched like cold apples we kept stuffing back into our pockets. Before leaving we stood together on the slab and looked up through a gap in the branches at the crushed velvet sky.

"S'ah-moon," said Freddy.

"Where?" I asked.

"There." Kitty pointed and it seemed natural that for once she had not asked for a translation but had understood him on her own.

I looked and couldn't see it. Then I could. Glittering ivory rind. I exhaled. My breath ghostwalked hoarily out of my mouth and expanded, dispersed, vanished. A sense of limitless increase.

We were five and seven and seven, out of sight and out of earshot of our parents. Out of their thoughts, perhaps, too. As free children we were accustomed to this. I shivered and reached out, not for Freddy's hand but for Kitty's, and she held it and squeezed back.

You couldn't do that with Fred.

Eight

L ISA, SWEETHEART, could we get a little water for Miss Manseau, please?"

Mr. Charles's bass rumble is pitched discreetly low. I wasn't aware of him getting up from his desk, but now I see him standing once more in the doorway to the outer office. My pulse throbs behind each ear. The blood peals there.

"Thank you, honey," he says to his secretary, and then he is coming back toward me with a plastic cup, his gait too purposeful and swift for this cramped room: I see him passing right through me, holding the shining white cup and striding clear through my person without spilling a drop, as if I am vapor, as if we exist on different planes.

"Here." He hands me the cup. Warm tap water. Metallic-tasting, welcome.

"Thanks."

"Lightheaded?"

"No. Mr. Charles, what—"

He holds up a hand. "Just take a moment. Drink some more water. No rush." He returns to his chair, sits sorting through papers. The newspaper clippings. I have read them all multiple times, can conjure their words, bitter as ink on my tongue. Thirty-year-old white male. No permanent residence. No occupation. Drifter. Collected cans. Reported to have been staying, since September, in an apartment over a garage located on an auto salvage lot owned by Ronald Ferebee, also the owner of the adjacent house where he lived with his wife and their twelve-year-old grandson, James Ferebee. The missing boy.

I sip. Mr. Charles doesn't look up; he seems really to have become absorbed, and I wonder if this is the first time he's reading the articles. The window behind him is a narrow slab of fading light, grave-marker gray. I drink some more. I'm not really lightheaded, just the air in here is overpoweringly close. I want to ask why it smells of bananas. Maybe Bayard Charles is potassium-deficient. I remember my hunger, the fact that I haven't eaten anything since that meager breakfast: egg, grapefruit half, toast. No wonder I felt a little faint. Sip by sip I drink until the water is gone.

"I'm fine now," I say.

He looks up from the articles, smiles in a way that seems weary, resigned.

"Mr. Charles. You were saying. You think Fred should enter a plea. Meaning saying he's guilty? I don't . . . You haven't even talked with him yet, you don't know his side of the story. You haven't met him. You haven't asked me anything about him."

He clears his throat. "Miss Manseau, understand. The reality, the way assigned counsel works in this county, we don't have the resources. No way we can meet with every client before their court dates. I'm not saying I like it that way."

"So what, you just advise everybody to enter a plea?"

"Don't misunderstand. I'm not ready to advise anything yet. But you should prepare for . . . I won't say the worst. But for a difficult road.

Do you want me to level with you, Miss Manseau? If you'd rather be kept in the dark . . . but I don't think you came all this way just to have me sugar-coat things. The charges I read you, that's just the arraignment. You oughtn't be surprised if the D.A. brings additional counts at indictment." He rubs his chin. "I'd expect it."

I concentrate on looking him in the eye. I don't trust my voice to ask what additional counts he foresees.

"If I thought," he continues, "sugar-coating had practical use, I'd do it in a heartbeat. But I've never known it to help a client's case. Miss Manseau, understand: we're dealing with the death of a child, a minor. When the medical examiner's report comes in, the D.A.'s going to be combing it for any reason, any evidence at all that would support his bringing some kind of wrongful death charge. In all likelihood we may be looking at negligent homicide. Maybe man two."

"Man two?"

"Second-degree manslaughter. That's a class C felony."

"Manslaughter's . . . less than homicide?"

"Opposite. Criminally negligent homicide is a lesser charge than manslaughter. Class E. It's early days, a lot's going to depend on the examiner's report, whether the D.A. thinks he's got enough cause to convince a grand jury." He throws his hands wide, shrugs. "*Maybe* it's going to amount to nothing. *Maybe* we'll learn . . . oh, the boy had a preexisting condition, was going to have an aneurysm, say. No matter what, no matter where he was or who with."

"But that's . . ."

Mr. Charles closes his eyes. "But that's unlikely. And there's something else," he says, now addressing a spot above my head, "that I'd prepare for."

The blood slams heavily again behind my ears.

"You've been reading the papers, following the news? Given the fact pattern of the case, certain questions have been raised about the nature of your brother's relations with the deceased. Again, we're waiting here for the medical examiner's report, but you can believe the D.A. is going to be looking closely at any evidence, anything that might come up in the report that might be indicative of abuse. Of any kind." His eyes fasten on me. "You're here, you said, because you want to offer information about your brother. To help me understand him—that right? You said you wanted to 'explain certain things.'"

Another pause. I know this is my cue to speak. I cannot.

"I wonder," he suggests, "if there's anything you want to tell me about your brother's history. Anything about his prior relations with— boys, children."

"No."

"Nothing you want to mention?"

"Nothing to mention."

The air is thick.

I make it clearer: "There is no history."

I say it as firmly as possible, all the while knowing it is not precisely true. Or may not be precisely true; the truth is I never knew. But I cannot keep my thoughts from wandering to the story of the family—an old Batter Hollow family with a son—that took Fred on vacation with them the summer he was twenty-three, the summer after Neel died. All I ever knew for sure was that the family brought Fred back to Batter Hollow after only a few weeks. "The trip ended early," June told me over the phone in a voice like milkweed. I thought she would explain, but she trailed into silence. Then, her voice seeming to dwindle into even frailer wisps: "He seems . . . sad, Ayv."

The next afternoon I sat across from her at the kitchen table, having wrested myself from Dennis's and my apartment in the city and traveled grudgingly north to Freyburg. I sat there wary and a little resentful, summoned by what she hadn't named, waiting for her to explain, but she offered no more details—perhaps she lacked any—of what had happened on the trip, the reason for Fred's early return. I didn't press her. Out of sensitivity, I think. But it is also possible I also wanted to wound her a little with my deliberate incuriosity.

"Their son broke his leg," she finally explained. "It was only an accident, but the break was bad—he needed surgery, so they came back to the States."

"What do you mean 'only an accident'? As opposed to on purpose?"

"Of course not," she said. Then repeated what she'd said the evening before on the phone. "Fred seems so sad. He hasn't spoken since they brought him back." Sometime in the night he'd gone out to the tree house he'd built in the woods and stocked with army blankets; she hadn't seen him all day. "Not one word."

And I watched her knuckles whiten on the cup—she'd taken to using Neel's old soup bowl–sized teacup—each time she turned to look out the window at the dense woods behind the house.

Now Mr. Charles clears his throat. "Are you aware that when he was found the boy was wearing only"—he glances at his desk, finds the passage, reads aloud—"a pair of briefs and a single sock?" He gives me a quick look, his seed-eyes sharp, then scans the paper again and reports neutrally, "The temperature at the time they found him was thirty-four degrees. It had dipped to twenty-five the night before."

"A sock?" I whisper, but the word, malformed, flakes apart in the back of my throat. This hasn't been in any of the accounts I've read. I try to glimpse what sort of paper he's consulted. Some kind of police form, I think it must be.

"Also," he continues, "that investigators found, laid out on a table in the apartment where your brother had been staying, the skeletons of dead animals?"

How could I be aware of this?

He says the next thing almost gently. "Also pornographic materials."

I shake my head.

"You say you've been out of contact with him for two years?"

"A little less."

"Why is that?"

I can only shake my head again.

"And the occasion of your last meeting?"

"Our mother died. So I saw him then, he came home for that."

"For the funeral?"

"For her. We didn't have a funeral. He came to see her when she was sick and we knew she was dying. He stayed a few weeks and then he went to Cape Cod. It had all been arranged. He went to stay with a friend of the family, the son of people my parents knew. He's a house-painter. Fred worked for him. He's never been a big phone person. My brother, I mean. He doesn't own a cell. I did speak with him there on the Cape, a few times."

"When was the last time?"

"A few months ago?"

"Why did he leave?"

"I don't know."

"Were you surprised he didn't tell you?"

"I don't know."

"Are there any other living relatives?"

"No."

"Yet it doesn't surprise you that he'd take off for no reason, without letting you know."

How can I explain? Mr. Charles's voice is magnificently dignified, carefully stripped of inflection, but I see what he must be thinking, see the way the elements must be composing themselves in his head.

"Would you describe your brother as a drifter?"

"No." Something cracks and I look down: I've split the plastic cup. "He—we—it's how we grew up. Traveling, I mean. Our parents took us on lots of trips, camping and things. We'd make it up as we went, fairly unstructured. And Fred didn't go to school. Or only for a short time and then our parents—well, nowadays you'd say they homeschooled him. We had a lot of freedom. We were encouraged to explore."

"Explore?" Mr. Charles twists the base of a silver pen.

"We ... He'd spend, you know, whole days in the woods. Sometimes longer. It was normal for him." What is it I'm trying to tell Mr. Charles about Fred? *He shall have no master but Nature.* I wonder if Bayard Charles is familiar with Rousseau.

"You weren't homeschooled?"

"No."

"Why was your brother homeschooled and not you?"

"Fred is ... it suited him. He's different. He's always been different." I feel heat blossom on my neck at this treasonous confession. Even a word as vague and benign as "different" was never used in our family. But who am I betraying? Fred? Our parents? And suddenly I'm furious, because how am I supposed to help Fred without including this part of the story, without telling Mr. Charles the story?

The phone in the outer office erupts with another full-throated warble, but Mr. Charles, jotting quickly now with the silver pen, seems not to notice. "In what way 'different'?"

"Well ... he didn't start reading until late. He didn't talk much as a kid. I mean he never talked much, period, but especially when he was little, he was slow to begin talking and ... well, slow with lots of things."

"Are you saying he has some kind of disability? Are we talking about an individual of diminished capacity?"

"Yes. No. I mean, what is diminished? He's just different, he's his own way. What I'm saying is if you knew him it wouldn't seem strange that he took this boy to the woods. He was always going into the woods, into nature."

"Has he ever been diagnosed with a specific condition? Ever been evaluated that you know of?" Mr. Charles is leaning forward, more animated than he's been this whole time. "Do you know whether we're talking about a cognitive impairment, or something behavioral? Any mental illness?"

"No, not . . . I don't think so." I press my fingers hard against my bottom lip.

"You say he did attend some school?"

"Only for a year. Well—part of a year."

"When was this?"

I picture us down at the mailboxes at the end of Batter Hollow Lane, waiting for the school bus. Bracing for the school bus. "When he was eight."

"Was this a private school, some type of special ed?"

"No. Public. Freyburg Primary School, where we grew up."

"Why did he stop?"

I picture us sitting outside the main office, Freddy and me, swinging our legs on the little bench, waiting while Neel and June met privately with the principal, Freddy's second-grade teacher and the school social worker. Hearing Neel's raised voice right through the cinderblock wall. Seeing June's smile when they came out, an awful, crooked smile that tried to cover the fact she'd been crying. "It wasn't the right fit."

"Do you remember the name of your pediatrician?" asks Mr. Charles. "I assume your parents took you to the same doctor?"

I shake my head. "We mostly would go see Ginny Gann if we got sick. She was our neighbor, an osteopath? I think that's what she was. Like a family practitioner."

Writing as he speaks: "Still in practice?"

I have no idea. June will know, I think for a split second, then make the autocorrection: would have known.

NONE OF THE FAMILIES live at Batter Hollow anymore. The Shed was only ever sporadically occupied after Jim and Katinka left back in the mid-eighties. The Salinas-Buchbinders moved out of the Annex when Noah left for college. The Ganns, after so many years of providing a more or less cheerfully frenetic backdrop to my own childhood, eventually vacated the Classrooms to go west, I think, someplace like Seattle or Vancouver. And the Manseaus left immediately upon Kitty's finishing high school. They'd grown tired of the inconveniences of experimental living some years earlier, but waited long enough for Kitty to graduate with her class before they relocated back to Lower Manhattan, not far from the art gallery that had begun to show Don's metal sculptures. Their desertion came as a particular blow, not only because it vouched a loss of faith in Neel and June's way of life, but because it left them without any neighbors. Neel felt their move as both a philosophical and personal rejection, and it became one of the grievances he nursed with bitter dedication during his final years.

After Neel's death, June remained in the Office about a year before the isolation drove her to Freyburg Center, where she rented an apartment over the bicycle shop. Fred stayed with her for stretches of time, but by then he'd turned eighteen and begun traveling for long periods. Not independently, of course. Old friends of Neel's, many of them former Batter Hollow students, would offer to put him up and give him work as a favor to June. I never knew to what extent he was truly productive, earning his room and board, or whether these stints were more a matter of glorified babysitting. But I believe Fred must have been able to contribute meaningful work. He wasn't stupid and he wasn't lazy, and given the right kind of task he could be more diligent and thorough than most people. It seems possible that the great variety of experiences might have expanded him, too, made him more worldly and wise.

I can't account for all the places he traveled, all the jobs he held. By then I was busy building my own life with Dennis, working hard to become someone other than I had been: an adult, a wife, a music teacher. I do recall hearing about a stint he did on a lobster boat off Gloucester, and another on a maple syrup farm in Vermont. And I recall, of course, the summer after Neel died when that family brought Fred to the Magdalen Islands, employing him as a kind of companion for their twelve-year-old son. It was, June said, precisely his unconventional upbringing—the fact of his having been allowed to spend all those years ungoverned in the woods, hiking and exploring, foraging for wild strawberries and mushrooms, telling time by the sun— that made him perfect for the job. She told me about it over the phone, shortly after persuading the family to invite him, and she spoke in an excited rush, sounding happy and relieved and something else. Vindicated. As though reporting that Fred's upbringing hadn't been a disservice to him after all.

I was a newlywed that summer, having married Dennis six weeks before Neel's third and fatal stroke. Publicly, I joked I'd caused it. Privately, I believed I had.

By then Dennis and I were living in Queens, where he worked for Greensleeves, a green-energy consulting firm, and I led Clap Your

Hands! music classes for preschoolers at the Flatbush Y. I'd stumbled into the job, recommended by a family for whom I'd babysat while in college, and was somewhat surprised to find it suited me, both the consistency and the nostalgia, for I used many of the old songs and rhymes and handclap games that June had taught us when we were little. Every now and then there'd be a child who reminded me of Fred. The child could be girl or boy, black or white, shy or rowdy—none of this mattered. What would catch my attention was something less visible than atmospheric: a sense of profound detachment, an inability to participate with the rest of the class in any way, either to sing along or to sit still, and yet, from the moment I unzipped my duffel bag and began handing out rhythm instruments, a kind of intense rapture. I always found a way to let such a child have whichever instrument he or she desired, even if someone else had already chosen it, even if the caregiver tried to step in and mediate.

No, no, Robert, this nice little girl had the castanets first.

He should have them, I'd say, trying to project peaceable sagacity. And quickly I'd hand a pair of claves to the nice little girl, whose lip might be starting to tremble. *Hey, I bet you'd be really good at these.*

That Neel found my job an abomination factored heavily into why he and I were on less than stellar terms during the last years of his life. ("Cookie-cutter music," he called it, never mind that I'd learned most of it from June.) After he died, I made an effort to visit June at least every couple of months, but the truth is I found it depressing.

My mother was sixty-five when Neel died: young. Her hair, which still hung heavy halfway down her back, had turned a rich ivory. Its new paleness brought out the warm cork tones of her skin and made her dark eyes sparkle. She hadn't put on much weight as she aged, but the pounds she had gained looked healthy, softening her somewhat angular frame. There was no reason she couldn't have continued being active, doing the things she had done before his death: taking yoga, teaching figure drawing at the American Legion Hall, playing flute. But she complained of feeling tired and she complained of feeling old, and whenever I visited I'd find the kitchen table blanketed with old Batter Hollow yearbooks and newsletters, things she claimed to be in the process of cleaning out but which seemed only to accumulate in ever more precarious piles. And she never wanted to cook anymore.

We'd drive into Freyburg and have dry little sandwiches and wilty garden salads at the Front Porch Cafe, and then she'd say she needed to buy something, always something modest and cheerless, like toothpaste, and we'd walk to the five-and-dime, and then she'd suggest we check out the book sale table at the library, or browse the thrift shop, one thing after another until it was time for my train back to the city, and I'd come away feeling how attenuated her life had become, and how deeply she'd grown to dread spending any time at all back at Batter Hollow.

"You don't have to stay, you know," I finally told her. "It's not like you'd be hurting his feelings if you leave."

Her eyes went wavy but the rest of her remained composed and she returned my gaze so steadily that I grew hot and appended out loud what we both must have been thinking: "Like *I* did."

Because I'd gone away to college, my departure from Batter Hollow coincided with the Manseaus', and I think Neel conflated the two, experiencing my embarkation as another abandonment, if not an outright switching of allegiances. It's true that I grew close to the Manseaus during college, but as a result of happenstance rather than conspiracy. I attended New York University, mere blocks from their West Village apartment. Kitty had gone off to Oberlin, and Don and Meg, missing her, no doubt, took to inviting me for dinner every now and then. I loved to go. Their apartment, over on Jane Street, was modern, stylish, full of air and light. They always had interesting people over: grant administrators, civic planners, secular humanists—all these things I'd never even heard of up in Batter Hollow. And they treated me like an adult. It wasn't only that they assumed my interest in conversing with their friends; they assumed their friends' interest in conversing with me. They seemed to find it natural I would drink a glass of Rioja with them, keep up with the editorial page, have an opinion about everything from the Times Square renovation project to the Lewinsky scandal to what was happening in Kosovo. And, in no small part as a result of their expectations, I did.

Their older daughter, Ellie, the one who'd been in the Peace Corps, was living by then in Chad, where she did something with NGOs and microloans (more new vocabulary for me), but Dennis was living in Long Island City, and was sometimes at these dinners, often with a girlfriend. He had a succession of these, each one pleasant in a subdued sort of way. I studied them with surreptitious fascination, unable to suss out what made them particularly desirable. In the absence of more obvious charms, I invented all sorts of hidden attributes: they possessed scathing wits, cooked gourmet novelties, were terrors in the sack. That each must be in some way exceptional was a given, for Dennis, I was coming fervently to believe, might have had his pick of any woman in the city.

Dennis fascinated me. Initially I tried to convince myself it was just because of Kitty and the many ways they were at once like and unlike each other. His eyes were the same vivid chicory blue, but more deeply set, and awninged by thicker brows. His hair, once as blond as hers, had settled into a complicated honey brown. The most riveting similarity was the cleft chin. His was much more pronounced. I couldn't decide whether it was handsome or absurd.

But what fascinated me most was a quality he did not share with

Kitty: his modesty, his innate reserve. Dennis was capable of dazzling (as at our first encounter, when he tossed the white base of the lamp into the lavender sky), but never actively sought an audience or applause, so that even his starriest moments—whether of drollery or brilliance or bravery or benevolence—possessed a kind of stealth quality, with the result that when they caught my notice I felt specially rewarded, singled out.

Once I admitted to myself that I'd fallen in love, I fell as one does for every aspect of the man, however minute, and especially for those most foreign to me: his wingtips, his French cuffs, his taste for dark chocolate, his taste for octopus, the way his barber shaved the back of his neck, the crinkles that had already, at twenty-five, begun to etch the corners of his eyes. Each one of these in turn made blood rocket through my body. Long gone were the days when I joined Kitty in mocking him for attending Clenchbutt Academy; now I paged hungrily through his old yearbooks and drank in stories of his prep school days: the lab coat he'd stolen from a beloved chem teacher only to return it days later, tie-dyed; the beer bottle fight he'd broken up between classmates, which gave him the shiny raised scar on his left shoulder; the early-morning rowing in shells on the mist-shrouded Clembrook River.

I remember the first time I placed my finger in the lovely depression (I'd decided in favor of it) in his chin. We had already slept together but this felt more intimate, more riskily presumptuous even than that, and I could not work my voice above a creaking whisper: "How do you shave in there?"

When eventually I began staying the night in his converted warehouse apartment in Long Island City, I would lie awake, too incredulous to sleep, listening to him breathe and gazing out the vast bank of undressed windows, taking in the endless wealth of lights.

From this vantage Batter Hollow seemed poorer than ever. I went home for holidays with increasing reluctance. Neel, after years of mental sharpness, had at last grown doddery—and simultaneously more pigheaded than ever. The combination was hard on June. Still only in her late fifties, she tried to maintain her equilibrium, but the effort showed on her face and in her posture, and also in the way the house and grounds fell into disrepair. The Shed looked derelict, its two front windows having been smashed and replaced with plywood. A heavy length of gutter hung diagonally off the Classrooms. One side of the Annex had become streaked with green tongues of mildew. The Art Barn, victim to a fallen branch, had a hole in its roof. If the Office showed less obvious external decline, the inside reeked of neglect: peeling plaster, engrimed bathtub and sink, moldings darkly furred with dust.

Fred, though he still lived nominally at home, rarely entered the house. June told me he spent more and more nights in his tree house. "I think he's happy out there." But whenever I saw him he seemed more silent and remote than ever. He'd grown tall and broad-shouldered, with a strong neck and a fine, manly jaw; he might've been really handsome if not for certain oddities: his unwashed, uncombed, uncut hair; the habit he had of bouncing on the balls of his feet; the way his eyes would meet yours, at once shy and rawly eager, for just a second before sliding away again. I noticed a funny smell about him, too, like wet leaves and mushrooms.

THE PHONE IN Mr. Charles's outer office rings again and a minute later the young woman Lisa appears in the door. "Sorry to interrupt," she says. "But I've been asked to remind you that it's past five."

"What's that?"

"And I have class tonight."

"Hm?" Mr. Charles glances at her abstractedly, still keeping company with his most recent thought. Then his face clears. "Right. Right you are."

"And you're supposed to pick up cream cheese on the way home."

He looks nonplussed.

"For the icing? Grandma's carrot cake?"

"Oh," says Mr. Charles. "Ayuh."

Lisa gives a tiny roll of her eyes and retreats back into the outer office. So she is his granddaughter. So this is a family business.

Mr. Charles smiles apologetically, twisting the base of his pen and setting it down. "We'll have to wrap up now. This has been," he allows, "instructive."

"What happens next?" After sitting here for so long in the stifling banana air, I find myself unnerved by the abrupt dismissal.

"I'll get over to the jail tomorrow." He flips a couple of pages on a desk calendar, then confirms, "Yes, I should be able to meet with your brother tomorrow. We have your contact info? You gave it to Lisa?"

I explain that I am staying in Perdu this week, and although he should have my cell I write down for him again both my own number and Mrs. Tremblay's landline, adding what she said about the spotty cell reception out where she is. He stands and makes signs of closing up shop, straightening a few piles on his desk, tearing a slip of paper off a pad and folding it into his breast pocket, where I see he already has a little salad of other scraps.

"About visiting my brother—"

"Yes, yes, we can be in touch after I've seen him."

"No, I mean—*my* visiting him. How I haven't been able to see him? Because I'm not on the list?"

"Oh. Right. I should be able to . . ." His voice trails off as he re-deploys his pen and jots down something else, then adds that piece of paper to the others in his shirt. "Try calling after four, you have the number? Call the jail after four tomorrow. I should be able to get that taken care of."

I can hardly believe that dispatching this problem could be so easy—for him just a matter of making a call, when for me it has been an impossible plight. "Thank you." I reach out my hand, a little sick with relief. We shake once more and I leave, fairly tumbling down the stairs and outside where it is cold and dark and smells blissfully like nothing except cold, dark air.

In the morning Mrs. Tremblay sets before me a plate bearing an-other egg, hardboiled this time, and a slice of honeydew. She apolo-gizes for not serving toast.

"That's all right."

But she *tsk*s. "I put a piece in the toaster and then saw it was moldy. I just bought the loaf Tuesday!"

I commiserate with a like *tsk*, glad to find myself an ally of her disapproval rather than its target. She wears pale blue slacks, a pale pink sweater, and over these, an apron of yellow gingham. Outside the kitchen window the day looks as though it's been drawn with a crayon, the sky bright and scrubbed, the branches stiff at attention.

While I eat, she sips her coffee and leans against the counter, watching the bulbous little TV. It's showing the local news again, which makes me uneasy, but they're only airing a segment on how to buy your Thanksgiving turkey. We watch together as the reporter vis-its first a turkey farm, then a farmers' market, then a large chain store.

The segment ends with the anchorwoman back in the studio ribbing the on-location reporter about how he seems to be developing a little wattle himself, and as they go to commercial Mrs. Tremblay says, "I never like it when they do that."

I have never liked this either, the spiky banter, the false jocosity that seems to be the lingua franca of commercial news operations. I feel an unexpected glimmer of kinship with Mrs. Tremblay.

"Coffee?" she asks.

"Please."

Refilling my cup, she says, "You met my nephew," and for an instant I wonder whether she could possibly be Bayard Charles's aunt.

"I did?"

"You had a little trouble coming around the bend by Vincy Hill, I hear." Does she sound almost mischievous, letting this drop?

"Oh! That was your nephew? The man who stopped?" I try to remember his face, tucked back in the recesses of his hood. The spots of rain on his eyeglasses. "He was so nice. I didn't get his name."

"Ayuh. That was Bill." Now she's back at the counter, wiping it with a rag.

"How did he know who I was—or that you—?"

"Oh, well. Perdu's awful small."

I let that sink in. Impossible to tell, looking at her narrow shoulders and broad bottom as she rinses out the rag, wrings it forcefully and hangs it over the faucet, if she means this statement to be taken at face value or to suggest something more.

I thank Mrs. Tremblay for breakfast and try to carry my own dishes to the sink, but she intercepts me ("Oh, now. I'll do that"), removing them from my hands, and so I thank her again and excuse myself. I have just reached the doorway when the anchor says: "An update now on the death of young James Ferebee, the twelve-year-old boy who was found last Saturday in Meurtriere State Forest," and I cannot now leave without hearing what follows, even if this will give me away to Mrs. Tremblay once and for all. I turn back. She gives me a look. Then we both turn our attention to the screen.

"The boy had been missing for five days when rescuers found him unconscious in a creek bed seven miles from the nearest trailhead. He was brought to Criterion Regional Medical Center where medical staff declared him dead late Saturday night. Today, according to a spokesman from the District Attorney's office, the medical examiner's report ruled the cause of death to be cerebral hypoxia, a lack of oxygen to the brain. The report concludes the death was precipitated by an asthma attack triggered by the cold, wet environment in which the boy was found."

Oh, thank you. Thank you. Natural causes. The cold is to blame, the cold and the wet. Not Fred. Surely, whatever Fred did, whatever minor misjudgment he might have made in bringing the boy with him to the woods, things will go easier for him now.

The anchor continues. "The report also revealed evidence of a broken wrist, two broken ribs and contusions on the boy's face, torso and legs, all of which point to what appears to have been a harrowing series of hours, if not days, leading up to his death. Investigators are still working to piece together what took place between the time James Ferebee was seen riding in a car just blocks from his middle school in Perdu last Monday afternoon and the time he was found, five days later, clinging to life in Meurtriere State Forest. Friends of the family say that Frederick Robbins"—here the image cuts to Fred's mug shot, and it is as jolting as the first time I saw it: the severity not only of his hair cropped so close to the skull but also of his gaunt face, as if his skin, too, were hunkering close to the bone—"the thirty-year-old vagrant being held on charges of abduction, had spent weeks cultivating

the boy's trust, often inviting him into the garage apartment"—
and here the image cuts to an exterior shot of the place where Fred
had supposedly been staying since late summer: a listing, brownish,
aluminum-sided building, with a corrugated metal garage door domi-
nating the front, no visible windows, and an exterior staircase leading
to the second floor—"on the lot adjacent to the boy's home, where
Robbins had been temporarily staying."

The camera pulls back to show the lot in which the garage stands,
then pulls back farther to show a dark green ranch house, separated
from the junkyard by a cyclone fence: presumably the Ferebee abode.

Fred has spent so much of the last decade in reaches unknown to
me. I have never visited him in any of the places he has traveled. He has
never invited me. Nor have I tried, I realize, staring at Mrs. Tremblay's
old TV, to envision him in his surroundings. When he was working on
the maple syrup farm, I did picture him collecting a bucket of sap from
a tapped tree, knee deep in blue-white snow, but the image I conjured
was as pristine and idealized as an illustration in one of our old children's books.

When he was working on the lobster boat, I remember imagining
lobsters in their wooden traps and a boat riding spangled waves, but
never him; I gave no thought to where he stayed or how he lived or who
he interacted with or what they made of him. Same with the painting
gig on Cape Cod: I know he stayed in Dave Alsop's house, but not how
big it was or how close to the beach, or if anyone else lived there, or
what he did with his free time. I don't even know if it was a house, come
to think of it, or an apartment or a trailer.

Once I asked June how she could stand it.

Fred had been twenty-two that fall, working in a salmon cannery
in Kodiak, Alaska. I'd been up visiting my parents for the day. It was
after lunch. Neel had gone off to take a nap, and June and I sat on the

gray flowered couch having tea. Her box of stationery was on the coffee table, and I could see she'd started a letter to Fred in her beautiful, clear handwriting. Fred, of course, was no letter writer; she must have known he would not respond.

"Stand what?" she asked.

I tried to think what exactly I meant. Letting Fred go away, solo, into the immensity of an impartial world. Or rather, an all-too-partial world, a world that looked askance at the likes of Fred.

"Worrying," I said finally. "Don't you worry about him?"

"Ava." She pulled my arm very gently so that my hand came away from the earring I'd been twisting around in its hole. "If I thought worrying would help—if I thought there was even the slightest chance that my worrying would help Fred, I'd do it."

"But how do you know he'll be all right?"

Even as I asked, I knew the answer: she didn't. She and Neel had never known he would be all right, not during all those far-off days of childhood when he'd gone roving in the woods behind the cottages; not during the terrible long hours he'd sat in a classroom in Freyburg Primary, holding back tears, holding in the rhythms his hands wanted badly to tap on his desktop, holding off the stares and whispers of his classmates; not, for that matter, during the afternoons he'd spent lost with me up on the flowered couch, following my orders ("Get us some books, Freddy boy," "Breathe with your mouth shut") while I entranced him with stories of peril and pleasure, wound him round and round with my voice, led him down a branching path.

Now the TV is showing something else: a middle-aged woman in a down vest standing on the porch of the dark green house. "It's a tragedy," she rasps. "A wicked shame. He shouldn'ta died and that's all. The family don't even care what happens to the guy who did it. Nothing's going to bring Jimmy back." A caption at the bottom of the screen identifies her as FAMILY FRIEND. The camera pulls back then to show the front door behind her, with a quick glimpse of a face peering out through the side panel, before cutting to the studio where the anchorwoman announces, "As the family continues to mourn, a spokesman for the District Attorney's office says the investigation into the events that led to the boy's death will continue. In related news, we've just been told that the Arthur L. Humphrey Middle School will dismiss students one hour early today to accommodate those families and teachers planning to attend a public memorial service this afternoon."

Floating in the upper right-hand corner of the screen during this wrap-up is the boy's by now ubiquitous school photo. Round face like a bowl of cream, dark eyes and dark hair and those protuberant incisors, hinting at the beginnings of a grin. A ready face, a game face. The face of one who will be led.

Nine

THAT FIRST YEAR the Manseaus lived at Batter Hollow, Kitty and Freddy and I spent countless unstructured hours in Midgetropolis. We never told the grown-ups about our special place, never even uttered its name in their presence. "Want to go to M?" one of us would say softly, and we'd automatically drop whatever we'd been doing. Its magical properties grew and bound us to the place. I remember I'm the one who declared offhandedly, one December day as we approached the spot, "You can only get there through the Arch," and thus named the opening at the base of the two bent pines whose crowns came together. It was a fresh, chilly morning, the air tasting of tinsel, and we were well bundled in layers borrowed from the steamer trunk that had once been the school lost-and-found. Kitty and Freddy slipped through the opening between the trees after me, and from that day on we never entered Midgetropolis by any other route.

Already we'd begun seeing differently. There was a fat old lightning-struck stump that rose majestically from the forest floor, its splintered edges like crenellations, the white fungi that decorated its rim like heraldic pennants: this was quite plainly the Tower. One or another of us would climb up into it to serve as lookout or issue an edict; occasionally I'd stand up there and tootle my recorder like a medieval bugler signaling the start of a joust. There was a trio of sprawling, flattish, mossy rocks clustered down by the swale: these were our Thrones, richly upholstered in emerald velvet, each with a matching footstool. And the HOAGMAN APOC SAFE SPIRITS bottle became our Ark—this was what Kitty said you called the container for something sacred, in our case, a broad scrap of pale bark I had peeled, naughtily, from one of the silver birch trees, and on which Kitty this day inscribed a kind of oath: WE PROMISE TO DEADICATE ARSELVES TO THE LAND OF MIJATROPOLIS AND KEEP IT SECRET FOREVER NO MATTER WHAT HAPENS.

I helped dictate, and when it was done Kitty capped the felt-tip pen she'd brought and stuck it in the pocket of her peacoat. Then she withdrew from this same pocket a sewing needle stuck through a scrap of cloth and a book of matches. She displayed these on the flat of her palm and looked at Freddy and me with cheeks sucked solemnly in.

"Now," she explained, "we sign it in blood." She slipped the needle from its cloth.

We sat cross-legged on our Thrones, knee to knee to knee. Above us rose the pines, tall and muscular in their dark prickly coats. Above them the sky was drumskin white.

"First I'll kill the germs," Kitty announced, lighting a match and sticking the tip of the needle in the flame. She said we could start with me: pointer or thumb? I gave her my left thumb.

I was not happy about any of it: not her having sprung this on us; not her rather imperious manner; not her decision to start with me; and above all, not her having had the idea in the first place. It wasn't that I didn't like the idea. I was only afraid I'd never come up with an idea so good, so daring. What if Kitty found me dull or timid, unworthy of her friendship; what if she was growing tired of me?

So while she poked and pushed at the pad of my thumb for what seemed whole minutes, hurting me without managing to pierce the skin, I sat clenching my teeth and screwing up my eyes, determined not to make a sound. Finally she jabbed the needle in. I gave a little scream and opened my eyes. She squeezed and a drop of blood welled to the surface.

"Parchment," she demanded, holding out her hand toward Freddy, who was holding the birch bark oath.

At six, Freddy continued to be big for his age. He sat there on the flat rock with his legs crossed and his bare ankles sticking out from too-short tan corduroys and his hooded parka ringing his face with fake fur. His face was awash in tears. I was used to seeing Freddy cry— at that stage tantrums were a daily occurrence—but I had never seen him cry like this: silently, without histrionics or facial contortions, only a swollen softness, an overflowing sorrow that fed not on self-pity but seemed to tap deeper springs. He was crying for me.

"Parchment," Kitty repeated, apparently unaware that there was anything different about these tears.

They were an astonishment to me, the first evidence of empathy I'd ever seen in Freddy. In fact, I had worried about the way he sometimes seemed not merely unmoved but actually titillated when someone got hurt. Only a few days earlier, a bird had smashed into the kitchen window while we were eating lunch, and Freddy had laughed and flapped his wrists in excitement.

With an impatient sound now, Kitty snatched the piece of bark from his hand and rolled it against my pricked thumb, where the bright red bead had already almost dried. It left a rusty smudge.

Freddy gave a loud sniff and wiped his tears with the heels of both hands.

"If you're going to be a baby," Kitty said calmly, "you can't be in Midgetropolis."

"Yes he can," I contradicted. "He discovered it."

"We all did."

"He found the kettle. He found the floor."

We looked over at the stone slab upon which we'd erected our Midgetropolis house. Even in the midst of bickering, I knew we were all seeing it as we'd spun it out in our imaginations, and in language: its walls and wide hearth, its thatched roof and clay chimney pot, its flower boxes filled with marigolds and blue front door on which hung a brass knocker—all of this uniquely apparent to the three of us.

"Fine," Kitty huffed. "But if he doesn't put his blood on the parchment, he's not part of the oath."

I looked at Freddy. He'd stopped crying but along his jaw a few drops still clung like rain on the underside of a railing. I reached over and flicked them off.

"All right," I said, "but you go next. Show him it's not so bad."

With some bravado Kitty lit another match and re-sterilized the needle. Then she tried to prick her own finger, jabbing experimentally for even longer than it had taken her to puncture my skin. She couldn't do it.

"Want me to?" I held out my hand for the needle.

"Wait," she said, hunching protectively. "It's just harder to do on yourself."

"That's why I said you want me to?"

"No, I can, it's just . . ." She angled herself away and I got on my knees so I could peer over her shoulder.

"You're doing it wrong," I suggested. "You're trying to go in sideways. It's not like getting a splinter out."

"You're too close," she countered. "I can't see and you're getting your breath all over the needle. Now I have to burn off the germs again."

But she had another inspiration. She pulled up the leg of her jeans, exposing a little scab on her knee, which she picked off. Blood seeped to the surface. She blotted it with the piece of bark, and her mark came out better than mine.

"That's cheating."

"Blood is blood," she replied. And to Freddy: "Now you."

"No-ah needle," he said.

We helped him search for available scabs, practically stripping him: we pulled up the legs of his tan cords, took off his parka, pushed back the arms of his sweater. "Check his toes," suggested Kitty, and we removed his sneakers and socks, to no avail. "We'll have to prick you then," decided Kitty. "What finger do you want?"

"I do-ah," said Freddy. "I! *I-ah*." Striking his chest.

He scrambled off his Throne. Coatless, shoeless, sockless, he went stepping in the December woods along the muddy swale, the surface of which bore a lacy veil of ice, and plucked a jagged stone. Then he sat right down in layers of wet leaves and applied the stone's sharp edge to the smooth, flat plane of his inner arm, scraping and scraping back and forth.

It took him some time. Up and down the white limb he scraped, coolly, as though the arm were unattached to him or to anyone, as though it were inert, a piece of wood. He did not look up until he was done, until he had drawn blood. Then he tossed the stone away in the leaves, idly, without show, with no special force or flourish, and this seemed to me the crowning oddity, although I couldn't have said why.

He climbed back up beside us, offering the part of his arm where a little zipper of scarlet had risen up through a length of white-flaked skin, and I tried to catch his eye but his head was bent. Kitty pressed the birch bark to the wound, then pulled it back and showed us. Three spots of blood marked the parchment oath.

I looked at Freddy, who had surprised me twice in the space of ten minutes, first by weeping for me, then by displaying so little regard for his own pain. Now he was far from the trembling tears he'd wept for me; far, too, from the intense focus he'd shown while abrading the skin of his own arm. His eyes looked flat, vacant. His bare feet had gone bluish.

"Put your socks back on," I told him. "Where'd your jacket go?"

We helped him work the socks back over his frozen feet; we tied his shoelaces for him and retrieved his parka from where it had fallen. Kitty turned all motherly-efficient, brushing the wet leaves off his shoulders and telling him to lift his chin while she snapped his hood under it, so that I liked her again.

THAT EVENING NEEL, keeping Freddy company while he had a bubble bath, said, "How'd you get that on your arm?" I was reading in my bedroom across the hall and heard them through the open doors as clearly as if we were all in the same room together. Freddy had been making *chuff chuff* noises as he propelled his wooden boat across the surface of the bath, and every now and then I'd hear Neel refold the pages of his newspaper, but now the toilet creaked and I could picture him leaning forward from where he sat on its closed lid.

Neel generally made a point of attaching little importance to physical injury. If one of us came crying to him with a bruise or cut, he was likely to inspect it briefly, tousle our hair, and remind us that *life is inseparable from risk.* So when he put aside his newspaper to inquire about Freddy's arm, it got my attention.

"S'ah-scrape," said Freddy.

"What's that you say?"

"Ah-got s'ah-scrape."

It was still difficult for most people, Neel and June included, to understand Freddy's speech. By the time he turned ten, the problem had mostly resolved and only the habit of inserting extra vowels persisted. But for most of his first decade, I was the one who understood him best, and so ingrained was the habit of interpreting for him that I nearly called out from my bedroom, "He says he got a scrape!"

Instead I sat in wonder: Freddy had lied. For all his many failings, I had never known Freddy to be dishonest. In fact until that point I'd thought him incapable of deceit.

Later that evening, after Freddy had finished his bath, asked for and gotten a strawberry yogurt, flung it against the stove when told he had to sit at the table to eat it, spent fifteen minutes rolling himself back and forth across the floor, calmed down enough to go outside and look for the moon with Neel, then sat on June's lap while he drank a cup of water, and finally been tucked into bed, I stole into his room.

"Are you awake?" I could hear him slurping on his thumb as he often did in his sleep.

But, "S'ah," he answered, rolling onto his side and blinking shinily at me. I sat on the floor beside his bed where the moonlight fell in a thin channel.

"Did it hurt?" I whispered. "When you scraped yourself today?"

He returned my gaze so steadily that it prickled the base of my neck. For a moment I wondered if he was only pretending, all the rest of the time when he seemed unable to hold eye contact. After a moment he sighed.

He had a fairy-tale face, Freddy, a face of contrasts, pale and dark. He was sloe-eyed and slope-nosed and had a deeply bowed mouth. His breath often had a slightly sour scent that I associated with his thumb-sucking, but he had brushed his teeth before bed and now it just smelled of mint.

"Did it hurt when you went in the bath?" I pressed, thinking of times I'd had a scrape sting when it got wet.

He didn't answer.

"Did it hurt?" I repeated, my whisper close to a hiss.

But he only blinked. I brought my face toward his, leaning closer and closer until our foreheads touched, and our noses, too, and he did not jerk away and we were inhaling and exhaling the same minty breath.

What I meant was: *Did I hurt you? Did you have to make yourself bleed because you saw my finger get pricked?* And: *What else would you do for me?* And: *How responsible for you am I?*

Ten

I DRIVE INTO PERDU AT MIDDAY, telling myself I have no special plan. I might sit in the lone diner, order the soup and half-sandwich special, possibly stroll past the few blocks of shops or along the thin brown mill river that runs behind them, somehow biding the hours until four, when Mr. Charles told me to try calling the jail. But as I approach the coin-op news box outside the diner, my eye is drawn to the front page of the local weekly, the *Perdu Citizen.* I feed a couple of quarters into the slot and extract a copy. I know what I am looking for. There on the sidewalk, I flip through its few pages until I find the event listings, and yes, there it is: JAMES FEREBEE MEMORIAL SERVICE. THURSDAY, NOVEMBER 18. TIME: 1:30 P.M. LOCATION: BUCK WALLACE COMMUNITY CENTER.

My chest is thudding. I am going to attend. Not a decision but an imperative.

The day is sunny and brusque. I stand outside the diner, whose awning furls and flaps, the scant rectangles of newsprint snapping in the wind, the noon light spangling the page, my hair fluttering ticklish in front of my eyes, all of it combining to produce a feeling of near-vertigo that reminds me of the other night, when I slipped on Mrs. Tremblay's walk. Everything appears palsied, provisional, even the ink, spiky and smudged now in the corner where my thumb has gripped.

Inside, the diner is busy and warm and redolent of bacon and sugar. The sound of spattering grease pebbles the air. I stand by the PLEASE WAIT TO BE SEATED sign. A waitress calls, "Sit anywhere."

I slide into the only empty booth, a two-top against the wall. The customers at this hour appear to be mostly seniors, the men thickset and gravel-voiced, with baseball caps over their stiff gray hair; the women soft and lumpy in their hand-knitted sweaters. At the table behind me they are speaking of last night's hard frost, how it caught somebody named Emmy by surprise.

"Had 'em deliver a load of manure Monday," a man is saying. "Been sitting there ever since—"

"Sitting pretty," puts in a woman.

"—like a big lawn ornament," the man continues. "So last night, Emmy's getting ready for bed, hears on the radio the temperature's going to drop. Suddenly it hits her that pile of crap's about to petrify. She throws her coat over her jammies, makes Mort get up, has him out there in the dark with two flashlights, one in each hand, while she's shoveling shit over her seed beds for all she's worth." His laugh wheezes like a cracked concertina and is accompanied by his tablemates'.

I feel a prick of longing I do not understand.

The waitress, her hair in gray snails, takes my order. She goes. I wait.

Tables empty and tables fill. All around me, more people, more of the same: regulars, retirees with glasses so thick their eyes swim, distorted, behind the lenses. These are Fred's jurors. For all the visible indignities of age, they have about them a kind of collective grandeur.

How comfortable they appear, how established. They are that thing I will never be.

We must choose between making a man and a citizen. So quoth Neel, so we were raised to believe.

Food comes. Split pea soup and tuna on toast. I eat slowly, the *Perdu Citizen* propped against the napkin dispenser. I read as I eat but hardly know what I am reading; even as my eyes scan the print, my mind is elsewhere, turning that word—*citizen*—over and over, asking Neel, beseeching him: Why did you insist on making us unfit?

Around me the customers murmur, the waitresses joke. The diner is shot through with spooling gold light and the whole place smells of syrup and ham, echoes with the clatter of plate and mug. It's just the sort of place we would have gone with Neel and June on one of our jaunts; the sort of small-town place—entrenched, timeless, homely, unstriving—that I learned to love, but to love ambivalently, in wistful fashion, because it went without saying that in such places we could never belong.

As a freshman in high school, when I proposed trying out for cheer-leading, Neel and June were for once equally aghast. Cheerleading, they sermonized, represented the epitome of both mindless confor-mity and sexist stereotype. They had my attention: I'd found the ideal thing to rile them both. "You can't not let me," I said. "It's my choice"—a word I relished flinging back at Neel as often as I could throughout (and, disgracefully, beyond) adolescence.

When I did not make the squad, the humiliation was terrible. I had not only practiced the routine until I was sure I had it down, I'd scru-tinized every detail of the likeliest girls' appearance: their outfits, their high ponytails, their shimmery makeup, even the fetching way they chewed their lips and squealed with nerves outside the gym while waiting to be called in groups of eight. All of these I imitated as faithfully as I could and with what I believed a high degree of success. So when the list went up the next day and my name did not appear, it seemed the final proof of my intractable otherness—a residue that clung like a stench wherever I went and no matter how many times I tried to rinse myself clean.

Worse than the shame I felt reading the names of girls who'd made the cut were the palpable relief (from June) and vindication (Neel) I faced when I brought the news home.

"I'm sorry, Ayv," said June. "But to be honest, I'm also glad."

Neel crushed me in an embrace. I was as tall as he by then, and his five o'clock shadow ground against my cheek.

"Scratchy," I objected.

He let me go but couldn't help seizing my arm and giving it a pleased joggle. "I knew you could never pass for one of them."

"But why?" I moaned. "Why couldn't I?" I pulled the elastic from the ponytail I'd worked hard to mirror those of the girls on the squad and let my hair slop over my face. I was parodying despondency a little, in order to conceal my real despondence. "What's *wrong* with me?"

"You're free," declared Neel warmly. "Free from custom, free from pretense, and now free again from expectation."

Was he right? Was that true? Does the concept of such freedom apply when custom, pretense and expectation have never been yours to reject?

It was easy for Neel to celebrate their riddance from his own life; he'd grown up stultified by societal pressures, not only in school but at home. His parents, first-generation Scottish-Americans who'd owned a dry goods store, died decades before I was born, and about them I knew little. Except this: Neel had grown up addressing his father as sir. And this: on Sundays they always had a formal meal in the middle of the day, always with roast beef and turnips, which Neel to this day detested. And this: when Neel was a boy, his mother used to make him kneel on a cool oven rack as penance for misbehaving. June is the one who told me this last, and I remember staring at my father the next time I saw him, caught between pity and fascination, until he snapped, "What's so interesting? Did I forget to put in my teeth this morning?"

After Neel died Fred spent less time than ever under the Office roof. I knew June was lonely; I knew she worried about Fred, but any guilt I felt about the infrequency of my own visits I managed by not thinking about it, a feat that required I minimize my visits even more severely. Although I could easily have spent more time with her (it was only an hour and fifteen minutes from Grand Central to Freyburg), I made excuses as to why I couldn't get away: I was busy at work, my marriage needed attention, we had concert tickets, we had house-guests, we had the flu—anything to beg off going to see her more than once every three or four months.

When I did go, almost always alone (I was loath to remind Dennis of my strange and increasingly deficient-seeming origins), a knot would gather in my stomach as the train advanced north, a sense of duty and longing and apprehension all clenching there confusedly. Fred would pick me up at the station, invariably five or ten minutes after my train came in, taking the turn slowly and parallel parking in the tiny passenger pick-up area with geometrical exactitude, even though there were rarely any other cars and he might as well have parked head-on. After getting his license late, at age nineteen, Fred turned out to be a good driver, earnest and careful, but not a relaxed one; in fact, his prowess in maneuvering a car seemed a direct result of how unnatural he found the project, so as to require his complete, heightened concentration.

We never kissed or hugged hello. Swiftly and without a word, he'd come take my bags and put them in the trunk, always handling them with such gentleness that I was able to take this minor chivalry as a surrogate expression of affection. No matter how much or little time had passed since I'd last seen him, he always looked bigger than I'd remembered.

"Hey, good-looking," I liked to tease, an older sister's prerogative, when he came around and got into the driver's seat. He had June's stature, her long elegant back, and Neel's rampant curls, shiny as blackberries.

"Ah hi," he'd reply, ducking his head in a brief salutatory nod before giving all of his attention to driving. His sober response always left me feeling both frivolous and snubbed.

(But Kitty was the frivolous one, wasn't she, Fred? While I was— am still—almost as conspicuously solemn as you.)

More often, though, it was June who'd pick me up. Even during times Fred was nominally living at home, I might come to Batter Hollow and never catch sight of him. When I'd ask where he was, June would incline her head toward the window, and I got used to imagining him out there at all times. The idea of Fred seemed to exist throughout the woods, in every tree and rock, almost as though he had become one of those giants we used to pretend lived out there, spread across the whole area, large as a shadow.

On one visit June mentioned he'd been away in the woods without setting foot in the house for days. She said it mildly, as if it were normal, as if she'd trained herself to regard it as normal. "What about food?" I asked. "What about washing?"

"He'll come in by and by," she replied in the trailing voice I had grown to expect and abhor. We sat in the kitchen over tea and seaweed crackers. I'd been there maybe an hour and promised to spend the night. The rest of the afternoon stretched gray and infinite before me.

I pushed back from the table. "Think I'll take a walk."

It was autumn, not cold yet, the woods on fire with rosy orange light, the trees lit up like candles. I walked in and out of slats of sun until I came to his tree house, a platform with three sides built above the old swale. June hadn't told me which part of the woods to look in. She hadn't had to. What other site would Fred have chosen?

I hadn't thought of Midgetropolis, neither the place nor the word, in a long time. It formed on my tongue and dissolved. I recognized the swale and the shapes of things we'd given names: the Arch, the Thrones, the Tower. No one was around. I listened. The entire forest seemed to be listening to me. I climbed into the tree house—Fred had nailed pieces of wood for rungs into the trunk. I found his nest of army blankets, prickly with pine needles. I found an electric lantern, Neel's old pocketknife. I found a metal canister with a screw lid that contained a dozen plastic jelly containers, the kind they have in diners. I found the spread-winged skeleton of a bat. Its bones were not entirely stripped of carcass; leathery bits still clung in places, but not enough to hold it all together. Rather, the parts had been assembled in a corner of the platform with evident care, even—the word popped into my head and made me shudder; I didn't know why—fastidiousness.

Then my foot touched something buried under a heap of leaves, and when I brushed them aside I found the old Indian dolls that had been in June's family for generations. Their beautiful, serious faces had been erased, their clothes were in faded tatters, their beaded necklaces broken. The male doll's legs had been forced apart so that one hung limp, and most of their hair was missing; only a few straggly clumps remained.

I imagined for a moment Dennis at my side, sifting through Fred's things with me, and felt sick with relief that I'd left him in Queens. He had known Fred's strangeness as a child, had witnessed it in snatches, but I was desperate to keep him from knowing the extent of Fred's strangeness as an adult.

Buried underneath the blankets, in a metal box, I found a stash of papers. Old maps from our long-ago jaunts, disintegrating at the folds. Our entire collection of Ladybird books, and also *The Little Prince*, which I had read aloud to him years ago; and a Wildlife Sanctuary Guide, and a composition book.

I fingered the cover of this last, its mottled black-and-white design. Then opened it, my throat clogged and dry. There was Kitty's old handwriting. There were my old sketches. Stories and pictures documenting the games we'd played out here with Fred. I turned page after page, cymbals clashing in my chest. Halfway through the book, the writing mercifully ran out. Then it picked up again. Words and drawings in a different hand. Not Fred's. Someone else's. There was a date: July 5, 1998. The summer Neel died. The summer Fred had gone to the Magdalen Islands with that family, with their son. Hand-drawn maps, lists of words: carex, bulrush, spartina, Indian pipe. A sketch of a bird. A sketch of cows. Pages of tic-tac-toe. A page of hearts, drawn over and over. A page with a single heart shot through with an arrow. I sealed the books back in the metal box, buried the box back under the blankets.

At the house I did not tell June I'd found her old dolls, the knife, the canister of jelly, the box of books. I came into the warm kitchen where she was peeling apples and stood in the doorway and broke down.

She whirled around. "Ava?"

"What's the *matter* with him?" I choked.

"What is it, Ayv? What's happened?" She put down the paring knife and rubbed my back. I was doubled over, clutching myself around the middle. "Did you see your brother?" I could not speak. I shook my head. I tried to get myself under control.

"What's wrong with him?" I asked again when I could speak. My voice rasped; I could feel the fierceness of my own gaze as I looked at her, imploring.

She was quiet. "Let's sit," she said.

We sat in chairs by the stove. She was baking squash and the kitchen smelled like nutmeg. My face was wet, my lips and eyes swollen. June rubbed my back in slow circles while I regained the normal rhythm of my breath.

"He is difficult to love," June said after a while. Softly, softly she said this, as if it was a secret she had always meant to keep. A pause. Then: "That's not the same as unlovable."

That was the last time I ever cried for Fred.

Now in the diner I open my own composition book, Kitty's gift to me, and read over the few notes I compiled this morning in response to Bayard Charles's request for any helpful documentation of Fred's past. I tried to list all the different places he's traveled, the various jobs he's held along the way. But what good might this do, other than provide proof of his geographic instability? I tried to think of other doctors he might have seen, anyone who might have taken note of his apparent disability, but couldn't come up with any names other than our old neighbor.

GINNY GANN. HOMEOPATH? SEATTLE, VANCOUVER?

I cross this out. Wherever she is, whether still in practice or not, I think it doubtful she would have kept any medical records pertaining to Fred, let alone records of a sort that might help Mr. Charles defend him. But there is another, more troubling, reason I am hesitant to look her up. If it turns out she has saved records from that time, it seems likely some of them would document injury Fred inflicted on others.

My thoughts curve again toward the summer after Neel died, when Fred went with that family to the Magdalens. I have a dim recollection of meeting them at Neel's memorial service. The father remains an indistinct blur, but I have a definite image of the boy, twelvish, with pale, almost lunar hair, and of his tall, tawny mother, stiff-limbed and austere. It was my impression June never liked her, although possibly that's wrong, possibly it's borrowed from a later memory, once the trip was over, once Fred had been deposited ahead of schedule back at Batter Hollow. Amid some residue of blame, shame.

Had he been in some way responsible for the boy's injury?

He's the gentlest person I know, I have a memory of June insisting. To whom? And in response to what charge?

I try to picture Fred and the boy James Ferebee, but instead of the dark and ruddy boy they have been showing on the news, I see the milk-white boy of the Magdalens instead. I picture them deep in the forest, in motion. I picture them covering the seven miles the news reports say they traveled from the pickup truck they abandoned at the trailhead, walking along paths at first and then veering off, weaving among the trees, crunching through vast tracts of dry yellow and brown leaves, the forest like a giant's bowl of cornflakes—like we used to pretend back at Batter Hollow, Kitty and Fred and me, picking our way through the giants' breakfast in our soft sneakers on cold mornings, whispering so as not to wake the slumbering creatures, half believing we might one day really see them rise up through the earth. I picture Fred and the boy walking and weaving through the flakes of snow the papers say fell on Thursday night last, sifting through the sieve of branches, a dusting of sugar over the cereal of dead leaves. An inch of snow accumulated through the night: slow, slow confectioners' sugar coming down through the thick limbs of fir and maple and oak. I picture them walking all night long, staying in motion the way light and breezes and water keep moving, constantly, without tiring and without regard, much as the cold mountain air would have passed in and out of their lungs endlessly, steadily, ad infinitum. Until finitum.

I take a mouthful of soup. It has cooled to pastiness.

The waitress comes. "Anything else, hon?"

The unexpected sweetness of her address startles a lump into my throat. I look up at her and shake my head, unable to choke out words.

"Just the check, then," she answers for me.

I try to smile quickly before she turns away, then drop my eyes back to the composition book, where below Ginny Gann I have written:

FREYBURG PRIMARY. SEPT. 1984–DEC. 1984

The dates of Fred's brief, unwise enrollment in public school. "Unwise" being Neel's term for it from the beginning, and June's concession by the time the end of the year rolled around. Freddy made it through four months in the one-story sprawling brick building, where he'd been a large-boned, mop-haired, eight-year-old second-grader. I never saw him as miserable as during his short sojourn in public school—and I saw him there on pretty much a daily basis as long as he attended, since Kitty and I were fifth-graders at the same school, albeit housed down in the portables where the oldest students' classes were held. Freddy's own classroom, by a stroke of bad luck, was near the main entrance and catty-corner to the principal's office.

Kitty started going to public school in third grade, after a single year of "woods school," a term her parents used—not disparagingly, quite, but with a kind of detached amusement, as though they couldn't imagine what their thought process had been in deciding to let her spend her first year at Batter Hollow running wild with Freddy and me. As though the relationship they now bore with the people who had made that decision was one of fond bewilderment, a sort of *what-were-we-thinking?* mixed with *aren't-we-corkers-for-having-thought-it!*

If Neel took their change of heart, and subsequent decision to send Kitty to conventional school, as an insult, at least it might have bolstered his sense of exceptionalism. A sense I must have eroded a year later, however, by following Kitty into public school—the result of a protracted battle between me and my parents, and eventually between Neel on one side and June and me on the other, for my mother came around much more quickly. Neel's stance boiled down to: It's Our Duty to Keep Her From the Poisonous and Petty-Minded Influence of So-Called Civilized Society. June countered with: At Her Age Friends Are Becoming More Important and After All Kitty Seems Perfectly Happy There.

For a while Neel prevailed by claiming his position was the more philosophical and objective, but in the end he weakened under the dual assault of June's serene refusal to be converted and my own anything-but-serene insistence that he was ruining my life. He threw in the towel just in time for me to be registered for the start of school in September, and I'm afraid I was not very gracious in victory.

"You always say people should be allowed to do whatever they please so long as they're not hurting anyone else or themselves," I reminded him in cocky singsong. It was the eve of my first day of fourth grade.

"Ava, my girl"—he spoke with effortful jocosity—"in public school you won't be allowed to do whatever you please. You'll have a tidy little list of things you *are* allowed—forced, actually—to do, and a great long list of things you're not allowed to do or think or say or ask or—"

"But *that's* what I please, Neel. That's exactly what I please!"

"Bosh."

We were sitting out back at the picnic table, Neel on one of the benches, me kneeling up on top. Generations of Batter Hollow students had carved their initials into the warped and silvered wood, and as we talked I followed the irregular grooves with my fingernail, like the needle on our record player, as if by so doing I could make audible a record of Batter Hollow's past. The sky was still aglow, barely, with a soft periwinkle light, but across the field the woods was sunk in darkness, and fireflies were beginning to test their lanterns over by the mock orange bush. Freddy and June were inside the house, dancing to the stereo. Jazz, heavy with horns, floated out the open windows.

"Just remember," said Neel, "everything will be on a schedule. Your every action ruled not by nature but by the clock. You'll sit at a desk according to the clock, you'll be herded off to kick a ball according to the clock, you'll eat lunch according to the clock, you'll even—"

"I'll even pee and shit according to the clock, I know, I know! You've told me all this stuff!" (I did not believe he could be right about this last—Kitty had only laughed uproariously when I repeated his words to her—but even if he was, I had determined that my enthusiasm would remain undimmed.) I reached over and gave his cottony curls a consolatory pat.

Neel harrumphed into his cup, a massive lavender teacup, more like a bowl, that had been made by a former student and from which he always drank his evening Postum. Just now it served also as a kind of a face shield; I couldn't read his expression, only the corrugations of his forehead. Was he laughing? Was he upset?

Over his head, inside the house, I could see June waving her arms in a jazzy hula, her long hair swaying from side to side, and Freddy in pajamas bouncing up and down on the couch. I could not imagine

Freddy doing anything according to the clock. For a moment I stung with remorse; in the morning I would be leaving him behind.

As I was determined to do.

"Dance, Neel," I commanded, standing on the picnic table and snapping my fingers. "C'mon!" Shaking my shoulders and hips like I'd seen Jim and Katinka do at our Batter Hollow bonfires, when everybody came and toasted marshmallows and danced under the stars. Neel laughed, as I had meant him to. I hopped down and helped him to his feet and he danced with me, wagging his broad bottom like a parody of dancing; this was his only move on the dance floor, and it never failed to make Freddy and me dissolve with laughter. Only this night I found his awkwardness poignant as well as funny. It seemed unfair and even pitiable that Neel, despite believing so fervently, so faithfully, in "nature," should possess so little natural grace.

That was a mostly happy night. Or I see it so, gazing back at it now from this little diner booth. I look back once more at the few notes I have jotted down: a sparse mess of garbled shorthand. How could anyone who wasn't there hope to understand?

Who could ever tell a story complete?

Eleven

THE PARKING LOT outside Buck Wallace Community Center is packed. By the time I arrive, cars have improvised spots along both sides of the tree-lined street, and I find myself pulling over in what is really no more than a shallow ditch. As I head back down the road, the nearer I get to the white clapboard building, the more I find myself not alone but part of a convergence. Men and women and boys and girls—we are all walking slowly, singly or in pairs or in clusters, gathering more thickly as we near the high arched double doors. And although I am here of my own volition, I am struck by the discomfiting impression, as we all keep approaching from various directions, funneling toward a single point, that I am caught up by some force drawing us inexorably, nearing a destination toward which we have no choice but to proceed.

Once when Freddy and I were about nine and eleven, we had a music festival at Batter Hollow, an all-day out-of-doors event with a soundstage and colored tarps and picnic blankets crowding the meadow. It was huge. Alumni from every decade of the school's existence had come. There were bluegrass bands and Afro-pop, reggae and rock. It was hot and dusty and by late afternoon all the kids were practically drunk on lemonade and watermelon and brownies and sun. One of the last acts was a funk band, and as soon as they started to play, that was it for Freddy. He began dancing in his wild, transported way, and then pushing through the crowd until he reached the very edge of the stage. I threaded after him, apologizing to the people he'd stepped on, worried he'd try to climb right up with the musicians. Once he'd reached the edge of the stage he stopped, although he did hold onto the vibrating platform with both hands, as though he needed to feel the music inside his body.

This funk group seemed to be playing one endless song; it went on and on with no clear sense of shape, at least not to my ear, no sense of approaching a climax or circling around to a resolution. I began to lose myself in the tapestry of sound, letting it ripple over and through me, jabbing here, twisting into smoky coils there, then undulating apart. It occurred to me the musicians were making it up as they went along, and the freedom and difficulty of this amazed me. Standing so close, I could see the way they communicated with one another, laughing as though the melody had made a joke, then shaking their heads from side to side as though the music testified to some unspeakable profundity. During a long solo, the drummer craned his face skyward, eyes closed, sweat streaming, lips parted in a grimace or wince. When the music stopped, I clapped almost as enthusiastically as Freddy, whose elbows pumped and whose face had given itself over to a loopy, beatific grin.

As the musicians started putting away their instruments, someone in the audience yelled, "More!" and someone else, "Do another!" and quickly the whole crowd took up the chant, "Encore! Encore!" and began to clap rhythmically. Although I wasn't trying to match the crowd's rhythm, my own clapping got somehow conscripted into the mass beat. I tried clapping off the beat and couldn't. I found this weirdly displeasing, even debasing. It reminded me for some reason of the mechanical rides, the hippo and race car, in front of the Grand Union. I stopped clapping and wiped my hands on my pants. Around me the tidal throb continued along with the shouts of the smitten, insistent crowd. I looked over to see what Freddy was doing, and he wasn't there. Then I saw he was there, but no longer standing: he lay writhing on the ground in a kind of a fetal ball, eyes squeezed shut, hands clamped over his ears, mouth open in an inaudible squall.

I felt closer to him in that moment than ever before or since. I had the sense that I understood, implicitly and absolutely, the cause of his anguish: the loss of the band's free and boundless improvisations, replaced by the tyranny of this rhythmic clapping. It was as if in this one instant I'd been given the power to realize the crucial thing about my brother: that his odd and persistent compulsion to drum, to beat and tap and kick at things, was not pointless and arbitrary, not simply an annoying tic. He needed to disrupt order and pattern, to search out and produce irregularity, randomness. He had a horror of anything lockstep. I loved him searingly in that moment.

In a way, it is the complement of that moment in Midgetropolis when Kitty pricked my thumb and Freddy cried. Funny that my own revelation came years after Freddy's, when he was supposed to be the one deficient in empathy.

BUCK WALLACE COMMUNITY CENTER must once have been a church, with its high, intricately arched windows of leaded glass and its floor plan like a cross, but instead of pews there are metal folding chairs, and instead of an altar there's a stage with an American flag and an upright piano and a podium. Next to the podium stands an easel displaying a poster-sized likeness of James Ferebee—the same school portrait, as if no other photograph of the boy exists. On the floor beside it, a metal pitcher holds white lilies. Other, smaller bouquets in plastic and paper sheaths have been laid along the edge of the stage.

The building is not large; the downstairs is already filled. Newcomers are being directed to a balcony, and I let myself be carried along. At the top of the narrow stairway I see that it, too, is filling. I should go. Who am I to take a seat from one of the good citizens of Perdu? I turn, but my path is blocked by the people coming up behind me. Then an elderly woman in a coat the color of a daffodil slides over on the bench where she is sitting. When I hesitate, she looks up at me and nods.

I sit. The woman holds a program in her blue-veined hands, a simple photocopied sheet. I hadn't noticed these downstairs. When she feels me looking over her shoulder, she angles the paper discreetly, almost inadvertently, allowing us both to read. The hospitality of this gesture seems to reside not simply in its generosity, but also—more so—in its tact.

First the waitress's "hon" and now this. No—first the man who pulled over in the rain yesterday to help me free my tire from the ditch. No, first Mrs. Tremblay's small talk this morning, allowing me to be her ally in the grievance over moldy bread. And before that Bayard Charles with his plastic cup of water, his promise to get me on the list. And Kitty coming over with the composition book. And Dennis, my husband, my love (all at once I wish he were here, wish I'd asked him to come, wish I trusted him not to love me less if he knew Fred more!), topping off the fluids, leaving the chocolate bar on the dash.

So much kindness.

The service begins with a song I do not know, a hymn, I think it must be, played on the piano by a classmate of James Ferebee's (as the program tells us) and sung, it would seem, by everyone. From either side of me, from behind me and down below, voices rise in unison. Every last one of Neel's diatribes against conformity, against civilized society rains down upon me now. Every last one of the scores of people packed into this building seems to know the song except for me. I am revealed. I half expect to be asked to leave. I do not belong here. We do not belong, Freddy and me; not belonging was our bread and butter.

And in fact my silence does not go unnoticed. My daffodil-coated neighbor, without interrupting her singing, turns her program over. The back is printed with lyrics. She extends the paper toward me in her blue-veined hand. In embarrassment and under duress I take it and add my voice to the rest, faltering and small. But the melody proves easy to learn, and by the end of the song I find I am singing not simply out of politeness. Our voices in this vaulted place are rough-hewn and sterling, and I, who am accustomed to singing with others only as the Singalong Lady, find surprisingly exultant the way our voices flock together to hold the song's last note.

Now begin the speakers: the middle school principal, the boy's homeroom teacher, his gym teacher, his school bus driver. Each in turn mounts the stage and we hear a parable, a poem, a testament to his ball handling, a description of how he always liked to sit in the back of the bus going fast over the potholes, so he'd get bounced out of his seat. We hear how Jimmy—they are all calling him Jimmy, and he is becoming Jimmy in my mind, the pieces of a real boy converging, constructing someone solid and singular—was crazy about motorcycles and monster trucks, how he loved being allowed to drive some of the junkers around his grandpa's lot, how he'd looked forward to getting his permit in a few years and then his license and one day having wheels of his own.

The last speaker, a squarely built, older woman, has a wide face and a chin that flows pigeon-like into her neck. She has to catch her breath before introducing herself as Jimmy's first babysitter, back when he was a "little nipper." She says how Jimmy liked her to sing to him, that there was one song in particular he'd always ask for. Says how he'd sit on the floor, thumb in his mouth, take out the thumb to say, "Do Joe again," then stick it back in. She acts it out for us. She is a wonderful storyteller, this wheezy old woman, because while she talks I am seeing it, seeing just what Jimmy must have looked like, the way his fat little legs would have stuck out before him, dimpled at the knees; the way his hair would've curled long over his ears and down his pipe cleaner neck; the way his lashes would've cast fringed shadows.

Then she begins to sing the song she says was his favorite, and it's one I know, "Old Joe Clark." It's one I actually do when I'm being the Singalong Lady. A rollicking tune, the children love it. I pass out all my clappers and shakers and tambourines and they get up and dance. But this woman doesn't do it that way. She slows it down, turns it into a kind of ballad or spiritual, almost a dirge.

Ole Joe Clark he had a mule
Think her name was Sal.

Her singing voice is fine, full-timbred and with a husky warmth, yet bell-like on the high notes. It reaches effortlessly up to the balcony, curving lush and full across the rafters.

Heard he loved that dirt' ole mule
More'n any gal.

Perhaps it has to do with her vivid portrait of him as a baby—seated on the floor, gazing up, riveted by her melody—but one feels she is singing specifically and exclusively to him. One feels he must be here, unseen, listening, drinking in her voice that is for him and him alone. I get the queerest feeling that we are the ghosts, shadowy, insubstantial, congregated here only to witness the living communion that is occurring between this old woman, this newly dead child.

The song has many verses, and as she continues, never varying her tempo or the tenderness with which she delivers each note, another sound becomes intermittently audible, gradually increasing in volume and frequency: sniffles. Little moans. Here and there a sob blossoms and is suppressed. Some of the weeping emanates from people who sound as if they lack practice crying; men, their sobs have a raw, amateur quality, the more heartrending for it.

The woman comes to the final refrain:

Fare thee well Ole Joe Clark

The sweetness of the notes compounds their loneliness. They soar and fade like the burnt, spent ends of fireworks, their ashy tendrils scribbling slowly toward the ground.

The light outside has lessened. The diamantine windowpanes glitter and a rusty pink has bled into the lower rim of sky.

Soon it will be time to call the jail.

Fare thee well now I say

It comes to me why I am able to visualize Jimmy in such vivid detail: it isn't Jimmy, but Freddy I am seeing. Freddy's long lashes casting shadows; Freddy's sweet plump toddler legs; Freddy's thumb, glistening and pruney in the corner of his mouth. My own story obscuring the view. And it is Freddy I am mourning here, at Jimmy Ferebee's memorial service, Freddy in his crinkly plastic diaper with his uncut curling hair soft against my chin as he leaned back against me on the gray flowered couch to see the illustrations as I read.

I am mourning Freddy who is gone, and aching for Fred who resides at this moment a few miles from here in a long yellow building set back from the road, and both feelings, I fear, are discreditable and blameworthy here, in the Buck Wallace Community Center on the occasion of James Ferebee's memorial service.

But perhaps not. Perhaps it is through my feeling for Freddy, the boy I have known, that I am able to feel for the boy who is a stranger to me, and for all the strangers here. How many of them, my neighbors on this bench, and on all the seats above and below, knew him? I consider the daffodil-coated woman sitting on my right, her blue-veined hands now folded in her lap. Is she here because of some connection with the family, or simply because she is a member of this community? And in that way, connected.

Behind me someone sniffles. How many in this room are thinking of someone else right now? Are we not all guided in our grief by the constellation of associations sorrow brings?

Fare thee well Ole Joe Clark

The babysitter's voice sends the line once more with a kind of ascetic radiance throughout the room, until it gives way to a fragmentary pause, a controlled particle of silence, itself expanding from floorboards to rafters, filling the space with a great and ruthless nothingness. Then she brings the tune home, lays it to rest—

Haven't got time to stay.

II

DENNIS

WHEN AVA ARRIVED HOME after a week in Perdu, she looked physically reduced in a way Dennis couldn't put his finger on. Less like she'd lost weight than like she'd lost density. When he lifted her in an embrace, it was like lifting pumice.

"How are you? I missed you." He set her back down and peered into the pale oval of her face. "Hey," he said. He touched the corner of her mouth as if it were the location of a secret on-button. That was an old joke between them, and she smiled. "How was your drive?"

She considered the question, did not answer, and after a moment went on tiptoe and kissed his cheek.

"Are you hungry?" It was eight. He'd already eaten: first a hamburger and later some leftover antipasto and then some salsa and chips. With Ava away, he'd been sort of drifting from snack to snack all week; now he tried to think what real food they had in the house.

"Just tired." She bowed her head and leaned slowly forward until her face landed on his chest. He could feel her nose pressing into his sternum. A pantomime of tired: this was her little slapstick.

With one hand he lifted her hair off her neck, with the other traced the knobs of her vertebrae there. "Do you want some tea? A drink?"

She straightened. "A shower." She said this apologetically, also determinedly, and headed up the stairs.

They had talked little while she was away. Once a day or every other day, but briefly, and even then in conversations punctuated by silences. He knew she'd met with the lawyer, knew she'd managed to visit Fred twice. She said the cell reception was spotty up there, that the landline at the inn wasn't private. She said it wasn't even really an inn, more just someone's house.

"Like that B-and-B we stayed at, that time in Maine?" Dennis asked. "With the Weimaraners and those zucchini pancakes?"

No not really, she said. Not like that.

"And Fred?" Dennis asked. "How did he seem?"

This part of the conversation occurred a few hours later as they lay in bed, her head, still damp from the shower, resting on his shoulder, spreading a circle of chilliness through his undershirt. "Ayv? How was it seeing him?"

She said something tiny beneath his chin.

"What, Ayv? I didn't hear."

"Bad."

"Why bad?"

She nipped him through his shirt, and despite the gravity of the topic he smiled. It was a classic Ava reprimand: nonverbal, to the point.

"I mean bad in what way?"

But now she rotated her head so her face lay flush against him, her mouth effectively stoppered in the crevice between his chest and his arm. This gesture, too, he felt, was not without some bleak humor. Ava had little gift for verbal jousting or repartee, really for witticism of any kind—except a particular strain of deadpan physical comedy. It had taken Dennis a long time to pick up on her latent clownishness, and when he realized it for what it was, it had sent his growing affections for her through the roof.

In the beginning, when he had first begun to think of her as something other than Kitty's brown-haired, brown-limbed, woodland-creature friend, he'd liked how still, how inward and even recessive Ava could be. It suggested a kind of integrity, the absence of a need to perform. Not that he thought about it precisely in those terms.

He'd been twenty-one the summer Ava first blindingly caught his eye. About to start his senior year at Columbia, he'd been saving money by living at home; it was the longest stretch, actually, he'd ever lived at Batter Hollow. Ava, fourteen, seemed unaware of her effect on him, the fact that where once she'd blended unremarkably with the other denizens of Batter Hollow, a hodgepodge of shadows at the periphery of his family's glow, this summer she emerged for him, appearing suddenly as neither a woman nor a little girl but as something unclassifiable: simply, conspicuously *herself*. Dennis found this quality not just arresting but frankly and vexingly erotic, a response he could not—for all his considerable self-reproach in bed at night and in his morning shower and in the afternoons when he'd retreat from the day's heat, sprawling in front of the window fan in his loft bedroom in the Art Barn, fortified by a couple of FrozFruit bars and his dog-eared copy of *The Dancing Wu Li Masters*—successfully quash.

That was the summer he made the giant four-square court, though neither four nor square accurately described it. The old court, located down below the meadow on cracked blacktop, had seen plenty of action back in the days of the school. Even in more recent times, it remained popular. Dennis had played four-square down there with Kitty and Ava and Fred, as well as Noah Salinas-Buchbinder and the Gann kids, whenever he'd been home on school vacations.

Occasionally Jim and Katinka would join in, too. But the painted boundaries of the four squares had become so faded and chipped away, that if you didn't want to spend half the game arguing whether the ball had bounced out of bounds, you had to remember to bring chalk each time. The free-spirited, communal Batter Hollowans, Dennis was quick to realize after his family moved there, bore no less competitive drive than his team-spirited, clannish Clembrook classmates. If anything, he mused, taking particular note of the Gann kids, with their feral mops of coppery hair and their freckled, near-translucent skin, the way they shoved and shouted at one another during these disputes, the absence of boundaries—whether painted or figurative—might encourage even greater ferocity.

It was precisely one such quarrel, resulting in the youngest Gann getting a bloody nose (whether fault lay with her brother's elbow or her own unbridled emotionalism was to remain forever unresolved) and running up the hill toward the Classrooms, crying for her mother, that inspired Dennis to redesign the court. "Would you guys want it bigger?" he polled all interested parties. "Not bigger squares but more of them, so you wouldn't have to wait as long to get in?"

"I would," said the second-youngest Gann, who tended to put in the second-most time waiting on line to play, and with a few more nods all around, Dennis's proposal was ratified.

He devised a round court with a central circle for the king, surrounded by six numbered wedges for the other players, each working their way up toward the king's spot. With a piece of sidewalk chalk, a compass fashioned out of a length of clothesline and a broom, and Kitty and Ava enlisted as helpers, he plotted first the outer circumference, then the king's inner circle, and finally, using some rudimentary geometry and a paper plate folded in sixths ("Fractions!" shrieked Kitty and Ava with earsplitting zeal), divided the remaining doughnut shape into equal sections. The circle's diameter was nearly the full width of the blacktop. With an old can of purple house paint, and Kitty and Ava as his able sous chefs (so they dubbed themselves, pronouncing it like Dr. Seuss, a point on which Dennis did not correct them), he rendered indelible the lines they'd traced in chalk.

Now, after a hot morning's work, the three of them sprawled in the shade at the edge of the blacktop, surveying the results. Or Ava surveyed the results. Kitty surveyed her own legs, picking at dried speckles of purple paint, while Dennis surveyed, as unobtrusively as possible, Ava. She wore a pair of black gym shorts and a gray T-shirt that might have been a boy's, and the plainness of her dress only accentuated what Dennis had recently come to realize was her stealth beauty. She wore her dark hair long and loose, and it glowed in the July sun like the grooves in a vinyl LP. Her feet were bare, her toenails unpolished, her soles dirty. Her only jewelry was a sailor's rope bracelet, equally dirty, on her left wrist.

Dennis wanted to bite it. He hoped this did not make him a pervert. The trouble with fourteen, he thought defensively, was that although she was barely a teenager, she looked like the girls—women—he knew at Columbia. She seemed, since the last time he'd seen her, during his winter break (*had* he seen her then? . . . yes: he was able to dredge a memory of the girls coming in from a sledding afternoon, waddling into the Art Barn kitchen in their puffy snow pants, heating hot chocolate on the gas burner, blowing their noses boisterously, leaving milk and cocoa powder slopped all over the stove), to have shucked off some kind of chrysalis, emerging to stand as tall now, and as—what was the word?— *developed* as many of his female classmates. Perhaps feeling his gaze, Ava turned from where she sat and acknowledged him with a look of such guileless geniality that he scrambled to his feet and began balancing the broom handle on his palm.

"The first time we saw you, we thought you were in a circus," said Ava.

He had no idea what she was talking about, which he conveyed by pulling an exaggeratedly daffy face without taking his eyes off the broom.

"Literally like the first day you came. You were moving furniture and stuff into the Art Barn, you and your dad and this other guy—bald? Short?"

"Uncle Chris?" said Kitty.

Ava shrugged. "We thought you were like acrobats," she went on, and Dennis was keenly aware of her watching him, and of the fact that he'd removed his shirt earlier, in the heat. With great concentration, he transferred the broom handle to his chin. "One of you," she continued, "I think it was you!—juggled a lamp."

"Where was I?" demanded Kitty.

"You were in the tree," said Ava, and Kitty said, "What tree?" and Ava said, "Sassafras, ass," and Kitty said, "Oh my God! I *remember* that! And Freddy totally hit me in the face!" and Ava said, "And I died," and Kitty said, "Poor Bird—but it was my face!" and the two of them were in stitches and Dennis had no idea what they were talking about; they'd slid far from him into the land of girl, where they conversed at girl-speed in girlcode about girlthings.

That was pleasant, too, and probably just as well. Crickets or what-ever played their tiny string instruments, and the day smelled sweet and empty as funnel cake, and the broom bobbed against a sky that spooled out above them, blue.

"Sick! Can we use it?" One of the older Gann kids had wandered down, either Drew or Al; they looked too alike for Dennis ever to feel safe guessing.

"No," he said, letting the broom fall from his chin, pleased at how long he'd managed to balance it there, chagrined that Ava hadn't seemed to notice.

"Why not?"

"Got to dry first."

The Gann, hands on hips, circled the freshly painted court appreciatively. He was about sixteen or seventeen, Dennis figured, with a heavy ledge of a brow, a pug nose, a jutting chin and a mane of rough red locks; his appearance was almost vulgarly masculine, and evoked in Dennis an embarrassing, primal competitive urge. Though nowhere near as tall as Dennis, the Gann kid was noticeably more built, a fact that could not escape notice since he was wearing, yes, a muscle shirt. It showed off his sculpted upper body to great effect.

"Seven players?" asked the Gann. "Who goes in the middle?"

"See the crown?" Dennis pointed at the little three-pronged coronet he'd painted in the center of the king's circle.

"Sick."

Dennis couldn't help being gratified by the praise. "It should be usable in a few hours," he offered. "Say after dinner."

"You girls going to play?" asked the Gann, turning toward the corner of the blacktop where they lolled, their legs splayed indifferently before them.

Kitty shrugged. "Probably."

The Gann sucked his teeth. *"Probably?"*

"I might have to wash my hair," she said in a passable Mae West, churning her shoulders, and the girls brought their heads together, his sister's the color of ginger ale, Ava's the rich brown of a cola, and released their intoxicating bubbles of laughter. Dennis was beset by a medley of responses: a thirst and a revulsion, as well as a confounding surge of sympathy for and resentment of the Gann who'd triggered in them this maddening mood, in which they became as irresistible as they were unreachable.

The Gann, however, seemed undaunted. "What about you?" he said, prodding Ava's ankle with his own bare foot.

"Maybe," she replied, and it might have been no more than a mindless aping of Kitty, but Dennis caught in her voice a flirtatious note he'd never before heard Ava use. "If you don't kick me."

"Who's kicking?" The Gann prodded her again.

"Gross, your feet are filthy."

"'Filthy,' what are you, British?"

"Seriously, do you ever wash? Ever smell your feet?" And from where she sat, she lifted one tawny leg and toed him in the shin.

"Dude, smelled yours?" He clasped her ankle and held it, even as she tried to pull it back. They tussled a little, Ava trying to shove the Gann off balance, the Gann using her foot in order to maintain it.

"All right, all right," said Kitty after a minute, "get a room, why don't you?" and Dennis, fairly horrified at Kitty's making explicit what a moment before might have existed only in his head, had to turn away.

That was when he saw Freddy standing in the upper meadow watching them—how long had he been there?—and in the next instant come charging headlong down the slope, a darkly thudding blur, Freddy who at twelve was large and dense and unanswerable. He didn't exactly attack the Gann. It was hard to say what his intention might have been. He did not strike out with his hands, nor did he shoulder-tackle or head-butt; simply, he ran full-force into the older boy, his entire body the weapon—again, if that was even the intention. Dennis could not have said for certain that it wasn't just plain clumsiness, some kind of high spirits gone awry.

Both boys went down hard, the Gann landing with an alarming

crack on the asphalt, Freddy landing on top of him with a more cushioned-sounding oomph.

"Jesus!" yelled Kitty. She and Ava leapt to their feet. Ava grabbed Freddy's wrist and tugged him hard until he rolled off the Gann and then sat, slumped and sedentary, arms loose at his sides, neck bent so that the cotton wool of his dark hair flopped forward, obscuring his face. It was impossible to say whether he was sorry or sulking or scared or, for that matter, satisfied.

The Gann didn't get up. His eyes were closed. One arm seemed to be twisted under his body, and when Dennis crouched beside him—"I don't think you should move him," Kitty said sharply, though he had not been planning to—he saw, mixed in with the tangled red hair squashed between the boy's face and blacktop, an alarming dampness that was darker red.

"Someone go get his mother," said Dennis. Both girls fled up the hill.

Then there were still the crickets, still the fragrance of honeysuckle and mock orange woven through the July breeze, still the silken blueness of the sky. And the Gann, his pulse beating reassuringly in his neck, his breath rising and falling visibly in his chest, but the rest of him lying still and in such an awkward, incorrect manner that Dennis felt almost impolite, even prurient, watching over him. He could see a bit of ginger fluff on the Gann's upper lip and a large red pimple behind his ear.

There was Freddy, too, sitting behind him. Dennis looked over his shoulder. Ava's brother was still slumped in the same position, head bent low as if in shame.

"What were you trying to do?" said Dennis, as neutrally as possible.

No response.

"Did you think he was hurting your sister?"

No response.

"They were just horsing around, you know."

Freddy made a strange, creaking sound, and his hunched shoulders quaked.

Dennis wondered if horsing around was what Freddy had intended, too: just to join in what looked like roughhousing. He didn't know Freddy well, having caught only glimpses of him on his own school vacations, or having heard from his mother the occasional Freddy story, accompanied by soft, sorrowful clickings of her tongue, but he had known him for ages; had, in some small fashion, watched him grow up, and he could see how year by year Freddy was less a part of things, less included in the activities of the other Batter Hollow kids. How year by year Freddy was losing ground, becoming increasingly odd and unappealing—unincludable—in the eyes of the world, even this small, familiar world that knew him best, and Dennis, who had no particular interest in Freddy (no real liking for him, if he was going to be honest), felt for a moment the tragic unfairness of Freddy's lot.

Another sound rose up from Freddy then, a kind of heave.

"Look," said Dennis, "it's not entirely your fault. You couldn't have known he'd knock his head. Although, you are pretty big, you know? You're . . . a big guy. You should try to be more careful. Okay?"

With a raggedy gasp Freddy raised his head a little, just enough to peer up at Dennis through his dark fallen bangs, and his dark eyes were not wet, not worried, but shining bright with mirth. Dennis could see his long eyeteeth shining, too, both of them bared, almost rudely white and healthy. He was laughing.

Whenever Dennis thought about it afterward—and it did turn out to be one of those memories that bobbed up again and again over the years—he couldn't decide what to make of Freddy's laughter. Had it been chilling, a sign of a grievously dissociated mind? Or was it something more piteous and blameless, a sign of ignorance, innocence, of how little he was able to understand personal responsibility, or to feel for someone who'd been injured? Someone he had injured.

At the time, in confused revulsion, Dennis turned away. When he did he saw that the Gann had come to: he'd opened his eyes and was scowling. *"Fuck,"* he said, and, "Fuckin' that *hurt,*" and he pushed himself to sitting, ignoring Dennis's suggestion that he might want to lie there a little longer. And in that next small moment before Kitty and Ava and Ginny Gann and some of the other Gann kids came bounding down the hill toward the court, Dennis struggled against the sense that there *was* in fact something funny about the incident: the squat, muscle-bound Gann, trying to impress Ava with all the foot-smelling, ankle-grabbing finesse of a caveman, suddenly being flattened by the graceful blur of this huge, bumbling boy. Was that the joke, or was it even more rudimentary: simply the ancient infantile comedy of peekaboo? On-off. Here-gone. Permanence-impermanence. Ho-ho-ho.

In any case, as Ginny Gann knelt before her son—palpating with her clinician's impartiality the areas at the base of his skull and around his collarbones, looking into his eyes and asking him questions that he answered grudgingly, with robust adolescent embarrassment—Dennis was appalled to discover himself overcome with the urge to laugh. He suppressed it as best he could. It wound up sounding like a cross between a burp and a retch, and garnered suspicious looks from both Ginny Gann and Kitty, but the former quickly resumed testing her son's mental faculties, and the latter was diverted by one of the little Gann girls, who, seeing her brother alive and well, was now begging Kitty and Ava to swing her between them by the hands.

That evening after supper, most of Batter Hollow strolled down to the new seven-square court for its inaugural game. Dennis could not help but feel proud when, in addition to the kids, several of the grown-ups lined up for a position, too: Jim and Katinka, who played with rangy, cutthroat flair; Don, who compensated for the deprivations of middle age with the canny grace of a former athlete; June, who, though light on her feet, proved gaily inept at getting the ball to land within bounds; and even Marty and Pearl Salinas-Buchbinder, who so rarely left the quiet of the ivy-covered Annex, where they liked to remain ensconced among their books and papers, the chamber music they favored wafting softly out the windows. The Gann parents didn't come, but all the kids were there, including the one Fred had knocked down earlier, seeming none the worse except for a scrape, already scabbing over, at his temple. Meg Manseau, whose hips bothered her, and Neel Robbins, who was by then in his mid-seventies and the survivor of his first mild stroke, sat on folding chairs in the grass with the low sun at their backs, the midges arcing around them like pale sparks in the light. Dennis was given the honor of inhabiting the king spot first, but he didn't hold his position long, and as soon as he got out, Neel summoned him over.

"What gave you the idea?" He gestured toward the court with his huge lavender teacup, which still contained enough of his evening Postum to slosh precariously as he pointed. Though it was a warm evening, Neel wore a cardigan and had a light shawl draped across his knees. His hair, backlit by the setting sun, looked as gossamer as the midges.

"Well, it was partly wanting to see if there was a way to get more people playing at once." Dennis stooped a little to converse; Neel wore hearing aids now.

"Yes?"

"Yeah, with so many kids, the little ones especially get out quickly and then they have to wait in line. Also I'd been wanting to try out this idea from a class I took, the Art of Structural Design."

"Remind me, you're at . . . ?"

"Columbia." Dennis always had the urge to say sir when he spoke to Neel. A vestige, perhaps, of his prep school days; at Clembrook the boys had addressed the headmaster as sir. Neel, for all his strident refutation of such formalities, nevertheless seemed to wear a mantle of authority as plain as the plaid shawl now spread on his lap. A paradox, Dennis thought when he was feeling fond of Neel. Hypocrisy, he thought when he was not.

"Majoring in . . . ?"

"Civil engineering. In this class we talked about the ethics of design."

"Ah," crowed Neel. He raised his Postum in tribute, whether to the seven-square court or to the ethics of design, Dennis wasn't sure. "Chip off the old block," he announced, enigmatically (did he mean Dennis reminded him of Don and Meg, or could he in some addled, grandiose way be referring to himself, to the legacy of Batter Hollow, even though Dennis had never been a student there?), but Meg just laughed appreciatively and smiled up at her son. "We like him."

Dennis allowed himself to straighten now to his full, comfortable height and, surveying all the people playing or waiting for a turn on the court he'd made, feeling the sun baking on his back and the welcome chill of evening beginning to rise up from inside the earth, could not help basking in a sense of well-being. He had to admit, it felt good being praised by Neel Robbins. Whatever his feelings about the man, he was, after all, the paterfamilias of a vast community consisting not only of the people gathered here this evening, but all the legions of Batter Hollow alum who'd gone on to make names for themselves.

Not to mention he was the pater of Ava Robbins. Ava Robbins, admittedly too young for him, but ah! Long-armed and leggy, smooth and summer-brown of face, she was so alluringly, inscrutably serious: just look at her standing there now in line, one hand clasping the other elbow behind her back, feet planted wide, attuned to the game, attuned vigilantly, it seemed, to Fred, who'd made it to the number three square and was following the ball with a kind of jangling focus. Slack-jawed, he barked out one of his peculiar laughs from time to time, but on the whole was keeping it together and doing well in the game. Ava regarded Fred with such concentration she appeared oblivious to all else, insensible to anything not-Fred. When the ball next came to his square and he overshot, so that it cannoned clear beyond the asphalt court and bounced into the tall, prickly grasses down the meadow, her face crimped in a disappointment so reflexive it was as if she were actually wired to something: her brother, the ball, the disgusted groan of the Gann who went off to retrieve it.

Had Dennis ever watched anything with such concentration as Ava watched her brother? Even as he studied her, he could not help but be conscious of other things: the sweet July breeze on his arms; the pride that attached to him through the game being played on his court; his mother and Neel in their folding chairs beside him; the possibility that he might be observed, considered, by others. Although not by Ava. She was lost to herself. As if to confirm what he was thinking, a damselfly landed then on her head. Dennis watched as it folded and respread its wings, the needle of its body jewel-bright against her brown curtain of hair, and flew off again, unmarked.

It struck him that this quality of deep, obviating focus was something the siblings had in common, a kind of ingenuousness so pure it bordered on indecent.

THANKSGIVING FELL just days after Ava came back from Perdu. The Manseaus were hosting at their Jane Street apartment in the Village. Dennis and Ava had signed on to bring pureed peas, roasted root vegetables and apple cake. Dennis was clad in clean black jeans and a heathery green sweater Ava had picked out, Ava in a long brown A-line dress with blanket stitching and the amethyst drop earrings Dennis had given her on their seventh anniversary, purchased from the little cigar-scented antique shop in town. When they assembled in their front hall, loaded with CorningWare and a foil-covered roasting dish and the cake plate draped with a tea towel, Dennis caught sight of them both in the small mirror that hung next to the door and felt a heaviness in his chest. She had taken such care to adorn herself festively for the occasion, yet she looked so lost. He bent and kissed the top of Ava's head. "You're gorgeous."

She gave him a seven-watt smile.

"Tell me about you," he said in the car.

"I'm thinking about Fred."

"I know that. Tell me about Ava."

"Ava's thinking about Fred."

Miles passed.

"Do you feel like telling *what* you're thinking?" He knew that Ava had been able to visit Fred twice before she left Perdu. The first time, by her account, Fred had been essentially uncommunicative. The second time he had been worse.

She began a movement now that was like washing her hands in slow motion, her trademark and oddly sensual gesture of distress. "I'm scared for him. I'm scared for him right now in prison, and I'm scared for whatever's going to happen to him for the rest of his life. I'm scared thinking about whatever happened. And I'm angry, and that scares me, too."

"Why?"

"I'm not supposed to be angry at him."

"Why not?"

But she didn't explain. After a few more miles she said, "I keep trying to picture it, all different versions of what might have happened. He didn't tell me anything. He sat there in these clothes that weren't his, the terrible prison-green shirt and pants—why do they do that?"

"What?"

"Make them wear those clothes. Is it to punish them psychologically? It is a kind of punishment. I never thought of it before, until seeing him. It's a terrible thing, making them all wear the same clothes. Neel would have hated it!" She gave a rough little laugh. "Why can't they just let them wear their own clothes? I can understand no belts and zippers and things, but why not let them wear their own T-shirts and sweatpants?"

Dennis considered. "There might be security rea—"

"And he was *bouncing*—you know that thing he does when he's nervous, how he bounces his legs? He was bouncing everything, his legs, his back, his head—I was dizzy watching him. He didn't tell me anything ... and I don't know if *he* knows. I don't know if he even *knows* what happened. Oh, Dennis!"—a kind of horror seemed to loft this last utterance, his name, make it skitter wildly up an unstable ladder so that he felt an impulse to throw out a hand to catch it, catch her—"I don't know how his mind works!"

Dennis thought of pulling the car over, putting his arms around her, taking her face in his hands. He glanced sideways. Ava looked like a closed-up shop. Her knees were drawn in to her body, her feet up on the seat so she could wrap her arms around her legs. It was a child's pose. She looked straight ahead. Out the window the trees, lean and burnished, flew by.

"How can I help?" asked Dennis. "What can I do?"

"Nothing." Her voice thin and absolute. Then, with more warmth, "You're already doing it."

"What am I doing?"

"Loving me."

"That isn't anything," he said.

"It is," she corrected him. "It's everything."

DENNIS'S PARENTS' APARTMENT comprised two rooms: a small one in which they slept and a very big one in which they did most everything else. The sole apartment on the top floor of a five-story walk-up, it had a skylight, hardwood floors and one long cork-covered wall on which hung dozens of paintings as well as a lush vertical herb garden. By the time Dennis and Ava got there the other guests had already arrived. Kitty and Tariq had brought fourteen-month-old Dilly, who was walking around like a broken wind-up toy, with a steadiness of purpose and immoderacy of speed that were out of kilter with her sense of balance: every few seconds she seemed about to go over, but remarkably did not fall. Don's brother, Uncle Chris, was there, too, with his husband, Richard, and their eight-year-old daughter, Li-Hua. The other guest was Gerta Hauptmann, an octogenarian friend of the family who had worked as a photojournalist in the days when few women worked outside the house. She looked like an elegant puppet, with her hair like a skein of yarn and her little bent figure that seemed to be made of chicken wire, and she favored such long necklaces, featuring such heavy clay beads, that whenever she pivoted unexpectedly Dennis felt the urge to duck.

"Ava," said Meg in her soft taffy voice. This was after the initial greetings, the shedding of their outer garments, the setting down of their dishes with all the other potluck offerings already crowding the butcher-block island. "We were sorry to hear about Fred's troubles." She looked her daughter-in-law in the eye a moment before folding her in a second, prolonged embrace.

"Who knows?" Ava glanced down toward the sitting area where the rest of the company had gravitated.

"Just us, honey. Don and me. And of course Tariq."

Don was even more discreet, saying nothing to indicate he'd heard about Fred, just smiling at Ava, crinkly-eyed, with extra frequency and warmth, reaching out to squeeze her hand or shoulder from time to time, and refilling her glass even more attentively than was his wont. Tariq, handsome in his trim, hygienic way, offered her only his usual impeccable manners. Kitty betrayed her concern by planting herself loyally in Ava's vicinity and noting whenever Ava fell out of interaction for what struck her as too long, at which point she'd try to baste Ava back into the fold by sharing some anecdote about Dilly or, whenever she felt more drastic measures were called for, by plunking the child bodily in Ava's lap.

All their solicitude came as a relief to Dennis, who realized only now how much effort he'd expended these past few days, hovering in his wife's vicinity, trying to gauge and maintain the ideal balance between attentiveness and distance. For Ava never wanted comforting in the way his other girlfriends had. She reacted to the smallest expressions of his love with gratitude and sometimes tremulous awe, and anytime he offered more than she deemed sufficient, she would retreat, as if it overwhelmed her system. Dennis had taught himself to respect her need for distance, as he had done, for example, last week, in acknowledging her wish to map her own route to Perdu in an old-fashioned way, on a paper map. He understood that this self-containment was part and parcel of what he loved about her. But in times of duress, especially when all he wanted to do was step in and fix whatever ailed her, he found it difficult to remain both attentive and actionless.

Now in his parents' apartment, while others tended to Ava's silent distress, he let himself go off duty. He talked English football with Richard and Tariq (the former rooted seriously for Manchester United; the latter was a rabid Liverpool fan). He kidded around with Li-Hua (having recently discovered sarcasm, she deployed it hilariously, with a novice's enthusiasm and lack of nuance). He competed with his uncle Chris to see who could catch a cashew in his mouth thrown from the greatest distance. And when Dilly tugged on his pant leg, requesting an "'orsey ride," he let out a whinny and sank to all fours. ("'Orsey? What are you, raising her Cockney?" Dennis asked Tariq. "Is this a 'Go Liverpool' thing?")

Dilly was cutting a new tooth, drooling "like Niagara," as Don phrased it several times, and experimenting with biting down on an array of textures as she toddled around the room or was passed from lap to lap. She bit so hard on one of Gerta Hauptmann's clay beads that she broke it right off the string. "My word!" exclaimed the elderly lady, examining the shards in her palm, and then to Kitty, with well-mustered appreciation, "She has wonderfully strong jaws." To which Kitty responded with a scream: Dilly, thrilling to the attention, had tried out a similar trick on her mother's finger.

"No, Dillon," said Kitty gravely, and holding out her hurt finger to Tariq: "Look at the toothmarks! *Bad* Dilly. *Not* funny," she added, but the little girl only widened her bulldog grin.

"She's your daughter," said Don, lifting her delightedly.

"What's that supposed to mean?" demanded Kitty. "I wasn't a biter."

Meg cut in peaceably. "Maybe it's a sign that it's time to eat."

At the table—really three tables of slightly incompatible height and width pushed together and covered with a series of cloths—Dennis sat between Kitty and Richard and across from Ava, whose wineglass Don continued most attentively to replenish. Ava, he noticed, seemed to take each pour as a cue to drink, which she did with the air of an automaton. Somewhat guiltily, aware of how willingly he'd neglected her during the pre-dinner hour, Dennis began trying to calculate how much she'd had. "Don't forget your water, Ayv," he said, leaning across the table and sliding it toward her, a cue she responded to with equally mechanical obedience, picking up her tumbler and taking a sip.

There was no turkey, Don and Meg having been vegetarians for decades, but the table groaned under untraditional bounty. There were, in addition to Dennis and Ava's vegetables: a butternut-squash-and-zucchini galette, stuffed cabbage, two kinds of cornbread (Meg's, which was closer to a corn pudding, and Richard's jalapeño-and-cheddar contribution), green salad with pear and manchego, cranberry-orange chutney, potato latkes, and cold sesame noodles. For dessert there was the apple cake, chocolate-frosted pumpkin bars, and an old-fashioned icebox cake—a solo effort by Li-Hua, who, stripped from the moment of all sarcasm by her own blushing pride, recited from memory, at her dads' urging, the recipe: squirt whipped cream on chocolate wafers, stick them together in the shape of two logs, refrigerate overnight.

"I made those back in the days when we really had iceboxes," declared Gerta Hauptmann, and Dennis studied her wizened face across the table and did some math, trying to work out whether she was making a joke. She was so small that Meg had had to place a foam pillow on the chair for her, and now Dennis imagined her feet dangling above the floor. "I met your father, you know," she said then, turning abruptly to Ava on her left.

Ava, who hadn't said a word during the meal except to murmur thanks whenever Don filled her glass, frowned. The shell curve of her ear reddened. "My father is dead."

"Oh no," said Gerta. She gave Ava's arm a tiny, spirited punch as if to say *What a card*. "Back when he first opened his school, this was, a million years ago, and everyone wanted an article about it. That's when I was working for *Life*. Got sent up with a reporter. We took the train. Spent the day. I never wanted to leave."

"I didn't know that, Gerta," said Don.

"This was before your time—long before you were a student there." Gerta nodded at him and her heavy clay earrings swung precariously from earlobes that looked thin as paper.

"You wrote an article about my father?"

"Just shot it, dear. I took the snaps. But he had the right idea, I thought. Your father. Beautiful man. He reminded me of Oberon. The fairy king. Beautiful school, all that wilderness, the woods, the freedom, the children going in and out of doors as they pleased. None of them wore shoes, as I recall. They looked like fairies, too, little rascal fairies. Cobweb, Peaseblossom, Mustardseed . . . what's the other one named?"

Conversation around the rest of the table had ceased, and Gerta Hauptmann had taken on a new vivacity, the glow of her memory seeming to illuminate her bony features.

"Moth," supplied Tariq.

Gerta turned to him. "But the reporter felt otherwise," she recalled, frowning. "What was his name?" She appeared to consult Tariq. "He had terrible hands, I remember, quite hairless. And pink. Smug little hands. That was when all men wore hats . . . but I digress. Anyway, I was only the photographer. In the end, the words tell the story."

"What did he say?" asked Don.

"The reporter? He wrote a snide—oh, a sneering piece, full of moral stuffing and . . . what is the word? Certitude." She addressed Ava. "He said your father would follow his pupils into the woods, where they'd set up play areas, camps and forts and things, and observe them. Never interfere, not even when they got into fights. He said—this was the damnable line—he said your father was more primatologist than educator.

"Of course, it didn't do a bit of harm among those who really appreciated what the school was doing. My pictures didn't do any harm either," she added, demurely boastful. "Enrollment went up." Gerta's small fist thumped the table triumphantly. Cups rattled in their saucers.

And over the crumbs and cold, pooled coffee, a kind of fermata settled.

"Excuse me," said Ava. She rose and took two steps toward the narrow hallway that led to the bathroom, but teetered so alarmingly that Richard pushed back his chair and rushed to steady her. When she turned to thank him, Dennis saw that her eyelids were at half-mast, and her speech sounded occluded, as if she were balancing a plum pit on the middle of her tongue. So he rose, too, and saw her to the bathroom—that she did not object to his help was further confirmation of how past her limit she was—and from there proceeded with her to his parents' bedroom, where he settled her onto their bed, covered her with a woven throw, and lowered the window shade. On his way to the door, he heard her say, "Den," in a crumpled voice. He went back and knelt beside the bed.

Her eyes were closed, her mouth pinched. "I'm wretched."

Ambiguous little pronouncement: Verdict or complaint? Dennis stroked her forehead, hoping to make the vertical line between her eyebrows disappear.

"I don't want to lose you," she murmured.

"There's no chance of that."

"No, I didn't—I didn't want to lose you."

"What do you mean, Ayv?"

In a cracked whisper: "I didn't want Fred to move in with us when my mother died." From behind closed lids, tears. "I wanted to keep . . . I wanted us to be—"

Dennis passed his finger over her brow, willing it smooth. "Shh," he said, even though her words had run dry. What else could he say? "Sh."

In time her breathing eased into the rhythms of somnolence. He watched her tenderly but with curiosity, too. He had a thought about Ava, one that had occurred to him in the past but which he would never share with her: it was that sometimes she seemed to have her own small impairment, a milder version of what, in her brother, was more plainly, more problematically manifest. Yet would Dennis have ever formed such a thought if it weren't for Fred? Surely all husbands found their wives unfathomable to a degree. Surely everyone was a riddle, a muddle, a bundle of more or fewer broken parts. And just as surely, Ava saw in Dennis things she found inexplicable, without being moved to question his wellness, to wonder whether he was sound or impaired.

Ava slept, the line between her brows gone at last. Dennis watched her and marveled at the ludicrous dignity of the human face in repose: stripped of sentience, pared to its composite parts, a cipher.

• • •

BACK IN THE MAIN ROOM Dennis sought out his mother. Meg was at the kitchen end of the room, working on the redistribution of leftovers. He let her know where he'd left Ava, and Meg murmured, "Poor thing. She hasn't been sleeping well?" with such apparent cluelessness that Dennis was annoyed.

"Well, that and the fact that Dad was doing his best to get her sloshed."

"Oh, Dennis, he was not."

"He was topping off her glass every three minutes."

"He was a little nervous," Meg allowed, "a little ... misguided about how best to show his concern."

Sarcastically: "Ya think?"

"She didn't have to drink it," Kitty pointed out, sidling up behind him. She pried an edge of pie crust from its dish and chewed it smackingly by his ear. The three of them stood around the butcher-block island, where Meg had stalled in her task at the preliminary stage of simply gazing back and forth between an assortment of plastic containers and the serving dishes that had been cleared from the table. Everyone else had been shooed down again to the other end of the room, where they sank willingly onto the brown sofas there, beneath the skylight and the tall, graceful windows that gave onto the backs of the neighboring apartment block: a view of narrow gray and brownstone buildings; an intricate geometry of fire escapes; thoughtfully plotted miniature gardens and crisscrossing strands of holiday lights that had already, in the smoky light of late afternoon, twinkled on.

"What's that supposed to mean?" Dennis asked.

"Just that. Dad might have been misguided as a host, but Ava might have welcomed getting blotto." Kitty plucked an olive from the dregs of the salad bowl and sucked it impassively from between her fingers. Her flaxen hair, modishly cut, sparked out all around her heart-shaped face.

"A little harsh, no? Given what she has going on right now."

"I don't mean it to be harsh. But I don't think we're doing Ava a favor by ignoring her part in it. I don't think we do anyone a favor by absolving them of their personal responsibility."

"In what way is she personally responsible for her brother being in jail?"

"I don't mean that. I mean responsible for drinking as much as she did."

Dennis thought of Ava curled in drunken slumber on his parents' bed, of her garbled self-indictment and his own disloyal musings about how much she might share in common with Fred. He looked at Kitty now blithely feeding herself remnants of Stilton, nibbling up crumbs from the cheese board. "Certainly you've always made impeccable decisions under duress. What was that particularly impressive display of fortitude a few years back? When that dog-walker/musician guy broke up with you. Those were some solid choices you made, Katherine, giving up food and living on cigarettes and Ensure—"

"Dennis! I can't believe you would bring up Enzo." She glanced toward the other end of the long room, where Tariq was changing Dilly's diaper while she chewed on a board book. "I'm not saying I haven't made bad decisions in extremis. I *am* saying they were my decisions and I take responsibility for them. Just because Dad's clueless about refilling guests' glasses doesn't mean it wasn't Ava's decision to drink too much."

Dennis opened his mouth to return the volley, but was not sorry when their mother cut in. "Children," was all she said, in the gentlest of tones; nevertheless the utterance was as effective as it was concise.

It resulted in Kitty's and Dennis's exchanging the look they'd exchanged a million times: a look that did not forsake entirely their own lingering adversarial positions, but acknowledged shared amusement at their mother's mellifluous protest. More than once Dennis had wondered if this wasn't in fact the genius of Meg's mild rebukes: perhaps she knew full well that the absurd softness of her appeal brought them together in silent laughter.

Kitty fished a piece of oil-soaked arugula from the bottom of the bowl and licked it off her fingers.

"Stop eating everything," ordered Meg. "What are you, pregnant?" Kitty's hands dove into her trouser pockets. Meg turned to Dennis. "You're the engineer." She handed him the stack of plastic food containers. "Figure out what to do with these leftovers."

"Not actually an engineer," he demurred, accepting the assignment nevertheless. Dennis had dropped out of graduate school after one semester, sick at last of books and theories, impatient to get his hands on actual *things*. Score one for Neel Robbins, he'd grudgingly thought, while Don and Meg made valiant efforts to hide their fretful disappointment. Luckily, he'd had to temp only a few months before landing a job at the green-energy start-up Greensleeves.

"Kitty, you go see if anyone needs anything. Where's my grandbaby? Oh, having her bottle. Li-Hua looks like she's dying of boredom. Why don't you go ask Tariq to let her finish feeding Dilly?"

A single grin passed between the siblings. They loved this about her, too: that beneath the dulcet tones lurked an efficient brigadier general.

Afternoon progressed toward evening. The sky turned dusky, unfurled pennants of pink, then went swiftly, definitively black. The lights outside multiplied, illuminating other holiday gatherings in the apartments across the way, while above the rooftops and stretching west they plotted a pointillist picture of downtown. Gerta Hauptmann left first, ushered into a Gramercy-bound cab. Soon after, Chris and Richard and Li-Hua headed off for the F train back to Jackson Heights, and then Don and Tariq pulled wool hats on over their twin pates and went out for a walk with Dilly, who'd begun to fuss, in hopes that the motion would make her fall asleep. In the bedroom, Ava slept on. And in this way, Dennis found himself once again alone with Kitty and Meg. As if by prearrangement, the moment the umbrella stroller had been maneuvered out the door, the two siblings and their mother launched into the discussion they'd been longing to have, no antecedent necessary.

Kitty turned to Dennis. "So is he getting out?"

Dennis shook his head: Fred was being held without bail.

"But I thought that was maybe going to change. At the pretrial hearing? Or detention hearing, whatever?"

It hadn't, though.

"Why not?" Kitty demanded. She was reclining on one of the brown sofas—they all were now: shoes off, feet up on the cushions, throw pillows tucked under various parts of their anatomies—so that the vigor of her indignation seemed at odds with the languor of her pose. "Is he a danger to the public?"

"It's because he doesn't have a permanent address, I think," ventured Meg. She and Kitty lay at opposite ends of the same sofa, and Meg stroked her daughter's stockinged foot. "It makes him a flight risk."

"Also no ties to the community," confirmed Dennis.

"Oh. That's how *law* works?" Kitty drawled the noun, leveling accusatory looks at Dennis and then Meg, as if they might be the very legislators responsible for these rules. "So, what—you can't get bail if you're homeless?"

Dennis explained what Ava had told him the lawyer told her: "It's not cut-and-dried. It can depend on the nature of the crime, the way it's playing out in the media, the feelings in the community, the whim of the judge. Apparently in Criterion, it's not even a judge-judge. It's a lay magistrate. They don't have to have any legal training. The guy in Perdu, the magistrate there, he's a local businessman."

"What kind of businessman?" Meg asked.

Kitty snorted. "Does it matter?"

"Ava said he owns a hardware store."

"Jeez. Well, what about the lawyer?" asked Kitty with new animation. "Is he any good? Do the *lawyers* in Podunk have to have legal training?"

"Careful," said Meg, tweaking her big toe.

"What?"

"You're sounding like a snob."

"I'm seriously asking!"

Dennis, from the adjacent sofa, considered his little sister. He was accustomed to people referring to her, almost matter-of-factly, as a beauty. Even Neel used to call her Bonny Kitty. Much of her charm resided in her energy: the liveliness of her chin, with its defiant whisper of a cleft; her high, smooth forehead pleating in consternation; her bright chicory eyes flashing at you expectantly; even her nose was lively, now wrinkling, now flaring. But he saw it as too much performance, for he'd seen it too often performed. And he could not shake the conviction that she was enjoying being outraged at least as much as she was genuinely experiencing outrage; that her sense of injustice and her indignation on Fred's behalf thrilled her.

Meg gave Kitty's foot a reproachful little slap, but added, "Denny, love, how *is* the lawyer?"

He told them what little he knew: that Ava hadn't much liked Bayard

Charles at first, that she worried he seemed quick to enter a plea, but then he'd gotten her name on the visitor list so she could see Fred, and now she thought he was becoming more invested in the case as he learned more about Fred, his background, the way he was, his peculiarities.

Dennis used that word, there in the living room on Jane Street: *peculiarities.*

No one said anything for a moment.

Then Kitty propped herself up against her end of the sofa and looked pointedly at Meg. "Mom? I know we're not supposed to talk about it, but what *are* his 'peculiarities'?"

Meg gave a slow, considered nod. Yet all she said was, "I don't know."

"But you know what we mean."

"I do." She squinted, as if into the vaults of memory. "But Neel and June never wanted to talk about it. I mean they didn't want to give any sort of name to his . . . his condition. They wouldn't have liked even that word. And it was . . . a politeness, or really a form of respect—"

"What, not to mention it?"

"I was going to say, to try to see it the way they did: not as a 'condition' you could separate out and—I don't know, analyze, treat—but as part of the wholeness of the boy. Of Fred."

Kitty turned to Dennis. "Do you know?"

"Know what?"

"Does Ava ever talk about it?" put in Meg.

He hesitated, seeing the territory before him suddenly strewn with mines. He and Ava had made a practice, all these years, of eliding the subject of Fred. For Dennis it was simply a matter of following suit, deferring to his wife's implicit wishes. He'd perceived how she worked to minimize his interactions with Fred, the way she'd encourage him to stay in the city whenever she traveled to Freyburg, or ask him to accompany her only when she knew Fred was away. Initially these efforts had struck him as odd. After all, Dennis had known Fred growing up; what was there to hide? (Although the fact of their families having known each other so long might explain why they never discussed his condition, parsed his Fredliness; it obviated the need. This might even, it had occurred to Dennis on occasion, be one of the reasons Ava had married him.) Later on he found her behavior insulting: Did she think Dennis insensitive, intolerant? Did she think so little of his love for her that she imagined he'd be easily put off? But eventually, as Dennis became more intimately acquainted with Ava's own flickering strangenesses—the tiny foibles and quirks that set her apart from the world, that seemed to provide her with some necessary shade, as if she were a rare, delicate mushroom—he came to understand. Or to believe he understood.

It was not Fred himself that Ava wanted to keep hidden. It was that part of her she feared bore too strong a resemblance to him, that indistinct part that his presence might amplify, lend clarity and prominence.

Dennis recalled the confession she'd made earlier, lying on his parents' bed. *I didn't want Fred to move in with us when my mother died.* Well, neither had he. So it had all been pretty convenient. Only now, two years later, did he wonder: How much of her disinclination stemmed from fear, fear of what might happen to their marriage, fear of whatever conclusions Dennis might form if not shielded from the daily reality of Fred? He shifted uncomfortably on the brown sofa, perpendicular to where his mother and sister lay cozily entwined. Did he bear some of that burden of guilt? Had he too readily accepted the solution of Fred's going to work on the Cape? By the time he'd learned of this plan, it had all been arranged, apparently by June herself. But were he and Ava supposed to have countered with an offer of their own?

No one—not June, not Ava, not Dennis—had mentioned the obvious: that Fred was good with his hands and the routines of manual labor. That Dennis was just starting his own home insulation business. That if Dave Alsop was willing to put Fred on his housepainting crew, Dennis might as easily offer to put him on some jobs closer to home.

"Hello?" prompted Kitty. "What does Ava say?"

"Nothing."

"Do you have a thought?" Meg went back to stroking Kitty's foot. "Dr. Manseau?"

"Not actually a doctor." Kitty's degree was a master's in psychology.

"But you must have covered some of this in school. What might a diagnosis be? If you had to hazard a guess."

Diagnosis. That word even more of a betrayal than "condition." And yet—Dennis glanced toward the hallway that led to the bedroom—mightn't it also be a help, their speaking in these terms? Ava had said the lawyer asked some of these same questions.

Kitty turned up her palms. "I used to think he must be a little retarded," she confessed. "I mean"—her cheeks pinked—"when we were kids. Now I'd say cognitively impaired. But I'm not sure. Even back then, it was like . . . he always seemed so out of it, and then he'd go and surprise you. As if he hadn't missed a trick, as if he'd been understanding everything all along, picking up on even more than a typical kid."

"A savant?" mused Meg.

"You're free-associating, Mom. Do you even know what that means? I don't remember anything that would count as signs of savant syndrome, so much as . . . sometimes he'd just surprise you with how aware he was. As if he knew more than he let on." She seemed to be remembering something. Dennis wondered what. For his part he saw again, in a frieze as sharp as it was unbidden, Fred at twelve kneeling in his hapless way—large and heavy and soft—on the freshly painted seven-square court, his head bowed, his face obscured by that dark froth of bangs, and then peering unexpectedly up at Dennis, his eyes dark and glittering and full of laughter.

"Is it some kind of autism?" Meg wondered. "Aren't some autistic people extremely smart?"

"Asperger's," suggested Dennis.

"Or another form of high-functioning autism," said Kitty a bit officiously. "I don't know, in school, when we were learning this stuff, I mean I do remember thinking about Fred, actually, how he seemed to fit a lot of the symptoms. Maybe he's on the spectrum. There's also"—she snorted—"pidnose. PDDNOS. 'Pervasive development disorder not otherwise specified.' As you can see, it's a really well-understood area." She let her head clunk back theatrically on the armrest.

"The question is," said Meg, "could any of this help him now?"

"I don't see how," said Kitty, "if he's never been diagnosed. I hate to say it, but don't you blame his parents?"

"You have to understand," said Meg in her languid way, neither defending nor condemning, "Neel and June had beliefs about all that—about so-called experts, and labeling, and the medicalization of personhood."

Kitty snorted again.

"No," Meg reproved her softly. "They weren't superficial beliefs. They'd come to them with a lot of thought."

"But you and Daddy left Batter Hollow. I thought you decided it was dumb."

"It didn't ultimately feel right for us," Meg agreed. "But who's to say it was wrong for them?"

"I'll say it. It was gross negligence. Like Gerta Hauptmann's reporter-guy said." Kitty, becoming more exercised, sat up now. "I remember that year you let me stay out of school and go running around with Ava and Freddy all day long. Fine, none of us got hurt, but we could have."

"Remember, though," objected Dennis, "you're looking at it through the filter of a helicopter mom."

"I'm not a helicopter mom."

"Excuse me, you're the mother of a young child in the twenty-first century living in Park Slope, which happens to be the epicenter of helicopter parenting. You can't help but be influenced by today's norms."

Kitty ran her fingers through her short hair. "Okay, fine. But that's not even my point. It's not just that we were left to do our own thing. Although yes, sue me: I do believe children need care and supervision. But on top of that. It wasn't just that they wanted us to have freedom. Neel had this way of observing us."

"Pick an argument," snapped Dennis. "Did you want to be supervised or not?"

"I mean this *way* of observing us. Like a primatologist."

"And you a bonobo."

He expected her to stick out her tongue at this but she was earnest now, ruminative. "I mean it's one thing to be an educator and observe students. But to regard your own children with, with ..." Her hands groped the air as she searched for the term. "... *professional remove.* Isn't that unforgivable?"

"What are you guys talking about?"

They all started.

Ava emerged from the darkness of the hallway and stood shyly just inside the large, lighted room. Clutching the plaid throw around her shoulders, she shambled forward a few steps, sleep-disoriented and blinking.

Meg righted herself on the sofa. Dennis and Kitty stood with awkward simultaneity, as if caught engaging in illicit behavior.

"How long have I been asleep?" Ava stopped partway into the room and squinted uncertainly at them. "What's unforgivable?" she asked.

III

KITTY

THEY SET OUT for a walk together on the morning of the shortest day of the year, Kitty and Ava with Dilly in the backpack. Kitty and the baby had come up the day before in order to attend one of Ava's Singalong Lady sessions at the Freyburg Library, an experience that proved electrifying for Dilly. Unable to remain in Kitty's lap, she'd meandered around the circle of parents and children all seated on the rug, shaking the maraca she'd been given from Ava's duffel, and dancing, along with a few of the other toddlers, in the primal way of their kind: they were fat-bottomed vaudevillians in their diapers, yet somehow lithe as sea creatures. She eventually planted herself directly behind Ava, who sat cross-legged strumming her guitar. There Dilly became transfixed, letting one plump starfish hand drift and settle on Ava's shoulder.

Kitty and Dilly had spent the night in the Annex's guest room (which Kitty could not help thinking of as Noah Salinas-Buchbinder's old room), where they'd eschewed the portable crib and deliciously shared the bed, then risen to see that during the night the world had been dusted with white. "Snow!" Kitty cried, holding Dilly up to the window. "Snnooow," her daughter echoed reverently. After breakfast the three ladies bundled up and set out the back door. The meadow, as they crossed it, was fully bathed in golden sun; it steamed damply, the snow already melting, but when they came to the mouth of the old woods path, they could see pennants of white extending in the long shadows beyond each tree.

Ava had made one trip back up to Perdu since Thanksgiving. Kitty was able to glean information a question at a time. Ava had stayed at the funny little guesthouse again. ("I thought you hated it?" Kitty said; Ava responded simply, "It's not that bad.") Yes, she'd seen Fred again—twice. No, he hadn't told Ava anything about what happened. He looked thin, thinner even than in November. As with the first visits, he'd sat hunched in his prison greens, bouncing his body, looking at his feet, mumbling only a few fragments of speech and then only snatches of nursery rhyme—*Here is the church, here is the steeple*—and something else, a sentence he repeated several times, which Ava hadn't been able to place at first: *Where I live everything is so small.* Only with Fred it came out: *Ah-where I live-ah everything is so ah-small.* Only later, during the eight-hour car ride home, by turning it round and round in her own mouth, did it dawn on her: a line from *The Little Prince.*

"I remembered it," she said, "from reading aloud to him when we were small."

They walked in silence along the snowy path. It was colder the deeper into the woods they went.

"And what comes next?" Kitty probed gently.

Ava stopped, confused. "In the book?"

"No, I mean—will his case go to trial?"

Ava released a humongous breath. It hung white and shapeless in the air. Dilly made a gleeful sound, then mimicked the huff, tickling Kitty's ear. "Unclear," said Ava. "The lawyer's getting his own medical expert to examine the results of the autopsy. Supposedly it'll help him decide whether to advise entering a plea."

"So that's good, right? I mean he's being aggressive, proactive?"

Ava nodded. "Yes, I'm liking him more. Apparently most assigned counsels would never even suggest something like that, bringing in an expert, because of the expense. Dennis and I said we'd pay."

Lo-Impact Solutions was still a young, one-guy operation, and Ava could hardly pull in much as the Singalong Lady. Kitty said, "Tariq and I would really like—"

"Thanks." Then perhaps in apology for cutting her off, Ava leant close to Kitty and kissed her. A rare occurrence. Kitty was moved.

"Me," said Dilly. Kitty could feel the weight of the backpack shift as her daughter craned forward, and Ava, laughing, went on tiptoe to kiss the baby. Dilly was at the stage where she liked to offer the wettest, innermost part of her pucker, and Ava—poor physical-contact-averse Ava!—came away duly slimed. Kitty caught her eye as she did her best to inconspicuously wipe off the saliva, and in the next instant both women were helpless with laughter.

"Ha!" chimed Dilly, stiff with delight. Kitty felt the entire backpack spring to attention. "Ha! Ha! Ha! Ha!"

Each puff of mirth perforated the air. Kitty could tell, by the distribution of weight and the pause between Ha!s, that her daughter had flung back her head and was watching her cottony breaths vanish one by one. Dilly's vigor delighted and humbled and sometimes frightened her. She could not imagine letting this girl run free.

They walked on, down the path that curved through the woods, pointing out rabbit prints and deer scat to each other and to Dilly, stopping to watch a flock of cedar waxwings scatter, startled, from a holly bush. How clean the world was still! How clean the world was here, in Batter Hollow, only a few hours up the Hudson from Brooklyn, but somehow further distant. Kitty closed her eyes and drew in a breath, silvery, astringent. Oh, this world that continued to produce waxwings and berries, toddlers and snow! This woods with its snow-frosted carpet of leaves, its great columns of trees, its immaculate hush, broken now by the chitter of a chipmunk, the coo of a dove, the fall of a nut.

"I forget how much I love it here," she declared.

"You don't love it here."

"I do!" protested Kitty, laughing.

"But you never come," said Ava.

"Oh, Bird," sighed Kitty.

Yet it was true. Ever since her brother and sister-in-law had moved back to Batter Hollow two years ago, she'd rarely come to visit. Highly understandable, she thought, since first she'd been pregnant and then a new mother, and still seeing patients throughout all of it except for a measly three-month maternity leave. But perhaps Ava was more aware than Kitty had realized that the reason her visits were so infrequent was not strictly a matter of logistics.

"Really," Kitty had said dryly, when Dennis told her they'd bought the old Annex, the ivy-covered whitewashed brick cottage that had for so many years housed the quiet and stately Salinas-Buchbinders. "Why'd you do that?"

"We like it here." She heard in his plural pronoun fathoms of spousal loyalty she thought squandered. Or not squandered; that was too harsh. Misspent. "It suits us," he went on. "And of course it holds so much meaning for Ava."

"Of course."

If he perceived in the flatness of her echo a note of aspersion, he did not comment. Taking her cue from him, she allowed her feelings to remain unarticulated. To him. To Tariq she confessed she was furious: at Ava for her solipsism, which apparently had the black-hole-like ability to bend other bodies toward it, and at Dennis for proving himself thus bendable.

It was morbid, regressive, was it not? This she demanded of Tariq. To move back to the forsaken grounds of her father's glory days, to a place that had already, by the time she and Ava were children, been inhabited as much by echoes as by real people. And to drag Dennis away from his job with Greensleeves to a place he bore almost no connection to, a place so dilapidated now that four of the original five cottages had been razed, and the unpaved lane that led to the remaining cottage had become roughly pocked and gouged. Besides, Kitty, newly pregnant when they announced the move, could not help taking their desertion personally.

Back when her best friend and brother had first become a couple, some seven years earlier, Kitty had been publicly magnanimous and privately titillated, but in any case genuinely excited. She'd been living in Boston, interning at a residential treatment center for addicts as clinical training for her master's, and was therefore not only physically distant from the courtship but also sleep-deprived and overcaffeinated, factors that somehow combined to cast news of the romance in a rarefied, fantastical light. Ava and Dennis? Her jaw fell open. *Ava* and *Dennis?* How bizarre, how unlikely, how very nearly incestuous. And how the pairing seemed to confer a new, exalted status on them both.

That Ava could rise, in Dennis's eyes, from the drear, sexless ranks of kid-sister's-immature-friend; that Dennis could emerge, in Ava's eyes, from the uninspiring role of best-friend's-boringly-conservative-brother—these facts foretold limitless possibility, not just for them but for everyone, for the general human capacity to metamorphose. Kitty could hardly imagine the two of them finding each other attractive. When she summoned to mind their most deeply defining characteristics, she could think of nothing but Dennis's preference for the mainstream, his essential squareness; and Ava's inability to pass for mainstream, however hard she tried.

And she had tried painstakingly hard. Kitty thought of the time she'd gone out for cheerleading, their freshman year of high school. She'd known Ava wouldn't make the squad, no matter how perfectly she executed the routine or reproduced the hairdo. She'd watched her friend practice and prepare, all the while biting her tongue, for how could she say there was no point, that there hung about Ava at all times an aura of otherness? It was more than the mere fact of her provenance. Yes, kids knew she came from Batter Hollow, but they knew this about Kitty, too, and it proved no liability in her case.

How painful was it to remember the time Ava, as a junior, had fallen hard for Chris Rachette, a three-varsity senior with ruddy cheeks, ripped jeans, a Saint Christopher medal and a black Miata. The way she'd hung about his locker, gone to his games, angled for rides in his car. He must have thought she was cute, must have had a taste for the quirky, because he'd encouraged it; Kitty saw with her own eyes how this was true, how he'd stretch his arm up the wall and lean in, how he'd bestow on her his famous lopsided grin, how he'd once used his own finger to brush aside a strand of Ava's heavy dark hair. And what had Ava done? Written him a letter. Kiss of death. Long, earnest, heartpouringly honest. Not popped on impulse through his locker vent but delivered to his house through the U.S. mail. Envelope, stamp, formal, legal, the act intractably committed and radiating intent. What was Chris Rachette to do after that but start ignoring her in the halls, answer her greetings only when they were unavoidable with a vague *hey*, take Stacy Figueroa to the prom?

Kitty remembered the aftermath, too: Ava flung sideways across Kitty's bed, shaking with sobs, crying like her stomach hurt, and her face, when she lifted it from the bedclothes, blotched pink and white, a mask of agony. "Chris Rachette's a big dick," Kitty had soothed. "Really. He's just a giant penis. He's a big doody." This last elicited a soggy laugh, as she had hoped it might. "I'm serious. I'm going to get a red Sharpie and write B. D. on his forehead."

So there was this, too, the history of her pity for Ava, informing her response to the news that Ava and Dennis were dating, fanning her happiness, however skeptical, for them, and allowing her to put her reservations aside. But when they announced, only a few months into it, their intention to wed, she felt her hackles rise. "Why marry?" she quizzed Ava over the phone.

"Because we want to," Ava explained, slowly, absorbedly, as though the words' simplicity belied complicated origins. "We've talked about it, Dennis and I, about how it feels right, to us both, not to be formless, not to be casual about what we feel." She went on with the explanation at some length, in increasingly meandering and vague fashion, never coming out and saying what Kitty believed was really at stake: Ava's determination to refute her parents' choice. If Neel and June had elected not to marry legally but to live outside the social contract, then Ava would hasten to marry early and secure a spot within it. All that talk of "we" and "us both" was smoke screen, or else self-delusion; Kitty felt sure this was about Ava's desire, period.

"Why marry?" she quizzed her brother next, determined to get at least one of them to examine the decision critically, and reasonably confident that if she could engage Dennis in a conversation he'd begin to see there were other, more favorable options.

But Dennis, in what must have been an act of unintended gallantry, did Ava one better. "I want to," he said. Simply, but with such finality that even Kitty knew better than to press.

The wedding took place a few months later on a sleety afternoon in March. A bare-bones ceremony at City Hall, with sandwiches and cake at a restaurant afterward. Ava was twenty-five, Dennis thirty-two. She wore a sleeveless white sheath, daringly simple and beautifully cut, if rather too bare for the wintry weather; the whole time they were in the restaurant she never warmed up. Dennis looked euphoric in a dark suit and flowered tie. He spent some untold portion of the reception, before Kitty herself rid him of it, with some older relative's coral lipstick print on his cheek, and something about his unknowingness, his blithe ignorance of what was all too plain to others, made her, unexpectedly and with startling force, want to weep.

Neel was less than two months away from his third and fatal stroke, but of course no one knew that then, and at the reception he yet managed to hold court, still imposing in his wheelchair, his white curls still buoyant, if more sparse, and the unparalyzed side of his face alternately scowling and twinkling as various of the guests came to have an audience with him, bending or kneeling by his chair. Irony of ironies: the great iconoclast authoritative to the end. When Kitty stooped to kiss him he beamed with lopsided vitality. She could not help finding his visage a little frightening, but made herself smile back. "There she is," he declared with what seemed proprietary satisfaction. "Bonny to the end."

June was there with him of course, looking a little tired, Kitty thought. They'd also brought Fred. Kitty, who'd seen him only a handful of times since she'd gone off to college, didn't recognize him at first. At twenty-two he was rakishly, jarringly handsome in his sports jacket, jeans and high tops. Her first impression was that he'd changed, emerged, outgrown his tics and quirks. But then she saw how he ducked his head and swung it away, in almost equine fashion, from those who attempted to engage him, and how he kept close to his mother the whole afternoon, and how he appeared to vibrate compulsively on the balls of his feet. When she went to say hi, he bobbed his head quickly in her direction and then seemed to scan the air above her for someone or something he'd rather see.

Also in attendance were the extended Manseau family, a few former Batter Hollowans, and a substantial number of the bride's and groom's new friends: Dennis's colleagues from Greensleeves, Ava's from the music conservatory, various others they'd met in school or through work. The new friends, taken as a whole, were ethnically and professionally diverse, yet comprised a single aesthetic, Kitty thought. She had the odd notion they'd been chosen and assembled in order to signal a specific message, something to do with how Dennis and Ava were choosing to regard themselves, or how they themselves wanted to be regarded.

Kitty did feel some pleasure for her friend. It was the pleasure of relief. After so many years spent striving for normalcy, for acceptance by the normal, Ava seemed radiant with achievement. Still, what Kitty remembered most indelibly about the day were the goose bumps on the bride's arms.

Yet now, these seven years later, she had to admit their marriage worked. Or seemed to—for what can you ever know of a marriage from the outside? Not that it matched her ideal. Compared with hers and Tariq's, or Don's and Meg's, or even Neel's and June's, Ava's and Dennis's relationship seemed careful, modest, polite. Almost *enacted*, rather than messily lived. Like a child's notion of the institution, safe and steady. A pageant played in dress-up clothes. Yet she could not deny that the kindness between them was palpable. So, too, the love.

And today, tromping through the woods with her daughter on her back and her old friend at her side, drawing the tinseled air into her lungs, she found she could not summon her old indignation at their having moved back to the obsolete school grounds. The absence of the familiar cottages was sad, but Dennis and Ava had made a snug home of the former Annex, and the woods was clean and grand. Dilly had begun to sing, quietly, interiorly, some barely recognizable version of one of the Singalong Lady songs from yesterday, and Kitty could tell by the way the baby carrier jounced softly on her back that her daughter must also be trying to replicate the hand gestures Ava had done. The path rounded a bend and led them into a shadier part of the woods. Instantly it was chillier, bluer, the firs more closely clumped, a heavier mosaic of snow patterning the ground.

"It's great here," said Kitty, stopping to rest. Walking with Dilly was a workout. "I forget how peaceful it is."

Ava gave her an odd look.

"What?"

"Do you ever think about it? What we did out here, what we did with Fred?"

A kind of blankness came over Kitty, a blankness that was necessary if she wished to mute her irritation, for Ava was always saying odd things without warning, unreasonably expecting others to think and feel the same as her.

"Don't you know where we are?" Ava asked, and there was an expectancy in her tone that irritated Kitty further.

"Er . . . nature?"

Ava looked at her levelly. "You don't recognize it," she said, without humor, without bitterness. And she turned and faced the area to the left of the path.

Kitty followed her gaze. Trees, bushes, rocks, leaves. Then she spied a kind of platform thing half hidden in one of the hardwoods. A tree house, she thought. But why should she recognize a tree house? They'd never had one in childhood.

"Um, no?" Kitty shrugged, laboring to keep it light.

"This is where we had it." Ava continued to look not at her friend but at the snow-dusted patch of woods. "This was Midgetropolis."

• • •

THEY HAD PLAYED HERE nearly every day the year the Manseaus moved into the Art Barn. Once Kitty started going to Freyburg Primary, the time she had for their games back at Batter Hollow was more limited, but she and Ava and Freddy had still spent many long Saturdays and Sundays in Midgetropolis. And they kept this up even after Ava joined her in public school. Fred joined them, too—for a bit, anyway.

During the brief period when all three attended Freyburg Primary, they would set off together down Batter Hollow Lane in the early morning, kicking up loose stones when it was dry, squelching through mud when it was not, swinging their canvas schoolbags and plastic lunch boxes at their sides. The girls walked down the middle of the lane, while Freddy always went down the side, running a stick along the trunks of trees, his attention held by the arrhythmic pattern of bumps traveling from the stick up his arm. By late fall the morning sunlight would cut almost sideways through the leaf-purged branches, and their own movement past the trees created strobing light, which seemed to excite Freddy: he'd speed up his walk, break into a trot and then a run, still holding out his stick so it smacked the trunks, bumpity-bumpity-bump, working himself up into a ululating yell, a sound Kitty found unnervingly indeterminate, pitched midway between euphoria and distress.

At the bottom of Batter Hollow Lane, where they waited for the school bus, Freddy would use his stick to strike the row of mailboxes, going up and down in no particular order, sometimes slowly and sometimes practically in a frenzy. Kitty and Ava would stand several feet away, "smoking" twigs they'd snap off a juniper bush and "light" with pine needle matches, affecting world-weary, hip-jutting slouches and puffing out wisps of ersatz smoke. "Will you shut up?" Kitty would sometimes call over her shoulder, "you're giving me a headache." But both the words and jaded tone were as transparently artificial as her cigarette and stance; it was all charade, and anyway she knew Freddy wouldn't pay her any notice. For all the gaps in his mental faculties, whenever he was engrossed in something he had really singular powers of concentration. Plenty of times Kitty had tried to get his attention only to give up with a disconcerting sense of her own inadequacy.

The school bus driver would not allow Freddy to bring his stick on the bus, setting off a series of tantrums. The first day, the driver, a sinewy older man with one cauliflower ear, wound up forcefully wresting the stick from Freddy's hand and throwing it out the door. Freddy had wailed and rocked and hit his head with his fists all the way to school while Kitty, seated with Ava across the aisle, burned with embarrassment, some pity for Freddy, and anger—this last divided between the bus driver and Freddy. The second day, despite their having rehearsed a more favorable scenario with Neel and June the night before, Ava and Freddy together in tears declined to board the bus, leaving Kitty to slink on singly and ride to school by herself, burning once again with embarrassment, pity and anger—this time, more of the pity directed toward herself and the anger divided now between Freddy and Ava. The third day saw Freddy left behind alone, bellowing, jumping up and down, waving his stick and behaving generally so much like Rumpelstiltskin at the end of that tale, that as they pulled away and he got smaller and smaller through the bus's rear windows, Kitty could not choke back a hot throatful of laughter, and Ava refused to speak to her for the rest of the day.

By the second week of school, Neel and June had worked out an arrangement with Freddy. It involved his depositing his stick in a kind of quiver constructed of cardboard and attached to the mailbox post with pieces of twine. Each afternoon when the bus brought them home, the stick would be waiting there for him, so that he could return up Batter Hollow Lane repeating his tree-knocking ritual in reverse.

Kitty was nine then, nearly ten, and felt confused admiration for the vast patience Neel and June and Ava afforded Freddy. The confusion had to do with her belief that she could never muster such patience, and a measure of scorn that they did. Why put up with all Freddy's shenanigans? Why give in to his ridiculous insistences? She felt sorry for them, and this gave her an elevated feeling, the impression of being more knowing and sensible than the Robbinses, yet she derived no pleasure from this feeling of superiority.

She tried some exploratory complaining. "Why does Freddy have to ride the bus with us?" she asked her parents. "He's always kicking the seat in front of him and he makes weird sounds. Humming and stuff. Why can't Neel and June just drive him?" Don and Meg would answer, as she had known they would, "It may be good for him to be around other kids more"; "Just ignore him if it bothers you"; "Perhaps Neel and June think it'll help him adjust." It wasn't that Kitty expected them to solve the school bus problem, but she hoped for some sign that her parents, too, harbored doubts about the wisdom of the Robbinses' choices. Some sign that they, too, disapproved.

Certainly someone ought to disapprove. Someone ought to tell them how bad things were at school. Kitty and Ava were in fifth grade that year, the year Freddy, for a handful of months, attended the second grade. Kitty and Ava were up in the portables, a cluster of classrooms separated from the rest of the building by a gravel path and flight of steps. It was great being in the portables, great being the oldest kids in the school. They got to go straight from the lunchroom to recess whenever they were ready, without having to line up and be dismissed like the lower grades. And they had the best teacher, Mr. Yeltsov, who called all the kids by their last names and who played music while they did their math modules—not children's music but his own tapes that he actually listened to in the car on the way to work (he'd told them this), things like Kate Bush and the Talking Heads and The Police.

But several times a week an aide would come up to their portable and interrupt class, asking if she could "just borrow Ava Robbins a sec?" Mr. Yeltsov's jaw would jut sideways and he'd give a brusque nod, and then Ava would go off with one hand gripping the other, the bunched fingers twisting slowly to and fro. She'd return ten or twenty or forty minutes later, her face somehow narrower and paler, and she'd shake off Kitty's questions, her demonstrations of sympathy, even her most general efforts to provide good cheer. After a month or so they stopped pulling Ava out of class, but then it was worse because Ava (along with all the other fifth-graders) would still hear about whatever trouble Freddy had gotten into, only now it was through gossip and Ava could do little but sit helpless, cheeks burning, while the whispers flew. Among the Freddy stories that circulated around the school were these: he'd been made to sit out in gym for the entire class and then cried so hard he threw up on the wrestling mats; he poured a foil dish of tempera paint on one classmate and spat on another; he got caught pocketing coins from the Estimate Jar on his teacher's desk; he wandered away from recess and turned up fifteen minutes later banging away on the metallophones in the music room; he wandered away from recess and turned up four hours later in a residential neighborhood over a mile from school.

He got a reputation for being violent (or as the kids repeated to one another, *That Freddy Robbins is vicious*). Kitty knew what they meant but also that they were wrong. It was more that he was unbiddable. When allowed the freedom to which he was accustomed, Freddy was peaceful almost all the time. Only when made to comply with order and rules, systems and rigor, did it become impossible for him to keep still. The final straw occurred in December. While lined up in the hall with his class, about to head to music—his favorite part of the school day, especially when they got to use the rhythm instruments—Freddy, with no apparent provocation, turned and pushed the girl behind him. She landed face-first on the buffed linoleum and broke her nose.

The school requested parental consent to have Freddy evaluated for an Individualized Education Plan, consent Neel and June declined to grant. Instead they withdrew him from Freyburg Primary, forevermore to be schooled (or unschooled) at home.

Ava, asked to make a choice, said she wanted to continue in public school.

"Now I feel rotten about it," she confided to Kitty, right after announcing her decision to Neel and June.

They'd come out to Midgetropolis, where they were sitting on the slab, Kitty trying to start a fire in the hearth with a pile of pine needles and a magnifying glass stolen from Mr. Yeltsov's room. All autumn the girls had been practicing their pyro skills, experimenting with different forms of tinder and different types of lenses.

Freddy played by himself a few yards away, spinning himself round and round down by the swale. Every so often he'd lose his balance and topple over onto his back, where he'd lie serenely a minute before rousing himself to spin again. It was a cold day and bright in the startling way of the shortest days of the year. Wood smoke stippled the air. One of the cottages must be having a fire—evidence that another world, the real one, existed just through the woods—but the smell blended happily with the girls' thus far unfruitful efforts to kindle their own; instead of undermining the validity of their imaginary domain, it seemed to enhance it.

"Neel's mad." Ava looked miserable.

"Did he say that?"

"Of course not. He just got all stiff and polite. And then he was 'busy' all of a sudden, and he went in his office and shut the door. He never shuts the door all the way, not unless he's on the phone and Freddy's having a tantrum."

"It's silly for him to be mad," said Kitty. She'd never ventured direct criticism of Ava's parents before, not even in its mildest, commiserating form. "After all, they said you could choose."

"Guess I was supposed to choose what *he'd* like."

"It's your life."

"I know. I told him that!" Ava wiped a tear furiously. "You'd think he'd be happy! 'People should be free so long as they're not hurting anyone or themselves.'" She quoted Neel in a bilious, mincing voice, then picked up a handful of pine needles and flung them.

"Watch the fire," Kitty protested, neatening the remaining needles with the side of her palm.

"He's such a hypocrite! He can't even admit I'm right. He can't admit I might genuinely have a different choice than him. I hate Neel! People should be free so long as they think and feel exactly like him, is what he means! Fuck him! Fuck Neel!"

Kitty was scandalized and exhilarated by this open rebellion, but before she could think how to respond, a great whooping sounded behind them. They looked over to where Freddy stood, and he flapped his arms at them violently and fell backward, plank-like, his body sending bits of dry, rotted leaf into the air. For a moment all was still. Then a decidedly festive chortle issued forth, and Ava and Kitty turned back to their as yet imaginary fire.

"What about June?" asked Kitty.

"What about her? Neel's God, nothing else matters."

This was interesting, too. "But do you think she supports you?"

Ava shrugged. "Who knows? She'd never say. Neel doesn't come right out and say, either. He's just all 'Oh! Oh! I've got to go do something in my office now.'"

It was electrifying to see Ava mock her father. She scrunched her neck, beetled her brow, and made ridiculous, jerky gestures that somehow, despite the fact that Neel never literally did any of these things, captured the essence of his disgruntlement. Kitty cracked up. Ava looked startled, but within moments hilarity swept over her, too, and both girls were howling.

A batch of crows lifted out of a nearby tree, trailing a clutter of cawed rebukes. Something about the birds—their indignant departure; their cantankerous voices—seemed a second wicked imitation of Neel, and plunged Kitty and Ava further into hysterics. "Oh! Oh!" choked Kitty, drawing enough breath between fits of laughter to repeat Neel's line as Ava had delivered it. She tucked her chin against her throat as Ava had, and there was vanity here, cruelty as well, for both she and Ava had slender necks, too long and smooth to bunch up like Neel's, so that the very imperfectness of their impression mocked his own imperfections more deeply.

Freddy, meanwhile, had drifted over to the stone slab and stood above them, grinning broadly and emitting the rusty hinge noises that marked his own laughter. Kitty felt the scrape of annoyance that always accompanied his intrusion on Ava's and her space. "Huhhhnn-hhhhnn," he gasped. His laugh alone would be enough to make life in public school disastrous for him, if ever he went back. He'd never go back, though, that was obvious. With his grating laugh and dumb smile, he'd be the one to fulfill Neel's wishes, roaming the outdoors without any mandate for unclocked hours, unmeasured weeks and months and years. "Neel must *really* like Freddy." Kitty made her voice go up and down, goofy, elastic. "He must love him best."

"I kn—I know!" shrieked Ava. "F—Freddy's their favorite!"

"Their golden child!" Kitty screamed. This, too, held cruelty. She knew it. But as she let herself be flattened by waves of laughter, falling backward on the slab, Ava joined her, the two of them laughing at the same vicious joke, side by side on their backs.

And Freddy, who would never be golden, never be favorite, never be easy to love, let alone able to understand the joke, joined in, too. His creaky *ha ha*s broke forth into full-on *Haah-Haah*s, and he sunk beside them, flapping his hands against his thighs, his jaw sprung so wide that Kitty could see all his teeth and little webs of frothy spit collecting at the corners of his mouth. Why did Freddy always seem nakeder than other people? His laughter, ignorant, innocent, unabashed, made the whole thing more mean and also more heady, and Kitty laughed and laughed until she ached so much she had to press her hands to her ribs like a bandage.

It was Ava who stopped first. Ava who righted herself, suddenly sober, rolled up onto her knees and brushed pine needles from her hair. "Stop laughing, Freddy," she said quietly, and he did, or tried. A few rusty bleats escaped. Ava put a hand on his knee, and although he did not like to be touched, in this instance he let her. Kitty sat up, too, and leaning back on her hands she watched them, brother and sister, the one struggling to quell his braying, the other bowing her head over her own hand where it rested on his corduroy kneecap.

And there Ava sat, straight-backed and still, concentrating with such grave dignity that Kitty couldn't stand it. Or couldn't stand something. Some underlying unfairness about the whole thing. Hadn't Ava also laughed? Hadn't she just a moment ago been rolling around on her back beside Kitty? How did she manage to switch off so quickly, switch allegiances? What made her and how dare she decide to become, all on her own, serious? And however did she know when it was all right to touch Freddy? For that matter, how did he know her touch was meant to protect him—because wasn't that it, really? She was protecting him from laughing at his own expense. Protecting him—the realization came in a noxious spurt—from Kitty herself! Kitty and all others who would hurt him: his would-be mockers and judges, the untold legions of the unkind and unknowing.

Kitty got to her feet. "You're so self-righteous." It was a phrase she'd heard her mother once say to Ellie, her older sister now living in Central Africa. "All of you Robbinses are."

Ava said nothing. Her face had resolved into an expression of almost consecrated seriousness; her very posture transmitted wordless reproach.

So Kitty left them there, brother and sister, sitting on the slab as the day grew dark. She turned heel and walked away, but with the vexing feeling that they had turned from her first. She would never forgive them, she decided, threading her way through the trees and over the cold-hardened path, although she might pity them in time; yes, she might eventually grant them that, crippled as they both were by their family's proud eccentricity, its strange pieties. She stalked out of Midgetropolis and out of the woods and straight back to Batter Hollow, where the chimney smoke turned out to be coming from the Art Barn and her mother turned out to be making kale pie, and she threw herself into the rocking chair by the stove—"I hate the Robbinses," she muttered—and rocked in it violently until Meg said in her mild way, "Don't take your anger out on that chair," upon which she sprung from it and tore up the stairs to her room and threw herself furiously down on the bed, with a great groaning of springs that reminded her despicably of Freddy's laughter.

Too often it was like that: Ava being her friend and then pivoting to become Freddy's sister instead, as if these were two different people, and always, *always* it contained a kind of censure. For why should being Kitty's friend prevent her from being Freddy's sister? What about the one could not accommodate the other? Yet Ava's actions suggested their incompatibility. Worse, they suggested that Freddy, drooly, tantrumy, stick-beating Freddy, was better, truer and somehow more worthy, than Kitty. Which was crap.

THEY FOUND IN MIDGETROPOLIS, in addition to the kettle and the SAFE SPIRITS bottle, other objects strewn about or half buried in leaves and dirt, and sometimes these discoveries had an enchanted feel, and sometimes they felt sinister. No matter how often they'd hunted out there, exploring and excavating the same patch of woods until it seemed nothing could have escaped their notice, still new objects managed to turn up from month to month and year to year, as if the earth itself was relinquishing them gradually, hesitantly.

Ava said the items they found must be relics of old Batter Hollow students. She liked to speak as if their ghosts still lingered in the woods, keeping watch from behind the trees. But Kitty scoffed. "How can they be ghosts? They're not dead, just grown. Think of my dad." For her, the various objects were clues about something larger and older than Batter Hollow, linked to the fantasy they'd indulged in on the day they founded, or found, Midgetropolis: that of the slab being a giant's grave marker, evidence of a whole hidden network of behemothic tombs, a vast underground mausoleum, branching beneath the forest floor. In any case, they took pleasure in being a little scared by the items that turned up.

Once they found something rigid and black and full of holes. "Burnt metal," said Kitty. "Or plastic," guessed Ava. "Pick it up, Freddy," she ordered in that mild, offhanded tone he almost always obeyed, and sure enough he lofted it, dangling the thing by what seemed a tail, so that Kitty screamed, "Rat carcass!" and Freddy, screaming, too, flung it away. On further investigation, digging it up with sticks from the damp leaves among which it had fallen, they decided it was only an old rag petrified by some tarry substance, but even then it made them shudder; there was something in the splayed, stiffened, ruined look of it that seemed not simply grotesque but malevolent. Freddy in particular remained really terrified of the rag, which they left lying where it landed, hidden behind a bush.

Other artifacts were less patently spooky. Once they found a couple of cans with their labels still mostly legible. SWEETHEART BEANS, one read, and WEARWELL MOTOR OIL. Another time they found the plastic yoke of a six-pack and an empty whiskey bottle small enough for a doll. Another time it was a pair of cat-eye glasses with one earpiece missing. The girls took turns sashaying around Midgetropolis, holding it like a lorgnette and saying, "Jolly good," and "Where did I put my wellies?"

One afternoon when Kitty and Ava were finishing up sixth grade, thinking with excitement about the new school they would attend in the fall and getting used to that exotic term, "junior high," Kitty spied the tip of something pink poking out of the wet earth by the swale. It turned out to be a plastic barrette, the sort a little girl might wear. (Kitty and Ava were by then styling their hair with blow dryers and mousse.) It had two rows of tiny teeth and was shaped like a bow. "Yours?" she joked.

Ava swiped the object from Kitty's hand, spit on it, rubbed it on her jeans to remove the more tractable bits of black soil, then leaned over and fastened it roughly to a piece of Kitty's yellowy-white hair.

"Hey!" Kitty yanked it out, then called over to Fred—they were just beginning to call him Fred instead of Freddy—"C'mere. Come over here a sec. I want to make you pretty."

He did not glance up from where he was sitting, arranging baby pinecones on the slab. At ten he was supposedly showing signs of being gifted at math. This was according to Ava. Kitty remained skeptical. But Ava said no, Neel had noticed something in him, a kind of attentiveness to patterning, and had helped him make certain connections, with the result that Fred was now obsessed with Fibonacci sets, pointing them out wherever he spotted them, in the petals of lilies and asters, the spiraling seed heads of coneflowers, the complex architectures of cauliflower and pineapples and artichokes.

Now Kitty went over and stood behind him, inspecting the design he'd made for evidence of brilliance. He'd arranged the baby pinecones from small to large. "Wow," said Kitty, "that's really good."

"Leave him alone," said Ava.

"Now don't freak." Kitty addressed Fred, ignoring Ava's admonition. Leaning over, she extended the barrette on the flat of her hand. Fred looked, then reached. Swiftly, Kitty closed her fingers. "It goes in your hair," she explained. And cajolingly, "Want to look pretty?"

"Just let him be," repeated Ava, but she sounded bored and did not stir from where she sat.

Kitty knelt and gingerly picked up a lock of Fred's hair. He did not protest. It was thick like June's and curly like Neel's and far softer than she had imagined. Fred quivered slightly and lengthened his neck toward her as she combed her fingers through it. "What nice hair you have." He sat immobile, his very stillness a kind of permission. She began to work out the many tangles, trying not to pull. "When's the last time anybody combed this?" she murmured. "Or washed it?" The only sound he made was that of his stuffy, clotted breathing. Never before had he submitted to her like this, as he occasionally would with Ava, and Kitty was intoxicated by the novelty of his trust. Once she'd worked through all the snarls, she fastened the barrette on this tuft of hair, and it poked straight up from his crown, a little topknot. "Voilà," she said. "Now you're Fredericka."

With a loose, spreading grin, he reached up to feel what she had done, but, "No!" she reproached, "you'll mess it up!" and seized his hand midair. This, she knew, was risky; he was liable to yank free and strike out at her, but he remained wondrously docile and let her pull him to standing.

"What are you doing now?" asked Ava apprehensively, but she still lolled on her Throne by the swale.

"Come," Kitty coaxed, and as he reached up again with his free hand, she was quick to grasp that one, too. "You'll ruin it," she clucked. "Come, we'll take you to a mirror. Now don't touch. Isn't he pretty?" she demanded, leading him toward Ava and then past her, to the edge of the swale. She pushed the back of Fred's neck and made him bend down toward it. "Look," she urged, "you can see your reflection in the water." The swale that day was no more than a muddy trickle; she was play-acting. "Isn't Fredericka pretty?" she insisted, bending over and pointing at the glistening rocks and leaves as if his image were available there.

"Ah-yeah!" he agreed, nodding so that the topknot flopped. "Pretty Fred-ah!"

"Fred*erick*a."

And he married his own laugh to hers, his with its wheezy, broken sound, hers glossy and hard, and then he began to dance, comically, maniacally: kicking up his boot-clad feet and pirouetting with an invisible skirt held in his fingertips.

"Fred." Ava sighed. "Don't be a dope."

But, "S'ah'm Fred*erick*a," he corrected her, and laughed with great gusto, a spit-flecked, braying sound, embarrassing yet unembarrassed. So Ava, rolling her eyes, smiled in spite of her disapproval, and when Fred began to urge them, "Come-ah on! Ah-dance-ah!" both girls obeyed, joining Fred in his spastic movements. Distinctions between whose laughter and dancing were forced, falsified, and whose helpless and ingenuous became blurred, even for Kitty, so that by the time they all collapsed, panting, on their Thrones, she was legitimately confused about her own intentions. Had all her participation been in mockery of Fred, and in some way, more to the point, of Ava? Or had it at some moment morphed into them all three just having fun? And how bedeviling not to know her own mind.

In any case, the "Midgetropowaltz," as Kitty christened it, established a beginning. The barrette, the dance, the persona of Fredericka—together these formed a blueprint they were bound to follow. The next time they came into the woods, Kitty brought a composition book. "We have to write things down," she said. "The life and lore of Midgetropolis." They all signed their names inside the front cover, and she began to keep a record of what they did. "You do the illustrations," she told Ava, who was good at drawing and who, with finely lettered captions, made a visual inventory of all their most important artifacts and landmarks: the kettle and the SAFE SPIRITS bottle and the scary tarry rag; the Thrones and the Arch and the house itself, drawn with a real fire blazing in the hearth and the pilfered magnifying glass nearby. And she began to do illustrations of the character of Fredericka, who emerged, both in Ava's drawings and Kitty's storylines, and also, especially, as enacted by Fred, as a kind of cheery yet hapless maiden, eternally trusting and endlessly susceptible to spine-tingling scrapes. Forever and deliciously at the mercy of evildoers, forever in peril.

After this, for as long as they continued to play in, or play *at*, Midgetropolis, they played this game. (How long had they continued?

Had the game ended sometime during seventh grade, or eighth? Surely by high school the girls must have outgrown its appeal and begun leaving the woods to Fred alone, not knowing and little contemplating whether their withdrawal relieved or saddened him.) They never gave it a proper name, the game, never mind that it had its own book, its own narrative with a plot that repeated in an endless loop. Never mind that it had its own protagonist, if not quite heroine: Fredericka was too much a victim for that. The game hinged on Fred's willingness to assume the role, with Kitty and Ava taking on the parts of minor characters, sometimes Fredericka's tormentors, sometimes her rescuers. They took on, too, the job of encouraging or badgering, whatever might entice Fred to play. Which he did, readily, allowing himself to become the object of both their fawning adulation and their teasing, the membrane between the two kept crucially thin and unstable.

It was a kind of gentle persecution, what they did to Fred, what he permitted them to do. Fredericka, they persisted in calling him, and he responded as if delighted to be in on the joke. To be the joke. The more he claimed the role for himself the more they showered him with approval, and they wooed him further into the game by promising to make him their sister. One day he let them mousse his hair and make up his face. It fascinated Kitty that here in Midgetropolis, so long as he was being Fredericka, he'd let them touch him unrestrainedly.

Kitty had him tip back his head and hold still while she painted his full, slightly chapped lips. The sun cast spears through the treetops overhead, making him close his eyes, and she could see through his violet-veined lids the quick darting movements of his eyeballs, like the slippery hearts of small creatures. His skin was as smoothly transparent as a fairy-tale maiden's; he had no visible pores or oily patches, none of the angry little red spots Kitty and Ava had both lately developed. They considered this absence, then painted them on, pimpling him all over with dabs of scarlet lip gloss, and when he protested—"What-ah, you guys ah-doing? Quit-ah, quit that, guys!"—they leapt, shrieking, out of range of his flailing arms, saying:

"Look-ah: look-ah your brother's-ah face-ah!"

"Gross-ah! Get away-ah from-ah me-ah!"

Only when he began to tear apart the Midgetropolis house—heaving the kettle into a bush, scattering the leaves they'd laid out to make a bed, kicking and stomping the pinecone-and-pebble border that marked the hearth—did they try to pacify him, clucking, "Freddy, Freddy, don't be mad, we'll help you wash it off," and led him down to the swale, which was flowing this day with spring runoff, so that they could scoop handfuls of cold water and scrub the marks off his face. "See, Fredericka? You're the prettiest sister of all."

Spring set in more deeply. Flowers nosed through the clutter of the forest floor, trees put forth curly young leaves, and the stone slab of their woods house roasted in wanton scraps of sun. Here on a hot day in May, Kitty and Ava persuaded Fred to let them paint his toenails blue. Another day they dug to the bottom of the old steamer trunk where, below the many decades' worth of former students' abandoned hats and gloves, they found a pile of brightly colored squares of silk, which they brought to Midgetropolis, thinking of the children who had played with them long ago. They spread these silks on the stone slab, apple green and yellow, purple and rose and peacock blue, and with these slippery squares they draped Fred, tying a turban on his head, a sarong around his middle, a cape around his neck. When he went to scratch his ear and knocked the turban loose, they scolded him in silken voices, guiding his hand back down to his side. They made the turban secure once more and scrutinized him—"Hold *still*, Fredericka!"—so intently he squirmed.

"He's a sheik."

"A sheikess."

"*She's* a sheikess."

"Where's her harem?"

"That would be us, doll."

They lifted their T-shirts and, humming "Streets of Cairo," did belly dances. The sight of their own flat bellies, recently discovered as assets, delighted them. Kitty pushed her pants low to expose her jutting hip bones; Ava copied. These, too, had recently made their presence known, as had the sparse, coarse, curlicues of hair sprouting on both of them just below. This secret they had shared a few weeks earlier in Kitty's bedroom, standing before her mirror and comparing subtle differences in color and amount. Now, as they bared their midriffs to each other and to Fred on the stone slab, that private knowledge tinged their song with lewd laughter.

"We're Salome," said Kitty, circling her pelvis.

"As in lunch meat?"

"Dolt. As in the dance of the seven veils."

"Whatev."

They snatched up the extra silks and twirled them around their heads and past Fred's face. The light shone through the cloth and cast colored shade and Fred closed his eyes and smiled his terrible, open-mouthed, trusting smile as they let the silks billow up and fall against his skin.

"He's a genie," said Kitty, grabbing the kettle.

They rubbed it.

"Now you have to grant our wishes," they informed him.

He laughed in his Fredly way, disorderly and unhinged, and the turban shook loose again from his hair.

Clicking their tongues, they swooped in to fix it once more. "You keep messing it up—no, no, just . . . hold *still*," they repeated, batting his hands away, until, "You hold him while I fasten it," said Ava, and this time when his hands floated back toward his head, Kitty stepped in and bound them at the wrists. "There, that's better." His hands were held fast behind his back with the red silk. Because he was Fredericka he let her, but as soon as she stepped away he began to strain at the knot.

"You can't tie him," said Ava.

But, "You're our genie," explained Kitty, very nicely, too, lilting and sincere, with her pale eyebrows lifted and her chicory eyes wide. "That means you have to do everything we say, okay?"

"Kitty . . ."

But Fred stopped straining and nodded. So he was in the game, still in the game, willing to play or willing himself to play, either one, small difference, and either way, *willing*, as anyone could attest.

"I don't think—"

Kitty spun toward Ava, cutting her off. "What do you want?"

"What?"

"What do you want from the genie? Come on, make a wish."

"Oh." Ava's eyes went vacant. Her gaze slid from Kitty to her brother in his turban and his bound hands, then off toward the trees. She did that irritating thing where she kneaded the fingers of one hand with those of the other. "Uh . . ."

"Oh my God. Is everyone in this family retarded?" Kitty swiveled back to Fred. "Lie down, genie."

"Don't we have to untie his hands?" ventured Ava.

"Of course not."

"But how's he supposed to—?"

"He's a genie," said Kitty, and clapped twice. "Lie down."

Without use of his hands he accomplished this more awkwardly than he might otherwise, and she could see him thinking it through, how best to do it. He knelt first, then tilted himself sideways, and finally, with little pricks of sweat breaking out along his lip and brow, worked himself into a prostrate position on the warm slab.

"Faceup," snapped Kitty. "Chop, chop."

He rolled with some effort onto his other side, arching his back for his hands, which were trapped underneath. Sunlight struck down at his face; he shut his eyes. Ava stepped over him, shielding him with her shadow, while Kitty darted away behind the bushes.

"What are you doing?" Ava asked.

"Nothing." Kitty was already back. "Okay, genie, now grant my wish: I want a kiss."

"Don't do that."

"Shut up. He wants to play."

"But he doesn't . . . He can't kiss."

"Of course he can. Can't you, Fredericka? You like being the genie, right? You like granting our wishes."

"S'ah-yeah."

"See?" Kitty knelt beside him. "Now pucker up. That means push your lips together. No, out. No, push them together and *out*. Yeah. But keep your eyes closed. And your lips. Oh my God, can you stop laughing for one second? Pucker." She was laughing, too, and now so was Ava, laughing in a protesty little way but still, whickering along with them, and the sun flocked them with coins of light and licked the colored silks, and the breeze that flittered through the woods smelled richly of dead pine needles and all the soft dense clumps of new-grown moss. Fred managed to stop laughing long enough to hold his pucker in place and Kitty whipped out what she'd gone to get from the bushes and kept hidden behind her back: the tarry rag, stiff as an old carcass, which she mashed now against his lips for a full second before leaping up and away, shrieking with laughter.

Fred roared. When he saw what he'd been kissing he sat up and began to spit, and then to cry and hack and heave and drool and gag and grunt and retch and groan.

"Kitty!" said Ava with such sharp reproach that Kitty felt unfairly maligned and also uneasy.

"It was a joke."

Ava knelt by Fred and tried to pick apart the knot that was still binding his wrists together. "I can't get it," she said miserably after a minute. Kitty came forward and gently pushed Ava's hands away. "I have longer nails." While she worked at the knot, she delivered a kind of patter. *Sorry, Fred. It was just a joke. You know that, don't you? You're all right. We were just playing, right?* And he calmed down while she loosened the silk, and nodded to each of her questions. When she saw the knot was undone, she did not announce it but, still holding the silk around his wrists, brought her face close to his.

"It's time for your reward now."

Something, fear or interest, flickered across his face.

"It's something nice, I promise."

"Ah . . ." He was still flushed from struggling and then from his violent reaction to her trick; his cheeks were stained pink and the bow of his lips was full and red and all at once with his dark and shining eyes he gave her a rare steady look.

Kitty bent, her heart gonging, and laid her mouth on his. Warm, soft, soft as a raspberry. She darted her tongue in and out and sat back quickly. "See?"

"Kitty," breathed Ava, horrified, furious.

They watched. Would he spit again, would he hack and gag?

"Fred, Fred, are you okay?"

"No, no-ah, no." He shook his head from side to side. "Not-ah Fred. S'ah Fred*erick*a."

IV

FRED

One

THE MAN SAID *Get up you have a visitor.*

He figured it would be the lawyer again who came yesterday but they went down a different hall and the man brought him to a different room. Instead of one table and two chairs, this one had a bunch of tables and a bunch of chairs, and lots of people sitting at the different tables, not just men in greens but women and some kids, too. Some of the people were wearing regular clothes like skirts and sweatshirts. Some were dressed fancy. One woman was wearing a red dress and sharp red shoes like she was going to a fancy restaurant.

He was standing there just looking at some babies, and there were people talking Spanish and people talking English, and people talking something else he didn't know what, and one man and woman, they were both crying and neither of them using any tissues, just their sleeves. It was funny seeing all these different kinds of people after days of having everybody be a man and everybody dress the same, either in blue uniforms weighed down with buttons and badges and zippers and snaps, all that sharp shiny metal that made you blink, or else like him in these loose green pants and loose green shirts that hung off you and smelled of cooked peas. And these black rubber sandals that weren't his either. Where were his shoes? He couldn't remember.

He was blinking his eyes, looking around the bright fluorescent room, searching for the lawyer. He remembered the lawyer from yesterday, or maybe the day before: a tall sit-up-straight man with little glittering eyes in his big dough face that hung in folds around his neck. The man who brought him in said *Don't see your visitor?* and he shook his head no but then he saw her.

His throat went *clank* like he was a metal bank and someone had stuck a big coin through the slot.

He had never called Ava because her number was in the little book back at Dave's house on the Cape, and he didn't know how she'd figured out where he was or what happened or how to find him or anything. He didn't know how she'd gotten herself here or how she could've known to come. But Ava always knew stuff he didn't know. Seeing her made him feel happy and scared. He started to rub his hands on the side of his pants. She was wearing a sweater that was brown, and pants that were gray. Some birds were brown and gray, and he wanted to tell her *Hey, you look like one of those birds,* but he saw that she had seen him now, too, and her eyes went all tilty, like a roof that was too steep.

She started to stand up and the man behind him said, just like he was cracking a stick over his knee, *Ma'am!* and she sat back down and the man said *That your visitor?* and he nodded and the man said *You go sit over there. Remember no touching.*

Also, in case he forgot, the rules were screwed right into the wall:

NO TOUCHING
NO FOOD
NO GUM

NO PROFANITY

REMAIN SEATED

NO LOUD TALKING/LAUGHING

VIOLATIONS OF VISITING PRIVILEGES MAY RESULT IN
    DISCIPLINARY ACTION AGAINST THE INMATE AND
    APPROPRIATE ADMINISTRATIVE OR LEGAL ACTIONS
    AGAINST THE VISITOR

He sat in the tan plastic chair opposite Ava's tan plastic chair and he swallowed and he folded his hands on his lap. He folded them with the fingers going this way and that way, every other one. *This is the church, this is the steeple.*

"Hi," Ava said. Softly. She must have been memorizing the rules before he came in.

He was looking at his hands, trying to remember how June used to do it, the way to fold them so you get the people.

"Fred?"

He could get the steeple. He could get the doors. He opened the doors and it was empty inside, nothing but smooth palms. He couldn't remember how to get the people.

"Hey, Freddy." That was her old-fashioned name for him. It got his eyes to jump up. They jumped up and saw Ava looking at him with her eyes tilted so steep it made him feel like he was sliding, so he started looking at who else was in the room. Nine guys in greens like him, and across from every one of them, visitors. In all, thirteen visitors. There was a baby bobbling on its mother's leg and it had sparkle things tied in its little pigletted hair. There was a woman with lips like a bitten-into chocolate when it's one of those chocolates that has raspberry filling. There was a man with a T-shirt with words and a picture. The words said *Sparky's Marina* and the picture was a fish standing up wearing a chef's hat and holding a spatula. His eyes were swallowing hard at all that color, all that noisy brightness.

"Freddy, please look at me," said Ava.

He looked at her and her eyes were tilted and sparkling with too much sadness and he felt like he was sliding fast, falling off a roof. He looked over her shoulder and studied the rule sign.

"How are you?"

He nodded his head. Once he started, he couldn't stop. Bouncy bounce.

"Are you doing okay?"

NO TOUCHING

NO FOOD

NO GUM

"Why don't you look at me, Freddy?"

He couldn't.

"Look at me."

He would fall.

"Please."

"Ah," he said. "Ah-fall."

"Fall? Did someone fall?"

He was nodding his head up and down. The rule sign was bouncing all over the wall. Darting up and jumping sideways, running slantways and scampering down. Breaking all the rules.

Ava was talking.

Our parents left us, she was saying. *They were poor. The cupboards were bare. They took us into the forest with them to cut wood, and they left us there to fend for ourselves. We made a trail of white stones, and when the moon came up it lit the stones and we found our way home.*

He knew this story.

"Do you remember being in the woods?" she was saying. "Did you talk with the lawyer about it? Bayard Charles? What did you tell Mr. Charles? Freddy, do you remember what happened in the woods?"

"Bread-ah-crumbs," he said. Nodding a little faster, bouncing his knees and his whole bent spine.

Bread crumbs, Ava agreed. *The second time they led us deeper into the forest, and again they left us to fend for ourselves. This time we tore off bits of bread to make a trail, but when the moon came up there were no more crumbs. The birds had eaten them up. We were lost.*

"Birds," he said. "Ah-lost-ah."

"Who is lost?" she asked. "Did you and the boy get lost in the woods? You and James, Jimmy. Were you lost?"

Nodding, bouncing. The rules scuttling and darting all over the wall, broken.

"Freddy, please won't you tell me what happened? What were you doing when they found you in the woods? Were you looking for the boy, for Jimmy?"

NO PROFANITY

REMAIN SEATED

NO LOUD TALKING/LAUGHING

"Freddy. Fred. Look at me."

Noddingnodding. His knees were bouncing. And his hands, locked together, bounced on his knees. *Here is the church, here is the steeple.*

"Why can't you look at me? Freddy, did you do something? Did you do something to make the boy run away?"

Open the doors. Where are the people?

"Did you hurt him? The doctor—they said his wrist was broken. And," she touched her side—

NO TOUCHING

"Two ribs. Do you know about that? Can you tell me? Did it happen by accident? Did he fall?"

He felt himself sliding. He would fall.

"Just tell me, please. Please. Fred. Tell me the story."

No, he said. He put his hands over his ears. *No loud talking.*

Hush, said Ava. *Calm down. Hold still. You want to hear more of the story?*

Noddingnoddingnodding.

Take your hands off your ears.

He let them fall.

After three days of wandering, we came upon a cottage made of bread, with a roof made of cake. Windowpanes of clear sugar. Remember? You broke off a bit of roof, and I began to nibble on a window.

Nibble, nibble.

Yes, I began to nibble and then we heard a voice come from inside the house: Nibble nibble little mouse—

No!

—who's that nibbling at my house?

"No!" His voice roared out of him. It scared him. "No loud-ah talk-ing!" He banged his hands over his ears. It didn't help. He banged them again and banged them again and he roared and roared and roared. "No loud-ah talking! No loud-ah talking! No loud-ah talking!"

The man hurt him when he tried to pull his hands off his ears.

Another man had to come and hold his other arm.

They held his arms behind his back again, like in the woods.

It took three men to get him out of the room.

Two

In his whole life he'd only ever known three people who re-minded him of the Little Prince.

The first had been Kitty the day he'd met her, twenty-five years earlier: the day she'd sprung down to the ground from the sassafras tree with her short star-colored hair and her pin-striped conductor's over-alls and her bare feet and he'd hit her cheek with a wooden spoon. Never mind that the Little Prince doesn't have overalls. Or bare feet. She had been like the pictures of him in Neel's book that he had first seen when he was very small and Ava read it aloud to him up on the couch. She was like the Little Prince in more ways than her hair, al-though he could not have said how. Something unfamiliar and brave and a little fierce about her, and she sometimes talked in riddles.

The second person had been Thor, but he didn't like to think about Thor.

The third person was brand-new and standing there right this sec-ond: the girl beside him at the bar. She, too, had short star-colored hair sticking out in tufts around her head. She wore a stretchy denim jumpsuit that clung to her, and she also talked in riddles. She kept calling him Sailor.

"Hey, Sailor," she said. "What's that you're drinking?"

When he didn't say anything back, instead of cutting her eyes and sucking her teeth, she turned to Dave. "What's the matter with your friend?" she asked. "He shy?"

At first he hadn't liked how dark it was inside. When they first got here, him and Dave and Dave's friend Umberto, the summer evening had still been light, and the bar was so dark he was afraid he'd bump into things. He had to hold his hands out like a mummy while he walked, and then he did bump into something, a man, who swiveled his head around like an owl and looked Fred up and down. Fred said, "Ah-sorry," but by then the man had already turned back around.

They got seats at the bar and Dave and Umberto ordered beer, and Fred asked for a Mountain Dew and the bartender said we don't have Mountain Dew, only Sprite. And Fred said to Dave he was just going back outside to the deli on the corner, which he'd seen when they were driving up, so he could get himself a can of Mountain Dew. But Dave had taken a handful of Fred's shirt, not roughly but in a way that meant they were friends and everything would be okay, and Dave said, "Just have Sprite, okay? It's the same thing."

So Fred got Sprite but it wasn't the same thing. For example, Mountain Dew had caffeine and Sprite didn't, and also Mountain Dew was special because it had real orange juice in it. He mentioned this to Dave, and Umberto said, "Bullshit," and Fred said no, it wasn't bullshit, you could check the ingredients on the label, and Umberto said, "Remind me why the fuck we had to bring this wacko," and Dave just clapped a hand on Fred's shoulder and said, "Okay, Buddy, I believe you, let it go."

The reason they had to bring Fred was Fred couldn't be left alone anymore in Dave's house on the Cape.

The reason they had to be in here was they had to meet a friend of Umberto's that Umberto had some business with.

But when they first came in, Fred really hated to leave the summer evening's hay-y smell and the last snips of light blinking like sequins on the surface of the mill river that ran through the town. Fred knew it was a mill river from his map, one of the boxful from the old house that he had taken with him when June died. A shoe box stuffed with maps she'd picked up at gas stations when they were little, when their family used to go on trips. Some of the maps were still smooth and crisp to the touch, others were faded and soft as silk. These were easy to fold back up again, but also easy to tear, and he was careful to handle them gently whenever he went on a road trip with Dave. He would pull out the right map for wherever they were, find their position, ask Dave the name of where they were headed, and trace their route, counting up the miles between exits and intersections, those tiny black numbers inked in be-side stretches of highway like a secret code. June had taught him they were mile numbers. She had taught him how you could count them all up and know how long your journey was.

Sometimes he could see how near they were passing to someplace he'd been long ago, someplace June had marked with a pink or yellow highlighter pen: a state forest where they'd camped, a college town where Neel had given a talk, a beach where they'd swum. Sometimes, to pass the time on those long trips, he would read the maps like they were picture books with illustrations too tiny to see. He'd spend long minutes with the map held close to his face, smelling the musty sweet-ness, filling in with his memory the microscopic details: the green tent they'd all slept in; the college students with their fringed jackets and

Frisbees; the peanut butter sandwiches they'd eaten on the beach and the peppermint stripes on the umbrella and the cut he'd gotten on the bottom of his foot from a piece of glass.

The town he and Dave and Umberto drove to was called Perdu. This word was printed in the smallest-sized letters on the map, next to the smallest-sized dot. A blue thread ran beside it. Fred had looked up from the thread and connected it to the narrow mill river running alongside the car. The map didn't show the low brick buildings backed up along its far bank, or the laundry blowing on lines that ran between these buildings.

It had taken a long time to get here from the Cape. They'd driven all day, and he hadn't liked going from the car immediately into the dark of the bar with the noise from the jukebox filling the room, fuzzing up against the wood-paneled walls and thudding in his ears, and he hadn't liked the noise of the people who laughed in rough, sparky barks. "We get it. We know you don't like it," Dave had finally said. "Quit saying so over and over." But it really made him think he might puke, and at first he'd had to cup a hand over his nose to try to block the smells of spilled beer and old fry grease and sweaty bodies.

He told Dave he was going to wait outside, but Dave pointed him toward a barstool. "Just grab a seat. You're okay." And Dave turned out to be right as usual, because after a while his eyes adjusted and his ears and nose adjusted, and he saw that all the bottles on the shelves behind the bar, with their different colors of glass and their different shapes, were like a city, with a pretty skyline he could lose himself in, trace with his eyes, another kind of map. And he drank more Sprite and had some wings with bright orange sauce that wasn't too spicy, and Dave and Umberto had some wings and some drinks that came from one of the pretty bottles behind the bar. They also had some more beers only this time they called them chasers.

Umberto's friend who he had some business with still hadn't come in, but three girls came in, and they seemed to know Umberto. They walked in a swirly way toward the bar and pressed themselves up close to it, somehow making room where there hadn't been any, and now two of them were sitting on the stools that Dave and Umberto had been sitting on, with Dave and Umberto wedged in behind them like almost-right-but-not-quite jigsaw pieces.

The one girl with star-colored hair didn't have a seat. She was standing tucked up close to Fred, and he didn't want to give up his stool so he didn't smile or look at her when she said hey Sailor to him, but after she turned to face the others he snuck looks at her short, pale hair that stuck out around her head just like the Little Prince.

He wanted to tell Dave about it, but he didn't know if Dave would say, "Cool, Buddy," or "Not now, man," or worse, nothing at all, just eye him coldly like the owl man and swivel his head back around. Dave was capable of all three. Fred met Dave at Neel's memorial service. Both Dave's parents had been Batter Hollow students, and Dave said he himself had gone there as a little kid, right before the school closed. Fred's first memory of Dave was actually at the gathering after Neel's memorial service, a big party back at Batter Hollow that wound up stretching late into the night. Dave had been a skinny guy standing outside in the dark, leaning against the wall of the Shed, smoking with the lighted end of his cigarette cupped inside his palm. That's when he came up with the name Buddy. "Hey, Buddy," he'd said when Fred wandered by. "Sorry about your old man."

He stuck around a few weeks after the memorial service, staying in the abandoned Shed and doing odd jobs for June, replacing the rotten wood on the front porch of the Office, fixing the gutters, patching the roof. Then he got a call to paint a house back on the Cape and he left. But later, when June got sick and had to lie in bed all the time, she called him. Well, first she had to call Dave's mother to get his number, and then she called Dave on the Cape and they talked. She asked Fred to leave the room while they talked. When she hung up she called for him to come back, and he sat in a chair pulled up to the bed and she lay there with no hair and her skin the color of beeswax on the pillow, and she said Fred was going to have a job and a place to live on the Cape. He was going to help Dave paint houses and he was going to stay in Dave's bungalow with him. And she would make sure Dave got some money every month and Dave would make sure Fred had clothes and food and whatever he needed. After she told him this she looked like she might fall asleep, but instead she reached her hand out from under the sheet and touched Fred on the knee.

"You always liked the Cape," she said.

Then she closed her eyes for eleven seconds and just as he was counting twelve in his head she opened them again and said, "You always liked the ocean."

Then her face sort of crumpled, and her yellow skin looked like a candle someone had taken a fork to, and she didn't smell a thing like June.

"Hey!" The star-haired girl whipped her head around. Fred had leant in close to the girl's hair; he'd been smelling it. It smelled like raisin cookies. Now he sat back quickly on his stool, careening his gaze over to the bottles behind the bar, tracing with his eyes the rise and fall of their glass silhouettes. *Bumpity bumpity bump.*

"Don't think I don't know your type," the girl added more slowly, looking him up and down. But not like the owl man had looked him up and down. With her it was more like he was a path in the woods she was thinking she might go down. "You get me, Sailor?"

He didn't know if he got her, but he nodded, which was something he'd learned to do whenever people asked him a question that didn't make sense or spoke in riddles. Then he was afraid he might keep bobbing his head up and down the way that felt good but Dave had informed him was *a little weird, Buddy*, so he looked away again, back toward the skyline of colored bottles.

"You always this talkative?"

This was a joke and he knew to smile. "Ha ha," he added after a moment.

When she smiled, one cheek got a dent in it, curvy and dark. It was a little like the dent in Kitty's chin. He wanted to put his finger in the dent. He turned away from her and touched his glass of Sprite instead.

"You must have a secret, huh? That's why you're so quiet. So what is it? How come you won't tell what you're drinking?" She leaned over right in front of him and he could see, because she had not zipped her denim jumpsuit all the way, where a shadow slid down between the tops of her small breasts. She closed her hand around his glass and slid it toward herself, brought it to her own lips, slowly, slowly, and drank, keeping her eyes on him the whole time. "Hm." Sounding surprised, she set the glass back on the bar, tipped her starry head to one side and narrowed her eyes at him.

His Adam's apple slid up and down his throat. "Ah, have you-ah, ever read *The Little Prince*, by-ah, Ant-ah, Antoine de Saint-Exupéry?"

Her eyes popped big like in a cartoon. "It talks!" she screamed. She reached around and whacked her friend, on the next stool, with the back of her hand.

"Ow. Bitch." The friend rubbed at her shoulder and looked over at them both. Her eyes, beneath heavy lids, had a mean look. They were the color of a bruise.

The third girl was busy laughing at something Umberto said.

"Sailor boy can talk!" announced the star-girl. "Listen to this." And to him, "Repeat what you just said."

"Ah ..."

"Ask me that thing again."

"Ah, are you-ah, familiar with-ah, that book? It's-ah, a novel by-ah, by-ah, by-ah, Antoine de Saint-Exupéry."

"Dassant eggs-*what*?" She yelped the last word so high he flinched. "You are priceless. You kill me, what language is that?"

"S'ah not-ah a language," he explained, and she let out a happy scream and gave her friend another whack. This time her friend shoved her back. She stumbled against Fred, who steadied her.

"He was-ah a writer," Fred said. "And-ah a pilot. In Africa. You-ah, you-ah, look like the drawings of-ah the little prince."

He talked on then, wanting to explain about the book, which he had never read through all by himself but which Ava had read to him long ago, and whose illustrations and sweet pervading sadness had made a lasting impression, so that now he liked to bring the book with him wherever he went, and sometimes he would flip through and read himself a line or two—he liked where the snake says, *It is a little lonely among men*—or just page through the pictures, and as he talked to the star-haired girl about the book he noticed it was unusual he wanted to talk so much; noticed, too, that as he went on the words began to slip more effortlessly out of his mouth, following smoothly upon each other without needing those little pockets of air to come between so many of them. But he also noticed how his voice got lost in the surge of the jukebox and spikes of laughter throughout the bar, lost in the tumult of milling bodies that flashed in and out of the corners of his vision, heavy with sweat and muscles and fat; lost, too, in the glint of pint glasses bobbing along on trays held high, and in the glint of tongue studs and nose rings and the neon Genny Light sign over in the little box window, so that Fred had to look back at the bottle city again, rest his eyes by letting them travel the miniature glass skyline, and while all this was going on, the girl with the Little Prince hair leaned in and laid a hand on his crotch.

"Ah," said Fred. He looked down. There were her fingers, idle and innocent.

"How you doing there, Buddy?" This was Dave, standing over him, breathing the smell of liquor against the back of his head. "Time to get going." Dave rocked forward on his feet, stumbling against Fred's stool, then straightened again. The girl's fingers slid lower, worked into the crevice between Fred's legs. Fred wondered if Dave saw it. Dave should see it. Then he could say *Hey!* if it wasn't okay. He could say *Hey, that's a little weird!* the way he did whenever Fred forgot and started bouncing his body or making sounds he didn't realize he was making. Then Dave would just say in a bright friendly voice, *Hey!* or else more quietly but still friendly, *Hey, quit that, quit doing the bobble-head thing,* or *quit humming,* and Fred would quit.

"Ah . . ." said Fred. The girl's hand grew heavier, massy and warm, and her fingers rippled against his thigh. He tried to see the girl's face but she was turned away, talking to her friend with the mean eyes, as if she had no idea where her hand had gone or what it was doing, the fact that it was moving, kneading at his crotch and he felt like dough and the smell of yeast flooded his nose and made him sway on his stool. He shut his eyes.

He saw June in the kitchen, bent over the table, working a great mound of dough with the heels of both hands, a thin cloud of dust floating in the light above the table, pale flour stars, pale galaxies of flour dust revolving slowly about her.

He saw Neel coming upon him in the upstairs hall. *Like stars,* Neel said, understanding. Freddy just sitting with his arms loose at his sides, watching particles of dust in a slant of light, each tiny mote made gold as it passed through the shaft. *They're like the stars and the planets revolving in the universe,* Neel said, squatting, and there without hurry they watched the galaxy ballet. Perhaps, said Neel, the dust in the air in the upstairs hall *was* another universe, every bit as complicated and populous and full of mysterious grandeur as their own. Freddy liked it when Neel spoke to him this way. The words he didn't know had shapes and colors and he could taste them. *Populous* was white and puffed as popcorn. *Grandeur* was green velveteen, mossy on his tongue.

Perhaps, said Neel, one of those specks of dust was a planet like this one, with a little boy like Freddy on it. And to him, Freddy was a giant—so unimaginably large that he could not even be seen. *Imagine,* Neel said: *too big to be seen.*

Fred opened his eyes. There were the bottles, the anchoring rows of bottles behind the bar. He found it necessary to shift on the barstool, to give the star-girl's hand more room, to give himself more room within the confines of his pants.

He looked at her again, at the back of her head all tufted with yellow. He did not think you could do the thing she was doing absent-mindedly, or do it with your back turned, or while you were talking to someone else. But the star-girl didn't seem to be paying him any attention. She was busy singing along with the song on the jukebox now, together with her friend, leaning her mouth toward the invisible microphone her friend was pretending to hold.

Fred let his eyes close again and pressed himself into the slow heat of her hand.

"Come on," repeated Dave, "let's go." He gave Fred a poke between the shoulders.

"Ah-where?"

"Dude. Some address, I don't know. Umberto's friend."

Fred had gone on road trips with friends of Dave's before. They usually went in winter or when the weather was bad on the Cape and they knew they wouldn't get any painting or roofing work. They would drive north to Maine or New Hampshire, or west to New York, and once all the way up to Canada. Always in a rattling car, radio stations coming in and out, noisy windshield wipers and Slim Jims and Combos from rest stops. Cold water in the gas station bathrooms, cigarette smoke in the houses and apartments, nights spent sleeping on somebody's couch or floor or in the backseat. The car lighter forever getting pushed in and pulled out, its glowing orange spiral pressed to the ends of the cigarettes Dave and his friends smoked. Fred rode in back, where he'd crack a window when he started feeling sick and suck cold whistling air into his lungs until someone told him to shut it.

There was always a purpose to these trips, although Fred never usually understood exactly what. There was a destination they had to reach, something that had to get done once they arrived. *Going to see a girl* someone used to know, or to *get some papers signed*, or to *visit some property* or *check out the product* or *pick up a delivery* or *sell a pair of skis*. One time Umberto had been going to *buy a painting*. They drove all the way up to Lake Placid and the whole way there everyone kept mentioning the painting Umberto was going to buy, and then when they got there they met some people and went to a party and then to another party somewhere else and they all slept on the nubby orange carpet in someone's basement, and then the next morning it was time to head back, and in all this time Fred never saw the painting.

On the drive home he'd asked what was the painting of?

Dude, what?

Fred said, *The-ah painting you-ah, you-ah, went to buy. Like-ah, what-ah was it of?*

Umberto said, *Your mom.*

And everybody laughed. And it had been a joke. And Fred had known to smile.

The first few times Dave had to do a road trip after Fred started living with him, Fred stayed on the Cape by himself, but that hadn't gone too well, even though Dave had gotten him all set up with Campbell's and Chef Boyardee and Dinty Moore, things that would be easy to heat in a pot on the stove. The first time, Fred hadn't realized the gas was on even though the burner wasn't lit and when Dave came home he kept saying *Jesus Christ, Jesus Christ, can't you smell that?* running around opening all the windows and both doors, saying *Jesus Fuck, the whole place could have blown. Hell yeah, I'm mad*, he'd said when Fred asked if he was mad.

The other time Fred stayed on the Cape alone, Dave went out and got Hot Pockets and Easy Mac and frozen pizza and they made a plan that Fred would just use the microwave and not even touch the stove, but for some reason Fred got the feeling that the gas had been left on; he kept checking the knobs on the stove but still he was scared, he kept thinking of Dave saying the whole place could blow, and his body started shaking so bad he had to run out of the house and not go back inside without Dave, which meant he had spent two whole days out in the cold, walking around the empty town with no tourists, waiting for Dave to return; two whole nights in the backyard wrapped up in a drop cloth he found in the shed, shaking with cold. The third day some cops and EMTs came to Dave's house and found him huddled on the gravel. They said they'd gotten a call from a neighbor and they talked to Fred and checked out the house and told him it was safe to go inside, but he still wouldn't go in, so they wound up calling Dave, somehow they got his cell number—Fred didn't know it—and Dave had to come back early from his trip. *Hell yeah, I'm mad*, he'd said again that second time.

After that Dave said it was easier for Fred to come along on these road trips. Sometimes Fred had to wait in the car, especially when they were meeting someone somebody had business with. Fred figured that was probably what was going to happen now in Perdu. They would leave this bar that his eyes and nose and ears had gotten used to, and get back in the car and drive to some house on a dark road or some apartment complex with spray paint on the doors, and then Dave and Umberto would go inside and Fred would have to wait in the car, and it would be for a long time, he was pretty sure, and without the radio to keep him company, because Dave didn't keep the keys in the ignition anymore since that time Fred had gotten tired of waiting and taken the car for a drive.

"No," said Fred.

"What?"

"I-ah, I'll ah-stay."

"You can't stay," Dave began, putting a hand on Fred's shoulder, pulling at his arm. But Fred knew how to make himself heavy on the stool, and then he heard the star-girl say, "Aw, Dave, let him stay, he's having fun," and Umberto say, "C'mon," looking at Dave with eyes flat as coins, jerking his head toward the door, and the star-girl say, "What's the matter, you jealous? 'Cause you *know* I'll take good care of him." Then the mean-eyed girl turned out to be crying, and Umberto and the other girl were already walking toward the exit, Umberto with both hands on her bottom, and Dave was sighing and the star-girl was saying, "Go. You have your fun, let us have ours. He can crash at our place tonight."

Dave said, "What do you want to do, Buddy? You sure you don't want to come with me?"

"Ah," said Fred. "Ah . . ."

"He's fine," said the star-girl. "Aren't you, Sailor?" Flashing her dimple, removing her hand from between his legs.

"Ah . . ."

"Just go," said the other girl, sniffing. Her hair hung over her face and she was playing with a straw wrapper. Dave hesitated. Suddenly she turned and shoved his chest with both hands, hoarsely shouting, "Fucking *leave*."

Dave went.

THAT NIGHT FRED STAYED with the star-girl. She said her name was Loreen Ferebee. Her bed was a mattress on the floor.

"When-ah, when are they coming back?" Fred asked when she turned out the light.

"Who?"

"Ah-Dave. And-ah Umberto."

She whispered, "Fuck if I know, Sailor," and climbed on top of him. Beginning to move, she whispered, "Fuck if I care."

Later she rolled away, sat on the edge of the mattress and said, "Huh." Shaking a cigarette out of its package, she looked at him sideways. "You ever been with a woman?"

That was one of those questions that might be a riddle, so he thought awhile, but he couldn't figure it out. "Yeah."

She shrugged and smoked. "You got nice equipment, I'll give you that." She smoked a little longer, then stubbed it out and went to sleep.

In the morning the sky was no color, and rain was tapping against the box fan that sat in the window. He was lying on a mattress on the floor. The star-girl was asleep beside him. He couldn't remember her name. He knew she told him the night before, but it always took him a while to remember a new person's name. He didn't know what he was supposed to do, if anyone would be mad if he got up and walked around or left, so he lay there and waited. He had to pee, but he held it. He looked around from where he lay. On a dresser across from the bed there were glasses and bottles and an ashtray and a framed picture of a boy with dark hair and big front teeth. There was a TV on the floor, and a chair, and everywhere else all over the room clothes slumped in piles like exhausted children. He turned and watched the star-girl sleep. He saw she was older than he'd realized in the bar, not really a girl. And her hair was no longer star-like. It lay squashed against her head, limp and dark at the roots. And it didn't smell like raisin cookies. Just smoke.

Three

BESIDES WHAT HE WAS WEARING, this is what he'd brought with him from the Cape, all zipped into his orange knapsack:

- extra pair of underpants
- extra shirt
- extra pair of socks
- toothbrush
- toothpaste
- razor
- *The Little Prince*
- seventeen single-serve packets of grape jelly and eleven single-serve packets of strawberry jelly and two single-serve packets of syrup collected from diners
- Neel's pocketknife with the toothpick missing
- June's map of St. Lawrence, Criterion and Franklin counties

He didn't bring extra pants or deodorant, because he'd forgotten to, and he didn't bring the rest of his clothes or any of his other things like the box that held the letters June had written him when she was still alive, and the rest of her maps, and the pictures of their family, June and Neel and Ava and Fred, at Batter Hollow where he had grown up. He didn't pack any of these things because he hadn't known he wasn't going to return to the Cape. If he'd known he wasn't going back he would have brought them, and also the notebook where he wrote down important things, for instance important telephone numbers, for instance Dave's and Ava's.

But it turned out not to matter what he'd packed and what he'd forgotten, because he didn't have any of it, because the orange knapsack was still in the backseat of Dave's car, and Dave and Umberto didn't come back the morning after they left the bar, and they didn't come back all the next day. Or the next night, either. During this time it rained steadily and Fred stayed inside the apartment with the star-girl (*What's your-ah, name again? Oh my God, for the hundredth time, Loreen Ferebee, want me to write it down?*) and the other girl, the one with the bruise-colored eyes. Her name was Tonya or Tee and she spent a lot of time walking loudly around the apartment, her bare heels banging the floor, sending shivers through the wood.

The long, narrow apartment was on the ground floor of a house that backed up on the mill river. It was dim inside, the air gray and almost grainy, and it smelled like mice and like milk that has turned. It was split unevenly into two rooms: a big one with a mini-kitchen and a beanbag chair and a bed and a table with folding chairs and a TV, and a small one with a dresser and a TV and a mattress on the floor. The small one was where Loreen slept. Each room had one window. The big room's window looked out the front, onto a street of attached houses. The small room's window looked onto a row of metal garbage cans chained to an aluminum fence. Through the links in the fence you could see the narrow river, and the window fan blew in a breeze that smelled like boiled cabbage and feet. When Fred said, "Pee-yoo," and pinched his nose, Loreen said, "Paper mill. They shut it a few years back, but the river still stinks."

Even though the apartment had only two rooms, Tonya or Tee paced it like she was waiting for something to happen. Like she was waiting for someone to burst through the door. Fred had the feeling if someone did she'd punch them in the face. She passed back and forth through the skinny archway that connected the rooms. This archway had no door, only bare hinges and long strings of red plastic beads hanging down, and every time she passed through it, the beads would spatter and rattle. Every now and then Tonya or Tee would take a rest and sit down, only to spring up suddenly and start pacing again. "That *bitch*," she would say, suddenly backhanding the beads and appearing in Loreen's room. Or else she would say, "That *ass*hole."

"I know," Loreen would answer calmly. "She is a bitch." Sitting on the floor like she liked to do, with her eyes closed and knees pressed out like butterfly wings, the bottoms of her bare feet touching. She'd take in a long, slow breath and let out a long, slow breath, as if nothing mattered. Nothing in the world. Her hands palm-up on her knees. "He is an asshole."

The first time they had this exchange, Fred thought it was a joke so he said, "Ha ha." But Tonya or Tee whipped around and glared at him and he could see it wasn't a joke. He swung his gaze away and bobbed his head: little bounces, very fast, so the rainy window danced on the wall. Then—he was relieved—the crack of her heels on the floor as she spun herself around again; the clamor and crash of beads as she propelled herself back into the larger room. Fred began to hunch his shoulders near his ears whenever she veered close, whenever she said, "I can't believe they *did* that!" the "did" so sharp he saw it snagging, ripping her throat. He tried not to look directly at her. Once he did by accident and she caught him. Her heavy lids drooped even lower, and her eyes were like the holes of guns. "What is. Your fuck. Ing problem. Retard."

He ducked his head, clasped his hands. His heart thudded and his breath went shallow. *Here is the church, here is the steeple,* he told himself, hearing June's voice, seeing June's hands as he put his own two pointers together and made them into the steeple, until at last Tonya or Tee moved away again.

Once she punched the wall behind him. Once she threw an ashtray in his general direction and the contents went flying, the bent stubs of cigarettes skittering across the floor, the ashes ghosting up into the air and then settling back down, coating Fred's tongue, stinging Fred's eyes.

"Take a chill," Loreen said when that happened, and this time her voice did not have a nothing-matters lilt. It was flat and hard. She had been painting her toenails and now she looked up and pointed the tiny brush at Tonya or Tee, and a blue vein like a river on a map stood out on her neck.

For a moment everything froze: the girls, the TV, the rain outside, the blades of the window fan. Fred tried to stay frozen, too, to hide in the stillness, but an invisible siren was blaring closer and closer until it was right inside his head and he could not help clapping his hands over his ears.

Then Tonya or Tee yanked a raincoat off the back of a folding chair. "Fine. But he's not staying," she said, jerking her chin toward Fred. "I want him gone. And if those assholes don't show up with my shit by tomorrow, you're paying me back." And she pushed out into the noisy downpour, letting the door swing shut with a smack.

When she came back hours later she was holding a sopping paper bag and clown spikes blackened the skin under her eyes. It was dark by then and Fred cowered because she'd said he had to be gone and he was not gone. But she didn't say anything about finding him there. She didn't even look at him. She just climbed onto the mattress where Loreen and Fred were watching TV and she put her head on Loreen's shoulder. "How can he fucking like that bitch," she said, tipping the bottle whose lip poked from the top of the bag and drinking. "How can he fucking like her better than me."

"Shh," said Loreen, without taking her eyes off the TV. She put one arm around Tonya or Tee and with the other hand took the paper bag and tipped it toward her own mouth.

Fred inched away to the far corner of the mattress, where, leaning against the wall, he wrapped his arms around his drawn-up knees. He watched the huddled girls and the cold blue light of the TV flickering over them like rain and he felt something but he didn't know what. Like a metal machine was cranking inside his chest, its handle turning and turning and he couldn't make it stop.

THE WHOLE TIME he was at their apartment, this is what Fred did:

- eat cereal
- watch TV
- sleep
- watch the drips collect along a seam near where the ceiling met the wall and then drop down onto a rolled-up towel that Loreen had put under it
- try to tell if the drops were falling in any pattern he could measure by counting the seconds between them
- decide that they were not
- try not to look at Tonya or Tee

- look out the front window and try to see Dave's car
- count how many cars drove by in an hour: 23

On the second morning Fred again woke first. For a long time he just lay there, not moving, like he had the day before. He looked at the box fan and the dresser and the glasses and the clothes and the framed picture of the boy and now they were all a little familiar. He did an experiment of lying very still, almost frozen, to see if time would speed up and then maybe the next time he moved Dave would already be walking in the door, coming to take him back to the Cape.

He lay as motionless as possible but time didn't speed up. Maybe because he still had to breathe, and his heart beat no matter what.

The sky was no color again this morning but the rain had stopped and the window fan blew warm, sour-smelling air around the room. Then remembering what had happened the night before, he slid his thumb into his mouth.

During the night Loreen had climbed on top of him again. This time she had whispered instructions and placed his hands where she wanted them to be, and moved his hands the way she wanted them to move, and one time, surprising him with her quick strength, she rolled both their bodies over together so she was under him. She showed him what she wanted him to do and doing it was not hard but it made him breathe loudly and it also loosed up other noises from his throat, which made her whisper, "Shh . . . be quiet . . . come on, shut up . . . you'll wake her . . ." and he tried to be quiet both because he didn't like the noises he was making and because he didn't want Tonya or Tee to wake up. When the noises came out of him anyway, Loreen had pressed her small hand over his mouth and her fingers were like chicken bones, and he had the thought of sucking the meat off them, like the wings in the bar that had been covered with not-too-spicy orange sauce, and he thought of Dave, how Dave had come up behind his barstool and lurched forward and rocked back and said, *You sure you don't want to come?*

You sure? Had he been sure? Who knew. Sure or not, he hadn't come. He'd stayed in the bar with the girls and gone home with the girls and Dave hadn't come back and now he was here on this mattress on the floor in this sour-smelling apartment in this town with the blue thread running through it on the map and without his orange knapsack and Neel had a word for that: *consequences. Let him live,* Neel's voice came thundering into his head, as if he were here somewhere nearby, *with the consequences of his actions.*

And if he doesn't understand? If he doesn't get what those consequences will be? That was June. Her voice coming from the next room. Because now he is Freddy, with the moon in his window and his thumb in his mouth, drinking in the sounds that sift through the wall between his bedroom and his parents', and if he doesn't understand exactly what they are saying, he does know how to listen for clues that they are talking about him. And it gives him a flutter when he hears his own name: *Freddy,* says June—so they *are* talking about him. He rocks himself from side to side and slurps at his wrinkled thumb, listening for all the *he*s and *him*s that follow, each one sending a little gush of heat through his body. He is in two places at once! Here in his small captain's bed in the darkness, and also in their mouths on the other side of the wall. He is in their conversation, cupped by their voices, cradled at the center of their thoughts.

Nature teaches all children what suffering and pain are. Neel again. *If we let it. Give him the opportunity to experience the consequences and he will learn.*

What if he doesn't? June. *What if he can't?*

Risks are inseparable from life.

Stop quoting at me, Neel. I'm trying to have a conversation. With you, not a dead philosopher. Who managed to be very certain of his hypothetical children. What is it? "School them in hardship—"

School them to *hardship. Actually, "School them to the hardships they will one day have to endure. Harden their bodies to the changes of seasons, climates, and elements, as well as to hunger, thirst, and fatigue; dip them in the waters of the Styx."*

The Styx, Neel. Do you hear yourself? He's not your experiment, your test case. He's your son.

And Freddy, swaddled in blue shadow and watery moonlight, tucks his thumb neater into the warm purse of his mouth and sucks and drifts, content to float away on the raft of those words: *he's your son.*

But there is too much drift. Dave has drifted away, in his rattling old car, along with Fred's orange knapsack, and *The Little Prince,* and June's maps and Neel's pocketknife and all the single-serve packets of jelly and syrup, and he hasn't come back, and that is called consequences, and *Hey Sailor, where'd you go?* this was consequences, too: Loreen putting her hand on his cheek now and making it so his face looked back at her; Loreen rising up, arching forward and rocking back, pressing her small fingers against his mouth, pushing his lips hard against his teeth, slipping her fingers between his lips and inside his teeth for him to suck and taste and they weren't like chicken wings but like his thumb, salty and then wet and slick and faintly sweet with his own saliva; Loreen whispering *shh* even as her own breathing became raspier, and then she let out a little string of moans and their sounds spilled loose together; and their slippery skin slid between them; and the warm paper-mill-smelling air blew in through the window, with bits of wetness getting sucked between the fan blades so a spray of sliced-up rain speckled his back, until there came between them a shuddery collision in the windy dark hot small room.

After a minute she sat up and lit a cigarette.

That's more like it, Sailor. Blowing out the match. *That's what I'm talking about.*

ON THIS SECOND MORNING, he lay there sucking his thumb while all the pieces of the night washed over him, and then all the pieces of the day before and the night before that and the day before that and of June's yellow face and Neel's pocketknife and the bar with its bottle skyline and the lost jelly and syrup and maps and dust motes and the tiny wet stars of rain prickling his back. Finally he had to move, to pee, and he got up and did. At the far end of the front room, he saw the bed where Tonya or Tee slept was empty. He was relieved. She must have gone out again in the night. He helped himself to some Cap'n Crunch, which he could do because it was the second morning and he knew where it was kept and also that he was allowed to have some. The milk carton had been put back in the fridge empty.

He ate the dry cereal with a spoon, standing up, looking past the fan blades out the window. No one was around. The sky was very pale, although in the far distance there began to be some colored streaks. He looked at the chain-link fence and the clotheslines and the electrical wires and the flat, brown mill river, until all those long, straight lines began to make him feel dizzy and anxious, and he turned around and continued eating with the cluttered dresser as a table. First he had to push aside some glasses and a bra and an ashtray to make room for his bowl. Then he ate while studying up close the picture of the boy with the dark floppy hair and the big front teeth. The boy looked him right in the eye, smiling, not a big smile, just a chink. Like he knew a joke.

"What time is it?" asked Loreen, her voice froggy. "Jesus, Sailor, you always get up this early?"

"Ah-no." Fred wondered if his crunching had woken her. Cap'n Crunch without milk was pretty loud.

Loreen got up and went to the bathroom. Through the open door he could hear her peeing. Then he could hear the toilet flushing. It flushed a long time without stopping. Then he could hear the scrape of the toilet tank lid being taken off and the flushing stop and the scrape of the lid going back on. She shuffled back into the bedroom, sat on the mattress, picked up a bottle of cola that was on the floor and took a swallow.

"Who-ah," he said, "who-ah's that boy?" Holding the picture out to her.

"Put it back. That's Jimmy. My kid."

He put it back. "How come-ah, how come I never ah-saw him?"

She looked at him a long minute. Her hair was squashed flat on one side, sticking out on the other. She shrugged. "Staying with my folks right now." She searched with her hand for something in the sheets and found it: her little green lighter. "Anyway, you should be worrying about things that concern you. You know what day this is?"

"Ah-no."

"Sunday. Your asshole buddies took our money Friday. Now it's Sunday." She ran her thumb over the ridged metal wheel and made a flame lick out. Then she let it go. She did this again several times, making little tongues of flame and killing them. He began to feel dizzy and anxious again. She gave a little laugh through her nose. "Maybe you're supposed to be our collateral."

He didn't know what collateral meant but it seemed like she was mad now, too, like Tonya or Tee, because she had said asshole, and she was looking at him as if she'd just now noticed something bad about him. "What-ah, what do you mean?"

She gave another laugh, this one like a crumb had gotten stuck in her throat. "Collateral damage, more like." She leaned over and picked up the plastic tube thing she kept by her bed. She held her lighter to the little metal cup piece and stuck her whole mouth into the tube and sucked up thick white smoke. The water in the tube made a gurgling noise. She lifted her face and said in a voice that was like a skinny tunnel, "Ayuh. They must of sailed without you," before letting out her breath in a too-sweet fog.

The Cape had sailboats. Did she mean Dave had gone back to the Cape?

You always liked the Cape. You always liked the ocean. June told him so, after her hair had all gone to wisps and her face lay yellow on the pillow.

"Well, you can't stay here, that's for sure." Loreen gurgled into the tube and then released another plume of sticky smoke. "Even if you do have your *charms*."

Later she said she was going out. She went in the bathroom and stayed there for a while and when she came out she looked again like she had that night in the bar: her hair was star-shaped, sticking out around her face in pale, stiffened tufts. She wore a black leather cord around her throat with a teardrop sparkle hanging from it and a denim dress that came to the top of her thighs. "Goin' to see a man about a dog," she said, looking at herself in the mirror. Then she slung a purse over her shoulder and left.

Fred wondered if he was supposed to leave now. He curled up on her mattress and wrapped his arms around his knees and hoped Tonya or Tee wouldn't come in. He wished he had his notebook with Dave's phone number in it, and Ava's. He wished he had June's letters and her maps. He wished he could see June, even if her face was yellow on the pillow and she didn't smell like June. Even if her eyes wouldn't stay open long.

A sharp bang shook the whole house. Fred's body startled. He braced himself. What would come next? Another bang? Someone charging through the door? He waited, frightened, listening for pounding footsteps, furious voices, battering fists, but there was nothing. Only the drone of a car engine, dwindling.

A bird, Fred soothed himself, curling his body tighter. Only a bird. And saw himself sitting at the kitchen table in the Office with Neel and June and Ava, a dark hurtling shape cracking against the window beside them. All of them had turned to look and there was nothing, only the sassafras tree and the eggshell sky.

And then June, realizing what had happened, made a sad sound with her tongue. "A bird."

"A bird what?" said Ava.

Neel said, "Think."

Ava said, "What are you talking about?"

But Freddy knew! It was exciting and funny, because so often he didn't know things that other people did. But he had understood the hurtling motion, the thud of the small body stopped by glass, even before June said *a bird*, and he flapped his hands at the wrists and laughed. He knew what a bird felt like, too, because he had held one in the woods, a small bird he found on the ground with no feathers and purple soft skin and a translucent beak. He'd built it a nest of grass and leaves, and placed a berry beside it. Humans shouldn't eat berries they found in the woods because they might be poisonous, but the same berries that could kill a person could be good for a bird. Later when he'd come back to see how the bird was doing, the berry was uneaten and a flea was crawling across its eye.

Fred must have fallen asleep because the next thing he knew he was waking stiff and pasty-mouthed in the hot gray box of a room. Loreen was standing above him, gleaming with sweat, and she dropped something heavy on the floor beside the mattress. "Looks like I was right. You've been ditched."

He looked over the edge of the mattress. His orange knapsack.

"It was on the doorstep." She shrugged. "Along with, thank God, Tonya's shit." She set the other thing she'd been holding, a small package wrapped in brown paper and string, on top of the TV. Picking her way across the mattress in her platform sandals, she positioned herself in front of the window fan and plucked at the front of her denim dress, trying to let the breeze go down her neck, but it was too tight. Giving up, she braced her palms against the window and leaned into the fan, head tilted back, eyes closed, her sticky bright throat curved forward like a bent pipe. Fred lifted the knapsack onto the bed and recalled the sound he'd heard after the scary bang: the low whine of an engine and the whoosh of tires fading down the street.

"Dave-ah left it?"

"Apparently. It's yours, right?"

"Ah-yeah."

"Left it, left you." She gave a little snort. "You're lucky, though, Sailor. Lucky I like you." Her eyes still closed, she tilted her head this way and that before the heavy blades of the fan. The stiffened spikes of her hair remained immobile in the breeze. "Found you a place to crash."

Four

HE SAW THE BOY through the toaster-sized window in the bathroom of the garage apartment. Some speck of movement caught Fred's eye as he stood groggily in front of the toilet, and he turned to see someone climbing on a pile of car parts. At first Fred couldn't tell it was a person. He thought it might be a scavenging dog or even a coyote—he'd spotted these, along the rim of the soybean field out back, a few times while walking in the still-misty morning or as the light drained from the evening sky—but when he looked more closely he saw that it was a boy on all fours, using his hands to help him scrabble up on top of a rust-flowered hood. It was barely past dawn. The sky was milk blue. Late September, as far as he could guess. Middays still got hot, but the evenings were getting cold and the morning air could be stiff with chill.

The boy, in a short-sleeved shirt and jeans, continued his nimble, almost delicate climb over disembodied fenders and doors and grilles. Fred thought he could see, through the bleary glass, feathers of breath coming from the boy's mouth. Every now and then he'd stop, pick something up, and hurl it toward the stand of trees that huddled thinly along the rear edge of the auto salvage yard.

Fred had been staying in the garage apartment a few weeks already by then. This was the place Loreen had found for him to stay. Until Dave came back. That's what Fred said, when she told him he could stay there: *Until-ah Dave comes-ah back.*

"Sure," she said, "whatever you say." She led him up the metal staircase that clung dubiously to the outside of the building and pushed open the unlocked door. "Ta-da. Not bad, huh, Sailor?"

He followed her. It was dark inside. She was speeded-up that day, walking fast and talking fast and cracking her spearmint gum. "You're totally lucky because Ed, who was here for like ever, took off a little while ago and my dad hasn't had any luck replacing him. He says if you keep an eye on the place and haul trash once a week, you can stay until he finds a paying tenant, which means forever because come on, no one's going to rent this place. I mean, it's nice though, isn't it?"

Even after she switched on the light, the apartment had a murky, underground feel, with its dark paneling and swamp-green carpet. A long plaid couch hugged the opposite wall. With its sagging cushions, it looked like a mouth hanging open. Beside it was a door, taken off its hinges and set flat on crates. Doorknobs still stuck out of it, one above, one below. At the back of the apartment was a single window, long and narrow like in a camper, and a sticky band of sunlight fell across a kitchenette: sink, counter, hot plate, mini-fridge. Fred recognized the smell of Borax from Dave's bungalow on the Cape, and layered over that was the half-sweet smell of damp particleboard.

"Whatcha think, Sailor?" Showing her gum, a skinny neon-green wad imprinted with tooth marks.

What did he think?

You always liked the Cape. June had said that, reaching forward to touch his knee.

Fred thought of the Cape, its beach plums and scotch broom and salt sting in his lungs; the quick-vanishing footprints of piping plovers as they ran along the wet strand; Dave's house with its swollen moldings and grains of sand caught between the floorboards and warped windowpanes with tiny bubbles trapped in the glass; the ocean always in the distance, muscular and tossing.

There was no ocean here. Even the skinny, snaking mill river seemed far from this room above the auto salvage yard. They'd walked a long way to get here from the place Loreen shared with Tonya or Tee. Fred wasn't sure he'd even know his way back.

"Well?" she said, doing a twirl with her palms held up to the ceiling.

"S'ah . . ."

"I know, I know. You're like, how'm I ever going to *thank* this girl? Well, don't you worry about that, Sailor. I got some ideas. Let's just say I got that one covered." And with a laugh and another flash of her bright green gum, she stepped right up close and stuck one of her small hands quick down the back of his pants.

The first few weeks she came over often, never at predictable times, never for more or less than a few hours, always leaving him exhausted and with some new minor scrape or bruise. On the first visit she showed him how the couch could open up into a bed and it had stayed in that position since. Each time she came she'd say, "Brought you a present," and then take out an object from her bag: a candle in a jar that smelled like pineapple when it burned, a tube of Vaseline, a pair of furry pink handcuffs, a black satin eye mask. One time she brought a razor and shaving cream, but instead of letting him use these on the beard that had grown thick over the past several weeks, she insisted on shaving his legs, straddling his waist as he lay back and bending forward over his shins. Another time she flopped on her stomach diagonally across the couch-bed and went through his wallet, taking out his driver's license (*Oh my God, you look like Lurch*), his old Freyburg Public Library card (*This is so cute it makes me cry*), the business cards he'd picked up in diners from Lake George to White River Junction (*You got a fetish?*), and the whole wad of paper money that was everything he'd earned that summer painting houses with Dave (*Who'd a thunk?*). She put everything back except the money (*So I can bring you food*), and the next time she came she did bring him groceries, which she presented to him one at a time, pulling each item out of the bag with eye-rolling flourish, as if she herself were joyfully amazed to discover its contents: milk, Cap'n Crunch (*I know you like this stuff*), frozen pizzas, frozen chicken nuggets, canned peaches, bread, peanut butter, toilet paper and a case of Genny Light (*I bet no one's ever treated you this good, huh, Sailor?*).

"Ah-thank you," he said.

But most of the time he was alone. Fred had never lived alone. All the travels he'd done in the past had been supervised by someone his parents had known—friends, former students, friends of former students—and always before, in each new place, he'd been expected to do some kind of work: fill bait bags for the lobster pots, haul buckets of sap to the sugarhouse, clean out gutted fish at the cannery, stack baled hay on the loading dock, even babysit, sort of, which was maybe the best job he'd ever had. It wasn't real *baby*sitting, though. Maybe it wasn't even a real job. He wasn't sure because they'd never given him money and they'd brought him home early. Usually he didn't like to think about it, but now in these days when he was so much alone, he found his mind wandering to the time he'd accompanied a former Batter Hollow family to the Magdalen Islands as a companion for their son. Thor had been a skinny twelve-year-old with the lightest eyes Fred ever saw and hair like dandelion fluff and a small, pale mouth.

Thor was the second person he'd ever met who reminded him of the Little Prince.

"I really don't know what to do about him this summer," Fred had overheard Thor's mother telling June. This was before the trip, before anyone had the idea of Fred going along. Thor's mother taught college, and so did Thor's father, and they looked like brother and sister because they were both tall, sandy-colored people with long, narrow faces. The mother lowered her voice a little. "He has no friends, really. No one we could ask to come along. He's too old for a sitter, but we can't just send him off by himself, and of course Roger and I both need to spend a good part of each day writing."

The two women had been sitting at the picnic table behind the Office, pitting cherries for pie, and Fred could hear them because he'd been lying on the roof outside his bedroom window, a thing Neel and June had asked him not to do because it was dangerous and also the slates were fragile. But he could not help it: the feeling he got, lying on top of the house with his body at that steep angle and the clouds like pieces of cotton scudding close to his face was so intensely like the feeling he used to get when he played in the woods with Ava and Kitty and they'd make him lie on the stone slab and stretch a silk above his head and then let it go, let it float down slowly, *Lie still, Freddy, or we'll have to tie you*, and the colored square would grow larger and larger as it neared, finally blotting out the world as it settled over his face, burying his eyes and nose and mouth in soft, sunlit color.

"Freddy's been going off by himself for years," offered June. "Since he was younger than Thor is now."

There followed a silence. Then June spoke in a rush, and Fred could feel her blush mottling his own neck. "Not to compare—I'm not saying Thor ... well, I just meant, if Freddy could handle going off on—"

"No, that's all right," said Thor's mother. She trilled a little laugh. "I take no offense."

There followed another silence. He could hear them pitting the cherries, tossing the fruit in one bowl, the pits in another.

It was Thor's mother who broke this silence, her voice scurrying to mend. "What you and Neel have done," she began. "I mean, who doesn't admire ... You don't just talk the talk—so many people spout principles. You've done such an incredible job of letting him"—she gave a laugh—"be!"

Fred felt dizzy on the sun-baked slates, as if the roof had pitched itself steeper. He closed his eyes and held tight, pressing his fingertips against the crumble-toothed edges.

"Well," said June.

Then nothing for a bit. Just the sound of cherries and their pits.

Thor's mother said, "A lot of families would've sent him somewhere."

June did not reply.

"Not that you and Neel ever ... it's just admirable, what you've done."

Still nothing from June.

"I don't know that Roger and I could've managed ..."

Be quiet. Fred could feel June think it, sharp as the blade she slid into the cherry.

"The toll it must take on other ... well, everything else."

Be quiet! It was Fred's own thought now, surging through his body straight down to his feet, which kicked, his heels landing hard against the slates. Bits of shingle skittered down the roof, bounced over the gutter, rained onto the lawn.

Thor's mother let out a cry.

"Fred!" said June, sharper than her knife. She stood and turned in a single motion toward where he lay on the roof.

"I had no idea he was there!" Thor's mother pressed a hand against her heart.

Fred, shinnying down toward his open window, set more flecks of tile spattering noisily down.

"Oh, Frederick Robbins," said June. He scrambled over the sill and fell into the cool shadow of his bedroom. When he peered back around the curtain he saw her still on her feet, gazing up at his window, and was that a smile tucked in the corner of her mouth?

Somehow this had all led to (or anyway not prevented) Fred's accompanying Thor's family on their trip to the Magdalens for six weeks that summer. The entire time Thor's mother addressed Fred in a slow, loud voice with oddly formal precision and bestowed on him endless little pinched smiles that made a groove appear between her eyebrows. But Thor's father treated him easily, almost offhandedly, and the two boys—the twelve-year-old and the twenty-three-year-old—were given leave to spend the greater part of most days out-of-doors, exploring, so long as Thor wore his protective clothing: long-sleeved shirts and pants of special lightweight fabric that blocked the sun's harmful rays, and a khaki hat with a wide brim all around, because his skin was so sensitive to burning. "It's very, very important he wears his hat," Mrs. Thor told Fred (unsure what he was supposed to call Thor's parents, Fred called them nothing, but thought of them as Mr. and Mrs. Thor). "You understand, right? I cannot stress it enough."

They had suited each other, Fred and Thor, neither having much use for conversation, both preferring to be outdoors rather than in, both content to walk without talking for hours on end. Fred helped Thor make a good bow and arrow with Neel's pocketknife, and together they used the compass Thor's father lent them to navigate daylong hikes, on which they explored wind-battered bluffs and dank beach caves and trails of crumbly red sandstone. Sometimes they'd invent games—races, scavenger hunts—or dare each other to jump, to climb, to roll, to balance, or make up obstacle courses and then take turns navigating them backward, or with eyes shut, or with eyes shut and both hands clasped behind their backs.

When they got hungry they'd open Fred's orange knapsack and eat the butter and salami sandwiches and small hard plums and Pal-o-Mine candy bars Mr. and Mrs. Thor had packed. When they got tired they'd lie down wherever they were and drink in the scrubbed landscape, spread thickly with buttercups that shone like wet paint, and studded in the distance with figures of cows, dainty as toys. And always beyond them, in whichever direction they looked, the sea and sky running through their endless repertoire of blue.

They did not get bored.

Mrs. Thor insisted on Thor spending part of each day doing his summer reading, which consisted of three books his school assigned to all entering seventh-graders. Mr. Thor suggested they take a book with them on their excursions, but when it became clear, after a few days, that Thor had progressed no more than a page, Mrs. Thor made a rule that he had to spend two hours each afternoon back in the little gray chalet they were renting on Havre-Aubert.

During those hours, Fred was unhappy. After so many years of spending so much time alone and never once wanting for companionship or direction, he encountered for the first time unwelcome idleness. He couldn't sit inside with Thor, in the bland silence of other people's reading and writing—Mr. and Mrs. Thor each in their respective rooms, bent over stacks of books and loose papers, and Thor in the small living room curled on the couch, motionless except for the turning of pages and the minuscule movements of his lips as he read. Thor offered Fred one of his other books, but after a sentence or two the printed words and their meanings seemed to part ways and the object to become a taunting, dumb thing, inert on his knees.

He would wander outdoors then, into the world in which he'd always felt at home, with its indifferent warmth and its equally indifferent harshness, its ceaseless, ceaselessly amazing changes. It didn't care whether it disappointed or delighted you. It didn't care whether it held or harmed you. Neither did it care if you stroked it or pounded it, gouged it with your fingers, broke off bits of it and flung them as hard as you could. Everything was part of the world, him included. He never didn't fit when he was outdoors, never didn't belong. There was always somewhere to go in the world, always something to do, if only walk, if only rest with his back against a tree. If only lie with his ear pressed to the earth and listen to the faint sounds inside it: insects crawling, roots extending, subterranean moisture dripping. How could he ever be lonely in this world? How could he ever be bored?

But that summer in the Magdalens, on the island of Havre-Aubert, during those hours of the afternoon designated for reading, he did feel lonely and he did feel bored. It was the first time he'd ever truly known either of those states, and it was a result of his having experienced something else for the first time: a friend. Sometimes by the time Thor put aside his book and came outdoors, Fred was so eager to see him he'd pick him up around the middle and spin him around.

In the rented chalet, Fred and Thor shared a bedroom with a bunk bed, Fred on the bottom and Thor on top. They didn't talk in bed, not because they weren't allowed but because neither of them was a conversationalist. But sometimes they'd rap messages to each other with their knuckles through the bedpost. Thor tried teaching Fred Morse code, but it made Fred's forehead hurt to practice it (the effort of trying to bind rhythms to meaning when all they wanted to do was shimmy free), so they sent nonsense messages to each other instead:

dit da da dit dit
da dit da dit da dit dit dit dit

Whole conversations they'd have this way, and Fred profited more from these nighttime knockings than from any spoken conversation he'd ever had. They contained their own private jokes, long spells of syncopated intensity, and confessions of nameless melancholy that echoed long after Thor had fallen asleep. Lying there in the narrow bedroom with the moon slopping its light through the window and Thor's breath falling gentle as snowflakes down over him, Fred knew for the first time the gladness of sharing wordless agreement with a kindred spirit.

Never would he have wished what happened the fourth week of their stay, or maybe the fifth—at any rate the last, because they'd had to leave almost right away then, ahead of schedule, so that Thor could see a specialist back in Boston where the Thors lived. Never would he have allowed to happen what Mrs. Thor thought was all his fault (never mind that she did not say this aloud; it was there in her voice, in the terse control with which she addressed him after that).

He had come, Fred, over the wind-scrubbed hill with its sweeping silvery grasses and down the footpath to the back door of the chalet with Thor in his arms; Thor with his own arms still behind his back, bound at the wrists; Thor white with pain (strange that his skin could get any whiter) but uncomplaining except for occasional keening sounds that issued thinly from his tight mouth as Fred carried him from the place where he had fallen all the way back to the rented chalet. He didn't know how far he walked, only that his back ached and his legs felt watery and the sun had slid lower in the sky before they crested the hill and the back of the little gray chalet came into view. Only that by the time he reached the back door, his shirt, even with the strong, drying wind, was soaked through with sweat.

He did not have a hand free for the doorknob, so he thumped it with his foot. Mrs. Thor came rather quickly and opened the door and cried, "Roger! Roger!" and went to lift Thor from Fred's arms, but Thor gave a kind of scream that made her freeze. Instead she led them with a weird catch-step, almost skipping, to the couch, where Thor had earlier that day left his summer reading book splayed, as his mother had more than once scolded him about, facedown. Now whisking the book away, she directed Fred to set him down—"Careful! Careful!"—and flew to position herself between them, so that Fred stumbled backward a little.

They had been playing one of their dare games. It had been Thor's turn. The dare was to walk twelve paces back, parallel to the edge of a sandstone cliff, without looking. To prevent peeking, he'd worn a red bandanna knotted around his eyes. To make balancing harder, he'd worn a blue bandanna knotted around his wrists behind his back. The bandannas were Thor's, part of his sun protection gear. The idea to use them as binding was Fred's, but Thor had eagerly agreed. He'd even asked Fred to tie the knots for him.

As Thor took his backward paces, he strayed from his parallel path, veering nearer and nearer to the line where cliff met sky. Fred, his stomach fizzing with excitement, had exclaimed, "Ah-whoa... ah-whoop!" with every step Thor took, flapping his hands in a kind of projected ecstasy, for when it had been his own turn just minutes earlier, the dizziness of stepping backward, blind and buffeted by the stinging salt wind and the rushing sound of the sea below, had been a glory to him.

Thor, sightless, threw his head back, the sun irradiating his translucent nimbus of hair, and let out his own loonish chortle at the sound of Fred's whoas and whoops.

Then he disappeared.

Astonishment beat wings inside Fred's rib cage. He gasped for air. He gasped again. He felt not fright but the shock of the sublime. In that single, shining, ruthless instant life was no less good, no less strange, no less fierce, no less fine, no less clear, no less impenetrable than it had been the instant before.

Was this what made Fred hateful?

That Mrs. Thor found him hateful—had found him hateful all along—seemed clear to him now.

Not that he tried to describe this feeling or even tell this part of the story to Mrs. Thor back at the chalet as she grabbed a kitchen knife and cut through the bandanna that bound Thor's wrists, nor when she flung the ruined cloth to the floor and handed the knife to her husband, who'd come out of his own study yawning as though he'd been taking a nap. He didn't try to explain what happened when Mrs. Thor sank to her knees beside the couch, weeping and stroking Thor's hair, nor when Mr. Thor came back into the room after placing the emergency telephone call and then remained in the doorway, his arms folded across his chest, looking grimly at Fred. He hadn't tried to explain while they all waited for the emergency men to come and strap Thor onto their black and yellow wheelie thing (*Fractured patella*, the man at the island medical center would say later. *Completely shattered . . . surgery advisable . . . Prince Edward Island . . . airlift . . . as soon as possible . . . if you'd rather . . . notify Mass General . . .*), nor during the ferry ride back to the mainland with Mr. Thor, nor at the hospital where they met Mrs. Thor in the waiting room, and the two grown-ups walked to the opposite side of the room and spoke in quiet voices while Fred sat where he'd been told, in the pink chair next to the vending machine, jiggling his knees and bobbing his head, finding comfort in the rhythm.

He didn't try to explain how giddy, how gorgeously hollow-boned and glass-skulled it had made him feel to witness Thor-there and then Thor-gone, while everything else in the picture remained exactly as before.

But he saw from the way Mrs. Thor looked at him from across the hospital waiting room that she knew. She could tell that the first thing he'd felt was wonder. That his first sucked-in breath had been one of elation.

Only in the next instant had Fred gone to the place where Thor had stood moments earlier and seen how the red sandstone must have crumbled suddenly away under his feet. Only now did he realize they'd seen a sign, elsewhere on the island, warning of exactly this: a yellow sign with a silhouette of a person falling backward off a breaking bit of cliff. Fred squatted by the newly gouged edge, some yards from the former edge, and looked down. He did not know what he expected to see. Perhaps nothing. Perhaps just emerald waves frothing around the base of the cliff. An empty sea, a beautiful day. Perhaps Thor's disappearance would continue, seamless and sublime, into the future.

But no. The cliff face was not that sheer, and the boy lay humped on a ledge no more than a dozen feet below Fred. His wrists were still tied behind his back, but the red bandanna, the blindfold, seemed to have shaken loose in the fall. At first Thor lay so still, Fred was reminded of the bird he'd once found, featherless and damp, with purply skin and a translucent beak, and how he'd built it a nest with his own careful hands, and how it had been dead the next time he went to see it. Then Thor moved. He rotated his body sideways and tried to sit upright, but it must have been hard to do without his hands. An enraged cry tore from him, making Fred leap back in fright. There followed a series of thin, almost watery mewlings, and Fred crept back to peer over the raw red gash where the ground used to extend. There was Thor, curved now in an awkward crescent shape, propped on one elbow, his thin chest heaving with quiet sobs.

Fred scrambled down the steep slope and dropped onto the ledge. He worked on the knot that held Thor's wrists fast, plucked at it with his fingers and then with his teeth. It was no use. So Fred tried to lift Thor to his feet, but as his right leg began to straighten, Thor's face crashed shut like a pair of cymbals and went shiny with sudden pricks of sweat. He stood there leaning against Fred, panting, eyes squinched shut, his face awash. Fred gathered him in his arms as gently as he could, cradling him baby-style, and began the difficult zigzag climb up the crumbly slope.

They said nothing to each other, Fred and Thor. Once they'd regained the level top of the cliff, Fred headed back in the direction of the chalet. They crossed a string of meadows, each one a basin of silvery grass. Butterflies quavered like material bits of light, fragments snipped from the sun. Fred put one foot in front of the other, over and over. It was what he had to do. He breathed heavily through his mouth, trying not to jostle. In his arms Thor breathed more shallowly, the tiniest wire of keening noises emitted from between his clenched teeth. Their hearts beat nearly chest to chest. Fred's own pounded hard with his labor, but he could still feel, between the close walls of their bodies, Thor's beating softly. No matter that his back ached and sweat stung his eyes: this was a kind of elation, too. This was a kind of glory.

ON HIS FIRST DAY in the apartment above the garage, he had unpacked his orange knapsack and made two stacks on the rug. One for *The Little*

Prince and June's map and Neel's pocketknife with the toothpick missing. The other for his clothes. He sorted and lined up on the kitchen counter the single-serve packets of jelly and syrup, and in the bathroom he arranged his toothbrushing and shaving things on the back of the toilet. Whoever had stayed here before had left in one cupboard a box of crackers and a box of pasta along with some canned food, soup and olives. In the other cupboard he found some pans and plastic plates and utensils, and also matches, a can opener, and a stack of the kind of magazines that showed naked bodies. He found a drawer full of supermarket coupons and rolls of flypaper, and another drawer with a rust-stained dish towel. Wadded on the floor of the closet were a thermal shirt, a wool hunting jacket that reeked of smoke, and a green coverall; on the shelf above it, a lightbulb that tinkled when he shook it, a straw boater with a punched-out crown, and a dusting of dead moths. That was all.

The morning he looked out of the bathroom window and saw the boy climbing the junk heap, it had been over a week since Loreen's last visit. Possibly over two weeks. The milk, the Cap'n Crunch, the bread and the peanut butter had run out. The nights had gotten colder and Fred had taken to wearing the wool hunting jacket to bed. After the first couple of nights, he didn't notice the smell so much. A baseboard heater ran along the wall, but he couldn't find a way to turn it on. At Dave's house, there had been a knob on the wall.

When Fred thought about Dave, he'd get the feeling again of a little hard machine inside his chest, the handle cranking and the metal gears biting.

Loreen's dad was named Mr. Ferebee. He was a large man in a dirty green coverall with short white bristles growing on his face and neck and out of his ears. Some of the time he'd be in the office in the garage beneath the apartment where Fred was allowed to stay. Some of the time he'd be out roaming the salvage yard, picking up and setting down parts, or leading another man or two over to the big aluminum shed out back. Other times Fred didn't know where he was; for days at a time, the salvage yard would remain deserted, the corrugated garage doors padlocked shut and a heavy chain strung across the mouth of the driveway. Mr. Ferebee spoke hardly ever. When he did, his voice was like a foghorn, and it delivered no more than one or two words at a time ("Nope," "Ayuh," "Trash day"). He blew his nose by pressing a finger against one nostril and exhaling sharply through the other, regardless of whether he was standing out in the yard or inside the garage. He rarely looked at anyone, addressing his sparse remarks into the middle distance. The few times he did look at Fred, it was in the silence immediately following an utterance, and he kept his chin tucked tight against his neck and moved only his eyes, which were droopy and red-rimmed, with half-moons of white showing beneath the eyeballs.

The first few weeks Fred had hoped maybe Mr. Ferebee would give him other jobs on the lot. He would've liked to try taking apart some of the junked cars or sorting the loose parts, but Mr. Ferebee let him know he had better keep his hands off anything but the trash, which he was to haul from the garage to the Dumpsters at the end of the driveway by the end of every Tuesday.

With nothing else to do, with Loreen's visits having dwindled or stopped (Would she ever come again? Had she forgotten or grown tired of him? Did he even miss her company? He thought of the neon green gum shooting across the cavern of her mouth, the black satin mask she liked to fit over his eyes, the pineapple wax she'd once dripped on his stomach, her strange, excited laugh when he'd cried out, the hungry concentration on her face while she peeled it off after it had cooled), Fred had begun filling his time by taking longer and longer walks. Sometimes he'd stick to the county roads, where he'd take refuge on the narrow, weed-congested shoulder whenever the occasional logging truck or baler rumbled past. Sometimes he'd pick up the mill river, which ran as a muddy creek beyond the auto salvage yard and wound snakily, eventually straightening out as it neared town. It was here on the residential streets that he noticed, some mornings, bins of cans and bottles at the curb, and he began to carry with him a garbage bag he took from the garage. Sometimes on the Cape he had gone with Dave to the grocery store and they'd fed their empty cans and bottles into machines that spat back tickets you could use to buy food. He found machines just like them at the grocery store in Perdu, and fed the cans and bottles in and it worked. He bought more Cap'n Crunch and milk and bread and peanut butter and also, thinking of June, a bag of carrots.

One morning he found himself across the skinny river from the back of a house he thought was Loreen's. It was hard to tell because all the houses here were the same and they were all stuck together in a row, and also the chain-link fence between the houses and the river made them all look blurry. But behind this one house was a clothesline hung with all different pieces of Popsicle-colored underwear and he thought of Loreen's green and purple bras and her pink and turquoise leopard spotted panties, and he stood there a long time, waiting for what he did not know. He just watched, his hands in the pockets of the smoky wool jacket, the blades of grass at his feet sketched white with frost. The river, sluggish and low between its banks, stank of cabbage. After a long time he heard a police siren, far off, but still: he turned and hurried away.

Other times he'd walk in the opposite direction, away from town, cutting across the soybean field that spread in rows beyond the salvage yard, and head deep into the forest. He'd come across old trails and follow them until they petered out, then forge his own. He looked for owl pellets, which he'd put in his pockets and bring back to the apartment to dissect. It gave him something to do at night, sitting at the table that was really a door. He'd soak the pellets in warm water and use the tweezers from Neel's pocketknife to take them apart, separating the tiny bones from bits of fur and reassembling the skeletons according to his best guesses: hare, shrew, bat, vole.

He did not think about what might happen next. He did not think about what might not happen next. One afternoon he opened up June's map and spread it out on the table, where he studied it for a long time. Then he folded it carefully along the creases and put it away. Inside his chest he could feel the nip of tiny metal teeth, the grinding of a tiny metal handle.

The morning he saw the boy Jimmy for the first time, he stood at the toaster-sized window in the bathroom and stared and stared. It was like a mirage. Like magic or a trick. Like seeing a boy standing at the edge of a cliff and then seeing only the empty edge of a cliff. He wondered if his eyes were fooling him, if it really was only a dog or a coyote, transfigured by the strength of his loneliness. It wasn't until the boy lost his footing, falling partway down the junk heap, and said, "Shit," the word distinct as a speech bubble printed on the vacant morning, that Fred stirred from the bathroom window, zipping his fly as he hurried to the door and jogged down the rickety metal stairs.

"S-ah hi," he panted, slowing as he came up to the heap, where the boy sat on a fender inspecting a gash on his shin. He'd pulled up his pant leg to expose the cut, but at the sight of Fred he quickly lowered it and got to his feet.

No smile, no hello. Narrowed eyes that pulled down a little at the outsides. Big full cheeks like he was storing nuts in them.

Fred had his hands stuck up under his armpits, partly because it was cold, partly because he was afraid he'd flap his hands if they were loose. "Do you-ah need a Band-Aid?" he asked.

"No."

"S'okay."

"This is private property." He had big front teeth. Even when he closed his mouth, a tiny bit peeked white through a gap in his lips. Fred had the thought he'd seen this boy before.

"S'ah, I know. I-ah live here." Fred nodded in the direction of the garage.

The boy glanced at the metal stairs that led up to the second-floor apartment. When he turned, Fred saw how half his jaw was covered with a bruise, greenish-yellow with age.

"That's my grandpa's garage."

"Ah-yeah."

"Yeah. So who are you?"

Fred let his gaze slide away, over the boy's head, over the pile of car parts, drawn toward the raw-looking sky. A ribbon of wood smoke crept from some unseen chimney, unfurling through the air. Fred's stomach growled. It was pretty loud. The boy reddened and a grin broke out across his face, sudden and unbridled, only to get muscled back with a scowl.

"Ah-Fred," said Fred, and immediately his stomach growled again, louder this time and longer. Fred listened to it thoughtfully. It was a thing kind of like farting. You couldn't spell the sound it made.

The boy seemed to fight a little battle with himself, working to keep the scowl in place, but the next rumble from Fred was too much:

he burst. His laughter was young and high and helpless. "Shit," he said finally, still giggling. His shoulders and belly shook with it. "You hungry or something?"

Behind the boy, behind the junk heap and the aluminum storage shed and the dark, jagged pines along the far edge of the lot, the sun was just beginning to bore tiny little holes through the morning pall.

In general, never substitute the sign for
the thing itself.

JEAN-JACQUES ROUSSEAU,
Émile: Or, Treatise on Education

V

THE
THING
ITSELF

I<small>T IS THE FIRST WEEK</small> of the new year and I am back in Perdu, back for a third time in Mrs. Tremblay's saltbox house, in the mauve-and-blue room with the burn mark on the carpet and the white rattan table by the window, but it is different this time. Dennis is here with me.

We were at home in the living room—this was yesterday evening, right after supper—and I had just put down the phone. "That was Bayard Charles," I told him. "He says there have been developments. Potentially good, he says, but he doesn't want to raise false hopes. Something in the medical examiner's report. I'm going to drive up in the morning."

"Okay."

"Would you come?" I was as surprised as he must have been to hear myself ask.

Dennis looked at me. "Of course." Then nothing, a very pregnant sort of nothing, during which we gazed at each other actively and dumbly. Then after a moment he said it again, "Of *course*," and we moved toward each other, fell almost literally into each other, our movements simultaneously tentative and urgent, and the waves that came over us were full of gratitude and forgiveness and remorse, everything mingled, nothing like the straightforward passion of our early years when sex had been celebratory and dirty, all swagger and prowess and culminating in splashy attainment. This was altogether a different thing, and if you'd told me at twenty-four that freighted, fraught intimacy could outshine the unencumbered kind, I wouldn't have believed it, but this was something fine. It was startling and heart-rending and lush with humility. We wound up on the brick hearth, my hair full of ashes and my head tender from where it had bumped against the andiron.

Being here is different this time, too, in that Mrs. Tremblay has warmed to me. Or perhaps it is more accurate to say I have warmed to her. At any rate I noticed some change the last time I came up, for five days in December. The absence of pretense was a relief: we both knew she knew who I was. Also I had a better sense of what to expect. The single-egg breakfasts were by then familiar to me, and seemed less parsimonious than endearingly prudent. I let myself move more freely through the house—not much more freely, but enough to make a cup of tea, say, in the afternoon, and on my last evening I had let myself read in the living room instead of up in the guest room. I sat on the couch across from Mrs. Tremblay in her recliner. We even made a little awkward small talk. I learned that the guest room had been her daughter's bedroom growing up, that this daughter now lived in Toronto, that she was an optometrist, married, and had two children, "one of each."

The same things that had seemed dismal and forbidding on my first visit had assumed a different cast by my second. No longer did the bedroom feel hauntingly barren, or the mustard plaid recliner grimly ugly. No longer did the sounds of Mrs. Tremblay moving about her kitchen (I still maintain she is uncommonly noisy in this regard) seem to carry reproach. Now I see my assumption on the first visit, that she must have looked at me askance, must have judged me poorly, was inextricably linked to my own judgmentalism, my limited vision of who *she* could possibly be.

When Dennis and I arrived here this afternoon, Mrs. Tremblay did not even bother removing her apron. It was the same bib apron of yellow gingham I'd seen her in before, and when she came to the door with it tied around her ample hips, I swear a lump rose in my throat.

"This is my husband, Dennis."

She extended her hand. "Mr. Manseau." It was at once a greeting and a correction. The house smelled of baking.

We are upstairs now, just the two of us, lying on top of the blue-and-mauve bedspread, resting before we head over to Criterion. We speak in low voices, as if not to be overheard, even though Mrs. Tremblay is downstairs in the kitchen and could not possibly hear. For some reason I have been taking enormous satisfaction in pointing out to Dennis every little detail I'd described to him previously. ("Did you catch the old-school telephone in the hall?" "That's the little wicker desk I told you I would sit at to write." "Doesn't her mouth really look like she's sucking on a hard candy?") Each one another proof that my stories about the place have all been true. From downstairs comes the sound of what could only be a drawer full of silverware being poured down a metal chute. I turn to Dennis. I have told him about this, too: the decibel level of Mrs. Tremblay's routine housework. "See!" I whisper, vindicated.

His eyes crinkle. He kisses me twice.

The ivy on the windowpane has gone skeletal with the season; leafless and scraggly, it has a wild beauty. Its tendrils whorl and grope across the glass. I think of the giants we used to pretend lived under the woods, stretched out in great warrens there; think, too, of the pair of crooked pines, bent toward each other like cupped hands. The ghost children we used to imagine peeking out at us from behind the trees, with their queer, grainy, film-projector light: the specters, we told ourselves, of former students. I think of those former students themselves, immortalized in black and white on Neel's office walls, extending back through the story of his life long before we came on the scene, before we even existed; I think of their hold on his imagination, as insistent and tenacious as the winter ivy. I realize my whole life I have thought of them as superior to us, to Fred and me. I have thought of them as Neel's preferred children: those Jills and Johns who populated his books, who populated Batter Hollow in its heyday, who *gave* Batter Hollow its heyday, gave Neel's philosophies form, outlet, life.

"It's snowing," says Dennis.

So it is. Flakes as fat as goose feathers. While I have been looking at the pane, he has been looking through it.

IN CRITERION WE FEED a nickel into the parking meter, cross the green, go up the narrow, wood-paneled, banana-smelling staircase, and open the door with *Bayard Charles, Esq.* stenciled on the glass. Inside, the same clutter as before. I watch Dennis take it in: the stacks and stacks of books, the file folders spilling their contents like sloppily assembled sandwiches, manila envelopes, legal pads, yellowing magazines and journals, also tabloids and circulars and shopping catalogs and phone books and bags from the drugstore and loose receipts, and under this thick, variegated blanket of paper the vague shapes of sturdier objects: treadmill, photocopier, bookshelves, filing cabinets, folding tables and chairs.

The granddaughter is installed behind the reception desk as before, reading in the glow of the amber-shaded lamp. When she sees us, she marks her place in her romance novel with a finger. "I'll just let him know you're here." We get a cursory flash of dimples before she ducks through the door.

"I'm having déjà vu," I whisper to Dennis, although that is not quite the right term for it. I feel as if I've stumbled onto a kind of loop, and a weird dread comes over me, as if I am trapped in a world I could never hope to impact, fixed in some unremitting, unvarying pattern. All at once I find myself thinking again of Freddy at the music festival when we were children; the way, when the audience began to clap rhythmically, he hurled himself, in a fit of agony or rage, onto the ground. Or that's not quite right, either. I'm not thinking—I'm just seeing him, *feeling* him as he was that day, curled fetally in the dust below the stage, his eyes screwed shut, his mouth agape, any sound he might have been making lost, ineffectual, within the noise of the crowd. Then I'm seeing him, feeling him on the day we met Kitty under the sassafras tree: her smooth, pert face and the roundhouse motion of his arm as he brought the wooden spoon cracking down upon her cheek. And I feel myself on the verge of grasping something vital about his need to disrupt, to alter. As if in another moment it will all become clear: I will be able to put into words—explain convincingly to others—why this impulse in him is benign, why it is natural.

A line from Rousseau muscles into my head, not one I recall Neel ever spouting, not one I'd ever seen burned into wood. I didn't even know I had this line stored in my brain, but it comes to me now as if from some deep recess of memory. Something about a child's wish to disarrange whatever he sees: *Whether he makes or unmakes matters not; it suffices that he changes the state of things.*

Isn't this really what he desired, to change the state of things? As a way of validating his presence, his mattering. Fred's rhythms—really his arrhythms, his drummings and tappings and bouncings and rappings, for which I'd long ago accepted the lofty, Neelesque interpretation that they were based in a need to resist order, resist the conventions of civilized society—were, I think suddenly, nothing so complex. That was a story we told ourselves about them, a way of ennobling the action and painting Freddy as a kind of idealized figure, the ideal Batter Hollow boy. In fact, while I knew I was never the model Jill for any of Neel's writings, I have long believed Fred really *was* his John, the closest living example of the model pupil he had in mind.

Yet it seems to me now that Fred's destructive urges stemmed from a more basic need: simply to know his own agency. To know himself not powerless. Which is not a quirk, an oddity, but a need we all share.

Oh! I think of Dilly now, biting down with her new white teeth on her mother's finger, and the delighted chortle she gave when Kitty screamed in pain and surprise: her utter and gleeful lack of remorse.

Through the window of Bayard Charles's outer office, we can see the snow falling under the streetlights. The flakes are smaller now and more plentiful than the goose-feather stuff. This snow will add up to something; already I see it is accumulating on the cannon in the green and on the tops of cars.

Bayard Charles comes out to greet us. The same looming figure, his sharp little eyes like caraway seeds tucked into a doughy bun. Hearty handshakes all around. He says *Mr. Manseau* and *Mrs. Manseau* and *Please, come in, Please sit down,* and we are in his inner chamber now. The condensed smell of cough syrup. The clutter, even more intense than that of the outer office. The little row of picture frames lined up on his desk, their backs to us. *Lisa, would you bring some waters, please?* and a few niceties about the drive, about the weather, about the new year, while we wait for the waters: warm, tap, served in plastic cups. *Thanks, sweetheart,* he says, and on her way out she shuts the door.

"Well," Mr. Charles rumbles in his sonorous bass. And folds his large, brown-spotted hands leisurely upon his desk. I understand that this is simply the tempo at which he operates, but I am too impatient not to prompt: "You say there have been positive developments?"

He looks first at me, then at Dennis, and nods, allowing an expression almost of amazement to settle over his face.

"Yes," he says. "Yes, I believe so. Including now something that came to my attention since we last spoke, just this afternoon." He taps a folder on the desk in front of him. "Might be game-changing. Don't say that lightly. Didn't expect . . . well, don't often see something like this."

In all, he tells us, the new developments number three.

First, the medical expert—the one Dennis and I have scraped to pay for—has been, Mr. Charles says he's pleased to inform us, very well worth it. The expert found, in examining the autopsy report, what he is willing to testify are clear indications that the victim's fractures (wrist and rib) are old injuries.

"Old?"

Mr. Charles nods, opens the folder, refers to the top sheet a moment. "It seems there's a kind of cartilage that gets formed during healing, and this stuff eventually ossifies into new bone tissue. And in both the wrist and rib fractures, this process was well under way."

"Meaning the injuries would have occurred when?"

"Hard to pinpoint, but well before the time the boy was found in Meurtriere State Forest. The more important thing is, well before the victim is alleged to have had first contact with the accused."

"Before . . ."

"Before your brother arrived in Perdu."

"Then someone else hurt him?"

He is quick to shrug. "Can't prove it was anyone's fault. Could be the result of an accident. Or accidents, plural." But, Mr. Charles says, further details in the autopsy report point to additional previously incurred injuries—"burns on both palms," he reads, "and scarring on the back"—of the sort the medical expert would be willing to testify are consistent with those commonly seen when there is a history of abuse.

"Oh. But . . . oh."

Dennis touches my arm.

Mr. Charles draws a breath and closes his eyes, as though his next utterance—and it easily qualifies as the longest unbroken sentence I have ever heard him produce—requires his full concentration. "Mr. and Mrs. Manseau, we may be looking at a case that would bring more light to other parties' liability regarding harm done to James Ferebee over the course of his short lifetime than to any such liability on the part of the accused." He opens his eyes. "Understand, other parties haven't been charged with any crime. They never will be. But that's not to say it wouldn't be deeply unpleasant for certain parties if any of these suggestions were to be raised—or even hinted at—at trial."

I think of the Ferebee abode, that dark green ranch house they showed on TV. The "family friend" they interviewed on the porch, her rasping voice, *He shouldn'ta died and it's terrible how it happened*, and the indeterminate face glimpsed fleetingly as the camera panned away at the end, the face of some person unwilling or unable to do more than peer out from behind the window beside the door.

"But it isn't up to the family, is it?" I ask. "Whether this goes to trial."

"Correct. It's up to the district attorney."

"And even if this changes some things, it wouldn't change everything, right? I mean, the other evidence, the other charges. The part that when they found James Ferebee he was . . . he didn't have any clothes—"

Mr. Charles raises a hand and closes his eyes, stopping me from going on. When I fall silent, he turns to the next sheet in his folder. This, it seems, is development number two.

According to the police report, the boy's discarded clothes—coat, hat, scarf, gloves, sweater, shirt, pants and one sock—were not found in a single heap, as one might expect, he says, if they had been forcibly removed and tossed aside. Instead they were found spread out, as if they'd been discarded an item at a time, to form a kind of trail.

"Like bread crumbs," I breathe.

Dennis looks at me curiously.

"In a manner," Mr. Charles continues, "not inconsistent with a poorly understood symptom of hypothermia." It seems that in twenty to fifty percent of hypothermal deaths, the victim may engage in a behavior known as—here he pauses to refer to the document before him, running an index finger methodically across the paper until he finds it—"'paradoxical undressing.'" Apparently hypothermia can lead to vasodilation, a surge of blood to the extremities, which makes people experience a surge of heat that can lead them to shed their garments. "Although not rare among victims of hypothermia," Mr. Charles reads aloud, slowing down now for effect, "the behavior is frequently misunderstood by law enforcement officials, who may mistakenly interpret it as an indication of sexual assault."

Now I cannot speak for fear of sobbing; in fact I have half covered my face with one hand (Dennis has the other and is squeezing it hard), so it is Dennis who asks, after a beat, "You said there were three developments?"

And now Bayard Charles grins, there is no other word for it, and he settles a hand on top of the great, bald dome of his head in a gesture that seems linked to his own elation, as though he must work to keep himself from springing out of his chair. "So I'm reading over the case, my own notes, the report of the state's medical examiner, the report of *our* medical expert, the police reports, the newspaper articles, what have you, and I come across this." He slides a piece of paper across the desk. Dennis holds it so we can both see it. Across the top it says PERDU, NY POLICE DEPARTMENT INCIDENT SUPPLEMENT REPORT. I skim what seems to be a collection of statements by witnesses who saw James Ferebee in a truck near his middle school on the afternoon of his disappearance. A few lines have been highlighted in yellow about halfway down the page: *Christine Davilla, 51, resident 903 Wynett Ave. Apt. 2, reports seeing victim driving white Toyota pickup approximately 1500 hrs headed west on Bridge Street.*

"Yes . . . ?" I look up, uncertain.

"Notice anything off?"

I don't. I'm trying to recalibrate the military time—is there a discrepancy around when he was last seen?

Dennis ventures a guess to do with direction. "I think on the map it looked like the state forest was north of Perdu?"

But we are both on the wrong track.

"Driving." Mr. Charles claps his hands once. "Says she saw the victim driving."

We both look again at the page.

"Now, it could be a typo. Clerical error on the part of the officer who took her statement. Or the witness herself misspoke. Except"—he pauses for a fraction of a second, demonstrably pleased; I can practically see him licking the cream from his whiskers—"I called Mrs. Christine Davilla this morning, asked if she wouldn't mind clarifying the statement she gave the police. Says no, not at all, she'd be glad to. And she goes on to repeat her statement, exact same way. Says the boy was driving the vehicle, she's one hundred percent certain he was in the driver's seat with the vehicle in motion. Says he was laughing."

"But how? He was only twelve."

"Ayuh. It's not uncommon for kids here to drive young, sometimes, if they're on the family property, kids as young as thirteen, fourteen. Families with farms, that sort of thing. Can't get your license till sixteen, but no one'll generally bother you about it if you're driving a tractor or a snowplow on family property."

"Did the Ferebees have a farm?" Dennis asks confusedly.

"Nope. But they have a lot of land. Auto salvage yard right next to the house. They'd get junkers in all the time that still ran. Apparently Ferebee used to let his own kids drive 'em around the lot, had 'em all learn to drive that way. Not such a stretch to think he'd let his grandkid do the same."

"At the memorial service," I remember, "they said something about it. That Jimmy loved cars, loved driving."

Mr. Charles spreads his hands as if to say, *There you are*, and sits back, his leather chair creaking. Behind him, outside the narrow window, snow tumbles fast and glittering under a pink cone of light.

"So the ramifications?" Dennis is working to make sense of the big picture. "On the case, I mean, if Fred wasn't the driver?"

Mr. Charles sticks a thumb in the air. "It gets rid of unauthorized use of a vehicle right off the bat." He sticks out his pointer, then his middle finger. "Puts serious holes in kidnapping and unlawful imprisonment, too. Realistically, those'd have to be dropped. Can't prove abduction if the boy was driving himself of his own free will. The witness says she's certain about the laughing, that he had the window open, the radio on. Most they could do now is place the accused in the vicinity of the boy. But when you combine testimony that has the boy driving himself to Meurtriere with the medical expert's testimony, what you're looking at is a volitional runaway."

"So that leaves us . . . ?"

The lawyer leans forward and levels his gaze at us both. "I hate, I mean I hate, to raise false hopes. Not my policy. Told your wife the first time I met her I don't believing in sugarcoating. But." He draws a long breath through his nose. "We could be looking at a full dismissal."

Something escapes me, a little broken peal of sound, equal parts laughter and moan of relief. Then, afraid I am letting myself get too happy too soon, I frown at the police report Dennis is still gripping. "But weren't there other witnesses"—I am trying to be a careful citizen now, to ward off disappointment by preferring caution and forethought to eager belief—"didn't other witnesses say they saw James Ferebee in the passenger seat?"

"Funny thing," says Mr. Charles. "Three other people gave statements putting him in the truck. Not one mentions seeing him in the passenger seat." He rubs a hand over his face. "Something I've learned, Mrs. Manseau. All my years of practice. We see what we expect to see. Human nature. We fit what facts we have to the story we've been conditioned to believe."

HERE IS MY FINAL CONFESSION.

I make it with a heavy heart, coming as it does in the wake of Fred's death.

We never did learn whether, in light of the new information Bayard Charles managed to unearth, the district attorney would have dropped all charges. I do know that Mr. Charles—with whom Dennis and I have remained in sporadic contact, speaking on the phone a couple of times last winter to tie up loose ends, exchanging New Year's cards just this past month, with brief handwritten messages of greeting—remains staunch in his belief that if the case had gone to trial, the jury would've acquitted.

A year has passed since the evening we left Bayard Charles's office full of unexpected hope. Dennis and I sort of staggered out onto the sidewalk with a kind of dazed buoyancy. We didn't know where to go next, what to do, how to feel. For a while we just walked, saying little, strolling through the Criterion town green in the confetti of the snowfall. We were well-bundled, and after the close air of the law offices, the cold night air felt good. It was strange not being able to share the heartening news with Fred right away, but we'd come to Perdu knowing the rules: we would not be permitted into the jail for visiting hours until Thursday. This was Tuesday.

Before we said goodbye, Mr. Charles promised he would go see Fred himself first thing in the morning, so at least we knew Fred would receive encouragement at the earliest possible occasion.

In the meantime, Dennis and I found ourselves unexpectedly on holiday—alone in a pretty, snow-coated world far from home with no obligations, nothing to do, the burden that had been weighing on us the past few months greatly dissipated. It had been a long time since we'd found ourselves on vacation of any kind, and that night in Criterion, crisscrossing with welcome aimlessness the paths that traversed the green, high above which had been strung holiday lights in all different colors, turning the tumbling-down flakes gold and green and pink and blue, we were beset by an unexpected sense of festivity.

We went to an Italian restaurant off the green, where more strings of colored lights festooned the windows, and the menus were printed on the paper place mats. We ordered pasta and champagne. "I don't think we have that," balked the teenaged waiter, almost as if we'd given offense, but he checked with the manager, who himself delivered the bottle to the table, himself very decorously popped the cork.

Dennis drove us back to Mrs. Tremblay's over the winding mountain roads, taking the turns with slow grace, shifting into low gear for the steepest climbs. I told him again my story of skidding into a ditch in the rain, and being helped by the man who turned out to be Mrs. Tremblay's nephew. Dennis told me again, "I'm glad you were okay," just like that, with the brevity and heartfelt simplicity that has at times left me lonely and frustrated, because isn't there more to it, shouldn't there be more delicate layers of tissue to tease apart and examine at length? But that night I liked his answer. It struck me that his answer likely came from the same place as Mrs. Tremblay's nephew's decision to stop and help me that day. I laid my mittened hand on my husband's leg and leaned my head back against the rest. I was aware of feeling confident that he would deliver us safely to the guesthouse, aware of being grateful for this confidence.

We spent the night exultantly under the mauve-and-blue bedspread. We kept the curtains open, and at some point the snow stopped and the moon came out. I rose and went to the window. We'd been sweating under the covers but the room air was frigid. Dennis came to the window behind me and wrapped his arms around my middle and we stood together, our hot skin rapidly turning cold, neither of us minding. We fit together, limb to limb, crown to chin, belly to back, and took in the shapes the moonlight mapped across the landscape: the white-iced pines, the slippery road, the mountains like torn paper pasted on the sky.

After a while I whispered, "It's awful, Den, isn't it?"

"What?" he asked, his mouth in my hair.

"The boy. Jimmy."

"Yes."

"To think how he lived."

"Yes."

"And died."

"Yes."

Across the road ran a barbed-wire fence: five rows of wire strung between vertical wooden posts. Each length of wire was encased in its own sheath of ice. The barbs were encased, too, each one a little frozen star caught on the staff. I thought of June then, teaching me to read music, and of Freddy naming the cows when he was five, and Neel saying *They don't say moo*, and I missed them all.

It was Bayard Charles who informed us. The phone rang early in the morning while we were still in bed. When we came down for breakfast, Mrs. Tremblay had already laid our places, put out a rack holding two pieces of raisin toast and poured our tiny glasses of grapefruit juice, but before we sat she said, "A Mr. Charles would like you to call," and she handed me the piece of paper on which she'd written the number. I started back upstairs for the hall phone, but she indicated I could use the one there in the kitchen. Then she took off her apron and folded it over the back of a chair and excused herself from the room.

Fred strangled himself with his prison pants, got them wet in the sink and twisted them into lengths thin enough to knot one end around a heating pipe and the other around his neck.

When Mr. Charles finished telling me, or when I had finished listening to what I could take in, I handed Dennis the phone and walked out the front door and crossed the street and grabbed onto the fence and brought my forehead down on the uppermost, ice-encased wire. I didn't know what I was doing or what I hoped might happen, except I wanted to feel something strong enough to interrupt the terrible current that had seized me through the phone line back in Mrs. Tremblay's kitchen. But this fence was not electric. I fell to my knees beside it, then lay on my back in the snow under the white empty sky until Dennis came with my coat.

Later, when Kitty heard what had happened, she said, "Why do they even bother taking away their belts and shoelaces if they can just use pants?" which is so exactly like Kitty I didn't know what to say.

Tariq said we might be able to sue.

Don and Meg sent sunflowers, a lot of them, and later, when Dennis told them he was scared and didn't know what to do, Meg took the train to Freyburg and stayed with us for more than a week until I'd gained back a few pounds and was bathing again and getting dressed again each day.

Even now, a year later, whenever I think of the industry and ingenuity Fred's act must have required, I am demolished anew.

I never thought my brother capable of such despair. Or of such resourcefulness.

I spent my life thinking of Fred as unreachable, but there is nothing so unreachable as dead. Only when the possibility of ever learning his account of all that had happened was extinguished did I realize how much I had been counting on it, holding out hope for it still. He would tell me. I believed this. In time, he would trust, speak, explain. Because I am Ava. His sister. His. I don't know whether to call that vanity or love, but until Bayard Charles's early-morning call, I'd had faith I would eventually hear Fred's version. He would convey it to me in his Fredly way, and I would translate for the rest of the world. I would help others make sense of him, reach him. I would help him be reached.

For why are we here if not to try to fathom one another? Not through facts alone, but with the full extent of our imaginations. And what are stories if not tools for imagining?

Here then is my final confession: I have written this entire account. Every word of it is mine.

The sections I have called DENNIS and KITTY and FRED: all mine. I started with what I knew and, keeping faith with that, imagined outward, not in order to rewrite or overwrite anyone's truth, but in order to understand all that I can, as well as I can. In the case of Dennis and Kitty, I had the great luxury of asking questions, and of showing them what I had written, asking them to make corrections, and then revising according to what they offered. In the case of Fred, no such luxury. I researched what I could and imagined the rest. It is the best I can do.

Eleven weeks after Fred died a package came to the house from the Criterion County Correctional Facility. His personal effects. It contained some familiar objects: his orange knapsack, June's map, Neel's pocketknife, *The Little Prince*. His wallet, empty of cash, but with his driver's license, old library card, and business cards from diners all over New England. The package contained unfamiliar objects as well: a black satin sleeping mask, a pineapple-scented candle, a woolen jacket stinking of cigarettes.

Mrs. Tremblay, of all people, filled me in a little about James Ferebee's mother, how she'd been a starter on the high school girls' basketball team until she got pregnant. How she'd lived at home with her baby and worked at the paper mill until it closed. How people said her parents kicked her out of the house for doing drugs. How after she left they had taken over the job of raising their grandson, for better or worse ("mostly worse, people say"), themselves.

I tried finding Loreen Ferebee. There were two public listings for Ferebee in Perdu, New York: Ferebee, Ronald and Ferebee Auto Salvage. The phone numbers were identical. Hands shaking, I dialed and got a recorded message, the voice that of an older man, gruff, terse. I left a message, said I was trying to reach Loreen. I was as much relieved as disappointed that it was never returned.

I did find Thor Anderson. It took me some time to remember his last name, and even then I wasn't sure I'd gotten it right until he actually came on the line and he said yes, he was the son of a Roger

Anderson who'd once attended Batter Hollow School. He was very nice when I told him who I was. I reached him in his dorm in Cambridge; he was a sophomore at MIT. He remembered a lot about the summer in the Magdalens when he was twelve, the long days of exploring the islands with Fred, the fact that the trip had to end early when he shattered his kneecap. I asked him if it had healed okay. Good as new, he said. "I run now. Not marathons or anything, but still. I have a five-K coming up in two weeks."

When I told him Fred had died, he offered his condolences and asked how.

"He took his own life."

There was a long pause. "I really liked your brother," said Thor. "He was a special person. He was really nice to me at a time when I wasn't incredibly happy. I wish we'd . . ." but his voice trailed off. "Well," he said, and I liked him for what he said next, the honesty of it. "I guess we wouldn't have kept in touch."

I tried learning more from Dave Alsop. I called his number on the Cape over and over but no one ever picked up. When spring came, Dennis and I drove out there. We found his address across the street from a trailer park. The bungalow was more broken-down and grimmer even than the old Batter Hollow cottages had been before being razed. Tires and hubcaps on the lawn. Cracked concrete foundation. Faded plastic awning over the door. There was a car in the driveway. It was two in the afternoon. The bell was missing—an empty socket gaped where it had been pulled out of its mount—but we knocked until someone came and peered through the screen. "Dave?" I asked.

"Yuh?" Bleary-eyed, scratching his bare chest, holding a cotton blanket around his waist. He welcomed us in, offered us beer. We declined. He popped the top off a can for himself and settled onto a gray couch. I had the strangest feeling looking at it. It was so threadbare that in many places, stuffing poked through the fibers.

"Who's there?" called a woman's voice from the other room.

"Just some old friends!" he yelled back. He smiled sheepishly at us. "Yvette," he confided, like this explained everything.

We told him Fred had died, and how, and where, and he said he was real, *real* sorry to hear it, but I had the distinct sense he hadn't actually taken it in.

"Dave, is there anything you can tell us about what happened?"

"No!" His eyes grew wide. He was all earnest affability. "No *idea*, man. I mean, offing yourself?"—he gave an amazed laugh—"In jail? That's pretty out there."

"I meant can you tell us anything about what came before? How he wound up in Perdu, even?"

"Oh!" Dave grinned hugely, like he knew we'd get a kick out of the story. "Met a girl. Yeah. We go on this road trip, right? And this *girl* we meet up in Perdu likes him. And your *brother*, he takes a shine to her. I guess he must of, because when it's time to split, you know, he's like, No way, I'm staying."

"Did you know her?"

He puffed dismissively. "Not really."

"When are they leaving?" the woman called from the other room.

"I don't know!" Dave yelled over his shoulder, then turned back and gave us a conspiratorial shrug.

"What?"

"Soon, baby!" He winked and did silent fake laughter, like the three of us were all in on some joke.

"My mother," I said, "made arrangements for you to get funds deposited in your account every month."

He looked amazed. Then he tipped his head back and studied the line where the wall met the ceiling, straining in an effort to retrieve the memory. "Oh, *yeah*," he said finally, beaming. "That's right. I guess that kept up for a few months after he split."

"Until his death," I said. Dennis and I had sat down with another lawyer in Freyburg, gone through the bank statements, the terms of the will and the trust. June had arranged for Dave to receive five hundred dollars a month. If Fred had come to Perdu in late August, as seemed to be the case, Dave had received five months of automatic payments after Fred stopped living with him. "That's twenty-five hundred dollars."

"Yeah, uh . . . I'll have to write you a check. For that amount. Yeah. I'll have to mail you that."

I peered a little closer at the couch. It was still giving me the strangest feeling. Now I noticed, and it activated the hairs on the back of my neck, a shape woven into the fabric on part of the back cushion that wasn't torn, a large petaled flower so faded you could barely tell what color the threads had been. "Where'd you get that couch?" I asked.

"The *couch*?" He looked around himself in disbelief. "Dude, this *couch*? I don't know. It's been here, man." He laughed. "It came with the *house*."

Later in the car, heading back to Freyburg, Dennis said he'd thought at that moment Dave had been seriously about to faint.

Dave never mailed us a check, as we had known he would not.

Any thought I had of trying harder to get in touch with Loreen Ferebee, I scuttled after that visit.

Instead, I took what I already knew, lined up all the additional pieces of possible evidence, opened the composition book Kitty had given me, and willed myself to conceive of what I could never know for sure, from multiple angles and with partially conjured ingredients.

Does that make this account dishonest? Would it have been more truthful if I'd remained within the confines of my own perspective? I don't know. Which is more wholesome: to subscribe to the limits of what we have experienced or seek with one's empathic imagination something more?

The story is not done, of course. What began as disconnected scribbling in the book Kitty first placed in my hands more than a year ago has continued to grow unevenly and untidily—no bakery box done up too squarely, this. I will continue the work of correcting the mistakes and filling in the gaps, returning to the places where my imagination and compassion have so far fallen short, for the rest of my life.

Neel would say *bosh*. Allow only experience, resist interpretation.

But is that natural? Is it human? Don't we all do this—make story—whether we intend to or not? Or have it another way: Isn't the extent to which we engage in this practice the measure of our humanity?

Neel and June believed people are free. Neel, a fundamentalist, believed this absolutely. June, agnostic, gave it the benefit of her doubt. But it remained in the end their creed, their faith. I give them credit for this. No one can say they didn't follow through. They believed they were giving Fred freedom from the label of a diagnosis. They believed they were giving me freedom from Fred.

I see now they were mistaken. We are none of us free. We are tethered by our connections to other people, those we know as well as those we will never meet. What tethers us is our ability—our responsibility—to imagine them, to fathom their lives, their circumstances, what we have in common, what sets us apart.

I have faulted myself for being too fond of stories, but now I believe the only crime is telling ourselves the story is done, the task accomplished. So long as we keep at it, mending and amending, being open to revision, there is no call for blame.

Almost daily now I find myself chancing upon new tendrils of story, new ways of thinking about Neel and June and Fred and myself and everyone I've ever known and everyone I'll never know. I try to discern between those tendrils that extend understanding and those that obscure, choke off the view. I try to cultivate the former and weed out the latter, remaining mindful that any certainty I have now might later wither or change course. I don't worry about this. I will work forever and gladly to better fathom my own husband, and also my old, vexing, beloved best friend, and my parents and brother who are gone from me, and Don and Meg and Tariq and little Dilly, who I am just getting to know, and the children I grew up with and the children with whom I make music now at schools and libraries around Freyburg, and their caregivers, too, the ones who manipulate their little hands for them, teach them to clap and cry *Hooray! Here comes the Singalong Lady*, and also James Ferebee, and his poor, damaging, damaged mother, and his grandparents, hidden behind the walls of their dark green house, and Dave Alsop and the woman Yvette, who called to him from the darkened bedroom at two in the afternoon, and his friend Umberto—if Umberto, or someone like him, even exists.

Umberto. Yes. Let me make one final confession. Umberto is completely made up, a fabrication, the only character I have invented entirely from whole cloth. Despite this, or because of it, I find myself particularly intrigued by him.

Funny—I have just thought of this now:

All my life I have wished others could better see my brother. If only they understood him more fully, how much closer to loving him they might be!

What then am I to think of Umberto, minor character that he is, crudely drawn figment of my imagination? I have portrayed him as simply cruel. Suppose I were to imagine him more complicatedly, more messily—suppose I were to undo the red-and-white bakery string? What if I willed myself to fathom more of his story, extend toward him the tendrils of my own sympathy exactly as I have ached, still ache, for others to do with Fred? I have no control over others, but I can practice in good faith what I wish all of us might do.

Umberto, yes. Umberto: you are my hope, my hypothesis. My Émile. Tonight I will go to sleep thinking of you.

ACKNOWLEDGMENTS

Several people kindly helped me navigate a few matters of law, law enforcement and the corrections system in upstate New York, chief among them Wes McDermott; also Darrin Bartolotta, Matt Brief, Paul Casteleiro, Mike Dorf, Jonathan Gradess, Cathy Miklitsch, John Peck, Ellen Schell and Ray Schlather. I was fortunate to be able to draw upon knowledge and experiences gained from the teachers, students and families of the Rockland Project School, formerly of Rockland Lake, New York, and the May Center, formerly of Arlington, Massachusetts. And I owe a happy debt to my parents for exposing me in childhood to several books about Summerhill, A. S. Neill's famous school in England, and his philosophy of "freedom not license." I spent many hours of my youth in rapt study of the photographs and stories they contained illustrating life at that school.

I feel ridiculously lucky to be the beneficiary of the talents and dedication of Cathy Jaque, Marc Jaffee, Sarah Stein, Geoff Kloske, Elizabeth Hohenadel, Allison Hargraves, Tabatha Paterni, John Burdeaux, and all those who care so much about books and do so much to champion them, both at the Karpfinger Agency and at Riverhead.

Barney Karpfinger and Sarah McGrath offered an abundance of inexhaustible, insightful, challenging, loving energies to this project and to me. Without them this would be a far lesser book, and to them I am most grateful.